TAKE ONE

by

# RAEGAN MATTHEWS

# Description

Brock LaDuece is a millionaire, but in name only.

When his father disperses an ultimatum clearly stating he must marry, if only to secure the future of his family's Fortune 500 company, Brock reluctantly agrees he has but one choice...

To find a woman his parents will love, even if he doesn't.

Brooke Malloy is over the childish clichés born from romance of any kind. Studiously overseeing the day-in and day-out operations of her parents' family-owned bed and breakfast has become her life's routine.

By mere chance, or her best friend's unwavering determination, Brooke finds herself front and center in the world of reality television.

When Brock and Brooke are thrown together after a heated one-night stand, only to come face to face the next day as opposing contestants on a failing reality television show, sparks fly. But not in a way either of them expected.

Facing each other again is tough enough, but doing so in front of hundreds of thousands of viewers who thrive on critiquing their every move, proves not only difficult, but their own hellish version of reality is in the spotlight.

# Rights

# Acknowledgements

Editing, Formatting, and Cover by: Rebel Edit and Design

http://www.rebeleditdesign.com


Proofreading by: Author Services by Julie Deaton

http://jdproofs.wix.com/jdeaton or
https://www.facebook.com/jdproofs/?__mref=message_bubble



Book Club Gone Wrong:

https://www.facebook.com/Bookclubgonewrong/?fref=ts

Thank you so much for hosting my release party and to all the wonderful authors who took time out of their writing caves to come and help celebrate the release of F*CK Reality. I appreciate you all!

# Prologue

*This is where everything gets fuzzy.*

*Brooke*

-

"Fuuuuck," Brock moans his frustration into my neck as he greedily thrusts his cock against my thigh.

We're both drunk, and I have no clue as to how we ever made it up from the hotel bar to his penthouse suite as quickly as we did. I suppose my lack of sexual adventure, coupled with our mass consumption of alcohol, had something to do with it. No matter, though, because as we sat across from each other at the bar downstairs, listening to those around us banter in their own drunken states, our attraction to each another was undeniable.

Now that we're finally in his room, alone *and* naked, the attraction has gone from subtle touches to blatant groping. And not because I have rose-colored beer goggles on, either. The man on top of me, fighting with a condom in one hand, while balancing his weight to keep from toppling me with the other, is hot—beautiful even.

*And, thank you, God. Even in his clumsy state of intoxication, he's an ace with his hands.*

"Hang on," he mutters as he lifts his body off mine—just enough he's able to sheath himself with the same condom he's been messing with for what feels like *forever*.

"Do you need a minute?" My question comes out as a drunken giggle. "Is this your first time?" Finding it incredibly difficult, I barely hold back voicing more jokes at his expense. We've been constantly at each other in interruption.

He'll kiss me, I'll kiss him.

He'll touch me, I'll touch him.

He'll laugh at me, I'll laugh at him.

It's turned out to be a game of whose determination to deter the other is greater. I'll admit to the possibility that I'm cheap and easy, too. But only because I've enjoyed every second of his body touching mine in play.

"You got jokes?" he attempts to sneer, but the break of his boyish grin ruins his objective. The question ends up getting lost in his slurred words, followed by his drunken laugh.

I love his laugh.

I love his smell.

I love his smile.

Apparently, after so many on-his-tab rounds of tequila, I'm a lover of all things Brock LaDuece. And, at the moment, I'm drunk enough to not be even a little ashamed to admit it. Tonight, the shots were good, the company was entertaining, and the likelihood of what would come later was promising enough to keep me toasting.

At least a dozen times.

"Ready," he directs as he positions himself at my entrance.

"Do it," I breathe, praying I end up enjoying his cock as much as I've enjoyed everything else about him.

When he finally thrusts his hips and slides inside of me, I hear a guttural hiss break between his grinding teeth, along with the violent curse he utters immediately after.

It's not every day, or any day for that matter, that I've been so boldly complimented on the feel of my tight, wet pussy. Or the silky strands of my long, dark, and shiny hair. Not to mention his constant verbal praise of my bronzed skin, perky chest, round ass, and shapely legs. He's done nothing but reference my appearance all night.

There may be a small, feministic part of me that would normally take issue with his way of expressing his desires, but only if I were sober—which I'm not—so *fuck it*. I've encouraged myself to revel in every goddamn compliment, even if most of them have been dirty.

"I've been worked up since I saw you sitting alone downstairs," he chuckles, pinching my nipple and licking the sensitive skin behind my ear. "Slow the fuck down."

When I don't submit to his demand, he stops moving altogether and looks down while putting his weight against me to keep me still. The lamp light next to his hotel bed is dim, but I'm still able to make out every glorious facet of his face and striking feature of his body. I shamelessly commit them all to memory.

His honey colored eyes are like glass; so reflective, I can see my own flushed image inside them.

His dark hair, nearly black in color, sticks out in every direction from where I've ran my hands roughly through it.

The strong line of his jaw, paired with the two-day darkened growth around its edges, heats my skin with every graze.

His glossy red, well-kissed lips stand out against his perfect white teeth. A complete contrast in comparison to his olive colored skin.

All of Brock is ... *too much.*

"I'm close," I cry out. He lifts his weight and begins to move again, my hips in sync with his, but powering through with more speed and added aggression. "Don't stop."

"Fucking hell, you'll pay for this," he threatens as his pace quickens to match mine.

Once his body carries mine to the brink of release, he drags me back when he suddenly slows.

My body tenses, clenching him tightly from inside in an effort to delay my orgasm for as long as possible. His hands grab my wrists and pins them over my head. There, he laces his fingers through mine, clutching them firmly. Our bodies are flush together by his weight, sinking me further into the lush hotel mattress.

Brock bends his neck to kiss me. The warm caress and soft touch is unhurried as his tongue slides deeply and forcefully into my mouth. The twisting duel of tongues continues before he pulls out and starts all over again. As soon as our bodies ignite with our orgasms, we both let go.

*Completely...*

# Chapter One

*It's three strikes you're out, right?*

*One week earlier...*

*Brock*

-

"Sweet mother in heaven. For the love of God, make it stop," I hiss at my cell phone lying next to me, buzzing its insistence. Obviously, someone expects me to answer, but fuck if I want to move an inch to find out who it is.

Opening one eye, I find the constant stream of my phone's vibration has forced it to the edge of my nightstand where it's now threatening to fall. My head is pounding, and my eyes are splitting, in sync to every beat of my heart.

Last night was yet another victory in way of mind-numbing sex. As it always turns out, the next morning I'm waking up sick from a hangover, but happily content in doing it alone.

"What?" I snap after I connect the call and *gently* brace it against my ear.

Pushing my morning irritation aside, I listen to Drew as he attempts to rein in his laughter.

After he's composed himself to his own satisfaction, he quips, "You brought that cougar from *Shooter's* home with you last night, didn't you?"

*Son of a bitch. Of course I did.*

Being a thirty-year-old bachelor, spending most of my evenings in the company of a variety of women isn't necessarily the abhorrent curse my family would like me to believe. The truth is they just don't understand. It's not as if my life is being spent as single and '*alone*' alone. That's not the case at all.

I have a strong center, which includes a close, tight-knit family. Even if they don't agree with my decision on giving up finding 'the one' to settle down and start a life with, I know if I ever truly needed them, they'd be there without question.

Same with my small group of trustworthy, long-time friends. Those men are more like my blood brothers. We've known each other most of our lives and have been through a lot, both separately and together.

"How drunk were you?" he questions, still stifling a laugh.

"Drunk enough," I openly admit, because I was. I was blitzed.

My active-as-it-can-be social life is what my parents pretend to ignore the most. I enjoy women because of their gentle nature, their soft bodies. And, if I'm lucky, their willingness to spend just one night and be on their way first thing in the morning, but I prefer them to leave sooner.

I wouldn't label myself a player by any means. I mean, I haven't completely given up on a future with only one girl, but I haven't found a woman who suits everything I'm looking for.

Sure, I'd like her to be both smart and attractive, but to be honest, I'm looking for a woman who possesses a great sense of humor. This characteristic has taken me a long time to admit. A lot of men my age desire full lips, round tits, and a nice ass. Maybe I'm getting older, or maybe I'm more old fashioned than most, but I like to laugh. I've been in the company of enough women to see that most are afraid to be themselves. If a girl has me laughing, she's already a candidate for a second date.

My life isn't all about a loving family, great friends, and finding laughs, though.

You've probably heard the idiom stating how money is the root of all evil. Well, in my case, this holds weight. In comparison to most other men or women my age, I'm rich. But not personally. I'm a millionaire in name only.

My stepfather, the only father I've truly known, is the rough and tough Chief Executive Officer and proud owner of Merritt Media.

Martin Merritt is a smart and savvy businessman. He started his company before I was born and has dedicated his life to making it all of what it is today. His determination in cultivating business relationships throughout this country has led to its strategic diversification. He's not only grown his business as a whole, from the first brick laid to the other buildings he holds staff in, he has also trained, mentored, and educated his employees to run the business seamlessly in his absence.

Are you bored yet?

Because I've heard this same speech from him so many times I can finish his sentences before he's finished speaking them. The first time he explained all of this to me, I was eight. The second time, I was eight and a half. Needless to say, Martin's been drilling this information into my head ever since.

After college, I immediately started my predestined marketing position inside Merritt Media. After many years of putting up with the exasperating duties and the hours I work to finish them, I'm considered only a favored paid employee. Hence, I'm rich by extension only. I don't make frivolous amounts of money; however, it's enough to pay my bills and allow me to live a life of menial luxury.

When I'm not working, I spend most of my time hanging out with my high school friends, Drew and Nick. Yes, I said *high school*.

One friend, of which is on the phone now, is using his antics to fray my already threadbare nerves.

"So, how was she? Did she show you her social security card as foreplay?"

*Mental note: Find new friends.*

"No, asshat."

"She leave early? Had to run home to feed her ten cats, I'll bet."

"You're an idiot," I charge.

This may make me sound like a pussy, but while I was away at school, I missed my friends and family. I hated not being around for their life's milestones; weddings, birthdays, anniversaries ... all of it. Because of my studious college class schedule, I wasn't always able to make it home enough.

While standing up and stretching, I stop my best friend with feigned denial. "Fuck you, Drew. She wasn't a cougar."

The asshat laughs again, seemingly not as sick this morning as I am.

"The hell she wasn't, Brock," he snorts. "Nick asked her how old she was when you left to get more drinks. She told him she was forty-one. Had to be lying. *Had to be.* I bet she was older."

*Forty-one?*

By today's standards, forty-one isn't old, but it would be a record for me. Older or not, the woman was hot. She was tall with long, red hair and a tight body, which enhanced her generous chest. Fuck, maybe it was all the beer and shots I had, but when she made her way over to our table, I didn't refuse her.

Last night, my buddies and I went to the new club located deep in downtown Dallas. I was wired from working another eighty-hour work week and was looking for an easy and fun way to release my tension.

"Why the hell are you calling me so early, anyway?" I clip, mentally cringing as I calculate how many shots we each must have consumed.

"Early?" Drew mocks. "It's almost one o'clock in the afternoon. What the hell have you been doing?"

Taking a quick look around my room, my eyes widen with anxiety, and the sharp pain behind both continues to worsen.

"Shit, I was supposed to meet my dad at the house for lunch."

"That was today, wasn't it?"

"Yeah," I confirm. "At noon."

"Martin's gonna skin your ass for this."

He's right. My father is probably sitting in his office at home right now, livid as fuck, contemplating all the ways he'd like to rip me a new asshole.

It has to be said that I hold the highest respect for Martin Merritt. Several times he's voiced his desire to one day have me take over his company, but with the constant stream of mishaps he views my life to be, he hasn't mentioned this being the plan in a long time.

I was only four when my biological father passed away. He died in a sad and tragic car accident, which left my mother in pieces. I don't remember a lot about what transpired directly after, but I continually give thanks to Martin for providing my mom with the life she most definitely deserved after suffering such a heart-rending loss.

"I gotta go, man. I need to call him so he knows I didn't forget."

"But you did forget," he insists.

"Right, asshole. Let me get off here already."

Drew shrugs off my urgency with his own. "Wait. Are we still on for the game tomorrow night?"

Apparently, the residual alcohol has a lasting effect on my memory. I have no idea what he's talking about.

Sensing my confusion, he adds, "Tomorrow night. We're meeting Cody and the guys for poker. You have time to sober up and get rehydrated by then, right?"

*Shit, the game.*

The first Saturday of each month is reserved for poker night. Each player buys in for one hundred dollars and plays until they've lost it all. If they choose to stay in, to win their money back, they offer up a bet of another variety.

These challenges can range from asking the little old lady at the post office if she'd be interested in going to dinner, to running through the aisles at Walmart, throwing random items into strangers' carts with a predetermined number of pieces you need to sneak in before you're inevitably caught.

To outsiders looking in, this pastime sounds both juvenile and ridiculous. To us, though, it's a pastime we've participated in since high school, and one we absolutely refuse to give up.

"I'll be there. What time?"

"What time?" Drew gasps. "Jesus Christ, Brock. It's the same time every month. Eight. Bring the beer. It's your turn."

"Right."

"Call me later," he insists. "Let me know how bad things go with Daddy Warbucks. Don't let him ground you, either. Not this weekend."

"Fuck you," I spit. "I'll call."

Before putting the phone down, I chance another look at the clock.

I'm so screwed.

*Shit.*

As I drive the long winding path leading to my parents' estate, I'm met with the sight of my bratty kid sister. Tate's sitting on the steps outside the front door, looking down, and picking something from the toe of her shoe. I can't see her face, so her mood is anyone's guess.

Tate recently turned sixteen. Supposedly, by the time my parents got married, they had decided not to have anymore kids. I mean, they already had perfection in me, so why risk it, right?

*Right.*

Turns out my mother, who has been known to be a little flighty, assumed she was going through early menopause and, taking her own medical advice, figured there was no way she could get pregnant. She was only forty at the time, and obliviously had grossly misdiagnosed herself.

At first, Martin wasn't happy about the pending arrival. However, it didn't take him long to figure out what a blessing it could be to not have to rely on his fourteen-year-old fuck up of a son to someday run his company.

That was until Tatum Lee Merritt was born.

My sister came into the world in the exact same manner she spends every day living in it. In short, Tate's a loud, crying, whining, pain in my ass. But, this said, I love her anyway.

To be fair, there are times she's not so nuts; granted, it's usually when she's sleeping. She loves who she loves in her own way and does what needs doing in her own time. Once recognizing her strong-willed personality and uncontrollable disposition, we all came to recognize, understand, and appreciate everything about her.

"Where the hell have you been, Brock?" the little tyrant clips as she remains seated on the stairs. Her hand comes up to shield her eyes from the mid-afternoon sun, probably to ensure she can scold me with those as well.

"Well good morning, my sweet sister," I salute.

"Dad's pissed. Livid, even," she enlightens. "He told me I can't go to the mall today because my asshole of a brother couldn't get out of bed to take me."

*Holy fuck.*

Strike two. This is something else I've apparently forgotten I was supposed to do.

"Why aren't you in school?" I question, realizing she's home on a Thursday afternoon.

My reasons for not being at work are legit. I took the rest of this week and all of next off for a planned vacation with friends, which was cancelled at the last minute. Tate shouldn't be here hassling me while I'm dealing with a goddamn hangover.

"It's spring break, dumbass," she curses again. "And now, thanks to you, a whole day of it's been ruined."

I narrow my eyes, always—*always*—hating my little sister's filthy, spoiled mouth.

"Anyway, why do you look like that?" She points, rolling her eyes from my head to my feet, annoyingly judging my ragged appearance.

"Grown up reasons, Tate," I vaguely explain.

Talking to my sister about being a responsible grown-up is the equivalent of her talking to me about a women's monthly period. She doesn't want to hear about having responsibilities and stress any more than I want to hear about tampons or cramps.

I narrow my eyes, not because of the sun's rays, but because this conversation, coupled with the hangover, is an enlightening shade of hell.

"Where's Dad now?"

Standing, Tate uses the palms of her hands to wipe the dust from her ass. Her shorts are too goddamn short to be wearing outside of the house or to the mall—or at all. Her blonde hair is swept up in a high messy bun, and her pink tank top reveals *entirely* too much cleavage for my liking.

Any other day I'd threaten to beat her ass myself if she didn't walk inside to change. But right now, I'm busy readying myself to get my own ass ripped for missing lunch with Dad. So, lucky for her, she's off the hook.

"He's in his office, but I'd steer clear if I were you," she tersely recommends. "I hear the weather in France is nice this time of year. You should move there."

Last year, my parents decided Tate wouldn't get the liberties of a car, her license, or legit dating privileges until she turned eighteen. I agreed, not that my two cents mattered, but I was a teenage boy once. My friends and I had one thing on our mind at all times. It didn't matter where we were or who we were with, it always came down to girls without clothes.

So, no way. Tate and boys are a cocktail for disaster.

Because my parents had her so late in life, they've regrettably sheltered her. Now that she's pulling away in order to state her independence, she's also starting to get into trouble. She's been caught missing curfew, sneaking out after our parents assume she's gone to bed, and sneaking boys inside after they've resided to theirs.

Wrapping my arm around her head, I pull her close and deliver a rough knuckle across her scalp. She's pissed and understandably so. But I hate when she's pissed at me.

"I didn't mean to forget, Tate. I didn't. Things have been busy at work, and last night I went out with the guys..."

That's all I get to say.

Pushing at my stomach, Tate frees herself and steps back. "Drew and Nick? I got stood up for a ride to the mall because you went out and got wasted with those idiots?"

*Ouch.*

Okay, right. Real facts and true experience may lead one to believe my friends are absolute idiots.

Drew Gables is a thirty-year-old unemployed wannabe professional golfer who was once an airman in the United States Air Force. When a fall from a building he'd been working on busted up his knee, he was honorably discharged and was happy to be.

He's probably lazier than most men our age, and he most likely drinks to excess more than once a week. He doesn't have a steady girlfriend, only because he won't put in the effort to keep one. He'd rather go without sex than put any time into a relationship that would last longer than the morning after.

All this said, Drew doesn't ask me for money (never), mooch off me (much), or piss me off (okay, sometimes).

Nick Givens is a little different, but not by a lot. Nick works at an automotive plant in Dallas. He just ended things with his longtime girlfriend, Katie, because she was asking for more than he was willing to give. Overall, he's a good man, hard worker, and great friend.

And no matter which colorful way my sister chooses to describe either of them—friends are friends.

"Don't dog the guys, Tate. You have no friends."

Her big blue eyes, which mirror my mother's, widen in surprise. "You did not just say that to me!" she shrieks. "Take it back."

Smiling smugly, I walk in front of her on my way to my father's office.

"I'll take you to the mall when I'm done here. You can't stay mad at me if I still do what I said I would do."

"Four hours later?" she snaps. "No one will be there! Everyone went this morning."

"Good," I return, as I imagine her eyes drilling holes into my back. "You're not dressed to go out, anyway. Change out of that costume and we'll figure it out when I'm done."

I hear her emit a sharp gasp before my name is loudly cursed. The sounds of her stomping echo off the heavy marble floor as she makes her way to her room, most likely *not* to do as I've just instructed.

*Such a pain in the ass.*

Walking up to my dad's office door, I find it's closed. Since he works from home, it's not surprising to find it shut. Normally I'd walk right in, but today I'm walking on eggshells, so I take the extra second to knock.

He doesn't answer.

This isn't unusual either. Once I've hit his shit list in doing whatever I've done to have pissed him off, my punishment is to be ignored. To this day, silent treatment—even at my age, given by my life's role model—still stings.

After pushing the door open, I step in and stop once I hear him on the phone. I don't focus on him directly since I can already see with his flushed cheeks, tight jaw, and narrowed eyes, he's pissed at me.

I'd be pissed, too.

"Right. Well, call me once you have her answer. We need this one, George. I trust you'll get it done."

*George.*

George McLain is my dad's right-hand man. For all intents and purposes, it's a job that should rightfully be mine. The problem is I've blown off enough lunch dates, ruined enough meetings, and fucked up enough paperwork that Dad's stopped trying to mold me into being him. Over the last year, my progress in taking things more seriously has gotten better, but in his eyes, I have a lot left to prove. Missing this lunch has clearly set me back.

"Sit," he clips once he disconnects his call. "Good to see you today, Brock. I thought you'd fallen into some self-serving hole and forgotten all about our meeting. Glad to know I was wrong."

I don't respond. If I do, it'll lead to an even bigger scene than the one unfolding now. I hadn't thought of our scheduled lunch together today as a meeting. I was off work, he knew that, so I was taking this as a time to catch up, father to son, but much to my dismay, I was mistaken.

Dad looks to his watch, shakes his head and *tsks*. "Two hours and forty minutes late," he tightly observes. "Were you aiming for a new record?"

My mouth opens to respond, but he lifts his hand between us. His dark hair, graying at the sides, his dark eyes, and his large frame slowly sit back to get comfortable in his black leather chair. He rests his elbows on the chair arms and runs his fingers back and forth over his bottom lip. He's thinking. This never bodes well for me.

"Dad, I wanted—"

"Don't," he interrupts, raising his finger in the air to silence me. "Don't say anything yet."

Adjusting my guilt in my seat, I brace. This isn't like the other times I've let him down. Not even close. Normally, he'd blow me off and move forward with whatever I had missed; be it a meeting, a call, a client, whatever … but this is different.

He's as livid as Tate said he was.

Reaching to his side, he opens his large desk drawer and tugs out what I know to be his best scotch and a single glass. I'm not being offered a drink of his expensive liquor. Any other time I would.

Another indication that Dad's fuming.

"You don't think much, do you?" he queries.

I sit in place, saying nothing as he shifts the items on his desk to make room for his drink. It's well after two o'clock in the afternoon, and he's hitting the hard stuff.

"Well, I've been doing some thinking for you," he tells me, setting his glass on the desk and opening the top of the liquor's carafe.

The sound of glass hitting glass clinks before the stench of liquor hits the air. I'm assuming he must know I'm hungover, and he's using this as an opportunity to taunt me.

Once he realizes I'm not about to interrupt, he questions, "Do you know who George is having dinner with tonight?"

"No," I reply, and I don't.

I don't like George, nor do I give two shits who he spends his evenings with.

"Sabrina Sandoval," he states. "Do you have any idea who she is?"

"The model?"

Sabrina Sandoval is an international supermodel who started her career fashioning lingerie. She's untouchable to any marketing companies or groups as she doesn't need them. Yet, George is apparently having dinner with her.

*Fat bastard.*

"Yes, the model," he confirms. "Do you know *why* George is having dinner with her?"

"He's going to ask her to join Merritt?"

He shakes his head. I'm wrong, but don't understand how I could be until he advises, "Because I couldn't count on *you* to do it."

*Fuck. That hurt.*

"Dad, I could've..."

His eyes narrow. "Could've what, Brock? Really? Please tell me what you could've done."

"Dad, I—"

I'm not able to finish with whatever I would've come up with to convince him of anything. Before I can get out so much as an apology, he declares, "Six months. That's how long you have."

I'm confused. "How long I have for what?"

Leaning back again, he takes his drink with him and clutches it tightly in his hand.

"You have six months to build a life outside of the one you're supposedly living in now."

"A life?" I question. Maybe he's already been drinking this afternoon; I just have no idea how much.

"A life," he concludes. "At least the start of one. An engagement."

Silence deafens the room, and the only sound coming from me is the wheezing I'm struggling to hide.

"An engagement?"

Dad continues as if I'm not totally fucking lost. "I'm not saying go out and knock some woman up by the time six months is over, by any means. However, knowing you as I do, you'll probably do exactly that just to spite me."

*What the fuck?*

"Dad?"

"Brock, son, if you haven't been paying attention, let me spell it out for you. I'm giving you an ultimatum."

"An ultimatum for what?"

Exasperated by my overwhelming surprise, he advances, "You need to find a good woman, settle down, and start a future. *Build a life.*"

"I have a life," I pointlessly explain. It may not be one he approves of, but it's one I do and that's what matters.

Now I'm no longer confused—I'm fucking annoyed.

Rolling his eyes and setting his glass on top of his desk, he braces his arms there as well. "Believe it or not, what I'm about to say hurts me, but I'm saying it for your own good."

Sensing my unease, he drops a bomb I hadn't seen coming, but should've. "How can I trust you to run this company the way I foresee it running, Brock, if you can't even manage a family?"

"So, if I don't do what you're *demanding*, you'll do what?"

"George is ready," he states quietly. If I'm not mistaken, I hear guilt. "He's learned everything I've taught him, and he's applied those lessons in a way I would if I were him."

"George," I repeat to myself.

George is my age, boasting the same education as I do. He's a go-getter, though. He's also my father's favorite, or for lack of a better term, his *pet*. My dad says jump, George not only asks how high, he asks how many times.

*Goddamn over achiever.*

"I see you're thinking, and I'd say slowly but surely, you're getting my point," he tells me.

The cogs of my mind must be whirling in a way he can see, spinning themselves around this bullshit scare tactic.

"Your mother worries. You're not living up to your life's potential, and it's starting to upset her a great deal."

Dad stands, taking his drink with him, and walks to the bay window of his office to look out.

His voice, laced with sadness and regret, reaches across the room with vague certainty. "I've loved you since you were a boy. I've always wanted good things for you and me for that matter. But, Brock..." He pauses, takes a drink, then a deep breath. He doesn't look at me before concluding, "I've never been proud of you as a father should be proud of his son."

*Fucking hell, that hurt, too.*

Angry and searching for cover, I mask my hurt. "Good thing I'm not your natural born son then. That should ease your disappointment a little."

He turns in place, and when his eyes meet mine, I find it's not only me smothered in regret, but both of us—and equally so. We're frustrated with each other.

Giving me only a few moments to reason with what he's doing, Dad leans his tall and broad frame into the wall while holding his emptying glass in front of him.

"Do you remember the last woman you brought home to meet your mother and I?"

*Oh, that's not fair.*

Apparently, he doesn't care to hear my confirmation, so he continues. "Cammie," he reminds me. "The waitress from Winston's bar. Was that her name?" Before I can so much as nod in agreement, he asks, "Do you remember how that evening went?"

"Yes," I confirm.

Though I've confirmed it, he presses forward with further reminders. "She thought Merritt Media was a company that broadcasted radio channels on the spaceships of NASA." His lips are tight, and the vein in his temple is bulging with insult.

Merritt Media provides its clients with a wide variety of marketing avenues. We represent celebrities of all kinds, garnering deals they couldn't otherwise reach for themselves. My father's contacts are strong; thus far his reputation is untarnished. I legitimately understand his concern for the future of his company and how my decisions could ultimately affect it. No one trusts a businessman with a woman on his arm who lacks common sense.

"I get it."

"Do you?" he counters, his eyebrows lifting in surprise. "Because it took you months to get that woman to leave you alone. Restraining orders were about to be placed, son. The woman was batshit crazy."

"All this happened three years ago. That's not fair."

"That's the whole reason I'm making this point. Don't you see?" He shakes his head while walking back to his desk to sit down. "Three years have passed since you've been in a committed relationship, and look how unhealthy the outcome of that one turned out. Somewhere, when I wasn't looking, you lost your way. I want to help you find it."

I don't comment. My feelings are hurt, and I'm a guy, we don't revel in admitting that.

"I want more for you than a waitress or a bartender, Brock."

Those positions he speaks so lowly of aren't worthless. They're real. It doesn't matter how little money may be in either occupation, not everyone works to secure a luxurious standard of living. Some actually want to do those specific jobs to earn their life's keep. Waitresses and bartenders included.

"So, six months to find what, Dad? A lawyer? Doctor? Because, to be honest, women like that bore the fuck out of me."

"Watch your mouth," he scolds. "I'm not saying whomever you choose has to be more of a success than you are," he explains to my insult. "I'm saying, at the very least, when they open their mouths to speak to or in front of your mother, they know what the word media in all aspect means."

"Fine," I clip, responding to a burden of fury toward my father I don't remember ever feeling. "Are we finished? I need to get Tate to the mall."

Dad's face gentles ever so slightly, likely because she's ridden his ass so much today. He's probably happy to finally have the little ice princess out of his hair.

"Six months from today, Brock. If you're not ready, everything you stand to inherit will be changed."

"Seriously?" I bite out. This is ridiculous.

"You'll inherit of course, but you'll get the same as Tate."

Which is enough to live comfortably, but not the vast fortune I once thought I'd receive.

"Got it."

"And don't test me. Don't pick up some random woman and throw a ring on her finger. The caveat to this agreement is that your mother has to approve of her in a way that will bring her peace in knowing you'll be happy for the rest of your life."

"Mom only?" I question. "You don't have to approve?"

"No," he returns too quickly. "I have no faith you'll pull this off. Thus, I don't necessarily plan to meet anyone."

Part of me is angry.

I'm a grown man, and the only father I've truly ever known still treats me as an errant child. Thus far, our relationship has always been good. Even as a kid, Martin Merritt ensured I never felt the void of my biological father in any way, and he certainly never set out to make me feel as though he was trying to take his place. Rather, Martin did the exact opposite. He sat back, helped me progress into a teenager, and let our relationship take its natural course. He made my life easier, if only because he made my mom happy.

The other part of me is disappointed in myself.

I've let him down. He's relied on me all these years to pull my head from my ass, and I haven't done it. If I'm being honest, I haven't wanted to. My life isn't his. I don't relish in working long hours forever, wining and dining clients, or spending most weekdays away from home. I do as I'm told, add input when I have it, but other than that, I have no desire in being his replica or clone.

However, at the same time, I also don't want to relinquish his company into the hands of another man. A man who technically only bests me because he has a wife, two kids, and lives in the suburbs of Dallas.

"Six months," I clarify. "I have six months to put a ring on a woman's finger. Mom has to approve."

"Yes," he nods. "I'm having Darrin draw up the contract."

This is yet another surprise—a contract?

"I'll be signing a binding agreement for this?"

"You will," he confirms. "Simple terms, but specific terms nonetheless. This way, there will be no way for you to contest my will should I pass..." He pauses and looks to the open door of the hall, probably listening for my mother, then continues, "...should I pass unexpectedly."

"You've really gone all out, haven't you?" My disappointment is etched with anger, the snide question meant to hurt.

"You've given me no choice."

"Right."

"If you aren't successful in this venture, Brock, I need you to know I still love you as I always have."

"Right," I snap again. I have nothing more to say.

"This is business," he adds.

"I get it."

Dismissing me, he nods to the door. "Now please, find your sister. Get her out of this house, and don't bring her back until she's no longer pissed at you."

"So, never?"

He laughs the first true laugh I've heard from him in a long time. I'm grateful to hear it, even if it is at my expense. It lessens the sting of the disappointment he feels for me.

"Tate loves you, as do your mother and I." Standing, I start to turn away. I don't get far before he adds, "I mean it. You're better than you're giving yourself credit for."

"Do mail-order brides still exist?" I joke, but then consider it as a valid option.

Dad shakes his head, pours himself another drink, and replies, "I don't know. But if anyone could have a woman your mother approves of delivered right to your front door, I have no doubt it'd be you who could."

# Chapter Two

*Brad Woodbury may or may not have cooties.*

*Brooke*

-

"Did you not hear me?" I snap my fingers in front of Samantha's face again. It's a futile effort as it does me no good.

The small faced, blue eyed, recently engaged woman appears sick. Her long, blonde hair is covering her face as she sits back in her chair and attempts to take a few deep breaths.

My friends and I are sitting next to each other in oversized, luxurious chairs at our small town's only salon. We're all getting pedicures before the party tomorrow night, which was planned to celebrate Samantha's marital engagement.

Supposedly, it's important to her to have the entire female wedding party go out and drink till we puke. She sold this to us as a 'bonding' experience. I'd settle for a stay-at-home evening, indulging in a few glasses of white wine, and playing mindless board games. Or maybe watching a couple of romantic movies. However, my ideas were labeled as boring and immediately cast aside.

"Am I really getting married? Are we really about to plan my wedding?" the bride-to-be asks, trading glances between myself and Addie as we flank her sides. "I mean, do you think Sean really loves me enough to commit to me forever?"

This is not the first time she's freaked out. Thankfully, she has months to prepare herself for the big day. She'll come to terms with what's happening, I'm sure, but it'll take some time. However, now that she's finally chosen her perfect wedding party, she's started having mini-rounds of nervous bouts, which have led to full-fledged meltdowns that ultimately required dark chocolate and cheap wine.

I look to her feet and conclude the paint isn't finished drying. If she starts to freak out like she did hours earlier, she'll ruin a perfectly good pedicure.

"Sam, breathe. Relax," Addie soothes, gently placing her hand on Sam's shoulder.

Addie's not so good with people crying. She sees one coming and, as a self-made rule, takes off in the opposite direction. Tears have no place on Addie's pillow unless they're hers alone.

I'm not great with soothing a sad soul either, but I'm better at it than Addie.

"You and Sean were meant to be together since the third grade, Sam. You two are going to be very happy." Addie throws in for comfort.

"Second grade," Sam corrects. "He sat by me in Mrs. Heller's class all year, remember? He always had something in his mouth."

"Glue," I remind her, my lips curling in disgust. "He went at it all the time."

"Glue," Sam repeats, finally smiling. "Yeah, I think I loved him even then."

"See?" Addie points out with her surprising second effort to comfort. "Breathe in and out."

All of us grew up in Peace Hope, Iowa where we still live today. It's a small and quiet place, which brags a population of four hundred and thirty-seven. It's a one stoplight, one church, one bar, and several farms kind of town.

My parents own and operate a quaint little bed and breakfast, just outside our city limits. Baskin Inn has been part of this town's heritage since my great grandparents had it built. They passed it down to their daughter, then she passed it on to my dad. I love the place, and I don't mind that I've finished college with a degree in business only to come back here to help run it.

My nineteen-year-old brother will be taking over as the rightful owner once he's ready. Until then, it falls on me to help my parents keep it up as we wait for him to finish college.

"Do *you* think I'm making the right decision?" Sam looks to me for guidance, but I don't answer.

I don't necessarily believe in love. Not to say I don't believe in it for others, but I've recently been burned. My ex-boyfriend and I broke up three weeks ago, so her asking me this at the same time I'm stewing over a broken heart and crushed spirit isn't a good idea.

"You're making the right decision," Addie assures with wide eyes, disciplining me because I've said nothing.

Jason Evers and I were together four, almost five, years. We met our senior year of college, located in the city not far from this one. From the moment I laid eyes on him, I thought he was beautiful.

His blond hair, blue eyes, and bronzed skin caught my attention at a fraternity party I let Addie talk me into attending. Before that night, I'd never been interested in anyone. I mean, I had a boyfriend or two in high school, sure. However, those relationships never lasted past a casual handhold or chaste kiss.

Living in a small town means you know everyone's business and they know yours. Privacy, in any realm, is never a guarantee. Because of this, I had kept my virginity, if only to avoid the loss of it becoming the town's leading coffee time gossip.

Once Jason and I began seeing each other though, it wasn't long before we started having sex. In the beginning, he was very sweet. He was the type of guy who bought you flowers, took you to dinner, then brought you back to his place for a drink before he took you to his bed. I loved him. I had nothing to compare our relationship to, considering I'd never been in one before. Maybe that's why I was so blinded by our young relationship.

Ultimately, as time went on, things between us changed. To this day, I'm still not sure exactly how it happened. At first, he started hanging out more with his friends, drinking, than spending quiet nights at home with me. I refused to believe it was because he wasn't happy, but looking back, that was clearly the reason.

Three weeks ago, I found him and a woman I'd never met having sex in the driver's seat of his expensive German car. When Addie called to tell me what she thought she was seeing, I rushed over to the bar where they were parked. The woman was mortified at the state I'd found them in. Jason was merely pissed at being caught.

The next day, I moved out of our small rental house and back in with my parents.

"Brooke!" Addie calls. I snap my head to find her and Sam staring at me with angry eyes. "Tell Sam she's not making a mistake."

"You're not," I wave them off with a hand gesture. "He loves you. He's always loved you."

Sam's eyes shine, welling with happy tears. "Are you going out with us tomorrow night? I know you hate bars, but the rest of the wedding party insisted we go to Cub's after dinner."

She's right. I *hate* bars. I'm quiet and reserved on most occasions. When all of the girls do go out, it's usually Addie who raises hell and brings unwelcome attention to our group.

"I'll be there," I assure, but wishing I didn't have to go.

"You're finished!" Shirley, the owner of Glamour Nails, happily exclaims as she runs the pad of her finger over Samantha's toenail to ensure it's dry.

"So pretty!" Sam returns, looking at her perfectly painted pedicure.

I move my gaze to Addie's fingers and toes, then laugh. Both are painted black.

When Sean proposed to Sam, Addie mourned over her jealousy and told me she refused to wear pink at the wedding. We both already knew before asking Sam's choice of wedding colors, she would choose pink and black. In sixth grade, Mrs. Lance forced us into creating our own do-it-yourself project where Sam, the most girlish of us three, insisted we plan our own weddings. Mine was simple—black and white. Addie's effort and imagination extended far enough to find a random bobblehead she coined as Elvis, insisting she'd be eloping in Vegas.

Sam, obviously, chose pink and black.

Turns out, lucky enough for Addie, the wedding colors are alternated between the five bridesmaids. Since I'm the maid of honor, I'm sporting pink. Addie will come up behind me in black.

"All right. Now, onto lunch," Samantha announces as she sits up to collect her things.

Addie follows up next with, "Thank God. I'm starving."

Addie works as a waitress in a truck stop about thirty miles from here. She makes good money and loves her job. She didn't go to college at the same time Sam and I did. She chose to stay back and help her ailing father heal after suffering from his second round of severe skin cancer. Now that he's back on his feet, he pays for Addie to take classes online here and there.

After Addie and I walk with Sam to her car, getting her situated inside, Addie turns to me and smiles.

"What are you looking at?"

If there's anyone who makes me nervous by delving out only a look, it's her. From personal experience, anytime she looks like this is when she's up to no good.

"I was thinking…"

"No!" I bark out.

"Come on, Brooke. Hear me out!"

"No."

I hate her ideas.

Opening my car door, I stare at Addie as she rounds the hood with her eyes never leaving mine. Once she's inside and buckled up, she exhales a heavy breath, then sits back to get comfortable.

"I know you and Jason just broke up," she starts.

I roll my eyes in reaction. She can't see it, and what I'd really love to do is close them and forget the world I once had with Jason ever existed, but I'm driving.

"Yes, we did. As in three weeks ago. So?"

"Don't get testy," she clips. "But Brad Woodbury may or may not have asked my mom for your number this morning when she went by the post office to pick up stamps."

Brad Woodbury.

Brad *Woodbury.*

*Brad...*

"Oh my God. She did *not* give him my number, Addie!"

Shaking her head, she raises her hands in surrender. "Don't get pissed."

"I'm not pissed," I calmly explain. "But if she gave him my number, you're paying for my new phone."

Brad Woodbury was three years older than us in school. He was the high school quarterback, as in he was the all-American boy this town adored. His long time girlfriend, Laura Pickett, was equally admired, but only because she was Brad's girl.

"Well, he's single. He divorced Laura and moved back home. He's working at the post office now."

"Does your mother hate me?" I question as I steer the corner to the restaurant and catch a glimpse of Sam waiting just outside its front door. She's on the phone, probably talking to Sean.

"My mom loves you," Addie boasts quietly.

She's right. I know Addie's mom loves me; she has since we were kids. More times than not, it was Addie's mother our friends flocked to for advice. We'd sit around her parents' kitchen table, chatting about whatever was going on in our teenage lives. Mrs. Tindal gave good advice.

At least I *used* to think so.

"I hate Jason for what he did," Addie continues. "You're still hurting. Mom knows what he did. Everyone does, and we all hate him for it. She thought she was helping when she told Brad to call you."

"Helping?" I scold. "You do know the rumors about him may be true, right?"

"Or they may not," she jumps in. "We don't know. We only know what we've heard."

"Rumors say he has herpes because Laura stepped out on him before they got divorced, Addie. I don't *want* to know if they're true or not."

Her lips tighten, and she keeps quiet, so I wait for her to say something else. When her eyes narrow and a small trace of a smile plays across her face, she finally admits, "Fine. You win."

"What?"

"My mom didn't give him your number, but she did tell him you were single. She said something about having you both over for dinner next weekend."

"No," I whisper between us. "Your mother is nuts."

"You should call her and fill her in on those rumors. If I heard her right, she's planning to make lasagna."

"Her best dish?"

"Told you, Brooke. She's serious about finding you a man."

A sudden rush of sadness falls between us. Addie senses this and her hand comes to my thigh, where she squeezes gently.

"I didn't mean to upset you," she says quietly.

The sting of tears threatening to release keeps my focus. Trying to hold them back is a feat in itself.

"I know you loved him, Brooke."

"I did, Addie. I thought…"

Wiping my eyes, looking out into the parking lot in front of us, I take a deep, but not so calming breath.

"You thought he was the one?"

"Yeah," I reply, shrugging. "Maybe. I thought if not the one, he was a good stand-in for the one."

"I'm sorry."

Pity coming from Addie burns. She doesn't do compassion. My best friend is fierce, so much more so than me.

"I say we go to Cub's Saturday night and make some noise. I mean, Sam's getting married. I think we're compelled to show her a good time while she celebrates."

"When did we all grow up?" I question softly, undoing my seatbelt and gathering my purse. "Really, because I miss playing with dolls."

Addie laughs. "We didn't play with dolls. We played with trucks, remember? That's how you broke your arm."

"Yeah," I remember, "don't remind me."

"You swore you'd fit in Jesse Kimble's yellow Tonka." She giggles. "Face first in the dirt, Brooke."

"I cried all the way home while you all laughed."

"You're still mad about that, aren't you?"

"Very," I pout.

Opening her car door, Addie wittingly suggests, "Let's go rub some food on those wounds. I'll buy dessert."

"Okay," I agree, slamming my own door shut and pinning her with a dirty look. "Extra chocolate, too."

"You'll need it because you should know..." she pauses, long enough to smile, "it's possible my mom did give Brad Woodbury your number."

*Damn it.*

# Chapter Three

*My friends dwell in very low places.*

*Brock*

-

It's been two days since my father sat me down and laid out my life's future plan without caring what I thought of it. Two days since I sat with his company lawyer with a contract in my hand, stating what I have to do to obtain his company as part of my inheritance.

When I called Drew to explain how lunch with Dad had gone, he didn't sound as surprised as I figured he would. It almost seemed as if he knew this was coming even before I did. Still, I'm struggling to process the notion I may lose all I worked for through college, as well as most of my adult life, to procure.

In many ways, I understand my dad's position. He has a lot to lose if I take over his company and fail. I don't blame him. On the other hand, it would be nice to know I was being given a fair chance to succeed.

"We said no girls were ever invited to poker, Nick," Drew blasts from his place next to me at the table, at the same time putting his cigar in the ashtray to his right. "Why did you bring her here?"

Nick, our mutual friend, the one Tate, my little sister, hates more than Drew, is also the one who just broke up with his longtime girlfriend. He's been sleeping his way through a variety of women he usually picks up from strip clubs or bars. Dallas is full of both, and he frequents them often.

"She'll be leaving as soon as the game starts. There's nothing wrong with stopping over to say hi, right?"

The currently indisposed woman here tonight is definitely one he met at a strip club. Her spray-on tan is orange in color. Her oversized chest and platinum blonde hair all scream 'Candy Land' or 'Shasta Sherry'. She's hot, I'll give her this, but definitely not my type—if I had a type.

"Someone wanna grab the other table and bring it in?" Cody invites while entering the room we all play poker in. His hands are full of chips, beer, and cigarettes.

Cody Miles is another mutual friend from high school, but one we were late in finding. Like women, believe it or not, men tend to run in cliques as well, only we're much less dramatic.

"Your girl is still in my bathroom. She's been in there for fifteen minutes," Cody informs Nick. "What the fuck is she doing? I gotta piss."

Nick shrugs. "No idea."

"Right, well, game starts in twenty. Can you go find her and help her find her way out?"

Nick grunts and mumbles under his breath, but soon stands and wordlessly excuses himself from the table.

Drew takes a drink of his beer, doing a shit job of hiding the smile he's got working behind the bottle.

"Why are you looking at me like that?" I question, surveying him with caution.

"Thinking is all," he casually replies, setting his drink down on the coaster next to him.

Pulling out our wallets, we all lay our cash on the table. Drew, me, Cody, Mark, and Nick have the process of this night down by routine.

"One hundred." I toss my twenties at Cody so he can exchange them for chips.

Drew does the same, but states, "I hope someone loses their bet, 'cause the dare I have tonight is gonna be a *big* one."

"Like your 'teepee Mary Williams's car' wasn't huge?" Mark laughs, knowing damn well that bet was a walk in the park.

Nick had Mary's car covered before the sun even started to rise. The rain that came early that morning, covering the paper and plastering it to the paint, was icing on the cake.

Turning in place and looking at me with curiosity, Drew smiles, and it's in a way I don't fucking trust or like at all.

"Think bigger," Drew tells the table. "That teepee shit was a joke anyway. I wasted a good dare."

"You did," Mark reminds him. "I told you to have Nick kiss the pastor's daughter."

Drew gasps. "She was *twelve*. Since when do we make dares that'll end us up in jail?"

Mark laughs, pointing to Cody, where they both say in unison, "Can I smell your car?"

I laugh at Drew's expense, remembering that very night well. Drew lost his hands at poker quickly and ended up placing in a dare to win his money back. Mark and Cody conspired before the rest of us had gotten here, and had already planned to set Drew up. It was a bullshit play, but the dumbass fell for their scam.

At the time, Mark had an aunt who had been visiting from out of town, staying at the Sheridan Suites. Somehow, they convinced my stupid friend to steal her rental car, already knowing cops wouldn't be called since they filled in his Aunt Midge prior to it. All in fun, she thought it was a great idea.

Turns out, Drew may hang with friends who know cars, but he most certainly doesn't have a clue about them himself.

In short, he approached the *wrong* woman who had just pulled into the hotel parking lot. She'd been driving a car he *thought* was the one he was supposed to take. When he got too close and she went to strike him, he cowered. Once Drew calmed her, he excused himself by stating, "I was just going to ask if I could smell your car."

"So fucked up," Drew mumbles as we laugh. "Too far. That dare went too fucking far."

Cody reels in his laughter then takes a seat. "As soon as Nick loses that woman, I'll need to check my prescription meds. If they're missing, she took 'em. What the fuck is he doing with her?"

Reliving the ultimatum given by my father, I'm all about watching from the sidelines as my friends enjoy the life I wish I still could.

Drew shrugs, but I answer. "He's having fun. Leave him alone."

"He said he may be getting laid off at the plant," Drew informs us. "If that happens, he'll move. You know he will. Nick hates Dallas."

Nick doesn't love his job at the well-known and well-developed automobile plant downtown. He does it for the money, not the rewards of sorting parts. He quit college his second year to come home and take care of his mom after his dad passed away. He's made no secret of his desire to get out of Dallas since coming back.

"He didn't mention anything the other night," I admit, feeling a little slighted.

We're not women; we don't share every miniscule detail of our lives. But being informed that one of my best friends could soon be out of a job would have been nice to know.

"He's nervous, Brock. He's thirty-years-old. No woman, no job, and no money."

"So he's you," I point out accusingly. "You have none of those either."

Drew scowls, but it's not serious. He knows he's a lazy son of a bitch, but he also knows his father has money, and eventually all of it will pass to him. Unfortunately for me, I'll be in apparent dire financial jeopardy if I don't marry.

"Do you have anything stronger?" I ask, aiming my question to Cody. The beer I brought isn't helping to settle my nerves.

"Top shelf, in the cabinet next to the fridge. Help yourself. No clue how long it's been there, but you're welcome to it."

"Check on Nick and what's her face while you're in there," Drew calls to my back.

Making my way into the kitchen, I flip on the light and go in search of the liquor. Three days ago, I didn't have a care in the world. Before my stepdad ruined any plans I had for my future, I would've just been another guy hanging with his friends. Now I'm a mess and trying to find anything to help numb my life's burdens.

"What the fuck?" Nick hisses after he opens the bathroom door, zipping his fly. "Shit, you scared the hell out of me. I didn't know anyone was back here."

My eyebrows lift in surprise. I shouldn't be shocked to see what I do; my friends are nuts.

"Don't mind me. I'm just gettin' a drink."

I lift the bottle in the air and do nothing to hide my smirk as his new flavor of the week comes out of the bathroom nearly naked.

*Yep, definitely a stripper.*

Her hair has that just fucked, mussed look. Being that she's not wearing a bra, her tank top does nothing to hide her arousal, and her small shorts hang low enough that it's safe to say she's not wearing underwear. She's also giggling incessantly as she grabs Nick's arm and walks up to stand at his side.

He ignores me and takes her mouth with his. Before I can look away, I see tongues in duel.

*Oh God. Too much.*

"Hurry your ass up," I interrupt. "The boys are ready."

At the same time I turn to walk out, Nick pushes the stripper out of his arms and states, "Don't lose tonight, Brock."

I stop at the door and narrow my eyes, knowing he can't see. I heard what he said. It's not so much his words I don't like, but the sketchy tone he used while saying them. Rehashing Drew's peculiar comment from earlier, I turn to face him.

Stripper has her hand down the front of his pants and the other up his shirt. She's standing behind him, looking at me with hunger.

*Fuck no.*

Man rule number one: Unless three started the party, another member cannot be included after. Not that I would consider touching her anyway, but still. Rules are rules.

Jesus, maybe we're more like women than we'd like to believe.

"What did you say?" I question, holding the bottle of Beam in one hand and a small kitchen glass in the other.

"Drew's hoping like hell you lose tonight, and you'll bet back in with a dare."

"Why?"

Nick shrugs, but his casual façade lies for him.

"Tell me," I clip.

"Just don't lose tonight," he says again, pulling the woman's hand from his pants and positioning her in front of him.

Nick's irritated. The man just had sex with a semi-hot stripper in a friend's bathroom, and yet he's annoyed.

My friends are nuts.

"Whatever," I snap first, then nod to her. "Get Candy outta here, and let's play some cards."

Candy's head rears back, her nose scrunches, and the rest of her face wrinkles. Not a good look.

"Who the hell is Candy?" she shrieks, her voice scraping my nerves with every word. "My name is Tawnya. With a W."

"Of course it is," I mutter to myself before leaving the two fuck buddies alone.

Two hours after Nick has sent *Candy* on her way and the cards are *finally* being dealt consistently, I sit back and revel in the slow burn of whiskey making its way into my system. The guys are all at ease, bantering back and forth. I'm trying. All I can hear, though, are the echoing words of my father's disappointment.

The way he *said* them.

The way I *heard* them.

The way he *meant* them.

"I'm out," I direct, pushing the rest of my cards in to fold. "Out of cards. Out of chips."

"Not out of time, though, right?" Drew attentively questions. He's looking at Nick, not me. "You're not leavin' yet, are you?"

Shaking my head, I answer, "No, why?"

"Because you still have a dare to play. If you think you can win, I mean," Drew baits.

*What the fuck are these guys playing at?*

A small string of curses come from Mark across the table as he sits next to Nick, but I can't hear what he says after. The added mumbles from Drew at my side aren't helping the tension at the table.

"What the fuck is going on?"

"You in or out?" Cody casually questions, holding the cards in his hand with impatience.

He's not buying into whatever bullshit the others are playing at either. His focus is rightfully on the game. With five hundred dollars on the line, he's always this serious.

Convinced I can win and beat these bitches at their own game, I sit up in my seat and declare, "I'll use my dare. Stack me in."

"You know the rules, right?" Cody asks, completely focused as he stacks my soon-to-be chips neatly in front of him. "One dare buys you back in for one hundred. The dare is in play only if you become the low man at the table *at any time*. No denying whatever the dare is or you're suspended from playing again for six months."

"I got it, Cody," I snap. "This isn't new. Stop talking and give me my chips."

Nick lights another cigar. Generally, he has but one to make him feel manly while playing cards, then stops. For whatever reason, tonight he's had three.

*What the hell?*

"Good luck, bro," Cody comments, shoving the chips in front of where I'm seated.

"You know..." Drew starts, accepting the cards dealt to him and looking at them in study with a haughty look on his face.

If only to wipe the smug look off his face, I appease him with, "What do I know?"

"That show is holding auditions in Dallas next week."

"What show?"

Nick holds his cards in front of him in obvious contemplation. When Drew doesn't answer, Nick does. "The marry me show, or some shit."

Drew laughs. "Marry a…whatever it is. Last year it was a plumber, remember?"

"What the hell are you two ladies talking about?" Mark asks, throwing his cards in and giving up his ante. "I've never heard of it."

"Yes, you have," Nick chimes in. "It's that Matt guy's pet project. He's the puke who hosts it. Hot girls, bachelor…"

My fingers tense, crushing the cards in my hand as I'm holding tight and hoping to fuck they aren't thinking what I'm afraid they are.

"Yeah, maybe," Mark shrugs. "Don't watch much TV anymore. Don't have time."

Drew, happy to explain, says, "I've got time, and those women are crazy hot. All of them are hoping to be the next television bride."

"Kinda sad," Cody says quietly, obviously not having a clue as to what's playing out. "A woman would marry someone she hardly knows for what? Fame?"

"Not this time. Fame isn't this season's premise," Drew answers. He tosses in his cards as well, leaving me and Nick in a standoff. "This time it's marry a millionaire, if you can believe that."

Surprised by the notion, Mark's eyes cut to mine. "Don't you gotta be single *and* never married to go on the show? Am I right?"

Nodding once, Drew refuses to look my way.

These bastards are thinking *exactly* what I was afraid they were.

"Don't even go there," I hiss in my best friend's direction.

Turning in his seat, Drew pins me with the most superficial, annoying smile the bastard can muster.

He leans his chair in my direction and says, "Then don't fucking lose the game, jackass. This is exactly where I'm going."

Slamming my cards down before it's my turn, which as a general rule you never do, I push my ante and bet to the center in frustration. I had a pair of eights, which would normally get me a win, but I've lost my concentration.

"That's a fucked up dare. We don't ever pull that shit," I clip, staring at each player in turn.

Mark's mouth is hanging open, probably because he knows he's won the pot, and it's a big one. Cody's jaw is ticking at the disrespect I've just shown to our friendly game.

Drew and Nick are smirking.

Nick clicks his tongue against his teeth while shaking his head, then states, "A dare is a dare. You bought in for it already. Not to mention, little brother, you've played a hand."

"Come on, Brock." Drew tries to soothe by slapping me on the shoulder. "You have nothing to lose, right?"

"Bullshit," I counter.

Drew looks clearly offended. "You didn't think it was bullshit when that woman nearly beat me to a pulp with her big, fat purse. Why's this bullshit?"

"Because it is," I aimlessly claim.

I have a fuck of a lot more to lose than anyone at this table.

My freedom, which I guess has already been challenged given the contract I've just signed for my father.

My dignity, which if I don't marry, will cause me to lose the position at Merritt Media. It's one I've worked hard for and will eventually deserve.

Not to mention, I risk losing my friends if these bastards continue to push me further.

"I won't lose," I tell them with confidence as I stack my remaining chips neatly in front of me.

After, when no one has anything more to say, I get up from the table and head to the kitchen for a breath of fresh air.

By the time I come back, the others have finished another hand and are now sitting around, bullshitting as they wait for me.

"Ready?" Nick queries once he notices I'm back in.

Taking my seat, I adjust my posture and abruptly return, "Deal the cards."

"Don't be that way," Drew whines. "Even if you lose, you win. Daddy Warbucks will be happy you're coming to your senses and seriously looking to get hitched."

"Fuck you," I reply, holding up a two of hearts and six of clubs.

The hand is weak—I'm fucked.

Tossing in the useless waste, I wait for the others to finish. During this time, I debate on whether I should walk away, leaving them to their game for six months without me. This oath we have to the dare isn't one anyone here takes lightly. We've seen men, far better players than us, be led out by pride and never to return because they couldn't handle even the smallest hit to their egos should they lose.

"Sweet," Nick drawls, pulling the stack of chips in front of him. "You wanna win, Brock, you've got a lot of work to do."

"Game's not over, dick."

All heads move toward the door, so I turn in my seat as well to find my sister Tate. She's dressed down, thankfully, and as her eyes round the table, a look of cutting condensation pierces the room.

"What are you guys doing?"

It's not surprising she's here. Through the years, it was occasionally my duty to watch over her when my parents insisted they spend time together, and the evening happened to fall on a game night. In order to not miss a play, I'd pack my sister's bag and bring her with me. She would bitch and moan, then threaten to tell our parents I was gambling. As long as I didn't drink and I kept the language at the table as clean as I could, she never ratted me out.

"How'd you get here?" I ask. All the others, except for Nick, ignore her and focus on the game.

"Jess is using the restroom. We're on our way to her house, and she didn't want to use a public bathroom on the way. We let ourselves in. Hope that's okay, Cody."

Cody nods. He's used to my sister's pushy and demanding disposition.

Nick's eyes widen. "Jess is here?"

Jessica Landry is Tate's older, more physically matured friend. That's to say she's still only eighteen. She's been a family friend since our dad hired hers at Merritt. She's a nice girl—albeit not so bright—and though I may go to hell for so much as thinking this, she's also hot as fuck.

"She just had a birthday, right?" Nick asks.

Tate's eyes narrow. She really doesn't have much love for my friends.

"Yeah, she did. So?"

"Nothing," Drew interjects, clearly seeing where this conversation is headed.

Setting the cards down, I turn further around in my chair to inquire, "You have a ride home from Jess's in the morning?"

"Yep. Dad's picking me up early and taking me to a job interview."

This surprises me, given that both my parents keep Tate on an extremely short leash. "Where's the interview?"

"Piney Hill Golf Course," she answers with an overly exaggerated smile.

"Why are you excited about working there, Tate? It'll be hot as hell," Cody responds, looking over at Tate. Seeing her animated expression, he raises his hand up to stop her from talking. "Wait, don't answer that. I don't wanna know."

She ignores his plea and answers anyway. "Young guys out in the sun all day. All tan and sweaty—*so hot.*"

"See? I didn't need to hear that," Cody moans.

Scoring my sister with a dirty look, I remind her, "No parties tonight."

Jess steps up from behind Tate and when I turn my gaze to Nick, it appears he has one thing on his mind, and it's not good.

"Cards!" Jess exclaims, looking over Tate's shoulder. "Can we play?"

The young girl is wearing next to nothing; a tight concert T-shirt, which displays her ample cleavage, as well as a short skirt, which showcases her long, athletic legs.

Nick continues to gape, so I tell her, "No."

"Your brother's playing for his life," Drew lets on.

Tate, though being a brat, clues in on what's off and doesn't take well to his tone.

Sibling protection hails. "Wait, what? What's that mean?"

"That show, the one with all those girls trying to get the one guy to marry them will be in town next week. Monday, I think," Cody explains before taking a drink of his beer.

"Shut up!" Jess exclaims. "Marry a millionaire! You'd rock that shit, Brock. You're perfect!"

*Approval from an eighteen-year-old girl who'd probably qualify as a contestant. Fuck.*

"Yep. And if Brock loses tonight's game, he's going to audition," Mark interjects, like he hasn't a care in the world. "Apparently, tonight we're playing for potential nuptials, not money," he complains, throwing his cards on the table while watching Nick rake in another stack.

Back to business, Cody dismisses the girls. "Let's move this along. Kids, you gotta go."

"Right. See ya," Jess replies.

Tate freezes. Standing rigid, her eyes don't leave mine. "Mom told me what Dad's making you do, and I think it's bullshit," she snaps. "She also told me you agreed. Don't agree to do something stupid, Brock. Okay?"

"I won't. Go have fun, but be safe."

Without saying another word, her and Jess file out, leaving me alone with the assholes who may have my best interest at heart, but don't have a clue as to how much I wish they didn't.

# Chapter Four

*Brooke*

-

"Christ, this place is packed!" Addie shouts out over the music, while pulling her purse in closer. "Look at all these people."

"What the hell is happening?" I ask, coming up to stand between my friends to get a better look.

"I have no idea," Sam replies. She's staring into the crowd with eyes wide as saucers. I don't think she's blinked once since we walked in. "Is someone having a party?"

On an average night, the one bar we have in town can be considered busy. This isn't that. Cub's Bar and Grill is *busy*.

More than half the faces looking back at us are unrecognizable. No way, the people of this rowdy and boisterous crowd hail from our small town. The band, which I assume is about to play, is setting up their equipment on the small stage toward the back of the room.

Both Monica and Valerie, Cub's wait staff on duty, appear to be running themselves ragged. Monica's red hair is thrown up with the sides threatening to fall from its clip, and Valerie's normally pale face is flushed as she bends to listen to the man who appears to be ordering a drink. He's also gazing down at her cleavage. I shudder to myself on her behalf.

"We should go. We can try the bowling alley. It won't be nearly as crowded," I decide.

"Not yet," Addie objects. "Wait."

"We won't get a table. If we do, there won't be enough room for everyone," I encourage, still hoping to persuade them to leave.

Sam jumps up and down in place, waving her hands around in the air, and smiles. "Look! There's Morgan and Amber. They found a table."

*Damn it.*

We were close to leaving, I know we were. Obviously, the rest of the group has arrived before us and secured a table near the back. After Addie turns back to me and gives me a 'don't complain, just go with the flow,' look, I follow closely behind.

I've known my best friend long enough to understand each and every expression she uses to spear me in these instances.

Addie's hand clutches mine forcefully, ensuring she doesn't lose me in the crowd. The brief glimpse of her other hand has her holding Sam's in the same brutal manner. We're single filing through the masses of dancing, laughing, and cheering patrons.

I'm, of course, still clueless as to why they're all here.

"Can you believe this place?" Morgan queries, smiling up at all of us as we stand around the table. No one's about to answer; we're all lost in our own thoughts of unorganized chaos.

The wall the table is backed against makes it a tight fit. There's an emergency exit behind where Morgan and Amber remain seated. Being that I hate crowds, Addie hates people, and Sam hates not being the center of attention at her own party, I suspect I could jar it open and make a break for it. I don't, though, only because Addie pulls my arm and I'm forced to take the open seat next to her. My back is to the crowd, so at least I don't have to focus on what may or may not be happening within it.

"What's going on?" Sam leans down to ask Amber, while pulling a chair out at the end of the table to sit.

"Do you know who Willow Ellis is?" Amber immediately questions back, looking first to Sam who shakes her head. After, her eyes move across the table to Addie who does the same.

I *do* know who Willow Ellis is. If I'm being honest, I consider myself somewhat of a stalker.

While working at my family's inn, I'm sometimes required to fill in for a variety of employee's shifts. This can entail working late evenings into the night, which is also when television's primetime shows are on.

Willow Ellis and Matt Sutton are considered America's television sweethearts who run the show, 'Marry A…'.

Each year, the show is based on a variety of everyday people who are committed to wed during its season finale. When I say everyday people, I mean just that. Doctors, lawyers, beauticians, etc. Last season failed in ratings because the plumber they chose looked so much like Mario the gaming character it was uncanny. And a little creepy.

The bride he ended up choosing flat refused to marry him and later became a celebrity for all the wrong reasons. Mario went home broken hearted, yet the blonde bombshell—I genuinely believe he fell in love with—went on to date, then marry a rich Italian playboy from New York.

As such, I'm waiting not so patiently for karma to catch on and kick her ass. Not only that, I want to see it play out on the small black and white television I watch from the reception desk at the inn.

"What about the show?" Addie inquires, her interest obviously piqued as Morgan had went on to explain without my hearing her.

"Well, they're here!" Amber exclaims, clapping her hands in front of her face like the cheerleader she most certainly was in high school. Her green eyes dance with excitement, and her blonde ponytail swooshes to her animated movement when she further explains, "They were supposed to scout the last female contestant in Des Moines this weekend, but word got out they were coming and it became too much for the camera men and staff. They all threatened to quit. So, they moved everything here!"

*Oh God.*

I'd like to roll my eyes in the face of her excitement, but I don't get the chance.

Addie turns in her chair, braces her hand on my forearm and declares, "We're applying."

No freaking way did I hear her correctly. "Oh no, Addison Tindal, we are not."

She smiles, reaches across the table to Amber's place, and yanks away the poor woman's only shot. She brings it to her mouth, smiles before downing it, then looks back at me.

"Live crazy, right? I mean, I've been telling you this forever."

"No," I flatly refuse, sitting back in my chair, and pushing my hands between us.

Standing up, Addie scans the crowd. I assume my crazy friend is looking for Willow and her group.

I'm not moving.

It's not happening.

The last thing I need to do is audition for a position on a show that could potentially set me up with some idiot I'd then have to seriously consider marrying.

*No way.*

"They aren't accepting any more applications," Morgan tells us. Her expression is one of pure defeat. She must have already tried to get in and was refused. "They're only here now to celebrate and wrap up before heading back to California."

"Pity," I smart, finally relaxing as I take in and exhale a needed breath.

"This is nuts," Sam exclaims. "Look!"

In unison, our heads turn in the direction of the stage. A woman I vaguely recognize is standing front and center. There's a short bald man holding a camera on his shoulders in the corner of the room. His camera's lens is aimed at her.

The woman walks back and forth, licking her lips for the crowd to appreciate. The gesture brings them to their feet, and shortly after, they start to cheer her on. Her long, red hair and pale skin come into contrast under the bright lights of the stage.

"Oh my God," Amber screams. "She's gonna strip."

"These people are crazy," I breathe. I squint, still unsure where I've seen her.

"Why does she look so familiar?" Addie questions quietly in my ear. "Did we go to school with her?"

Maybe that's it. Although, she looks a few years younger than any of us.

"Possibly?"

"Brooke!" I vaguely hear my name being called from behind me, but continue trying to place the stripper as she removes her shirt.

Her abs are tight. They're also decorated heavily in an array of colorful floral tattoos. She swings the shirt above her head before tossing it out into the crowd. The cameraman turns in sync with the crowd of onlookers before a group toward the middle quickly makes an attempt to grab it.

"Brooke!" another voice yells, this time louder, so I turn.

"Oh, fucking hell," I hear Addie hiss as we both turn to find my ex-boyfriend Jason walking in our direction.

"No," I mutter, but it's to myself. No way the others caught my hesitation. "He can't be here."

"The woman," Addie states. I turn to her as she continues, "That's the woman he was with..."

*No.*

It figures. I mean, it really would. My pathetic social life is coming to surmise my fate as the jilted lover of a man who left me for an apparent stripper. How lucky am I to get to deal with this mess face to face, *again.*

"Christ, I want to go home," I insist to my best friend, now standing even closer to me than she was.

"You're not going anywhere. Fuck that."

"Addie, please."

"Can someone tell me what's going on?" Sam questions. Her face is red from the body heat being generated in here. Crowds don't bode well for her anxiety, or mine.

"I want to go," I say again, grabbing my purse from the table.

By the time I turn back around, I'm too late. Jason's made his way to us.

His long sleeve shirt is free of wrinkles, surprisingly so, considering this chaotic crowd. His hair is neatly in place, as per usual. Unfortunately, so is his sweet smile I once believed was only for me.

The anger of rejection he recently exposed me to rises to the surface. My chest tightens, so I attempt to breathe deeply. My hands ball into fists at my sides as I turn to look at Addie. Her position is mirroring mine; a true friend standing by as back up.

"What are you doing here?" I snap, but I don't give him a chance to answer. "Seriously, Jason? You left me for a stripper?"

His jaw ticks and his eyes grow dark, no longer the sweet man I once loved. Now he's the adulterous man-child I hate.

"No, Brooke. Cheryl's not a fucking stripper. She's having fun."

"Fun?"

I point my finger in her direction as a gesture to prove this, being how she's removed her skirt and is prancing up and down on the stage wearing next to nothing. Her lace bra doesn't hide what's underneath, and her thong is hanging on by mere threads—literally.

"You cheated on then left me for *fun*?"

"I didn't leave you, Brooke. We grew apart."

*He did* not *just say that.*

"Did he just..." Addie's words get lost in my fury.

"I loved you!" I scream, loud and above the music, just enough to attract a small audience. "I loved you, and you had sex with that woman..." I point to the stage for emphasis. "You left me for a freaking stripper!"

"Calm down, Brooke," he placates, raising his hands in surrender. "I just wanted to talk."

My eyes fill with unshed tears that are begging to fall. "*Talk*?" I shriek. "Now? I gave you four years, Jason. I thought we'd—"

"We'd what?" he clips. "Get married? Have kids? Live the boring life your parents do?"

*Oh no. He didn't.*

Looking down, Jason's hand touches his forehead. "I'm sorry. I didn't mean..." When he looks up to watch me turn in place he pleads, "Brooke, wait."

He must think I'm leaving. I'm not.

As he takes two steps closer, his hand clutches my arm. I spring into a complete irrational reaction. The half-full glass of beer I'm holding shakes in my hand as I draw it closer to him. I take a deep breath before tossing its entire contents in his face. His eyes slam shut as the random drops continue spilling down his neck and onto his perfectly pressed shirt.

"She just..." Sam's speechless. This is new. "Oh shit."

Using his hand to clean the beer from his face, he opens his eyes.

"I hate you!" I yell, not caring about those witnessing my ridiculous behavior. "I hate what you did! Jesus, you two deserve each other."

The crowd around us steps in closer. The women are cheering me on, while the men are booing at what I've done. I don't care what anyone thinks. I need air.

Pushing past Jason as he says nothing, my shoulder meets his, and I hit it hard. I meant to.

"I don't want to see you again," I hiss into his ear. "You make me sick."

On the way to the bathroom, I hear footsteps drawing closer from behind. I recognize the click clack of high heel shoes and hope it's someone from our group. Then pray like hell it's really only Addie.

"Brooke," Addie calls from where she stands. "It's okay. No one's pissed. No one blames *you* for being pissed."

"I'm not pissed, Addie," I explain, now gripping the white porcelain of the sink so hard my knuckles start to burn. "I'm hurt. I'm humiliated."

She doesn't say anything other than, "I'm sorry."

"Did you see the woman he's with now?" My voice comes through with agitation. After only three weeks, the hurt is still so raw. "She's everything I'm not, Add. Everything I'll never be."

"You're right," she tells me. "And if you were her, I wouldn't want to know you."

The knock at the door saves us from further discussion. Addie opens it carefully, but doesn't greet whoever is there. When I peer above Addie's shoulder, I only make out what looks to be a blonde woman with big hair. She's also pressing on the door to enter.

I'm surprised when Addie steps back. This allows the woman enough room to squeeze through the door and into our small, cramped space.

"You're Willow Ellis," I whisper. "You're Willow..." I start to say again.

"Ellis," the woman says, smiling and offering her hand in formal introduction. "I am her."

"No way," I hear Addie mutter as she steps back into her position, guarding the door to keep the others out.

The knocking has become relentless, adding now a few curses from the women actually needing to use the facilities.

Addie ignores the activity behind her and states, "You're the woman from that television show."

Willow looks back and nods to Addie before turning her gaze to mine. "Sweetheart, are you okay?"

"She's okay," Addie answers, because I can't.

I'm starstruck.

For the first time in my life I'm coming face to face with a celebrity. I have no words. I'm sure my gaping mouth and speechless temperament is frightening her, but no way can I help it.

*No way.*

"I'm okay," I finally muster the courage to reply. "Jason and I have history, but I'll be fine."

Willow nods, keeping her eyes on me. "That was his name? Jason?"

"Yes."

"I hear you guys aren't taking anymore applications for this season," Addie casually points out. "But what about next year? I'd love to be on your show. How can I apply?"

I imagine my one-track mind friend would do well in the public eye. She would certainly bask in the attention. We don't have this in common. I've thrown a drink on a man I used to love only to find myself shamefully hiding in bathroom bar to avoid seeing him again for God's sake.

"You're technically seeing someone, Addie," I remind her, happy to have found my words. "Right?"

Addie narrows her eyes, this time using the 'shut the fuck up' expression I've come to know.

"Well," Willow starts, but stops. Her eyes come to mine, and her expression turns to all business. "*Technically*, your friend is right. We're not actively accepting any more auditions. We start with eight girls every season. We've already chosen them for this one."

"Yes," I reply. "I know. I've seen the previews."

"A fan of the show?" she recognizes while smiling. "Great!"

"I watch sometimes," I tell her. "When I can," I add, trying not to sound pathetic.

My head still isn't wrapped around Willow being here, standing in front of me, looking exactly like she does on television. She's so pretty.

"I want you there." My mouth falls open as she shocks me by further saying, "On the show."

"Wait, what?" Addie jolts, walking away from her place at the door to stand next to me. "You want Brooke?"

"Brooke," Willow says, using the name I obviously forgot to give her. "Yes, I want Brooke. I want the spitfire I just watched throw a drink all over the man who at one time broke her heart. I want the girl who didn't think twice about embarrassing the smug bastard who left his new girlfriend on a band stage to dance in front of a crowded room of rowdy onlookers that wasn't policed with security."

*Well, when she puts it like that...*

"Idiot," Willow mumbles.

"Bastard," Addie adds.

"He did break my heart," I admit.

However, seeing him again as I did, throwing a drink on him as I did, and finally saying my piece as I did, was therapeutic. I'm less hurt and more scorned. Everything Addie has been trying to tell me is true. Jason and I weren't supposed to be together. If we were, he wouldn't have done what he did.

Addie smiles at what she must believe is my self-realization. Willow's eyes narrow because she's obviously still pissed on my behalf.

"Bastard," Willow repeats Addie's conclusion. "Will you consider coming to Los Angeles?"

Shaking my head, I move to speak, but Addie steps in front of me first and responds with, "Absolutely."

"Addie!"

"She'll go." Addie turns to me, giving me a nasty look that Willow can't see before turning back around. "She'll go."

"Here's my card." Willow's long, red fingernails stand out against the gold and black card she's pushing toward me. "I'll call you in the morning with more details. I can also answer whatever questions you come up with before then. There's a catch, though, honey."

"What's the catch?" Addie asks, not giving me the chance.

It's a good thing Addie's thinking, too, because I'm a speechless zombie, holding the business card belonging to a woman who produces a reality television show. The same show I've watched, but never desired to be cast on.

"Well, we're set to tape next week. As in, *next week*. The only thing Matt and I have left to do is pick the groom. He's summarizing his interviews Monday and Tuesday, and then the candidate will be announced bright and early Wednesday morning."

"Shit, that's fast," Addie comments, but turns to look at me. "But you'll do it?"

"I don't know, Addie. I have to check…"

*What the hell am I saying?*

"No, I don't think I can make it," I curtly advise. "I have things to do."

"Willow?" Addie calls. The two exchange a look. "Can I get a minute in here alone with Brooke?"

And there it is.

That's all it takes.

Addie's mind is made up. I'll never convince her that this is a bad idea.

The worst ever.

Nothing good can come of it. But it doesn't matter. Seeing Jason tonight put another nail in the coffin which was once my life.

Dear Lord, I *hate* that man.

# Chapter Five

*Don't ask me if I know what the fuck I'm doing.*

*Brock*

-

"Own it, Brock," Drew demands. "You lost the bet. You know the rules."

I may have overreacted after losing the final hand of the poker game Saturday night. I threw my cards in, cursed the adolescent rules, then waited to see if my soon to be ex-friends were really going to go through torturing me with this ridiculous dare.

A dare which would put me in the spotlight of a ludicrous television show I've always—adamantly—refused to watch.

"You're trying to help," I explain what I know. "I get it, I do. But this is fucked."

"It's not." Drew shakes his head as he steps further into my apartment.

It's been two days of quiet peace with my friends. Two days where I contemplated this dare and if I should even consider it. Two days alone with my own reflective thoughts regarding my stepdad's disappointment and my mom's incessant worrying.

My contemplations weren't only about them, but Tate as well. So far, I've only played the role of a fuck up older brother, and I've done it with ease. I've never given my little sister reason to follow any of my leads by example.

When Drew knocked on my door this morning, I debated on whether to answer or not. Once I heard Nick out there as well, I knew I didn't stand a chance against the two of them together. Separately, maybe. Together, no way.

Nick looks around, taking in the state of my apartment. I haven't bothered to clean or straighten. Since I'm off this week, I thought I'd take some time to unwind and relax. Viewing my place through his eyes now has me second-guessing if all the deliveries in takeout and trips to the liquor store were such a great idea.

Finally, after a few seconds of keeping his mouth shut, Nick opens it with, "If Daddy Warbucks saw this place…"

"He'd have reason to be as pissed as he is?" Drew questions, eyebrows raised. He's readying for my reaction, but I don't care enough to offer one.

"We gotta go, Brock. And you're not ready."

"Ready for what?"

"We're meeting Matt Sutton's personal assistant in two hours. As in, you need to shower, dress, and put on a happy face."

"This is fucked," I tell them, refusing to move. "I didn't agree to this."

Drew sighs heavily, running his hands through his hair "You did agree. Brock, I know you think we're assholes—"

"*Fucking* assholes," I correct.

"Right." Nick steps in between us and stands too close for my comfort.

Nick places his hand on my shoulder and looks me square in the eyes. I've known him a long time, and I can't remember when he's been so serious, other than when his father passed.

"We're doing this," he says quietly. "But we're not doing it because we're dicks. We're doing this because we care."

Still standing behind Nick, Drew moves in closer as well. "We'll be downstairs. If you're not down there in thirty minutes, we're leaving."

"Thank fuck," I utter with relief.

Nick shakes his head. "No, Brock. This sounds like an ultimatum—"

"It is," Drew interrupts. "But if you don't get your shit together, we'll blame ourselves and rethink our friendship."

*Oh my god, my friends are starting to sound like women.*

"Seriously?"

"No," Drew replies. "But if you don't do this for us, then what hope do we have for our future?"

"Lead us, Brock," Nick dramatically states, covering his hand over his heart. "Help us."

"Jesus Christ," I mumble. I take the two of them in and think about how badly I need to expand my circle of friends. "Give me thirty."

"There he is! Who knows, you may not even get chosen," Nick says as encouragement, but he doesn't mean it. His smile lies.

"See ya downstairs," Drew calls back as the two idiots file out, closing the door behind them.

*"Do you have any future engagements which would hinder your ability to be on set for the nine to eleven weeks' time?"* the bald man asks as I sit across from him, waiting for him to stop prodding into my life as he is.

So many queries...

Question: *Do you have a girlfriend?*

Answer: Nope. If I did, my father wouldn't have forced me into this situation.

Question: *Have you ever been married?*

Answer: God, no. Same answer applies. Though, I don't tell him any of that either.

Question: *Do you have any STDs that you're aware of?*

Answer: Fuck no. No glove, no love.

Question: *Do you have any mental disorders we should know about prior to the show being taped?*

This is where I draw the line.

"Are we almost done here?" I abruptly question. He raises his eyes from his clipboard to find my disinterest. "I don't think I'm your guy."

"If you don't mind me saying so, Brock, but I believe you are," he returns with a smile. "Matt's all but decided you're who he wants. He mentioned your name again this morning."

"He didn't know me this morning," I state as fact.

The sudden inquisitive look on the man's face gives me pause. I'm quickly coming to the conclusion that my dear friends had already set me up; formal applications weren't needed in my case, apparently.

*Son of a bitch.*

I take a quick look around to the other candidates in this small lounge. Most are wearing suits. They're all tan with perfectly styled hair. Some even appear to have had manicures and facials. I look down to my dark blue Henley, which isn't even nice, and faded blue jeans, which have a few holes and tears, then smirk. I'm the only contestant in this room who doesn't give a shit.

Maybe that's what makes the theme of this reality television so *real*.

Sensing my inner discovery, Mr. What's-His-Name is, smiles again.

Standing up, he grabs his coffee cup and takes a quick drink. Before setting it down, he holds it to his chest and says, "If you don't mind waiting a few minutes, I'll tell Matt we've finished your interview."

Checking my watch, not giving two shits about the time, I counter with, "Five minutes."

As I sit alone, picking at the end of my shirt, debating on whether to pull the string, a tall, well put together man about my height and age comes to stand at my side. He's wearing a designer suit, coupled with expensive loafers. His face is closely shaven, and his smile is polished. He appears to be as I had imagined he would.

"Brock LaDuece, I assume?" Putting his hand between us, he offers it to me for me to take. His large faced, silver plated watch is another indication he's well-groomed.

Rather than continue to look disinterested, I stand and accept it. "I'm Brock."

"Matt Sutton, producer and host of the show."

"I'm still just Brock," I answer half-heartedly.

"Sit, please," he instructs, pointing back to my chair.

He walks around the table to the seat the interviewer—*damn I should have gotten his name*—was sitting and takes it himself.

As he flips through a manila folder, I catch the mug shot picture which had been taken when we arrived.

"You're a media mogul, I see," he casually comments, not looking up.

"My father is Martin Merritt, of Merritt Media."

"I see. So, as his son, this makes you his protégé?"

"As his stepson," I correct. "I'm his life's disappointment."

My reply forces his wide smile. His perfect, straight white teeth shine under the table's interrogation light above.

"Tell me," he insists, closing the file and resting his arms on top of it. "Why would you consider a position on a show such as this one?"

"Honestly?" I inquire. I mean, if we're being honest, I'll tell him.

"Absolutely." Sitting back, he rests his elbow on the chair's arm and crosses his ankle to his knee. "I'm curious. Generally, those we've interviewed are self-made millionaires. You're not. Your inheritance is what makes you different than the others."

"My father *strongly* urged me to find a woman and settle down."

His face drops. He must think I'm kidding. Fuck, I wish I were.

"He's threatening to take away my rights to his company, along with my inheritance, if I don't."

A look of understanding passes over his expression before he tilts his head to the side.

"Did you read any of the contract Tom gave you when you arrived?"

*Tom. Thank you for that.*

"I haven't," I admit.

Sitting up, he gives me a disappointed look. "In this contract, it states you must choose a woman from those we've selected. However, it doesn't mean the woman you choose will marry you. The catch is that if she were to refuse, the audience would choose for you."

*I did not know this.*

"This very same thing happened last year. The man chose, she denied. The audience chose for him."

"How'd that go?" I ask, oddly curious and internally berating myself for being so.

Matt nods with enthusiasm. "Very well. They're coming back at the end of this season to tape their follow-up episode."

I don't say anything in response. I don't know what to say.

"You're a good looking man, Brock. I have no doubt the women Willow has selected will meet your suitable expectations."

Shrugging, I admit, "My father won't care who she is or what she looks like as long as she makes my mother happy."

Matt's face once again turns to pity. "What about you?"

"I'll be happy to have all of this over."

Suddenly, he stands, extends his hand again, and waits for me to accept.

Once I do, he knowingly grins and says, "Well, let's start now."

# Chapter Six

*God, I love my dad.*

*Brooke*

-

"Dude, seriously. That woman is *hot*," Ashton, my nineteen-year-old brother, who I choose to believe will always remain a virgin states his observation as we all sit around my parents' dining room table. "I know she's gotta be old, but damn, she's still good looking."

I've been choking on my words, not my dinner, since I started to explain what happened at Cub's three nights ago. The only reprieve I've been granted is Ashton's continuous study of the magazine announcing this year's theme of the show.

*Marry a... Millionaire.*

I've tossed around the idea in my head so many times, and in so many ways, I can't remember all Willow told me. I know I have to decide today, though, as in *right now*. My plane, if I choose to board it, leaves tomorrow morning at ten.

"Ashton, put that down," my dad barks. He doesn't wait for Ashton to do as he's told, rather, he adds, "You have bigger things to worry about than the woman on the cover of that magazine."

"Dad, have you seen her?" my brother questions, lifting the copy of *Television Wild* and forcing my dad to look away. In the meantime, my mother's staring daggers at us all.

"This whole situation is preposterous! Tell me you're not seriously considering this crazy idea. Are you, Brooke?" she asks.

Mom hasn't taken this news well. Since I first explained Willow's offer, her lower eyelid has continued to twitch at a furious pace. For a few minutes, I thought she was going to pass out, but luckily the color in her face came back once she started steadily breathing again.

"I wasn't going to—"

"Oh, thank God," she exhales, interrupting me as she does. "You don't know that man they've chosen. And you don't know those *women,* either."

"Nora, stop it." To my surprise, it's my dad who intervenes again. He's been mostly quiet, not saying much since this conversation started. "Whether Brooke decides to go or doesn't isn't your decision to make."

"She doesn't know that city, Decklan Malloy! Do you want our little girl walking around lost and hungry in a strange place she knows nothing about?"

"Nora, please," Dad angrily begs. "Just stop."

"Dad?" I question. "You think I should do this?"

Directly following my question, my brother adds, "No way."

Ashton doesn't say this in a way as not to do it. He appears to be in as much shock as I am at the mere *idea* of our father entertaining me with his support in this decision.

"Brooke," Dad addresses. Before I turn to face him as he sits at the head of our small dining room table, he asks, "Is this an opportunity you think you'd *like* to consider?"

"What's there to *consider*?" my mother gasps, holding her hand to her chest.

Her long brown hair must be standing on end. She's got it pulled back away from her face that's aged at least ten years since we all sat down.

"What are you saying, Decklan? That she should go on some random low rated television show, meet her match, and do what?"

Dad throws a look to Mom, which thankfully keeps her quiet, but her mouth still gapes wide. I can't think straight with her constant interruptions.

"Brooke?" Dad prods for his answer.

Shaking my head, I explain, "I wasn't. I mean, until Addie—"

Obviously, Mom refuses to let this go. Cutting me off, she raises her voice to yell, "Addison Marie Tindal!"

Earlier this evening, I called my best friend. I strategically used several means of persuasive childhood blackmail and got her to reluctantly agree to having dinner with my parents. I was hoping either they would run her off, screaming for the hills and begging for their forgiveness, or calmly tell her me going off on some random little thought-out mission wasn't going to happen. I hadn't, however, placed any consideration into my father's peculiar reaction.

Addie comes striding in after hearing her name called. She bounces around the corner from the bathroom and quietly takes her seat directly across from me and next to Ashton. She up and ran once I brought up the show.

*Like the traitor she is.*

"Mrs. Malloy," Addie formally addresses. "Personally, I don't think Brooke going is a bad idea."

"You don't think this is a bad idea," my mother repeats. "And don't call me Mrs. Malloy!"

Now all the hairs on the back of *my* neck stand on end hearing the tone my mother uses. That same tone has always been saved for my brother and me when we found ourselves in a shit storm of trouble. Now it's aimed at Addie and, in reaction, my best friend sinks slightly in her seat.

"This was all your idea," my mom accuses her next. "I should've known. This has your name all over it."

Slapping his hand to the table, hard enough to rein in my mother's attention, my dad speaks to her directly. "Nora, for the last time, just stop. Let Brooke answer for herself."

"Yes," Addie agrees, shifting the focus from her back to me. "Let's hear Brooke out."

"I wasn't considering this, Dad, until Addie talked to Willow the next day and got the details."

"And?" he prods, coaxing me to continue. "Go on."

"Do you think it's a good idea?" I ask, genuinely wanting his opinion. "It would mean I'd be leaving the inn for at least two months."

Dad's lips draw in tight. It's always been my father, not my mother, who's pushed me away from this town.

Time and time again he's told me I'm too big for it.

*The people here are simple*, he's said.

*You have a good head on my shoulders*, he's told me.

*Go do what you're destined to do* was the best advice he's ever given me; I've never applied this to anything I've ever done.

"The inn will manage itself without you. Ashton can pull more of his weight while still maintaining his class schedule. And your mother and I can pick up the rest. Now, tell me..." He pauses, then directs, "What do you want to do?"

When I look down to my untouched plate, I aim to focus. Trying to explain that being away from this town for *any* reason would be good for *only* one is too tough for words. I need away from Jason and all the memories, good and bad, this town holds.

"I don't know what I want to do," I admit quietly.

My father, sitting next to me, brings his hand to my shoulder and squeezes gently. When my mom starts to say something again, he lifts his finger. She quiets, but audibly huffs.

"Brooke, look at me," he gently demands.

Tears spring to my eyes. Not from doubt of the show itself, but because the very thought of leaving either of my parents for more than a few weeks bothers me. When I look up, the gentleness I've always found on my dad's face is there. Always understanding and always ever-present.

"I think you'll do well in anything you decide to do. I've never seen the show myself, but I think if there's an opportunity that others don't get, you should take it. I'm not saying run off and get married—"

"Then what *are* you saying?" I ask as though those around the table have ceased to exist. This is a moment saved for guidance between a father and his only daughter.

"I'm saying Ashton, your mother, and I love you very much. We want what's best for you, and you're of an age now when you're the only person who can decide what that best looks like."

"Brooke," Addie calls. I turn to her. She holds the same expression as my dad. "He's right. You need to do what's best for you. Don't let my opinion interfere."

*There's a first.*

"I'll think about it," I tell them both.

When I bravely move my gaze to my mother, I find her mouth still open, but not in surprise. Her coloring is lost again, and her small body is starting to shake.

She's about to pass out.

Then again, so am I.

# Chapter Seven

*Out of sight, out of mind, I guess.*

*Brock*

-

Standing in front of the airport terminal, I take in the sight of my two best, albeit traitorous, friends.

Nick is looking anywhere but at me. If he were feigning a dubious whistle, it would be a fuck of a lot less obvious that he finds this entire scene hilarious. Drew continues looking at me, then to the door, and finally back to me, as if placing some internal bet whether I'll really go or make a break for it.

As if bets didn't just get me into this mess.

When I told my father my plan for the show, he gave me the same coarse expression he always does—half-hearted disinterest. After he approved a partially paid leave of absence from work, he shook my hand and told me to make good decisions. It was a mocking statement as he knew inevitably I'd be choosing a bride—a woman to bring home to my mother. His exact wish was becoming a reality, to my liking or not.

My mother, always overly dramatic, cried. She hates this idea more than any others I had growing up, and believe me, I've had plenty. To say me going on a reality show ranks higher than the year I brought home a family of baby squirrels is saying a lot. I was nine and didn't know any better, or probably did and didn't care. I'd trapped them in a barrel and had every intention of calling them pets. Her wordless reaction of heavy sighs followed by tears said enough. Needless to say, she was beside herself.

Tate reacted to the news I was leaving exactly as I figured Tate would. She was livid. She couldn't believe how far I'd sunken in order to get a date—her words, not mine. More than anything else, to me she's still a kid. Being so, I withheld all I truly wanted to say to her.

I can't get a date our father approves of.

I'm not able to make my good decisions regarding the women I sleep with.

I'm doing everything father says.

Unfortunately, though, I know my motives for going wouldn't appease her. I'm going to L.A. for a reason. Aside from a one week trip back in a few weeks, I'll be coming home a married man.

"You packed everything you need?" Drew asks. If I'm not mistaken, I'm sensing he's finally starting to feel a small version of remorse.

I nod, but don't say anything more.

"You nervous?" Nick inquires, still holding in his laugh. "I mean, not nervous about the plane, but you know, picking a bride."

"Fuck you," I flip back.

If he were anyone else, I'd punch him.

"I gotta go check in or I'll miss my flight," I advise.

"I'm not huggin' you, bro. I'll see you soon," Drew assures. "I'm gonna see if I can come visit."

"Maybe by the time you get there, I'll be less pissed," I advise curtly.

I shouldn't be pissed now, but I am.

I got myself into this, not them. Granted, they didn't steer me away and, months ago, they did fill out the damn application on my behalf, not to mention this whole fucking production was their idea of a perfect set-up.

Yeah, never mind. I should be pissed.

With Nick's smirk in place, I turn around to leave and hear, "Call us when you land."

# Chapter Eight

*Father knows best.*

*Brooke*

-

"Brooke, Ashton's waiting by the car to take you to the airport. Are you almost ready?"

I turn to find my mom leaning against the doorjamb of my bedroom and looking at me as she always does—with lots of love, but complete misunderstanding.

Her eyes are swimming with tears, and she's biting her bottom lip to control its constant quiver. My mom never understood why I've always made the decisions I have. The older I get, the more stress she puts on me to be like her.

Truth be told, I'm my father's daughter above all else.

In an effort to offer reassurance, I promise, "I'm going to call you every day. I'll text you, too. Don't worry, Mom. I really will be fine."

"Your father says this, too. But Brooke, I hate that you're leaving."

I knew she was going to make this hard. Dad told me as much last night after dinner, just as I was leaving with Addie to go out for a drink.

"I'll be back in a few weeks. They're giving us a five-day break, remember?"

"If you don't get chosen to be his *bride*, you'll be back sooner?"

Shaking my head, I advise, "No. The groom doesn't choose until the end. All of us have to wait to see what happens as everyone else does. I'm stuck in L.A. until the finale."

"I hope you're not *in* the finale, Brooke. Not in a way that changes your last name, anyway."

My mom still hasn't accepted any of this. I'm not confident enough to believe I'll be the woman at the altar. When Addie relayed all Willow explained during their conversation, she included such things as the professions of some of the contestants. They vary from hair dresser to veterinarian. She mentioned nothing of family-owned business owners who snack on cookies and ice cream while reading glossy glamour magazines and watching high school drama reality television to pass their time.

No matter what, this will be a good experience. I reassure myself of this for the hundredth time.

"All right, Mom. I'm finished here, so help me get my things to the car."

Without delay, Mom bends to grab one suitcase as I grab the other. We make our way through the house and into the foyer near the front door where my dad stands alone, drinking his coffee, and looking out into the driveway. Mom grabs me by the shoulders and pulls me in for a deep hug, which I return.

"I love you, Button. Be safe." She bids her goodbye through a broken voice.

Dad turns around and observes us with a small smile as Mom steps back, fidgets with her hair, and quickly walks away.

"She hates this," I prompt, walking closer to stand at his side.

Outside, both Addie and Ashton are leaning against Ashton's new truck. Luckily, they aren't paying any attention to what's going on at the front door.

My dad's still not said a word, so I ask, "You okay?"

Pulling his cup of coffee to his lips, he takes a quick drink then whispers over the rim, "No."

"Dad?"

Not looking at me, but out into the driveway, he explains his apprehension. "My girl is leaving. I'll never be okay with that."

"I'm coming back when it's over," I assure.

Throughout my life, especially as a kid, I've reassured him of this time and time again.

My first day of kindergarten, he had tears in his eyes.

He was so nervous for me to be around other kids my age. He said they all carried germs. The teachers at my school weren't considered responsible adults, but rather complete strangers. I'm not sure who between us was hurting worse when he and my mother dropped me off that first day.

My first middle school dance, he did all he could to keep his emotions in check.

That dance was the first time I had a reason to really dress up. I wore makeup. Before leaving the house, he told my mother to take it off. She fought to keep it and won, but he grumbled the entire way there and was waiting for me by the front door after Addie's mom had dropped me off.

My first date.

The night Tommy Gilroy picked me up in his parents' van, my father played his part well. He told Tommy if he brought me home so much as a minute late, he wouldn't call his parents to complain, but rather he'd call to inform them where their son's charred remains had been buried.

*God, I love my dad.*

"Do you remember when you were six years old and I took you to the state fair?"

I don't interrupt, but smile because I know where this story is going.

"It was just us. Ashton had chicken pox. He'd been miserable, and you and me needed a break."

"I remember."

When Dad looks over at me, I note his eyes are reflective. "I all but begged you to ride that pony."

"Yes," I concur, remembering my father softly nudging my back to leave him and walk toward the first pony I'd ever seen up close.

"I didn't want you to ride it. My heart broke at the thought, but my gut told me you needed to try."

"*Magnificent* was his name," I remind him. "He was so big. I was scared."

"You remember his name, which means he made quite an impression."

"I never got the guts to get on him, though."

"You never let go of my hand." My father remembers as well. "When I looked down at you and saw how nervous you were, I tried to reason with myself how important it was that I push you to do something you were scared of."

"I don't regret not getting on the horse, Dad, if that's what you're worried about."

No longer looking at me directly, he keeps his concentration outside. "I want you to live the life you should've been living here all along. I allowed you to hide behind your fears only because they were mine, as well. I should've been forcing you to face them as any other parent would have."

"You didn't let me hide behind them," I deny, but in part he's right.

To disregard my making excuses for him, he says, "Even if it's only for the next however many weeks, Brooke. I want you to experience things you wouldn't have the chance to otherwise."

"I will," I promise.

"And don't think about us back here missing you, either. We'll see you soon enough."

"I know." I concur.

"Just be safe. You know the rules. Act responsibly, be courteous and kind, but don't get taken advantage of."

"Hey," I call for his attention as I hear his voice starting to break. It's dropping with each word of last minute advice he's delving out.

"I love you, Button. Your mother and I both do. You're young and we worry."

"Dad, I'm twenty-six."

Finally, his head turns and it's then I see the expression on his face. He's scared. This isn't about the memory of a beautiful pony, my first day of kindergarten, or my first date. This is so much more, and he isn't handling it well.

"You'll still be my first born when you're fifty, and you'll *always* be my little girl."

His sincerity is too much. I drape my arms around him from the side as we keep our focus in the driveway, where Ashton has Addie in a headlock in play.

"God, that brother of yours will never change, will he?"

"Nope," I breathe out.

Thankfully, my brother will never change.

Turning further into him, I give my Dad a hug, tell him I love him, and walk out of his arms without chancing a look back.

"Woman, it's about time. Ashton's about to get his ass beat," Addie exasperates, fixing her hair and clothes from my brother's torment. "Are you ready to go?"

"I think so."

The sun is glowing, shining down so bright I use my hand to block its rays.

"You know Add's going with you to L.A., right?" my brother questions.

I *hadn't* known this. I immediately turn to her in time to see her throwing a sharp glare toward my brother. He shrugs it off as he always does.

"You are?"

"I am. It was supposed to be a surprise."

"How's that possible?" I inquire. I look back at the house to find my dad standing at the door, still drinking his coffee, but he's doing it with a smile.

"I took a leave of absence from work. Your dad insisted I go and watch over you."

"Watch over me?" I scoff. "You're the last person on earth who should be assigned to watch over me."

*My dad has lost his mind.*

Ashton's face is serious, and his words are confident as he says, "Not to supervise like you think. Dad told us he wants you to have fun, Brooke. Addie's going along to ensure you do."

Hearing this, I turn for the last time as my father's hand comes up from his pocket where he offers a wave and a smirk.

I return the gesture, but this time knowing I've been set up.

Addie and my own father have conspired against me. Apparently, if they have their way, I'll be living it up the entire trip.

I don't argue as I'm relieved I'm no longer going at this alone.

"Aren't you happy to have the company, Brooke?" Addie asks with concern.

"I am."

"Then, by all means, let's go get you hitched!"

Shit, I was happy until she put it like *that*.

# Chapter Nine

*My life is ridiculous.*

*Brock*

-

I haven't been to California since I was eleven years old and my parents took me to Disneyland one year for summer vacation. At the time, I hadn't realized there was any other purpose to this state's existence other than Mickey Mouse and Donald Duck.

Los Angeles is a madhouse.

To avoid not having to rent a car, I grabbed my suitcase from baggage claim and hailed a cab to the hotel.

Now that I've finally arrived, I'm finding the hotel lounge is flooded with people of all ages. Businessmen in suits, vacationing families, as well as a swarm of young women surround me. I keep my nose down to avoid looking at any one of them in particular just in case they're here for the same reasons I am. I'm not ready to face anyone from the show just yet.

"Brock LaDuece?" I hear my name called just short of where I'm standing. A thinly haired, middle-aged man wearing a hunter green polo and khakis extends his hand. "I'm Jerry," he introduces himself once I've returned his gesture.

"Yes, I'm Brock LaDuece," I confirm.

"Give me your bag. I'm here to show you your way to your room and go over what to expect over the next few days before the taping begins." He grabs the handle of my suitcase and adjusts the handle to his fit. "Come," He waves. "I've checked you in already. Thought I'd save you some time and frustration."

During the short walk to the elevators ahead, Jerry scans the crowd of women standing around a large seating area. A tall blonde woman I don't recognize stands on the wooden surface of a table while clutching a clipboard in her hand. Apparently, she's attempting to rein in the attention of the chatty women. Her efforts are for naught, as it doesn't look like it's doing her any good.

After hitting the button to the eighteenth floor, Jerry turns to me, rocks on his heels, and smiles.

"Another season starts," he utters, nodding in their general direction.

"Those are the girls from the show?" I question, already figuring that's the case.

He turns in place, taking them in. "Quite the lively bunch we have this year. Did you get a chance to review any of their faceless profiles on the plane?"

Nodding, I return, "I did. Thank you."

Technically, I'm not lying. I reviewed three and stopped. Nancy, Joelle, and Mary Ann did nothing other than jog my memory of syndicate rerun comedies I used to watch as a kid. There were no pictures of any of them, and though looks aren't always what's important, it would help to put a face to who I was reading about.

When the elevator door opens, I'm met with two women who look nothing like the plastic ones left in the other room. The dark haired woman looks up and smiles wide and friendly, whereas the lighter haired brunette doesn't offer me a second glance at all. She looks past me into the foyer of women still chatting along. Her face is expressionless, if not a little puzzled. She turns to her friend and narrows her eyes.

As I pass her, her shoulder catches mine, finally forcing her to look up and directly at me. She's cute, no doubt, but not in an overtly, obvious way. The tension around her exasperating beautiful amber eyes is evident as her mouth opens then closes quickly. I assume she was about to excuse herself for bumping me, but her friend clues in on my attention first.

"She's a little tired. Neither of us have ever been to L.A. Excuse us," the darker haired woman explains, grabbing her friend's arm and pulling her out of the elevator.

I lose sight of them too quickly and turn my gaze back to Jerry. He reads my aim wrong, thinking it was the girl who spoke that had my attention.

Shaking his head, he informs me, "She's not on the show."

"Figures," I reply anyway and let it go.

Pulling out another file from his briefcase, he hands it over for me to take. We've only hit the third floor and have stopped at each so I assume this is his way of not wasting time.

Opening the file, I skim through what looks to be a set of rules and regulations. Yellow highlighted marks capture my attention first.

"We'll be going over this in tomorrow morning's meeting. All of the contestants are required to attend. We're meeting in the Grande Room at eleven. Your meeting will be held separately at eleven thirty."

"Am I supposed to memorize all this?"

He laughs. "No. That's why I've highlighted the passages that pertain specifically to you. The rest are for the girls as well as the staff."

"There's a lot here," I comment, flipping through a few more pages, all of which are stapled to the top of the folder.

"It's the same contract you've already signed. There's nothing in there that'll surprise you later."

Jerry seems like an okay guy, so rather than continue charging him with a barrage of questions, I'll wait and get them answered tomorrow.

"This is it," he tells me as the elevator opens to a penthouse suite door. Reaching into his jacket pocket, he pulls out a plastic credit card key and hands it over. "This one is yours. You've got the Presidential suite for the duration of your stay. Full bar, hot tub, and other amenities you'll be able to find yourself."

"Nice," I say, looking around the area without truly seeing it. I'm too tired.

Slapping me on the shoulder, he informs, "If you need anything, you call me. My business card is by the hotel phone with my number in case you think of something before tomorrow."

"Thanks," I return.

"It's good to have you here, Brock. I'll see you in the morning."

Four hours later, I check my phone for the time. It's only eight o'clock, and I'm bored out of my mind. I've showered off the airplane ride, unpacked most of my things, and have perused through the entire suite. It's not home away from home by any means, but sure as hell beats the Red Roof Inn.

I receive a text at 08:07 p.m.

Drew: *So? How's it going? Have you met Mrs. Brock LaDuece yet?*

I stare at the text message notification as it waits for me to open it. I think back to the asshole who got me into this mess in the first place and wonder why he's not here. It should be Drew going through this, not me. If the situation were reversed, though, I'd probably be having as much fun with this as he is.

Me: *Kiss my ass.*

The phone rings in my hand so I answer it, if only to avoid the ringtone of Rocky he assigned himself months ago during a drunken poker night.

"You're going to be a stick in the mud the entire time, aren't you?" he starts before I'm able to say so much as 'bite me' or 'fuck you.'

"Yes," I respond with petulance as I stand to look outside the bay window of my room. The city looks crowded and busy; exactly the way I feel in being in it.

Drew sighs his frustration. "Consider this an adventure, Brock. You need a wife, they need a show. You get your pick of eight women—eight *hot* and *available* women. How hard can this shit be?"

"You'd think that," I answer.

Unbeknownst to me, my mind shifts back to the light haired brunette from the elevator. The way she looked around that room, completely uncertain and lost in a space filled with all those beautiful and confident women. I felt the same in that I didn't want to be there.

"Nick says to suck it up." I hear Nick in the background saying more, but Drew filters the translation as only he can. "Anyway, we wanted to call and wish you luck tomorrow."

"Thanks," I grumble, this time with less peevishness. Suddenly, I'm feeling like a kid at camp who wants to go home after only spending one night.

Hello Mother, hello Father, greetings from camp, *pick a wife*.

*This sucks*.

"Brock?" Drew addresses with question, his tone changing from jovial to serious.

"Yeah?"

"Make this work. Give it a chance. You haven't found a woman on your own, and you won't listen to my advice ever, but this time please hear me."

Looking to the floor, I rest my hand on my hip while gripping the phone to my ear.

"I will," I pledge. "How the hell did my life get to be this?" I ask in jest, but his answer is immediate.

"Because we let it."

I suppose we did. One for all, all for one, I guess.

"I have an interview tomorrow," he tells me quietly. I hear the regret in his voice, as well as his dream of being a professional golfer fade.

"Where?"

With more defeat, he responds, "Trade's Auto. Nick's trying to get me on. They had a structural change. He's not going to lose his job, thank God."

Shit. No matter or not, Nick hates his job. Drew will hate it more.

"If you need a reference, give them my mom. Don't give them mine. I have too many stories I could tell to get you out of it."

"Thanks, shithead. Take care and call me later," he concludes before disconnecting the call.

My forehead rests on the glass of the window as I continue looking down. I need out of this room and away from the ominous thoughts of marriage, kids, unemployed friends, and sure as hell, considering where I am right now, cute brunettes with hauntingly beautiful amber eyes.

# Chapter Ten

*Addie doesn't hate him.*

*Brooke*

-

"Holy shit, Brooke. Would you look at this place?" Addie gushes, lifting her arms around the room and twirling in place now that she's had time to look around and take it all in. "I mean, who lives like this?"

The hotel room is nice, but my best friend is being dramatic.

"Would you stop gaping? Come help me unpack."

When we arrived to check in to the hotel, the front desk clerk gave us our keycards while informing us we'd be sharing our room with another contestant from the show. Willow said my late arrival wasn't a problem, and that sometimes the girls do room together. It helps bond us, creating friendships in the face of adversity. I didn't understand, considering I don't plan to make friends. Not to mention, I'm thankful enough to have Addie here.

Our roommate's name is Ryleigh Summers. She wasn't here when we arrived earlier, and I didn't see her downstairs for the meeting we were late in attending. But, just like college, her first name was listed on the door to our room, so apparently, she belongs to us.

After check-in, Addie and I went downstairs for the first initial meeting Willow had called to order. She sent a mass text message to several of us. Some replied, some didn't. I can't put faces to names yet, let alone numbers, so I didn't put much weight into the person who texted back, 'Righty Ho!' or the other one who replied, 'I have cramps, can't make it.'

When we made our way into the lounge where we were told to be, we found Willow was standing on a table, trying to capture the attention of the many initial contestants, along with others who I assume were there for Willow's support.

Her arms were waving around her head, and for a few seconds I thought she was about to throw the clipboard she carried out into the crowd. It took her no less than forty-five minutes to quiet the group before she started to go over what we should expect to happen over the next few days.

All of it sounded ridiculous.

Meetings, paperwork, wardrobe, along with meet and greets between the contestants are all scheduled. By the time we'd finished, I couldn't decide if I wanted to poke my eyes out with needles or get so drunk I dreamed of being transported back home.

"Do you think that Ryleigh chick will care if I bunk with her?" Addie asks.

She's serious; I know she is. I'm a deep sleeper. When I'm sick or stressed, I have a tendency to kick like crazy. I even snore on occasion. These are habits of mine she's hated since we were kids.

"She doesn't know me, but do you think she'll care?"

"Probably," I reply as I heave my suitcase to my bed across from the vacant one. "Maybe she won't show up and you'll have it all to yourself."

"I want to know who the rich guy is. I'm dying to find out if he has a brother."

"Of course you are," I mumble, pulling out my now wrinkled favorite shirt and hanging it on a bullshit wooden hanger before laying it on the bed. "Do you not remember your boyfriend, Scottie?"

Addie must not have heard my flippant question. I hear her walking toward me before coming into view. She yanks a perfectly ironed shirt from my hands and tosses it to the floor to get my attention.

"Scottie and I aren't serious. We're growing apart," she tells me without a trace of sadness. "I need a change of view."

When I turn my glare at her, I find her smiling.

"What?" I clip. "What are you looking at?"

Grabbing my shoulders, she squeezes them while looking in my eyes. "You're going to lighten up. This is why your dad insisted I come with you," she reminds me. "Fun, Brooke. This is going to be *fun*. You're only twenty-six once. Live it up, woman."

"Right," I snip, then turn back to my bag. "Your enthusiasm is making me want to drink."

She laughs and points to the black mini-bar fitted beneath the hotel dresser.

"What's your flavor? We have..." She opens the door and rattles off four or five liquors I'm not familiar with, as I normally just drink beer. "Shit, I don't even know what to make with all this."

Setting the clothes down, I turn to my friend and negotiate. "It's only nine-thirty. We can sleep in late tomorrow. If you'd help me finish here, we can go down to the hotel bar and grab a drink."

"You'll wear this?" she asks, holding up a short, black pencil skirt. "And this?" she questions next, holding up a frilly, silk, short sleeve dress shirt to match. "Oh God. And these!" Now she's insisting. She's put together an entire ensemble in less than thirteen seconds.

To appease her and get her moving so I can have that drink I so desperately need, I agree. "Yes, I'll wear all of that."

"Sweet!" she enthusiastically exclaims. "I'll unpack the bathroom. That'll give you time to sort your stuff. Then we can sort mine."

About an hour later, we've got most of our things put away and we're standing near the door to leave.

"I've got everything, right?" Addie queries, checking the contents of her small black clutch purse. "ID, check. Lipstick, check. Money, check."

"Jesus, Addie. Enough," I quip with lost patience. The time I needed a drink was an hour ago.

"Okay, okay," she snaps back. "Don't get bitchy."

As soon as we're finally set to leave, the sound of the lock clicks and the door opens to a young, beautiful woman standing just outside of it.

Her hair is long, blonde, and curly. Her eyes are bright blue, sitting high above natural blushed cheeks. I notice her straight white teeth and overly generous chest next. Her skin is bronzed—natural or not is anyone's guess.

"Um, hi," Addie greets in surprise. It's obvious by her tone and lack of greeting she's taking in the woman's beauty as I just did.

"Hi!" the stranger greets back with excitement. Her shoulders shrug enthusiastically as her arms hang at her sides holding a large suitcase handle in each hand. "I'm Ryleigh."

"Our roomie," I reply. "I'm Brooke, and this is my friend, Addie."

"Girls, I am so glad to be here. I had a horrible trip, coming all the way from Louisiana. My mama cried and cried and cried. I almost missed my plane!"

I'm loving Ryleigh already. Her deep, southern accent, in addition to her sweet girl next-door appearance, is endearing.

"We were just heading to the hotel bar for a drink. Do you want to come?" Addie offers.

Ryleigh shakes her head and closes her eyes. "No, but thank you. I just wanna take a hot bath and turn in early. But I'll catch up with you two in the morning."

Addie and I step aside to allow Ryleigh to enter. She takes in the room and moves to her bed, throwing her luggage on top of it before turning around.

"Have fun, ladies." She bids us goodbye before Addie closes the door on our way out.

Addie has nothing to say until we're standing inside the elevator alone. That's when she turns to me with a mischievous smile.

"She's really pretty."

"She is," I agree. "I love her sundress."

"She has nice hair," Addie adds. "And her shoes were adorable."

"She has nice teeth," I include.

"And her eyebrows are perfectly arched, too." Addie grins.

When I face forward, taking in our appearance in the elevator's metal doors' reflection, I'm hardly able to control my laughter.

"You hate her," I whisper on a gasp.

"I so freaking *do*," she spits out, then busts out into a burst of laughter.

When the elevator doors open on the bottom floor, I look up and take in the man standing in front of us. He has dark hair, dark eyes, and a strong jaw lined with two-day growth. He's wearing a nice suit jacket, which defines his broad chest. His hand is holding a key-card, looking a lot like ours, only his is black.

Once he enters the elevator and stands between Addie and I, we both freeze in place, unable to move.

"I like his suit," Addie whispers from his other side.

My finger continuously presses on the button in order to leave the door open, but I multi-task to peer around him and look at her like she's crazy. He says nothing, but drops his head and pins me with a confused expression.

I'd be confused as well, considering this is where Addie and I are supposed to step off.

"He has nice hair," she says next. "And his shoes," she adds. "He has really nice teeth, too."

Finally, I break into a smile. My friend isn't crazy—she's nuts.

His head turns to her, where she ignores it and continues staring out the open door. Then his eyes come back to mine, a smile quirking his lips.

"But I don't think I hate *him*," she whispers, and I lose it. I can't stop my laughter.

It's a release of tension from the traveling, the tension of tomorrow, and the scrutiny of his gaze on us both.

Damn, it feels good to smile.

# Chapter Eleven

*Drinks are on me.*

*Brock*

-

I had every intention of spending the evening alone. No matter what my friends said, I was not going to look for a woman to spend my last night with before meetings began tomorrow. I had this.

That was until I saw the *same* woman on the *same* elevator *again*. The amber-eyed, light-haired girl who nudged me earlier was standing inside when the elevator doors opened. She didn't pay much attention. Her friend had no issue checking me out and any other time, I'd have manned up and taken the opportunity to talk to her.

But not this time.

As I reach my floor, I immediately hit the button to take me back down. I'm not sure what I expect, but if the bitch of fate is on my side, I'm hoping she's generous.

The elevator quietly dings before stopping at the thirteenth floor. When the doors open, there's a very tall, very blonde, very beautiful woman waiting with one hand clutching a purse as the other pimps her hair. Her eyes scan me up and down, assessing all facets of my large six-foot frame before she steps in and assures our destinations are the same.

"Nice night," she comments first, breaking the silence.

"It is," I agree, but wouldn't know. I haven't been outside of the hotel at all.

"Are you here for the show?" she questions next.

I don't want to divulge this. I hate being dishonest, but I don't know this woman and yet she's looking at me as though we're about to get acquainted. I've met women not so unlike her. If I'm putting forth effort to make a play, I'd like the recipient to make it interesting at least. I don't like to be chased. I do the chasing.

"No," I advise. "I'm here with my fiancée." Not a real lie, considering eventually I will be here with said fiancée.

*Jesus, I eventually* will *be here with my fiancée.*

Swallowing the creeping bile in my throat, I keep to small talk. "Are you here for the show?"

Her hand draws near her face where she plays with her metallic red painted fingernails and runs her tongue along her front teeth before answering, "I am."

Her sudden disinterest in me is welcome.

The elevator opens and I step back out into the foyer I had met Jerry in. The sound of high heels clicking on its marble floor echoes off the walls. When I round the corner and head back to the bar I just left, I find the two women I'm in search of.

The darker-haired woman is sitting next to the light-haired brunette who's ordering a drink from the waitress. Two men have already zeroed in on their entrance and are standing in close around their small table. They also appear to be chatting them up.

I have no right to be jealous. The fact that I am is ridiculous. But fuck it, I'm not going to dwell on it for long.

"You're back so soon," the female bartender greets as she leans her small but visible cleavage over the bar. "Another whiskey neat?"

"Yeah," I confirm. "Please."

Sitting down at the bar, I turn my chair slightly to ensure my view from here is good. The dark-haired woman is laughing out loud to whatever the man behind her just whispered in her ear. The light-haired woman is staring at her drink, maneuvering the straw around the edge of her glass. From here, it doesn't look as if she's paying attention to the gentleman pulling up a chair and taking a seat too close beside her.

Again, I'm not sure why I appreciate her disinterest. I've never met her. For all I know, she could have a voice that mirrors Minnie Mouse and a body marred with poorly thought out tattoos.

"Are you sticking around here a while then?" The bartender, who I may add has told me her name at least eleven times, inquires as she remains standing in front of me.

I keep my focus on the women's table and answer, "I'm not sure."

"Here's my number," she insists, sliding over a napkin with her name—*Julie*—on it with a heart dotting the *i*. "Call me if you're up for company later."

My thoughts filter through, wondering how many men have sat at this hotel bar with her name and number scrolled on a square, white napkin. Then I wonder how many have called and how many rooms, how many *beds*, in this very hotel she's been inside.

*No way.*

"Thanks." I graciously accept the napkin and silently vow to lose it as soon as I'm able.

"So, what do you do for a living?"

"Media," I respond, if only to satisfy her.

"Media," she repeats. "Like commercials and stuff?"

I bite my lip, not wishing for her to expand on what she thinks she knows. My father insists I find someone who knows what the word media means. I want to laugh, seeing this woman stuck as she is, but don't.

"Yeah, commercials and stuff."

"Two shots of tequila," a woman's voice at my other side orders. "The good stuff, please."

When I turn toward the woman, I realize she's the same one from the table I've been watching. I note she no longer looks as mischievous as she had earlier, but now a little exasperated. I quickly look back to verify her friend is still at the table. She's still not sitting alone; she has company. However, her face still shows complete indifference.

*Good.*

"Make it four," the woman tersely adds, then mumbles, "Ten if you got a tray for me to carry."

"Got it." Julie—now as I know her to be—returns with a bottle and lines up four shot glasses.

"Make it five," I toss out.

I hate tequila. If there's a drink that gets me wasted in a short quantity, Jose Cuervo does the job.

"And put them on my tab."

"Hey, thanks!" The woman smiles at me, then quickly looks to Julie. "Better make it six so I can down one with my new friend here."

Shit, she's getting the wrong impression.

To quickly divert her attention, I ask, "Are you here from out of town?"

"Yep. My friend is going to live it up whether she wants to or not."

She points to the woman I've been watching, and I nod.

"So far this trip, she's been a total downer."

"Tequila. You're getting your girl drunk," I accuse.

Lifting a glass to her lips, she smirks before quickly downing it. Once she's finished, she wipes her mouth with the back of her hand and admits, "I totally am. Wanna join us?"

I don't answer right away. Grabbing another glass, I tip it back and skip the lime and salt. It won't do any good. To me, tequila goes down as well as I figure airplane fuel would.

"Come on," she encourages. "Look at my girl."

We both turn in place to take another glance.

"She looks miserable," I advise. "She's not even trying to appear interested, is she?"

"Nope," she sighs. "She's totally not. Help me."

Turning to the now irritated bartender, I place an order. "Give us six more of these." I take out my wallet and throw down a hundred-dollar bill. "Keep them coming until this runs out, but before your twenty percent take."

"I think I love you," the woman at my side states. She extends her hand between us and introduces herself. "I'm Addie. I'm the devious best friend who's about to introduce you in a way that's sure to piss Brooke off."

*Brooke.* I like her name.

"Lead the way, Addie, soon-to-be-ex-best-friend."

She grins, grabs a few of the shots, and leads me back to the table.

# Chapter Twelve

*One tequila, two tequilas, three tequilas...twelve.*

*Brooke*

-

"You have fantastic skin," the man who introduced himself earlier as Charles Avery the Third whispers in my ear, while his hand draws in close to touch my face. "Flawless."

Immediately, I pull back and hear his sigh of discontent.

But really, that's his best effort to hit on me? I have fantastic skin? *Gross.*

The sad fact is I don't play the field as many other women do. However, I do play in the common sense club from time to time, and judging by his close examination of my facial pores, he's obviously not an active member. Maybe he was and has been rejected.

"I'm engaged." I try to speak the lie as truth, but it doesn't matter. He's not listening.

Just as he hasn't listened since I sat down and told him how my Great-Aunt Carol died in a tragic car crash yesterday. I spared no details, meaning I described her imaginary wedding ring being the only thing she had left behind to identify her. He didn't care about the fact he was hitting on a woman in mourning. Because again, he wasn't listening.

*What's the matter with these people?*

His friend, Jay, had followed him to our table and immediately came to sit at Addie's side. He's not shown any interest in her skin whatsoever. Jay's been nothing but sweet, even telling us all about his fiancée back home, who would be waiting for him to call her later. He's made no moves toward either of us. Seemingly, he's the only gentleman at the table, so much unlike his letch of a friend.

"Brooke, look who I found!" Addie exclaims, walking to us with two fists full of shots.

I'm not sure what's in them, but I'd be willing to consume each and every one in quick succession if it led me to passing out and forgetting this night ever happened. Maybe even forgetting why I stepped foot on the plane that brought me here in the first place.

*Jason.*

I blink twice in surprise when the man from the elevator earlier dutifully walks toward our table at Addie's side. His hands are also full of shot glasses, but he's also carrying a bowl with limes and a small shaker of salt. I blink again when he comes directly to stand beside me, looks down, and winks.

Carefully, he nudges his full hands in my direction, so I help him unload one item at a time. When we're finished, he licks his thumb and I watch with bated breath to see if he'll lick another.

So far, the vodka cranberry I've tried to finish hadn't been sitting well. Now, however, a taste of whatever is in those shots sounds delicious.

"Hi," he greets quietly.

"Um, hi."

As Addie takes her seat, she straightens the mess of limes while advising, "I found your man at the bar. He insisted on the tequila."

*My man?*

"Your man?" Charles, who I've forgotten was in the room, let alone still sitting beside me, questions.

I sit frozen in place as the man Addie 'found' bends to kiss my cheek, then leaves a burning hot trail up to my ear, where he whispers, "If you want to be saved, then go with me on this, Button."

*How does he know my parents call me Button?*

"Okay," I whisper back, heat racing up my spine in response to his touch.

Finished with his message, he stands straight, only to look down and offer another playful wink. By now I know my cheeks have reddened, considering all the blood in my body is rushing to cool them. He's made me dizzy.

Reaching for a shot, he slowly brings it to my lips in offer. I graciously part them before the sour taste of tequila hits my tongue then burns down my throat. The lime comes next. Again, he positions it at my lips and I open, held in rapture by his seductive way of doing so. His playful smile adds dimples, which are perfectly symmetrical on his beautiful face.

*Dear God, I'm still dizzy.*

When I look to my left, I'm relieved to find Charles has reluctantly pulled away. His back is against his chair, and his hands sit on his thighs as he surveys what's happening in front of him. I have more space than I've had since he arrived, and I'm thankful, but I'm sharing his confusion.

"I left you for an hour and you've made new friends, I see," the man, still holding my used lime rind, *tsks*.

My eyebrows furrow, and I move my gaze to Addie where she sits across from me, sitting up straight and smiling enthusiastically. When she catches on that I'm still stumped, she does the same that he had; she winks.

"Brock here has been looking all over this hotel for you, honey."

*Brock* interjects by bending down and resting his hand on the back of my chair before moving his face toward mine. His eyes shine with unheard humor. Unfortunately, my fuzzy head still doesn't fully understand the play.

His nose briefly brushes against mine. When he speaks, he's close enough for me to smell the alcohol on his breath. "I thought I told you to wait in our room and I'd come get you for a late dinner after."

Addie giggles. Charles growls. Jay sits in his chair, staring at his phone. I remain, like an idiot, unmoving.

Brock, *if that's his real name*, brings his hand between us, placing the back of his fingers across the apple of my cheek in a caress. Obviously, Addie set this up in an attempt to disengage the others, and she's done a fine job at that. The problem I foresee now is, I'm considering time with Brock will be a loss I won't want to endure when he walks away.

"Can I sit, or are you ready to come upstairs now?" he questions, raising his eyebrows, prompting me to answer.

"You can sit," I return quietly, in place of admitting I'd follow him wherever he wanted to lead. "There's a chair over there." I point to an empty seat at the table next to ours.

Brock refuses what I offer and points to my new friend, Charles, still seated at my other side.

He clears his throat before insisting, "I'll take his." Charles looks up, eyes venomous, as Brock continues with, "You were leaving, weren't you?"

A second or two passes and I'm undecided if I should stay or run. Finally, though, Charles straightens his sweater vest—*yes, he's wearing a sweater vest*—and scoffs to himself. His friend nods at him then stands as well before the two of them walk off together, most likely to find another woman with fantastic skin.

*Still, so gross.*

"Thank you," I sigh as I sit back in my seat. My nose still burns from where his grazed it, and my cheek still tingles from where his fingers had caressed.

Since the others have left, I assumed Brock's rescue mission was over and he'd leave. At the very least, I thought he'd take the seat I offered him at the other table. He doesn't. He does just what he said he was going to do and takes the closer chair Charles had been seated in.

"I found him at the bar," Addie tells me, smiling wide as Brock sits smirking with his arm draped over the back of my chair. "He looked lonely, so I nabbed him."

"I wasn't lonely," he retorts, then grabs a shot, and downs it quickly. "I was bored."

"Well, now you're engaged," she chides. "How nice is that?"

"Engaged," he repeats, looking down and suddenly defeated.

"Oh God. *Are* you engaged?" I ask.

Instantly, the skin of my neck, which he breathed heavily against earlier, heats with betrayal on behalf of a woman I've never met.

His expression fades as he looks up and smiles. "No. I'm not engaged."

"Are you here on business?" I query next.

I'm thankful for him coming to rescue me from Charles—a lie told or not.

"Yes," he confirms. "One could call it business."

"Evasive," I blurt. "So, you're here on business."

Brock's eyes fire at mine. A look of uncertainty passes between us before he says, "I'm trying to save the future of one."

"Interesting," I concede and let it go.

"Look!" Addie points to the other end of the room.

Our heads turn at the same time to find four middle-aged men setting up what looks to be a variety of band equipment.

"Oh, I hope they play the oldies," she cheers. "I love the Beach Boys."

Brock looks to me at the same time I turn my head to him. "She's kind of like that. How'd you know my nickname?"

"I told him on the way over." Addie interjects. "I also told him about Charles."

"And you do have lovely skin, by the way. *Flawless*," Brock voices with insincerity. When my eyes narrow, he laughs.

Then I do.

"We're almost out of shots. I'm going back for more." Addie stands, then looks down to where I'm sitting, closer to Brock than I should be, and grins. "Unless, of course, you'd rather we go back to our room to finish unpacking?"

"No," I reply quickly.

"All right." She smiles smugly. "I guess I'll be back."

As she walks away, Brock turns to me and questions, "What are you two up to in L.A.?"

Suddenly, the idea of being on that damn show sounds more desperate than it had an hour ago.

"Not much. You?"

"You asked me that, remember?" he counters to my embarrassment. "But I'm up to the same. Not much."

"Do you go around saving helpless women being hit on by creepy men often?"

He laughs again. So easy. So simple. I love that in a person, man or woman.

"I don't," he returns, swiping his dark brow with his large hand. He's nervous. I can tell. "But, when your friend gave me an in, I took it."

"An in?"

Leaning in closer, he brings the last of our first round of shots to my lips, so I part them. He's no longer looking at my eyes, but at my throat as I swallow.

"An in," he says again with conviction and seduction. Confident and demure—I can't fight this.

*Experience things you've never had the chance to.*

Dad's advice shouldn't apply here. He didn't intend for me to hook up with my first one-night stand, especially as I'm about to attend a meeting in the morning, which means to set me up to gain a perspective husband.

*But, damn it.*

"When in Rome," Addie interrupts, saying more with that statement than she could know.

Rather than bringing over fists full of shot glasses, she's managed to bring a tray of however many she can sit on top of it.

When she starts passing the drinks around the table, divvying them up in equal measures to all of us, she says, "I told the bartender you'd pay for these, too, Brock."

Brock sits back and smiles. "Of course you did."

"Bottom's up, ladies." Addie lifts her glass and readies the first of *so many* shots.

An hour later, we've added two additional tables to our group. Addie insisted on playing quarters, very well knowing my skill and aim are shit. We've consumed another round of shot glasses and are now teetering on the verge of very drunk and completely inebriated. My stomach hurts from laughing as much as I have, and my usual fair judgment has moved to the wayside.

Brock's compliments to my appearance haven't stopped since the others started paying less attention to us and more to each other. We've secluded ourselves completely, even in the middle of the chaotic crowd Addie's brought to the table.

"Are you having a good time?" he questions. His arm has been possessively draped along the back of my chair for the last hour.

"I think so," I reply. "I haven't had tequila since high school."

"High school?" he admonishes. "How's that possible?"

Shrugging, I return, "I'm a simple girl. I like beer."

"You're a cheap drunk, you mean," he corrects. He's joking, of course. "Or you're a really cheap date."

"I am that," I explain. He doesn't know me, or if anything I say is true. "I'm also really good with my mouth," I blurt next and hold in a laugh as he chokes on his beer.

There's no way to know if my flippant comment spurs his reaction or not, but once he's swallowed what he can, he leans in close. His eyes grow hooded and dark, and his voice is raspy and seductive when he suggests, "Come to my room after this."

All signs, every one my mind can imagine, point to this being a huge mistake.

"You want me to come to your room?"

"Yes," he asserts. "Stay the rest of the night with me, Brooke." Leaning in closer, his hand runs the expanse of my thigh. "Don't think about it. Go with your gut. Yes or no."

# Chapter Thirteen

*This is a bad idea.*

*This is a good idea.*

*This is a fucking great idea.*

*Brock*

-

"I never do this," Brooke insists in a lost breath. "I swear I don't."

She's pulling my hair as I've got her soft body imprisoned against the elevator wall. She says she never does this, and if that's the case, she's a goddamn quick study. Truth be told, she can confess or admit to whatever the hell she wants. At this point, I'd believe anything she said.

My hand is beneath her shirt, but still over her bra. Her chest is perfect. The weight heavy and the tips tight.

*Perfect.*

As we sat around the table throwing back shot after shot and listening to her friend, Addie, chatter on with all the people she pulled into our once small group, Brooke and I sat quietly side by side. Addie's endless bantering and crazy quarter playing skills wasn't what held my attention.

Brooke did.

The way she spoke, smiled, laughed. Every eye roll, every high five, every curse word—and it has to be said she doesn't curse well—had me putting forward my utmost attention.

She was my night's only focus.

Unfortunately, as the evening and drinks progressed, I wasn't the only man in the room captivated by her understated beauty.

Those idiots around us started to notice her as well. The quiet girl I had private privileges to no longer became just mine. Judging by the look on some of those men's faces, they were all interested to know if I'd share.

*That was a no.*

I don't mind competition as long as the prize includes everything I want for the night, and Brooke was definitely all those things.

So, I didn't give them any opportunities.

In reaction to their obvious interest, I did things I'd never done before. I was the first to make my intentions known. I acted ridiculous, staking my claim by grabbing her hand and casually leaning over to kiss her cheek, neck, and hand. Then I continued to dote on her. I didn't mind doing it, I just didn't enjoy feeling as though I *had* to. In my alcohol induced state, I may or may not have considered pissing on her to mark my territory had she not agreed to come up with me after the last round of drinks were finished.

"Where's your room?" she questions as I use my teeth and tongue to taste her neck. If I weren't so drunk, I'd savor the flavor of her skin.

Standing straight, but keeping my hand locked at her waist, I turn around and hit the button to the eighteenth floor. At the same time, I'm cursing the distance it'll take to get us there.

Lifting her head and using the pull of my hair as leverage, she asks, "Your room is the penthouse?"

I'm not sure if she's caught on to the reasons for my stay, and if I tell her, I'm afraid she'll stop what I've been looking forward to for the last three hours.

Thus, I don't hesitate to lie, "Yeah, company policy."

Her eyes narrow.

Apprehension and hesitation are settling in too soon. To avoid this, I step back into her and run my fingertips up the warm, soft skin of her thighs. Catching the hem of her short skirt, I raise it enough to get her attention. Her eyes close, and her lips form a subtle smile.

*She likes my hands on her.*

"Kiss me again," I demand, keeping my eyes open to gauge her reaction.

She doesn't comply, but rather reaches between us and uses her hand to cup my cock. In my painfully aroused state, her touch is threatening.

"Fuck, woman. You're killing me."

With her eyes still closed, she smirks, but this time she licks her lips.

"Yes, you're going to kill me," I confirm, not about to take my eyes from her mouth.

The elevator door dings before coming to a stop. At the same time, we step apart. Before the door fully opens, I notice she's panting as she adjusts herself to stand straight. She's also fighting to straighten her skirt. I'm standing in the opposite corner, wishing like hell I could help her out of it.

When I look up to find who's entered the elevator, I notice it's the same blonde who blew me off earlier. Her dress is wrinkled in the front, and her high heel shoes dangle from her fingers. The blonde's hair looks as if she's been thoroughly fucked. My guess is, shortly after leaving me to my business, she found herself some of her own and now she's unknowingly trying to ruin the rest of my night.

The ride up is quiet. I chance a look at Brooke and find her leaning against the wall, holding the railing with both hands. She's not smiling, and she doesn't appear to be having second thoughts. Instead, she's openly staring at me, taking me in, so I wink. Her face turns red at the same time the blonde clears her throat. She can see us in the reflection of the metal door, so I turn to look directly at her.

Once we hit the thirteenth floor, the door opens and the blonde moves to step out. Brooke then jumps, throwing herself into my arms. I grab her ass and kiss her hard, our tongues combat in equal thrusts.

"Hands," she utters, shifting her head to look down between us. "Touch me."

*Christ, this woman is relentless.*

The elevator dings again, so I turn to look up and quickly realize we're finally where we need to be. I don't put her down as I walk into my room. It's dark, but the lights from the city beam through the top to bottom wall of glass windows.

It's not until Brooke's legs grow stiff that I put her down and wait until she's balanced herself before letting go. When she starts to sway, I lean her against the back of the door. Without wasting time, I drop to my knees. As I do, she bends at the waist to help remove my suit jacket. I shrug it off before lifting her skirt and go eagerly in search of purchase.

Her thong is no challenge. One quick rip and it's gone, lying on the floor next to my jacket. As I move in to get my first taste, she drapes one leg over my shoulder and releases a loud, cursing moan into the room. Any other time, I'd coin this as a fake porn call, but hers isn't.

Her pink flesh is heated, wet, and sweet to taste. I dive in with added aggression, feeling my cock continue its painful twitch in spite of my effort to slow it down. As I continue baiting her to release, I look up and find she's struggling to remove her shirt. The material gets caught in her hair and she's fighting, and losing, the battle to release it. Her arms flailing above her head shouldn't be as funny as it is, but the fact she's losing a fight against a thin piece of material is amusing.

Figuring she'll hurt herself if I let it continue, I stand, push her back against the door, and take over. She doesn't give me time to enjoy the sight of her tanned skin and athletic build for long. Her mouth crashes against mine, and she takes it with fervor.

Once free of my buckle and zipper, everything I'm wearing falls to the floor. She's just finished unbuttoning my shirt through an uncontrollable giggle. I love the sound of her laugh. It's one of the first things that repeatedly caught my attention at the table. Any other time I'd be happy to hear it, but not now. Not when I'm naked.

"You're good?" I question, hoping to fuck all she is. My cock is waiting for the green light.

Nodding, she mumbles into my mouth and jumps from the floor into my arms. She weighs nothing, which is good considering I'm walking with her in my arms after consuming as much tequila as I did.

My hands grip her generous ass, and I waste no time in getting her across the room.

"I'm not a hooker," she announces. She pulls her head back, looks into my eyes, and runs her fingers through my hair. The small act of intimacy feels as if she's done it before, with someone else, and couldn't wait to do it again.

Unfortunately, not personally knowing her, I can only guess she's not a hooker. "I know."

"And this will mean nothing," she claims. The look of excitement she once had begins to fade now that we're in my room. I hate it. "I mean, not nothing," she corrects. "Just that, ya know."

"I got it," I confirm.

"Well, you say you do, but I'm not—"

"Are you finished?" I ask, hoping to shut her thoughts down so she can focus.

I've been with a lot of women, and sure as fuck more than my fair share. Brooke's apprehension, attached to her nervous chatter tells me she hasn't had the same experience with casual sex.

"I'm not a slut," she says next. "I mean I don't—"

"Brooke," I call for her drunken attention through my now unfortunate sobering state.

Her eyes slowly close, added tequila soaking through her muddled brain. At this point, I'm not sure if that's a good thing or not.

"I've only been—"

I don't want a list of partners, and I sense this is where her intent is going.

"Button," I whisper. Her eyes immediately open, so I smirk. She takes in a breath when I quietly observe, "There she is."

"You called me 'Button' earlier."

"I did."

Looking around my bedroom, she takes it in quickly before her lips crash to mine, and her legs stiffen to be set free.

"Sex!" she shouts with glee. "We're having sex!"

*The little drunken woman is all over the place.*

"We could have sex," I advise, "if you'd get your shit together."

Giggling, Brooke jumps on the bed and sprawls herself on top of it. The discussion leading us to this room had me forgetting she's nearly naked. Her tight body is spread out on my comforter with her arms stretched over her head. Her legs are closed, but her skirt rides up her thighs, close to giving me a glimpse of what's beneath it.

"Shit, my wallet," I remember. "Condom."

She laughs again. Fuck, I love that sound.

"I'll be back." I hate that I'm having to walk away for any reason, but seriously, I *always* use a condom.

After I've rummaged through my pants and found my wallet, I return. In the short time I was gone, I find Brooke's made herself comfortable. The pillows have been discarded to the floor; her skirt and bra are lying next to them, and the blankets hide her naked body.

An open bottle of mini-bar tequila sits on the table beside the bed.

"I'm not—" she starts, but I stop her.

"If you tell me you're not a hooker or a slut, I'm going to beat your ass red," I threaten, and her eyes grow wide. The thought excites her. "You don't look, sound, or act like either. I believe you."

"I wasn't going to say that," she huffs out, half-ticked as she sits up. "I was going to say I wasn't sure if you wanted more to drink, but I did."

Walking to the bed, depositing myself heavily on top of it, I roll into her, but stay above the covers.

"I'll drink from you," I advise, reaching inside the sheet and blanket in order to tear them from her body.

She laughs as I throw her legs over my shoulders to finish what I'd started. In and out, I thrust my tongue inside, reveling in her heavy gasps. Her hands run through my hair, stopping only when I've hit her spot. *The spot.* Her body is responsive, telling me what it likes. And fuck, the woman tastes good.

When I've got her close, with her legs shaking and her breathing labored, I release her to bite the inside of her thigh. She yelps, then makes a half-hearted attempt to get away.

*Not happening.*

"Want another taste?" I query. In the dull light of my room, I watch her eyebrows furrow in obvious confusion. My mouth gets close to hers, where I insist, "Lick my lips, Brooke. Taste yourself."

"Oh God," she whispers. Her eyes widen in disbelief.

"Do it," I encourage.

When she does as I've told her, my hips push forward. Her clit and outside center feels like silk, but not nearly as good as I imagine the rest of her will feel.

If I make it that far.

Grabbing the condom from the table, I use my teeth to rip it open. She lies beneath me, drunkenly smirking. I'm not amused.

"You have a nice tongue," she awkwardly compliments, causing me to lose focus with the condom. "I mean, you know what you're doing with it." She stops long enough to hate the silence as much as I do, then states, "I told you I was good with my mouth, too."

Taking in a deep, methodic breath, I ask, "Are you *challenging* me?"

"Yep," she answers assuredly, shimmying her body under mine. Inch by agonizing inch, I let her scoot down the bed from beneath me, using her hands and backside for balance.

No man would refuse Brooke's generous offer, so I close my eyes as she brings her face to my cock and grabs it with both hands. Her warm breath kisses it first before she sucks it in with one long, swift pull.

"Christ," I hiss, holding myself up by one arm. "Fuck! Do that again," I demand when she flattens her tongue against the underside and plays with the sensitive flesh.

With one hand wrapped around my length, the other massages my tight balls. The woman aiming to make me come down her throat claims to be no hooker, and I believe her. Yet, for reasons I don't want to think about, someone's taught her well. She's a god damn pro.

"Brooke, you have to stop," I seethe, but the desire to feel the back of her throat again pushes my hips forward. She's not paying attention, and if she doesn't, soon I'll empty into her completely. "Really. Stop." I thrust again as she giggles. The vibration nearly causes my release.

"Get up here," I snap with impatience.

Once she's settled herself beneath me, she spreads her thighs wide. I look down to find her eyes making fun.

"Hang on," I insist, lifting my body from hers, enough that I'm able to finally and *successfully* sheath myself.

"Do you need a minute?" she questions, still giggling. "Is this your first time?"

"You got jokes?" I spit, clenching my teeth and rubbing the pulsing crown of my swollen cock against her just as swollen clit.

If Brooke's this wasted and still spirited drunk, I imagine she could completely undo me sober. The very thought holds promise.

"Ready," I ask, finally closing in just outside her pussy.

"Do it," she breathes, sounding a lot like she's giving an order.

When I drive in deep, my jaw clinches. A muttering string of quiet curses breaks from my chest and I use it to get myself in check.

Her hips are flush against mine, meeting me in rhythm. However, more aggressively so. The feel of her, like velvet, fitted and ready, is already tempting my undoing and we've only just started.

"Fuck, you're tight, and so wet," I hiss, feeling the soft walls of her pussy pulsating around me.

Definitely not a hooker. She's killing me.

"I've been worked up for over an hour," I explain, pinching her chest and sucking the sensitive skin behind her ear. "Slow the fuck down."

She doesn't listen.

Her trembles of greed go into further frenzy as her hands explore my body. My back feels the spearing of her fingernails. My ass enjoys the pain of her heels digging in. My chest savors the feel of her naked body beneath it.

"I'm close," she cries out to my satisfaction. Slowing down, I wait for her release to back away. Obviously, she holds no appreciation for my wish to savor any of this. Her hips lift, and using mine as leverage, she moves faster from the bottom—back and forth, up and down. "Don't stop."

"Fucking hell, you'll pay for this," I threaten to no avail.

*She's an intoxicating combination of foreplay, sex, and rapid fire, all at once.*

Too fucking much...

When her body tightens, clenching me like a vise from inside, I pull out and grab her wrists, pulling them up over her head so she can't touch me.

Trapping her mouth with mine, I aim to quiet her moans as I thrust back inside of her. Within seconds, I realize it's too fucking late.

*I'm had.*

*I'm spent.*

*I'm taken.*

Completely.

# Chapter Fourteen

*And I thought this would be awkward.*

*Brooke*

-

"Woman, I bet I'm bleeding." Brock's words come out as a garbled mumble when he says them against my forehead.

He's still inside me and hasn't moved since we finished at the same time.

In all my years with Jason that never, not once, happened. I'd always finish first and wait for him to follow. Sometimes it took a while, as after I was done, I lost interest.

"Bleeding?"

Grinning, he pulls back and feigns a pained wince before replying. "I think your talons shredded my back."

"You don't say something like that to a girl you had sex with but hardly know, Brock," I scold. "Not cool."

"What do I say to a *really* hot girl I just had *great* sex with then?" he questions. And, if I'm right, he's being sincere.

Too sincere.

After spending time with Brock earlier as I did, I can see how Jason's version of us *growing apart* made sense. I would never *ever* have considered having sex in the front seat of a parked car like where I found him. At the time, the very thought would've horrified me.

That was until I considered having sex in a public hotel elevator merely because it wasn't getting us to Brock's room fast enough.

"Where'd you go?" he inquires, pulling me from everything Jason.

"Here," I cheerfully reply.

His neck rears back. The hair that's fallen to his forehead gives him a rugged, but boyish look. His cheeks are pink, and sweat beads cover his brow.

"I need to get rid of this." He carefully pulls out of me, and the empty feeling once he's done so isn't appreciated.

After he's out of bed, he doesn't turn back to look at me. He has a nice ass, and I'm not an ass lover at all. Nor am I a lover of all things cock. Women bug me when they go on and on about a man's dick and how lovely it is.

I hear the hotel toilet flush, and the light clicks off before Brock saunters back into the room. He's smirking at me, probably noticing I can't look away from his expansive chest.

Brock doesn't have the bulk of a body builder, nor the sinewy frame of a runner. He's somewhere in between. The definition in his arms, neck, and chest is thick and corded with veins.

Now that it seems I've worked off at least some of the alcohol, I fear this entire situation will get weird.

"So, I've never done that," I tell him.

He sighs as he comes to the bed, moves the covers, and lies down at my side. He's made no move to further touch me, which is fine.

The covers are pulled up to his waist before he turns his head and returns, "I think I got you've never done that. You've mentioned you're not a slut a few times now."

*Shit, I have.*

"I'm not sure how this works."

Really, I have no idea how *any* of this works. I don't want to explain he's only the second man I've ever had sex with, and that I waited until I was the ripe old ago of twenty-two before losing my V card to the only man I've ever loved. He wouldn't understand my reasons why, and I wouldn't relish in explaining.

"How what works?"

"This," I state, pointing around us in the bed. "I'm thinking I should go?"

Lifting his arm and settling it to rest beneath his head, he turns his gaze to the ceiling before asking, "Do you want to go because you want to go, or you think I want you to go?"

"I'm not tired. But maybe you are."

His head turns, that boyish grin comes with it as his eyes meet mine.

"I'm not tired, but I am starving. How about room service?"

"Breakfast with a lot of bacon?" I suggest, thinking the notion at this hour sounds ridiculous, but still good.

He laughs, drops his hands to his stomach, and replies, "Breakfast it is."

Jackknifing himself to a sitting position, he grabs the phone to make the call. Thinking this is a good time to plot my escape for clothes, I sit up and reach for the closest item within reach.

His shirt smells like he does. The size dwarfs my body, but it's enough to cover the most delicate parts of it. Once I have myself adjusted, I prop the pillows behind me to sit up and lean back against the headboard .

After he's ordered, he lays the hotel phone back in its cradle and grabs the television remote. He flips it to what I assume is a twenty-four hour sports channel, then fixes his pillows the same as mine and sits up next to me.

In the quiet of the room, I don't feel out of place. Though impossible, it's almost as if we've done this before.

"You watch baseball?" he inquires.

The commercial playing is one I've seen a thousand times.

"Sometimes I have it on for background noise."

"So, you *don't* watch baseball." He smiles. "Good to know."

"Do you watch game shows?"

"Sometimes," he says.

"Which ones?"

"Sometimes I have one on for background noise."

He's making fun.

"Music?" I ask, wondering what he'd listen to if he were alone. This topic could be a deal breaker. If he's into heavy metal, we're not a fit.

*What am I saying?*

We're *not* a fit. I don't know anything about him other than he's good with his hands and great with his dick. In my current situation, I don't have the right to get to know him. Nothing about what I'm doing in L.A. says this is a good idea.

"I like all music. Except that head banging shit."

*Damn it.*

It would've been better had he said he loved to head bang.

"What about you?" he asks.

Feigning boredom, I reply, "The same."

"I listen to a lot of vocalists. Too many to pick just one."

Curiously, I ask, "If you *had* to pick a favorite, though, who would it be?"

Studying the television, he says so quietly I nearly miss it. "Celine Dion."

"No way," I breathe, sitting up to get a better look at him. He can't be serious. "Celine Dion?"

"Are you judging?" he snaps, turning his face to mine and cocking a gorgeous dark eyebrow.

I bite my lip to keep from smiling before I counter, "I'm not sure. Are you serious?"

"She's talented. Her whole life story is inspiring. She's the youngest of *fourteen* kids. That's incredible."

I didn't know this about her, but I don't pay attention to the detailed lives of anyone else. Mine keeps me busy enough.

"So, you respect her," I summarize.

Flipping the channel to a gory scene in an apparent horror movie, he replies, "Fuck yeah. Her entire family lived and breathed music."

"I like Rihanna."

Rolling his eyes, he says, "That's easy. Who doesn't?"

"Where are you from? You're visiting Los Angeles, but where's home?"

"Dallas, Texas."

"Family?" I shouldn't be asking; I shouldn't want to know. But I'm curious. His admiration for Celine's family surprised me.

"Parents. Kid sister."

"Your parents are still together then," I assume, as he said 'parents.'

"No," he corrects. "My dad died when I was a kid. Martin raised me. I consider him my second dad, and he considers me the pain-in-the-ass son."

The topic of family has hit a nerve, and being that we just met, probably to never meet again, I shouldn't be so intimate, asking such personal questions.

"Your friend is crazy," he remarks out of nowhere. When I turn my face to his, I find his eyes are smiling. "The good kind of crazy."

"Explain," I insist.

A green plight of jealous tension sits heavily in my chest. I don't like recognizing it, nor it being there in the first place.

"I don't know her, but I'm guessing she has a good time wherever she goes. She told me she's attached, but it didn't seem like she lets her relationship status stop her from having men as friends. I admire that."

"She's a good friend," I return with honesty "She is half-crazy, though."

For the next thirty minutes, we sit side by side in quiet company. He's changed it back to the sports broadcast, following the scores at the bottom of the screen. I know this because every few minutes he mumbles something about a surprising score.

"There's the food," he tells me before throwing off the covers and making a move to stand.

I hadn't noticed he'd grabbed his boxers and put them on. Before he moves to the door, he turns in place and sets his gaze on my chest.

"My shirt looks good on you," he compliments.

Looking down at the gaping holes between the buttons, I don't make a move to close them. I'm comfortable. He makes me feel comfortable.

"Thank you." He smiles.

Damn.

# Chapter Fifteen

*Brooke and Brock act one, take two.*

*Brock*

-

Brooke's soft snores aren't what's been keeping me awake for the last forty-five minutes.

The soft and sweet mumbles she's been murmuring in her sleep aren't the problem either.

The reason I'm awake at this hour is because my mind won't stop racing.

After we shared a full plate of bacon and a few bites of whatever else room service brought up, we hung out in bed and talked. This is where I learned she had a great childhood, with a loving father she adored, a mother she tolerated, but loved all the same, and a pain in the ass little brother she despairingly admitted she wouldn't trade for anything. She has good friends she considers family, as well as a job working for her parents which she bears, but doesn't always want to have.

Spring is her favorite season because she likes the rain. She told me the sound of it hitting the pavement and windows calms her. Being outside, sitting in the sun comes second best in fun only to late night movies in bed, cuddled under the covers with whoever is willing to do so.

And, without having to tell me, I already knew she loves to laugh.

We're so alike. I'm not sure how she's truly real.

*If only she was a die-hard baseball fan.*

We can work on that.

As I turn my head to watch her sleep, which I'm sure isn't creepy at all, I hate the sun for coming up. I want to bottle this night, and not only remember it, but carry it through until the next...and the next...and the next...

Grabbing my phone for distraction, I check the incoming messages. I find none, except the one from Drew earlier, which stares back at me.

Drew: *So? How's it going? Have you met Mrs. Brock LaDuece yet?*

In a matter of hours, everything since being here has shifted. By no means is Brooke Malloy in love with me, nor am I with her. However, the compatibility and possibility factors that I've waited years to find and experience are all there—all coming one week too late. My remorse for tomorrow sits heavily between us. The bed isn't big enough to hold its weight.

Reaching for her hand, I take it in mine. She wears pink polish, which after knowing her for as little time as I have makes sense. Her angelic face is relaxed in sleep, her light brown hair falling haplessly against the pillow. Her long neck, leading to a chest reddened from my hands and jaw reflect back at me. I'd love to wake her, but I'm unsure how she'd react.

*What the hell, right?*

All of this will be gone tomorrow, forever filed away as a chance meeting and one-night stand that I should feel lucky enough to have had with a great girl from a happy home miles and miles away from here.

Deciding to press forward, I carefully and quietly move the sheet and slide it down her body. She doesn't move.

My hand runs the expanse of her naked thigh, making its way to the crook of her ass. Still, she doesn't make a sound.

My mouth finds her chest, kissing it gently before running my tongue over its now tightened peak. My cock swells. Her immediate reaction to my touch is enough to undo me.

Maybe, even with only knowing her a matter of hours, I'm already coming undone.

"Brooke," I whisper, as she begins to spread her thighs, getting comfortable beneath me. Her eyes aren't yet open. "You awake?"

"Hmm," she wordlessly acknowledges. Her arms wrap around my neck, and her head turns up in my direction.

"Look at me."

She does as I ask and smiles. I resent the realization, thinking the deep hue of her amber eyes will eventually come to haunt me.

"Good morning," I proclaim, once again hating the fact the hours have passed. I'm physically exhausted, but in no way ready or willing to sleep.

Her face inches toward mine. When I think she's about to kiss me, she moves her lips into my neck. Her fingernails gently scrape the skin of my shoulders, and her hips tense beneath mine.

"Condom," I whisper into her hair.

Reaching over to my wallet, I pull out the only condom I've got left.

*Better make this good.*

Once I've got it in place, I use my finger to test her readiness, only to find it was a futile effort. She's game.

"Yeah?" I question, waiting to secure the go ahead.

Nodding, she replies, "Yeah," before taking her tongue and running it slowly over my lips.

Sliding into her, I release a heavy gasp. For as long as I can remember, no woman has ever felt *so fucking good.*

"Easy," I instruct, this time hoping she listens.

Thankfully, she does and returns with a soft, "Easy."

Our bodies rock slowly in time with each other. We're relying on patience—a far reach from the drunken frenzy we shared only hours before. Each time as good as the other, but with an entirely different message.

"How are you here?" I ask myself more than her.

Yet, she answers. "I've thought the same."

Her lips spread quiet kisses against my chest. Her teeth sink in above my pectorals before her tongue moves in to soothe.

Grabbing her waist and taking her with me, I change our positions. Once I'm on my back, Brooke looks down with her hair in a tangled disarray. Any other woman I've been with would hate looking as she does on top of me, but Brooke makes it beautiful.

"Ride me," I demand, using my hands to guide her hips into a torturously slow motion.

When her body bends, she blankets mine, but holds me inside her with care. Her hands squeeze the straining muscles of my arms and she uses them to brace herself. I feel her mouth at my chest again; kissing, licking, searching. When she takes my nipple and bites, I jolt with its provocation.

Taking Brooke drunk was considered paradise. Taking Brooke sober is fucking *heaven*.

Sitting up, she removes my shirt from her body and tosses it to the side. With her chest on full display, she runs her hands up her body to touch herself as I lay under her and watch.

"Fuck, you're beautiful," I hiss, lifting my hips from the bed to drive deeper.

Brooke licks her lips again, this time with a knowing smirk.

"Touch yourself," I instruct.

Doing as she's told, I watch with rapt attention as she trails her fingers to her clit. Her insides spasm around my cock in reaction, and I've reached the point that I can't take much more.

"Brock," she moans, looking to the ceiling and rocking back and forth with fiery greed. "Shit, I'm—"

"Fuck!" I bite out. Grabbing her hips, I toss her over and adjust her beneath me again. Pounding into her with relentless thrusts, she scans my face with an intensity I can't understand.

"Don't stop," she orders as her legs wrap around my waist, where she locks her ankles together.

Without wanting to ever get away, I continue pulsing in and out of her with deep and penetrable pushes and pulls. In and out, quick and quiet.

"Goddamn it," I bark. "Fucking hell, wait."

She doesn't. Instead, Brooke's body further ignites, pushing me to the brink again and again before spiraling me into releasing all I have.

Somehow it's happened.

Somewhere it's real.

Both karma and fate are looking down on me and laughing their mother fucking asses off.

# Chapter Sixteen

*Wait, what? Say that again.*

*Brooke*

-

Brock's voice.

His smile.

His laugh.

His hands.

His body.

"She's awake." A voice across the room startles me from committing all of last night to memory.

As I slowly guide my gaze to the direction of the voice, Brock is standing outside the bathroom door, leaning his large frame against its jamb. He's holding a towel behind his head, running it over his wet hair again and again. Another lush hotel bath sheet is draped around his waist and knotted at one side. His cock punctuates the material, visibly straining at the front.

His tanned chest mockingly stares back at me. Even with so much distance between us, I clearly see I marked him. The dark purple hickey directly above his left pectoral was my mouth's favorite spot.

Clearing my throat and slowly making a move to sit up, I hold the bed sheet to my chest. My voice is coarse as I ask, "Coffee?"

"On its way," he assures. "I ordered room service before I showered. I wasn't sure you'd be hungry. You were sleeping and snoring, so I ordered for you."

"I don't snore," I weakly protest.

My objection is a lie because I *do* snore. Addie has taped this several times in the past, and to this day, still not-so-sparingly threatens to use this as evidence against me.

Brock starts to walk toward me, and I suck in a breath. I must look like a walk-of-shame-ready-to-bolt whore. I run one hand through my thick hair, then use them both to swipe the residual makeup under my eyes. The thin sheet slips slightly, capturing his interest. He cocks one eyebrow and knowingly grins, as if he's won some ridiculous game I didn't know we were playing.

Taking a seat next to me on the bed, Brock tosses the towel he was holding to the floor and turns his body in place. His gaze is assessing me as I do the same to him.

With kind eyes, he scans my face. "Stop thinking what you're thinking."

"What was that?" I counter.

"That last night wasn't as good for you as it was for me because I've been with other women."

It's a good guess, but I wasn't thinking this until now. As easy as it was being with him, I'm surely not the first woman to experience him the way I did.

"A *lot* of other women?"

He shrugs. At least he's honest.

"I should go."

"Let me feed you," he insists, running his finger against my bottom lip. "It's the least I can do."

My lips purse, so he removes his hand and smirks.

"You don't owe me anything," I smart.

"Oh, so last night was free?" he jokes, his eyebrows lifting in surprise. "And this morning? Two for one?"

I get he's kidding. His humor was as obvious last night. Brock's way of making me feel at ease was one of the reasons I agreed to come up to his room. But this joke isn't so funny.

Rather than revealing my insecurity, I quip back, "Yep, last night was on the house. So was this morning."

His sexy grin, the one I also fell for last night, comes to his lips before he inquires, "What do I get if I let you use my shower?"

"A clean breakfast buddy?"

"Dressed or naked?" he presses, staring at my chest without shame.

"Dressed."

He frowns. "Fuck it. Stay dirty."

"You're sick."

When he laughs, I narrow my eyes and hold my focus to his. My head pounds, but not so much as I assumed it would before I'd passed out in his arms a few hours ago.

"Get your ass up. Go shower. I'll wait out here for room service."

When I don't move from the bed, the sheet is ripped away. Suddenly, in the bright light of the day, I regret not putting his shirt back on after we had sex the second time.

"I'm going," I snap, grabbing the blanket, and at the same time using my shaky legs to stand.

Once I've got everything I need to shower, I turn back to find Brock watching. His gaze lingers on my exposed legs. I've been told I have a nice pair, but under his study, I'm convinced he agrees.

"I'll just..." I point to the bathroom, but awkwardly trail off. He breaks his gaze from my legs to lick his thick bottom lip before he curtly nods.

After I've showered, I process my hair as quickly as I can. The voices just beyond the bathroom door are jumbled. I can only make out pieces of what's being said.

"You're him," a man with a voice I don't recognize enthusiastically accuses. "The guy from that..."

Brock hisses something out in a dramatic whisper to keep the man quiet.

*What the hell?*

"*Dude*," the voice starts again. "You're the luckiest guy on earth. Have you seen those women?"

*Those women?*

"I mean, you're *soooo* gonna score a hottie."

"Keep your voice down," Brock seethes again. This time I hear him clearly. "Put the tray there and go."

*Room service.*

"Shit, sorry. I didn't mean to..."

The heavy, wooden hotel door slams shut, and my heart crashes repeatedly against my chest. Slowly but surely, bits and pieces of last night come together, cementing together what I've heard.

*Brock's the millionaire.*

It can't be. *He can't be.* Can he?

Last night, he said he was here on business. He said he wasn't engaged, which if he's on the show, then he didn't lie. He's not technically engaged *yet*. But he acted as if he wasn't here for an extended period of time— like he was only passing through.

*Freaking hell, Brock's the millionaire.*

I have no reason to be pissed or sad, yet my heart feels sick. Last night was great, being with him was...new and exciting. Yet, nothing we did was a promise of anything more. Last night was a great night of sex with a man I've never met and doubted I'd ever see again.

Physically, I'm exhausted. Emotionally, I'm close to the same.

Rushing around the bathroom to gather what little I've brought in with me, I don't pay attention to how I look before opening the door. It doesn't matter. I need to go.

"Your breakfast is..."

When the door fully opens and Brock's eyes come to mine, he stops talking. His jaw ticks, and a ruined expression washes over his face. I hate it. His sullen look tells me all my assumptions were correct.

*Stop thinking what you're thinking, that last night wasn't as good for you as it was for me because I've been with other women.*

Rather than stand too close, and to avoid facing the consequences of my colossal mistake, I push past him and make my way to the door. His hand reaches out to stop me. He pulls my arm and forces my body to his. My shoulder hits his chest. His dark eyes search my face for any chance I hadn't heard what I can't ever un-hear.

"It's too late," I whisper. "I need to go."

"Brooke, wait," he begs. But it's to no avail.

*Do you want to go because you want to go, or you think I want you to go?*

"I need to get back to my room," I insist, turning my focus to the door.

When he releases me, I move fast. With my shoes in my hand, I probably look like I'm fleeing a crime scene. And in a way I am. I'll pay for this later, I know it. Whether in mind, heart, or in the view of the critical public eye.

*Oh, so last night was free? Two for one?*

It's day one, and I've made myself the laughing stock.

# Chapter Seventeen

*That probably could've gone a little better.*

*Brock*

-

Fuck...

Fuck...

*Fuck!*

She heard every word that pimple faced bellman said. There's no other explanation. The beautiful, friendly, fun, and sexy woman who went into the bathroom to shower, came out as a timid, reluctant, and scorned one I no longer recognized.

Last night was a bad idea. I should've stayed in my room as I told myself I would.

If I had, I wouldn't have been so careless.

If I had, I wouldn't be sitting here stewing in guilt over hurting a girl I hardly know.

If I had, though, I wouldn't have met her in the first place.

Running my hand through my hair, I sit in this chair, only half-ass listening to Jerry as he continues walking me through what's about to happen this evening.

"You'll meet all the girls together first, then one by one tomorrow. There's nine this season," he says to my surprise.

"Nine?" I question. I didn't get nine files. I haven't read them all, but I can count and there were only eight. "How's it nine?"

"Late arrival. Willow added that last one."

I don't think Jerry likes Willow. He's shown contempt anytime he's talked about her this morning.

"Anyway, so tonight will be simple. You'll all meet in the Civic Room here at the hotel for a drink—no cameras, no crews, none of that. Just you and the girls."

"And what am I supposed to do with them?"

Jerry smiles, but my question isn't what he thinks it to be. After spending last night with a woman I hated watching walk away, my disdain for this dare has reached its limit.

If there's one woman like Brooke Malloy in this world, it's possible there's more where she came from. I was too stupid to realize this sooner.

"You talk, converse, carry on," he advises. "Get to know their names and faces. At this point, personal details don't matter."

"Those come later," I guess. It's the right one.

"Yes, you'll be required to date each girl once. With one exception."

"Exception?"

He nods. "Yes. If you know right away there's a woman you have no chemistry with, then you tell me, and I'll handle it."

"Got it," I confirm.

"If there's a connection, great. If not..." He moves his flat hand out to emphasize. "Then send them on down the road."

"Harsh."

"It's not so bad. None of the contestants will know once they haven't been considered. Their heartbreak comes at the end, and there they have each other to console."

"Except the one I choose."

Jerry smiles. "You got it. I should prepare you for something, though. Some of these women aren't necessarily here for you."

My confusion is obvious.

"I mean, sure. In a sense, they are here for you, don't get me wrong. I'm saying a lot of girls who audition for this show are also here for its notoriety. Last season, we had that plumber..." He rolls his eyes before continuing, "Willow was *insistent* we find an everyday blue collar prospect. Believe me when I tell you that poor man was as blue collar as they come. It turned out to be a fiasco."

Again, his distaste for the producer and host of this show is evident.

"Will you be having any guests join you for the duration of your visit?"

"Guests?" I don't understand.

"No one explained this to you?" he questions. I shake my head, and he goes on. "Family, friends, whoever you choose. We'll cover the cost. The process of the show can be daunting."

*It already is.*

"Some find having their loved ones within reach, even for a few days, helps to ground them. But please, no *personal* relations."

"Personal relations?"

"Two seasons ago we had that lawyer, Marcus Wellman. Do you remember?"

I don't, simply because I've never watched the show.

"Well, he had his ex-girlfriend flown in from Tallahassee. He told us they were still very close friends. When the other girls found out who was sharing his room, chaos erupted. The whole season was a public relations nightmare. Name calling, cat fighting, and threatened lawsuits had us busy for three months after the show ended and aired."

My interest in what he has to say is waning. I want to go back to my room and process, so I ask, "Are we about done for today then?"

"We are, but I'll need you to take these and look them over. Pictures are included this time. It's good to get a head start. So many girls, so little time, as they say."

*No one says that, Jerry.*

"All right, thanks." I accept the files with no interest in reviewing them.

"Well, then." He stands, extends his hand, and gives mine a firm shake. "We'll see you at six."

# Chapter Eighteen

*Here, hold my whorish, but now bleeding heart.*

*Brooke*

-

"All this isn't as heavy as you're making it out to be, Brooke," Addie soothes. "I mean, so what? You had fun, didn't you? You did something crazy for once in your life, right?"

There's a point she's trying to make, I'm sure. But I don't see it. I'm simmering over my loss of self-respect.

"Wait. You've never slept with a man you just met?" Ryleigh interjects, coming from the bathroom draped in a small, white towel. Obviously, she's overheard our conversation. "A hot, steamy, one night of animalistic sex with a stranger is good for the soul, woman," she adds.

I've hardly had the chance to introduce myself, let alone the opportunity to take in all her beauty. Right now is not the time.

Ryleigh's eyes widen as she waits for a response. When it doesn't come, she asks, "You've really never had one?"

I shake my head. Fortunately, she has no idea who we're talking about.

When I came back to the room this morning, Ryleigh had already left to meet some of the other girls for breakfast. Thus, thankfully, I had my best friend to myself.

When I walked in looking frazzled, Addie put forth her best effort not to laugh; however, she failed. Her flair for finding humor in my first adventure stung, bad. It wasn't long after when I finally broke down into tears of humiliation in knowing I was going to have to face him again.

Tonight, I'm sure.

Once she'd collected herself, I told her what I had done. Not only is Brock an incredibly handsome man we met in a bar by chance, he's also the man I'd be *interviewing* with to become his *wife*.

*God.*

None of this seemed to be a problem for Addie, though. She was elated I had a 'head start' with being the one he chose. Truth be told, I'm not here to be chosen. This was supposed to be an 'adventure,' nothing more. Not once had I given thought to being the one standing at the altar. Not as I left my house, not as I stood in the center of all those women, not even as I sit here remembering last night.

Adventure, damn it. That's it.

"Brooke," Addie lectures, still sitting on the bed, holding me at her side. "I mean it when I say this, so don't play it off as my crazy talk."

"Say what?"

My legs are folded and so far, I'd been looking down at my fingers, twisting them in my lap.

"Your Dad would be proud."

*She's nuts.*

My father would certainly *not* be proud of my recent, albeit only, act of slutism in its worst form.

He'd be completely mortified.

"Highly doubt this." I internally cringe as I stand. An image of my father's most disappointed expression crosses my thoughts with a degree of clarity I can't escape. "Addie, there was nothing about last night any parent would be proud of."

"I disagree," she objects as she gets up and adjusts the hair from my neck to my back. "I'm proud of you."

"You would be," I smartly return. "I'm not you. I get attached to people. You don't."

"This is true, but, Brooke, it was one night."

Honestly, I know this. However, stating the facts is one thing, *feeling* them is another.

"What are you wearing tonight?"

"Do I have to go? Am I required?"

Nodding, she sighs. "Most definitely required. It was in the contract, remember? All appearances are necessary."

"I'll wear a sack. A big one."

"You're talking crazy. We'll find you something perfect," she encourages. "I'm here to help you. I'll do whatever you need me to do."

This morning, after my initial breakdown, Addie physically put me back together and followed me downstairs as emotional support. There, this year's chosen women were herded into a small break room around the corner from the downstairs bar, or as I now refer to it as *the scene of the crime*. Addie was prohibited from going any further. A man named Jerry insisted I go in alone, but I wasn't alone for long. I met a few of the girls, and immediately observed some were more friendly than others.

Our bunkmate, Ryleigh Summers, just as I'd suspected in my short time of knowing her, is a social butterfly. She walked around to every girl, shaking their hand, and wishing them luck.

Emilee Cruz, a Hispanic goddess with perfect skin and seductive features, is the youngest in the group. She turned twenty-one just last week. She told me she auditioned for the show as part of her 'living life' new year pledge. She was really nice, but talked very quietly—awkwardly so.

Kylee Simmons is a *bitch*. I don't like to label women this, but some just earn the right.

My first impression of her would be to say she thrives in being the center of attention. Before the meet and greet had a chance to start, she had insulted one of the contestants I hadn't met. I never got the chance because the woman ended up in tears, wasn't consoled by anyone, and fled the scene as quickly as she could.

Kylee is tall, blonde, and fake; boobs, hair, tan, and possibly her ass. She's also, by pure and evil coincidence, the woman Brock and I shared an elevator with before our drunken sexual escapade last night. She didn't recognize me today, which isn't surprising. I didn't give her my attention as we rode to her floor. She didn't give hers to me either. We both had eyes for Brock.

*Brock.*

"I had fun with him," I admit, looking down then closing my eyes.

"Well, yeah," Addie tells me. "You got laid. That's *always* fun."

"No, Addie. There was more than that," I return. "I mean, yes, the sex was great, but the after was better."

Addie doesn't respond. When I look up, her eyes are wide and her mouth is hanging open. She also doesn't look like she's breathing.

Concerned, I ask, "What's wrong? What is it?"

"After was better," she utters. Once she's pulled herself together, she probes, "What do you mean *after* was *better*? What after? What better?"

Clearly noting she's stumped, I explain. "I mean after we had sex, we talked."

"Shit," she bites out, taking the seat next to me again and stroking the back of my head gently. "You're saying you two didn't, um..." She pauses and tightens her lips before stuttering on. "You two didn't...um..."

"Addie, what?"

"Hit and quit it. Fuck then flee?" she asks it so fast, I have to blink to keep up.

To her amazement, I answer, "No, Add. We fell asleep."

"But you *talked* first?"

"Yes."

"Damn."

"Then talked again after we..."

Her head rears back in shock and maybe a little bit of panic. "You had sex with him *twice*?"

"Yes," I answer. "Why do you look like that?"

"*Fuck.*" A thousand words she doesn't say slips through that one. Sitting up, Addie prods, "And you liked him?"

Yes, I truly did, which seems to be the bitch of this entire mess. Tonight, eight other girls who not only look like me, but are much prettier, will be vying for his attention. I know because I've seen them. We're all competing. My face will be lost to him within that crowd, and it sucks.

"I did like him. I mean, I do. He's really sweet and a lot of fun."

"A lot of fun," she repeats.

I wish she'd stop doing that. Her reaction to last night is disturbing.

Addie smiles with excitement, stands, grabs my hands, shakes them roughly, and bends her face toward mine. "Brooke, we have work to do!"

# Chapter Nineteen

*I just need a minute.*

*Brock*

-

"Initially, all of this can seem a little overwhelming." Willow Ellis states at my side as I stand in the valet lane of the hotel driveway. "I understand."

Desperately in need of a breath of fresh air, I escaped the barrage of questions those women were callously throwing at me.

*Do you own a house in Italy?*

*Do you spend winters in Vale?*

*Do you drive a fast car or luxury sedan?*

*Do you have a maid?*

There were a decent few who stayed quiet, but even those women were using the apparent leaders of the group as mouthpieces. I'm not sure which was worse, the boldness of those who pried for information, or those who sat back and listened.

"Yes, overwhelming," I confirm, because it's true. The whole night could be described as insanity.

"The girls will settle. Right now they're all scattering, trying to figure out if they have what it takes."

"Or figuring out the number of bills in my wallet," I return with sarcasm.

Willow laughs. "Being a woman myself, I can attest to the degree of strength it takes in competing with others. It's a process."

"A process?"

"Yes," she assures. "They're doubting themselves. All of them want something out of this or they wouldn't be here."

"I guess," I acknowledge. "Men don't act like this."

"Don't they?" she replies. "I think they do. Next year, if the show makes it, we're going to try your theory out. We'll have a woman in your place."

I don't care about next year, or this one, for that matter. My mind hasn't been on any of these girls. I'm still pondering over the one who ran out of my room this morning as fast as both her feet could carry her.

"That'll be interesting," I reply with disinterest. "Good luck with that."

"I heard some of them talking after you walked out," she tells me.

I can *still* hear them talking because they never fucking stop. I don't advise this; however, I do take some satisfaction in thinking it to myself.

"A few said you're everything they'd hoped you'd be."

Well, *none* of them were anything I'd hoped for. Sure, a few are hot, but nothing more than I've had at home. A couple were uncomfortable and shy; two were impossibly so.

Kylee Simmons seems to be the group's already self-proclaimed winner. When I walked in, she recognized me immediately. She walked to me like a lion would—circling her prey, playing with its food. I disregarded her every challenge and question. Ignoring her took effort and every bit of my patience. I don't lose my temper often, but in the face of that she-devil, it would be time well spent.

"The meet and greet is over in a few minutes, but there's one more girl."

*Great, another girl.*

"She sent a text earlier, asking that I excuse her, but I can't do that."

"You can," I assure her. I've had enough.

"I won't," she counters. "She'll be down soon."

Turning in place, Willow scans my face for a reaction. I don't have one, so she continues searching.

"Taping begins tomorrow. You have to decide who your first date will be. It wouldn't be fair to her if you didn't at least get to meet her as you did the others."

"I'll be back in. I just need a few more minutes."

Before turning around to leave, she smiles, but it doesn't reach her eyes. "Don't be frustrated. Today's the first of many to come. Matt's here to help you with anything you need."

"And you?"

Willow nods. "I'm here, too. I'm for them, though." She points to the door before turning in place and walking in the direction of it.

Once I know she's gone, I lean my back against the building and close my eyes, thinking how nice it would be to be anywhere but here.

*Do you go around saving helpless women being hit on by creepy men often?*

*I don't. But when your friend gave me an in, I took it.*

Fuck, this is painful.

# Chapter Twenty

*Nine girls + one guy = drama.*

*Brooke*

-

"Finally!" Jerry, the man I met earlier, meets me at the door to the room I was rushing toward. "Brooke, you were due here an hour ago," he scolds.

First indication tells me he's not only the facilitator for tonight's event, but a high-strung human being at that. His eyebrows are decorated in beads of sweat, and his thinning hair shines against a bald head with a glimpse of secretion as well. Though he's dressed in a suit, he's not attractive. My mailman has better features, and he's got to be at least fifty-five. This man can't be a day over forty.

"I'm here," I happily reply. "I talked to Willow this evening. She knew I was running behind."

"Willow," he sneers, his top lip curling as he does. "Well, you're here now, so let's head inside."

When I follow him into the area where I know Brock will be, my body rocks in place.

The women, contestants and otherwise, have separated themselves into two groups. On one end of the room, Ryleigh has made herself comfortable at a table with Emilee and a few of the other girls I remember thinking were nice.

The other table are those I didn't care for at all.

Kylee is first to see me arrive. She tosses out a dirty look, then bends to whisper into the ear of another plastic woman who I haven't met. Kylee's red dress, black stilettos, and heavy makeup scream slut, but I'm not one to judge. After last night, I'll never judge again.

Both Willow and Matt are standing near the bar, cuddling together, as if they're not amidst the chaos the rest of us are left to suffer in.

"Come," Jerry instructs. "Follow me. Brock's waiting."

*Brock.*

The initial confirmation of his attendance binds me into place. My feet are heavy, and my head is spinning. I haven't seen him since I fled, and there's no telling what his reaction to seeing me again will be.

I don't have to question this long because when I look away from Jerry pushing at my back, Brock rounds the corner. He's wearing another suit, this one better than the last. I find this one fits better, most likely because I know what's under it.

*Damn it.*

Along with the reminders of seeing him again, comes the memory of the way he smelled, the taste of his lips, and the thrust of his...

"There he is!" Jerry yells. Turning to me, he whispers, "I'm Jerry, by the way. We met just briefly this morning. I'm Brock's, for lack of a better term, bitch. For the next several weeks, I'm his bodyguard, fetch boy, and chauffeur."

I don't respond, or even get the chance because Jerry lifts his hand to his mouth, using his fingers to whistle loudly. When he does, he gets the room's attention.

Willow should try that.

Brock turns his head. His eyes narrow at Jerry, but when they come to mine, something else happens. As I stand across the room, surrounded by the exotic beauty of the others, I suddenly feel just as beautiful. Brock's eyes soften, and his head tilts to the side. His lips form the same subtle and boyish grin he had this morning as he stood in the doorway after his shower.

A small, pathetic wave of my hand greets him. Once I do, his grin morphs into a ridiculous smile. Initially, me showing up may have stumped him, but maybe he's happy I'm here.

"Wait here," Jerry instructs. "And take this," he says next, handing me a drink.

The gold liquid contents inside the red plastic cup holds zero appeal. After my drunken stupor last night, I'm thankful I didn't wake up sick. I dutifully hold it, though. It's giving me something to concentrate on.

Ryleigh stands from her table, leaving Emilee behind as she rushes to my side and emits a breathy, "Oh my God, girl. You clean up *nice!*"

*I* really don't. Addie did this to me.

My best friend insisted on not only what I should wear, but also how to fix my hair. It's swept up with small pins, decorated with diamond studs at the end. Long, wistful strands of it fall from the updo, framing my face and neck.

My vote of jeans and sweatshirt was immediately denied. Thus, this outfit isn't mine, it's hers. As cliché as it may sound, Addie borrowed me her favorite 'little black dress,' which thankfully fit me to a tee. It's not, in any way, risky or revealing. Rather it's simply stated and modestly elegant.

"Thank you," I respond.

A compliment given by her, dressed to the nines in her pale pink evening dress, says a lot, and in the face of this uncertain approach, I appreciate her for it.

"It's so busy in here," I observe, keeping focus on my new friend, rather than fall to intimidation with the stares coming from the rest of the crowd, namely Brock.

"I met him," Ryleigh whispers, bending close to do so in my ear. "He's hot."

A small sliver of possessiveness comes first, followed by a blistering bout of jealousy I have no right to feel.

"He's not much of a talker, though. He's hardly said a word to any of us."

The blistering jealousy morphs to irrational relief.

"And he's not sticking around here long. He told Willow he's ready to head up to his room. He's staying in the *penthouse.*"

This I already know, but I play it off with, "Nice."

"The girls love him already," she tells me. "I don't think any of us really believed he'd be much to look at, but he is."

"This is good," I casually return.

"They're going to be announcing his first date choice in the morning. I feel for the woman already."

Curiously, I ask, "Why's that?"

"First blood drawn," she replies. "These girls may be oh-so-pretty, but I've heard some of them talk about the others. Not nice," she *tsks*.

Oh God, I can imagine. Nine women, vying for the same man—a man who looks like Brock and has money. This is college cattiness 101. I've already taken the course, hated it, and assuredly dropped the class that followed.

"Well, at least you like him," I confirm, having nothing else to say. "That's something."

Ryleigh's eyebrows furrow. "You don't sound excited to be here," she observes. Her hands move to her hips, and she stares down at me with disappointment. "Are you still pining over your first-ever one-night stand?"

# Chapter Twenty-One

*Did you hear that? Brooke pined.*

*Brock*

-

"Interesting question." I step in to stand behind Brooke as to interrupt the conversation between the two chatty women. "*Are* you still pining over your first-ever one-night stand?"

Ryleigh's eyes widen, and her mouth hangs open before Brooke can answer.

When Brooke turns in place, I'm standing close. Too close. Without caring about the attention of the others who can see, my hand touches her hip and I hold it there as if I've done so a thousand times.

Her body heat burns my palm.

Her tremble scores my fingertips.

Her sweet smile cements to my memory.

"Hi," she whispers between us, then swallows hard.

Her eyes, shining with relief, look up at me before one side of her lips tip up into a knowing grin. She's busted. Her reasons for leaving my room this morning weren't just about *me* being here and why, but also *her.*

The first time I laid eyes on her tonight, standing across the room, nothing mattered. Her hypocritical leave from my room this morning was forgotten. The accusations held in her disappointed stare were meaningless.

She's here now, and I couldn't be happier to see her.

"Hi," I return, just as quietly as she did.

"This is Brooke," Ryleigh stutters, but gets herself together to finish introductions. "Brooke, this is Brock."

I'd spoken to Ryleigh earlier. Our less than cordial conversation was not her fault. As she chattered on about her family back in Louisiana, I stayed quiet. I missed what she was saying because I was sulking over an amber-eyed woman who made me laugh with her wit, smile with her awkwardness, and ache to touch her body.

"Hi," I say again, for lack of anything better.

As I stand close, the familiar vanilla scent of her hair, the delicate smell of her skin, and sweet musk of her perfume takes me in. Visions of her lying next to me in my bed come easy.

"Good! You've met." Jerry pops up at our side.

Taking a small step back, I keep my eyes on Brooke, and she does the same.

"We have met," I admit, in more ways than one. "Brooke..."

"Malloy." Jerry finishes before she can, then quickly admonishes, "You have her file. Did you not review that one either?"

"I didn't," I admit sharply, then press further in fun, in an effort to make Brooke uncomfortable. "I had a *very* late night and woke to a *pain in the ass* morning. I didn't get the chance to review anything."

Brooke's lips get tight, and her eyes narrow. Her look of disdain shouldn't be hot, but it is. I'm enjoying her pout.

"You have to read all the material I give you, Brock," Jerry drones. "There's information in those files that is important."

Taking my eyes off Brooke for the first time, I shift an icy glare in Jerry's direction. His incessant requests are wearing me down. As he takes in my expression, his face pales.

"Can I have a word with her?" I clip, turning back to Brooke and still not giving two shits about those who could be in witness. "*Alone.*"

Ryleigh replies, "Sure," at the same time Jerry returns, "By all means, you're the boss."

The two of them walk off in the direction of the crowd, leaving Brooke and I standing alone near the hotel door. My hand wraps around her wrist, and with not so careful steps, I lead us out into the foyer of the lounge.

"You owe me an apology," I start once we're clear of all others.

Her eyes narrow again. "A what?"

"You beat feet so fast out of my room this morning, I got lost in the dust."

Smiling, Brooke says, "Beat feet?"

Unable to control my urge to touch her, I take a step closer. Her back is near the wall, and if I keep pushing, I'll have her trapped.

"You left me," I accuse.

"I did," she returns. "The night was over."

"It didn't have to be," I insist. "I wanted to have breakfast with you."

The gears in her mind spin. She looks beyond my shoulder, rather than at me.

Reaching toward her, my hand holds her waist. When her back hits the wall behind her, our chests meet. I'm not about to give her too much room to think, at least not until I figure out what the hell is happening and how I feel about all of it.

Slowly, my eyes scan her face. My attention's captured when her pink tongue darts out to lick her bottom lip. Seeing this, I move my gaze to her neck, just in time for her to swallow. Her high heels add another four inches to her average frame, making her still shorter than me, but not by much.

"Come to my room," I insist, still looking down between us. When Brooke says nothing, I raise my head and push, "After this is over. I want you to come to my room."

Looking around the foyer, we both notice a few of the girls have started to file out of the lounge. No one but Ryleigh, followed closely by Kylee, offers us a second glance.

Rolling her eyes, probably at Kylee, she turns to answer with a stern, "No."

"Now you say no," I bait. "You weren't saying no last night."

She laughs, but it's not real. I sense contempt and maybe a little hurt. "You're here to pick a woman to marry. I'm not her."

"You don't know that."

"I do, considering you've already…" Her face turns a shade of pink, and she pauses before biting her bottom lip.

I'm already well aware that Brooke's not good with dirty talk. Her attempt last night was humorous, not erotic. I like that about her.

"We've already…"

"Fucked?" I charge.

"Yeah." The ire in her tone for my label isn't lost on me. "We've *fucked*."

Looking around again, we both notice more than a few of the girls are staring. I don't give a shit what anyone else thinks. I only care about what the woman in front of me does. I'm suddenly aware, I want the chance I deserve.

"We have a lot to do tomorrow. I should hang with Addie."

"The taping." I remember. "Come to my room for a drink. That's it. We'll talk about whatever you want."

My offer is tempting, and again, I note the thoughts are spinning behind her eyes.

Without giving another moment for her to contemplate turning my offer down, I demand, "Give me your phone."

"My phone?"

"I'm putting my number in it for you to text me later."

"You're bossy," she snaps, but she pulls the cell phone from her purse.

Checking the time first, she holds it between us. It's already closing in on eight. With any luck, we'll both be out of here within the hour.

I grab the phone from her grasp, where I find a picture of someone who could be her Dad and her. I study the image, framing her smile to memory, as well as the loving expression her father has as he holds her close at his side. I never had that, so I look at it with appreciation that she does.

Once I've finished adding my contact, I send a text to my number to ensure I have hers. "Will you come up for a drink?"

Her eyes roll again, but a small smile plays at her lips. "A drink is what got us into this."

"Maybe," I test. "But, from what I heard, you're still pining over your first-ever one-night stand, remember?"

Those beautiful eyes I saw my reflection in last night stare back at me, making it impossible to walk away. So, rather than do so, I wait.

Finally, she agrees. "I'll text you."

# Chapter Twenty-Two

*Mary Ann should keep her hands to herself.*

*Brooke*

-

Two hours later, I'm fidgeting as I stand outside Brock's penthouse suite. The marble floor may as well be a creaking, old, wooden plank that's walking me to future heartache. My hands are shaking, and my heart is beating faster than it did after finding out he was the millionaire bachelor.

I haven't given much thought to how Brock's made his millions and it doesn't matter. I don't care about money as a lot of women do. I never did. I only wanted to experience the adventure I promised my dad I would. Though, this isn't quite the adventure he probably wished for his only daughter to have. Admittedly, so far, I've enjoyed it just the same.

"Fuckin' finally," Brock greets, looking winded and a little exasperated as his door swings open. "Jesus Christ, what took so long?"

As he steps to the side, allowing me to pass, I don't take my eyes off him. I can't. Brock's rugged appearance makes my mouth water and my stomach flutter.

His hair is damp, his chest shining with drops of water he missed after his shower. The hickey I gave him last night stands out, and I smirk to myself in memory of how it came to be there. He's wearing a pair of black running pants with two thin, white lines running up the sides, and his feet are bare. He also smells like fresh soap and sandalwood.

*Mesmerizing.* He's managed to intoxicate me and I haven't had a drink.

"Gettin' a good look?" he quips, a knowing smile playing on his full red lips. "I don't mind, but—"

"I'm here," I press, trying to stay focused, "to talk."

Stepping in front of me, close, he looks down. His hand comes up to move the hair from my eyes, then he trails his finger down my temple to the apple of my cheek. His touch is soft and sweet. My eyes close, and my head tilts for added connection.

His lips touch the side of mine once, then pulls back to touch them again on the other. When I draw my mouth open to greet him properly, his tongue enters. Small thrusts of teasing twirls battle with mine in contest. Only a few seconds pass before his patience wanes, and his hand comes to hold the back of my head, clutching it tightly before I concede control and he takes over. Aggressively, he drives his tongue in and out as subtle moans emit from both of us. He tastes like beer. Foolishly, I'm lost in the moment, as if it's last night all over again.

"What took you so fucking long?" he breathes after pulling back, eying me with suspicion. "Two hours?"

*He's been watching the clock.*

I don't answer his ridiculous question. Instead, I follow his silent steps into the living room of his suite. I note his temporary place is much bigger than I remember and definitely brighter with the lights on. The main room's television is muted, but turned to the same channel it had been on last night in his room. Baseball stats run along the ticker at the bottom.

"Brock?" I call out, but he keeps walking, saying nothing.

The view of his back, sleek and powerful, emits another flutter. This time, not to my stomach, but between my legs. Once he's made it to the kitchenette, Brock rounds the breakfast bar and stops behind it.

This is good. I can't think clearly without maintaining at least *some* distance.

Doing all I can not to focus on his alluring presence, I set my purse down and get comfortable in one of the wooden stools across from where he stands.

"I may or may *not* owe you an apology," I start, picking up from where we left off downstairs.

His head tips to the side as though he's thinking; the same way he did when he saw me from across the room.

Regardless of how intimate I find his gesture, I power on. "I should've told you why I was in L.A."

"I'll accept your apology," he casually replies. Bracing both hands against the bar, he leans in to get closer. "And I'll apologize for whatever else you want me to, except last night. I won't be sorry for that."

Nodding my agreement, I say nothing. I won't apologize for that either. And, if I'm being honest, being that this adventure already has a predetermined expiration date, I'm willing to spend more time with him, doing the same thing we did last night. Again and again, if he's so inclined.

"So, you're here to find a husband," he smirks at my expense. "How's that even possible?"

"I'm not necessarily here to find a husband," I correct. "And how's what possible?"

"You're not here to find a husband?"

"No," I admit. "I came here because Addie talked me into it. I've never been spontaneous."

"Got that," he smarts. "You told me this repeatedly last night."

"Yeah." I wince. I was an idiot for running my mouth, admitting my inexperience.

"You're pretty," he compliments. "And fun."

When he stops talking, I choose to do the same. The smug way he's biting down on his bottom lip is a clear indication he's not finished making fun.

"Say what you're thinking," I demand. "Go ahead."

I hate guessing games. I'd rather just hear whatever he's pondering behind those beautiful brown eyes.

"You're hot as fuck in bed, too. One touch and you all but explode."

Scratch that, I *didn't* need to hear what he was thinking.

"Thanks?" That's all I've got. "You're not so bad yourself."

He laughs, and it's loud. His smile is wide, and his eyes are dancing.

When he brings his focus back to me, he continues with, "Jesus Christ, you don't have a clue, do you?"

No, apparently I don't. "A clue about what?"

"Nothing."

Staring at each other from across the small kitchen bar, he says nothing, and neither do I. This entire situation screams ridiculous. I've already had sex with the star of the show, the man who is here to pick a wife. Carelessly, we've crossed a line we can't uncross. I wouldn't want to, anyway. I had a lot of fun.

"I'm taking Mary Ann Steiner out Friday night for the first date," he informs me. "It was the girl Jerry suggested I use to 'get my feet wet,' whatever the hell that means."

A slight pang of jealousy knocks. The knock should go unanswered because, of course, he's taking Mary Ann on a date, as well as all those other women.

"Say something about it," he prods. "Tell me what you're thinking."

"Say what? What am I supposed to say? Of course you're taking her out. All those women are all here for you."

Walking around the bar, Brock prowls toward me. With his chest on full display, I barely hold my concentration. That small pang of jealousy turns to an unfounded rush of greed the minute both his hands touch my thighs. Then he spreads them, making room for his large body to lean in closer.

"Tell me, Brooke," he whispers, running his hands roughly against my jeans; back and forth, inflaming every inch he covers. "What did last night mean?"

"What did it mean?"

Hell if I know *exactly* what it meant. I've been listening to Addie, which has confused the ever-loving crap out of me. Her response to my first one-night stand, then the 'after' that concluded it, left me spinning.

"I don't know."

"I do," he counters. "I had a good time."

"I did, too," I answer immediately. It's the truth.

"This is so fucked," he breathes, touching his forehead to mine. "I've been here just over a day and I don't want to take the first girl out."

Mary Ann is gorgeous. She was one of the first women here I noticed. Her long, red hair is her most startling feature. No way it's colored, either, as her eyebrows are a perfect match. I can only imagine the *other* parts of her are a match, as well. And to think Brock might...

"She's very pretty," I tell him, downplaying my absurd jealousy. "She's a veterinarian, too."

"I like dogs, Brooke. They're the only animal which appeals to me in any way."

"Dogs?"

Shit, this figures. I love dogs. Not cats. They scare me.

"Cats creep me out," he advises.

*Well, of course.*

"And don't get me started on rodents."

"So, you go on your date, have fun, and you talk about dogs."

"She's from Missouri."

I hadn't known this. His knowing implies he's talked to her already, small talk or not. Again, that same jealousy flows to the surface. I quickly remind myself he's not mine. He owes me nothing.

"Missouri sounds nice," I offer, again in an attempt to hide my baseless hurt.

He studies my reaction, maybe waiting for me to admit there was more about last night than there truly was. It was random, a chance encounter which hundreds of people experience all the time. That was it. Nothing more.

*Right?*

"I should go." I start to stand.

After I've grabbed my purse from the counter, Brock steps forward, pressing his body flush with mine.

"When you walked in here tonight, you let me kiss you," he observes, "and you sure as hell kissed me back."

"Yeah?"

"Gratuitously," he adds with a smug smirk.

"Gratuitously?"

"If I would've put my hand up your skirt, bet you would've been ready for a lot more than my mouth on yours," he huskily decrees.

Sadly, maybe pathetically even, knowing he's here to date eight other women, he's still right. I don't admit this, but instead remain quiet.

"You like my mouth on you." He breathes the words against my lips.

Of course I do. I like *how* he puts his lips on me. The slow and sensual building of the kiss starts before diving into the heat and passion. I also like the way he touches me, his fingertips warm, leaving their prints to seep into every pore of my body in a way it misses him when he's gone.

"And I like having my mouth on you," he whispers, now against my ear. The shivers trailing down my spine incite the warm flutters of need I haven't been able to forget or deny. "Admit it."

Playing it off, I rear my head back. He straightens his so we're nearly eye-to-eye. "Yeah? I like to kiss."

Annoyed by my response, he steps back, running his fingers through his still damp hair. "You're not at the very least annoyed with any of this?"

"Yes and no."

Yes, I'm annoyed because I like him.

And no, I'm not, because we've just met, and there hasn't been much, other than sex and small conversation to speak of.

"I don't like that answer."

"It's all I have to give."

A soothing calm washes over him before he steps back into me. My back hits the kitchenette's counter as his body presses into mine. This time, I don't close my eyes to avoid him. This time, I meet mine with his and wait.

"Stay here tonight," he whispers softly, his nose grazing the apple of my cheek. "Don't think about it. Just say yes."

The palms of both his hands expand around my waist, his thumbs igniting trails of heat as they each caress the base of my chest. The now violent flutters in my stomach and the tingling between my legs cause me to sway. My breath hitches, and my thighs quiver in remembrance.

"If I do, it won't mean anything more than it did last night," I insist, convincing only myself. He's made no promises for more than sex, and I don't expect him to, being the reason he's here in the first place and all.

"It will mean something, Brooke," he corrects, whispering in my ear. "It'll mean I get to listen to you moan my name as I sink my cock into you again."

When I stop breathing all together, he smiles. The feel of his lips forming a grin against my cheek is evident. He's making it even harder to walk away.

Brock is sexy and playful. He's a beautiful man, in all ways. He's friendly, fun, and charming. He's boyishly adorable. He's also an inexperienced woman's personal cocktail for disaster.

And, of course, I'm already craving another drink.

So, I'm staying the night.

# Chapter Twenty-Three

*Rest in peace, Miss Piggy.*

*Brock*

-

The last time I was on a date similar to this one, I was a senior in high school. My ever-enthusiastic, matchmaking mother had just met a woman her age at the state fair. The same woman turned out to be a lot like my mother. The two hit it off like women often do, thus immediately delving into deep discussions about their children and what they think they know to be best. This is where my mother insisted I take her new friend's daughter out on a date for sushi because Charlotte,—*I think that was her name*—had never been.

Without feeling any guilt, I'll admit that Mary Ann is a nice girl. And, I'll give her this, she's also very pretty. She's successful in every way my father would appreciate, and sweet enough for my mother to adore. I'm sure Jerry chose her first for those very reasons. I'll admit, I thought if I enjoyed her company, then this date would lead to possibilities of becoming more.

Unfortunately, I've found I'm not the least bit interested.

"Sometimes, I get called out to the farms to birth them. My job is rewarding and also important."

*I'm sure it is, if you're a pig in desperate need of a mid-wife.*

When Jerry advised I'd be taking Mary Ann to Deangelo's Italian Bistro for dinner, I wasn't overly enthused. Of course he noticed, then quickly went on to explain Deangelo's is a quiet family-owned restaurant outside of the city. Thus, I knew ahead of time the forty-five-minute commute would most likely encourage conversation, as I'm sure all upcoming dates will. However, it ended up being forty-five minutes of awkward silence.

Between this afternoon's full-on meet and greet, which ended up feeling like speed dating and was taped with the cameras' lens in our faces, I'm already exhausted. Not to mention, I was given specific instructions on what I could and couldn't say or do during tonight's dinner.

*You can't ask her about her past relationships.*

*You can't inquire if she's been tested for any transmitted diseases, sexual or otherwise.*

*You can't reveal any of your personal fetishes.*

I'm not sure who put this list of dos and don'ts together, but whoever did has to be single, living alone, and caring for eight cats.

I meant what I told Brooke about cats. They're creepy.

"How many kids do you see yourself having?" Mary Ann asks the question before sucking in another noodle of her vegetarian dish of eggplant spaghetti.

Looking down at my plate of Italian sausage, I woefully recount her sorrowed story in regards to how viciously poor, wee piglets are treated before being led to their final resting place—a slaughterhouse.

Mary Ann's graphic description entailed how they must *feel* as they're taken to be destroyed. Not to mention her award winning play-by-play regarding the process of how blood is drained from their stiffened carcasses before they're laid out to be cut up into small pieces.

*Yeah.*

I push my plate away, wondering how to make a garden grow before responding, "Haven't given it much thought, I guess. Two? Maybe three?"

Her well-groomed eyebrow cocks. "That's all?"

"I didn't come from a big family," I explain, which is something she already knows.

I do know she came from a big family, though. She's told me about each and every one of her seven extremely successful siblings who are set to take over the farm this fall as soon as the youngest graduates from business school. They plan to diversify, expanding into crops, as well as more cattle.

*Dear God, can carrots be drained of their juices before being brutalized then murdered?*

Taking a healthy drink of wine, my thoughts wander to what Brooke could be up to tonight. When I said goodbye to her at my door this morning, she was distracted. She was too worried about being caught on my floor to give me the goodbye I wanted. Not so much as a kiss. I didn't like that. At all. And it won't happen again.

After we had sex last night, I didn't let her leave. Of course I didn't force her to stay, but I may have used my mouth to coerce her into coming back to me when she did make the attempt to get away.

I like her in my bed, and I want her there again tonight.

"Will you excuse me for a minute?" I ask, abruptly.

Mary Ann nods with a simple, "Sure."

Once standing, I turn to walk away. The one-man camera crew Jerry informed would be accompanying us tonight comes up slowly from behind. The onlookers of the restaurant don't hide their gawking stares as we walk from the dining room out into the small hallway near the back.

"Give me a few minutes?" I request, looking at Clive, the cameraman.

The relieved look he returns is immediate. Along with explaining that Clive would be accompanying us, Jerry also added that when either my date, or myself, requested cameras to be shut off, it was to be done so immediately. However, we weren't to insist this happen unless we truly desired absolute privacy. I don't know what qualifies as 'desire for privacy,' but I'll be using and abusing this privilege often.

"Any problem if I break for a quick drink at the bar?" Clive queries with a hopeful expression.

"None," I gladly permit. "I'll find you when we're ready."

He smiles, looks down, then raises his eyes to me. "I thought tonight was gonna go a lot differently, since you're so popular with the ladies and all. Glad it didn't."

"Hazards of the job, huh?" I joke. He's probably seen more than his fair share of outrageous behavior.

"You have no idea," he mutters as he brings the camera down from his shoulder and turns around to walk away.

With Clive gone, I don't enter the men's room as I had planned. Rather, I lean my back against the wall and pull out my cell phone.

The text Drew sent earlier still waits for an answer.

Drew 03:42 p.m.: *Are you still pissed at us? Thought I'd find out before booking a flight to see you in action, Romeo.*

*I've got your Romeo, asshat.*

I don't respond, not because I'm still pissed, but because my outgoing text to Brooke is my only focus.

Me 07:48 p.m.: *What are you up to?*

Straightening myself from the wall, I take a quick look around before heading back to Mary Ann. The immediate return of a text to my phone stops me.

Brooke 07:49 p.m.: *Hanging at the hotel bar with Addie and Ry. You're on your date, I presume.*

Me 07:49 p.m.: *Yes. An Italian Bistro. No one is talking about dogs. Mary Ann just told me how pigs are led to slaughter. She's a vegetarian. I ordered Italian sausage.*

My summarization of this date sounds ludicrous. Then again, everything about this evening has been amusing. Either that, or I'm already starting to crack under the pressure.

Brooke 07:51 p.m.: *Hope you weren't looking for her to give you a goodnight kiss. You're devouring Miss Piggy right in front of her.*

Looking up and stifling my laugh, I see a gentleman coming toward me, so I stand to the side before responding. I'd enjoy some safe, friendly banter between us. Another piece of her to savor. However, as shitty as it is, I have a date to get back to.

Me 07:52 p.m.: *You got jokes?*

Brooke 07:52 p.m.: *Lots.*

Me 07:53 p.m.: *Come to my room tonight at 11.*

Her response is immediate.

Brooke 07:53 p.m.: *All right, Hannibal Lecter.*

Her humor is only funny because it's not only awkward, but also distasteful. I smile briefly, then make my way back to *Clarice*.

# Chapter Twenty-Four

*His name is Brock, and he fits me in every way.*

*Brooke*

-

"Yes, Dad. I'm being totally responsible. *And* I'm having fun," I reassure him for the third time, all while sitting on Brock's hotel bed watching him slowly undress.

"Have you met the guy?"

*The guy.*

Funny how my dad insisted I fly out here, knowing I'd be meeting my possible marital match as it's being aired on a semi-popular television network, yet he's refused to acknowledge the star of this season has a name.

"Brock," I direct. "And yes, he's very..." I stop mid-sentence as Brock's shirt drops to the floor after he seductively unbuttoned it in front of me. "*Nice.*"

"*Nice?*" my father mocks. "I thought you'd have something more to say than 'nice.' Brooke, sweetheart, are you okay?"

Brock walks around the bed before I feel the mattress dip behind me. There, he positions himself on his knees and rests his chest against my back. Both hands trail slowly down my neck before he continues guiding them between the warm skin of my chest and bra.

*Sure, Dad. I'm okay. If I'm lucky, I'm about to be violated, too.*

I don't express this, I just answer as calmly as I can. "No worries. I'm having a really good time."

Brock's fingers twist both of my aroused tips, nearly to the point of pain before he strokes to soothe them with a gentle caress of his fingertips. I close my eyes and nearly avoid dropping the phone.

All evening, as I sat around drinking and playing cards with Addie and Ryleigh, I stewed over knowing where Brock was. Not to mention, who he was with. I thought about his hands on me, just as they are now, and hated the fact that Mary Ann was, in fact, somewhere on earth with those hands.

The promise for what was to come later tonight caused me to lose focus on a simple game of party gin. It was a mindless game that I didn't care about losing.

"All right, fine," Dad declares. "I'll tell your mother you're 'okay' and that Brock is 'nice.' But really, Button, if you're not okay and he's not nice, you'll tell me?"

"Of course I will, Dad," I reply, leaning my body forward then off the bed in order to break free of Brock's delicious distractions. "I'll call you tomorrow."

"Please," he begs, as he always does.

"I love you."

"Love you, too, Button."

The millisecond Brock overhears my father bidding his goodbye, the phone is snatched from my hand and tossed across the room. Thankfully, it lands on a pile of clothes with a quiet thud.

"You threw my new phone!" I shriek, but I'm barely able to get the words out.

As I'm psyching myself up to kick his ass, he forcefully turns me around and pushes my back to the mattress, only to then throw himself on top of me.

"Someone's date got him all worked up," I quip as he unzips my jeans with haste, then pulls them down my legs in one swift, and obviously, practiced move.

With fortitude, he runs his hands up my naked outer thighs, then counters my tease with, "Someone's mouth needs to stop making so much fuckin' noise so she can find a better use for it."

I gasp. Feigning insult, I dig further. "Mary Ann must not have put out. If she did, she wasn't very good. You're still all hot and bothered."

Brock sits, resting his ass on the back of his ankles. He looks over me for a few seconds, shamelessly surveying my best black-laced panties, then dives in to remove those, too. Before I can take off my shirt, or ask about his first date, his fingers pierce my inner thighs, holding them apart, as his mouth crashes down between them.

*Dear God, I'll never get tired of his mouth.*

"Jesus," I snap, feebly attempting to push my body up the bed to get away.

All at once, Brock is too much.

He's having nothing to do with my escape. The added determination of his tongue, thrusting in and out as though he can't get enough, is proof of this.

I gasp at the incessant invasion.

My neck arches and my fingers run through his thick mass of dark hair. He loves how I taste; he's told me this. *I* love how *he* tastes me. Fast then slow and all the ways in between.

He moans, I sigh. He sucks, I gasp. The tormenting pleasure pulls me forward then pushes me back. There's no set rhythm to his ministrations. Brock is everywhere.

A small echoing yelp breaks from my throat as soon as I feel his thumb adding pressure to my backside.

For as long as Jason and I were together, he never explored *that* area. Most likely, Jason assumed it was a no-go, as even he admitted he wasn't always gentle. With this being only the third night I've had with Brock, to include our drunken frenzy, I don't feel safe enough to go there with him...*yet*.

"Stay still," he growls, "until I'm finished."

*So. Freaking. Bossy.*

His thumb breaches the entrance and my jaw, along with every other muscle in my body, clenches.

"Brock," I bid sternly, staring up at the ceiling and hating that I'm going to lose my nearly sated status.

*And seriously, why are men so greedy?*

"I won't," he bites out, obviously noticing I'm tense. With his reassurance, my body relaxes. Until he adds, "But fuck me, Brooke, I want to."

*Shit.*

"Let me on top," I bait, hoping to sway his intent.

"When I'm finished," he hisses. I'm coming to learn Brock doesn't like to be interrupted.

Another finger replaces his tongue, callously dipping inside before searching to find the spot I *know* he works so well. His tongue flattens against then teases my swollen clit. Brock's warm breath cascades along my already heated flesh.

The stubborn man is making a meal of this.

"You call my name when you come, Brooke," he brazenly instructs. "Loud and clear, baby. I wanna hear you scream."

Listening to his encouragement, masked as invitation, my feet push themselves against the mattress. My hands grasp the sheets, my hips thrust harder against his mouth. With unrestrained abandon, I release a string of quiet curses before a weighted moan erupts from my parted lips.

At the same time, my body is hanging precariously on the edge of sexual frenzy, Brock's finger unexpectedly slides in to its fullest extent from behind.

*Never.*

Never amidst my most vivid sexual fantasies have I surrendered to such absolute submission. The stars are aligned, the twists of fate have gathered, and my body blazingly ignites. The perfect storm of desire, passion, lust, sex, and Brock are ruining me. An earth shattering guttural cry of ecstasy breaks from my chest—uninhibited and uncontrolled.

Seconds pass, yet I can't catch my breath. Thoughts cross, but I can't understand them clearly.

As soon as I open my eyes, I feel my face flush. Acknowledgment, embarrassment, and whatever else I've lost sight of come blaring to the surface.

*Oh God, no way I just did that.*

Crawling up along my body on all fours, Brock glares at me, but it's with hooded eyes. His body blankets mine before kisses me with a passion I know he never has. I would've remembered this. Biting, licking, sucking, taunting. Again and again until neither of us can breathe.

"That was the sexiest fucking thing I've ever witnessed *in my life*," he anxiously declares. "Christ, you're gorgeous when you come," he genuinely praises. "I want inside you," he demands before adding, "Deep, Brooke. So fuckin' deep."

*Well, when he puts it like that...*

"Condom," he clips hastily.

I could tell Brock now that on I'm on the pill and have been since I was fifteen due to irregular cycles. I don't, though. Rather, I watch with unveiled attention as the muscles of his chest and arms grow tight when he reaches into the bedside drawer.

"This'll be quick," he informs me as he rips the foil wrapper with his teeth.

Chancing to lighten the intensity of his mood, I run my first finger along his jaw, while at the same time, he aggressively works to cover himself. "As soon as you know when your next date is, let me know so I can be ready when you're done. I like having sex with you when you're this worked up. It's crazy hot."

"She mentioned *pigs*, Brooke," he angrily spits. "Being led to *slaughter,* for fuck's sake."

The startling realization that he spent his evening mentally dissecting animals makes me laugh. His typical ease in finding humor doesn't follow.

"Know what I did all night?" he teases, raising his hands over our heads and grabbing the top of the mattress for leverage. When he slides inside with furiousness, I gasp. "To escape *her*, I thought about fucking *you*."

I believe him, so does every inch of my body. His pounding is relentless, each drive harder than the last.

"I thought about *your* mouth sucking my cock from under the table," he hisses before biting down on the skin of my neck with frustration. "On the way home, I closed my eyes and thought of *your* ass. All the ways I wanted to take it, Brooke."

"Oh God," I breathe, unable to keep up with his rhythm and wrapping my legs around him to hold us both steady.

Without waiting to see if I'm close, Brock's body locks in place, his cock settles just as promised, deep inside. He releases all he has with a loud moan. "Fuck, why are you doing this to me?"

The room quiets. Neither of us put forth the effort to break the silence. His last compelling question leaves me speechless. His last vie for release has left him breathless.

A full minute passes. I know, because I've subconsciously counted the seconds.

"Fuck," he whispers against the material of my shirt. It's not until he does that I realize I'm still wearing it.

Brock's body shudders above mine. His hands finally release the mattress, and he positions his elbows on either side of my head. As he looks down, beads of sweat from his brow threaten to fall.

His eyes are hazy, soft, and sincere. "I thought about waking up to you again," he explains. "You left so fast this morning."

"I had to go," I defend.

Troubling times as this may be to explain what he doesn't understand. I need to address what's very recently been on my mind.

"I can't stay here every night. I have a best friend who came all this way to hang out with me. Not to mention a roommate who you're bound to end up *dating*."

"Dating," he grinds, pushing himself further inside me. My body is sensitive, sore, and tired. His eyes close, and he growls unsteadily into my neck, "Fuck me, you feel so *fucking* good."

Obviously, he has no intention of listening to anything I have to say. And yet, all the facts surrounding us remain true. Addie has been sitting in our room, hanging out with Ryleigh for the past two nights, delving out ridiculous excuses for my late night absences.

Pressing forward, whether he wants to hear this now or not, I advise him in a whisper because the truth of the statement hurts to say. "And I'll remind you, Mr. LaDuece, you're here to pick a wife. The future *Mrs.* LaDuece awaits, remember?"

His body locks, and he lifts his head from my neck to find my eyes. The dim light of his room offers little shield from the seriousness of his expression.

"We can talk about all that," he sharply informs.

I don't like his tone, especially not right now. Not when I can feel his dick continuously pulse inside me.

"But not now. Now, I want to fuck you again. So, let go of whatever you're thinking and stop talking about other women, or the *possibility* of other women while I'm inside you. Or anytime you're in my bed."

I nod, feeling scolded for merely being honest.

"Fuck it," he continues in a rush. "Don't mention other women *ever* when I'm with you."

He's pissed.

That's exactly what this is.

It's a side of Brock I haven't seen and shouldn't have, at least not yet, considering we've only known each other a few days. His eyes are dark; the look of adoration I had gotten gazed on me earlier as I talked to my dad is gone. The impenetrable lust I heard in his voice has all but vanished, replacing it all is insult.

"I'm sorry," I try to soothe. "You're right."

His features lose their tension, and he retracts his hips to pull out.

"Glad that's straight," he says. "I'll get rid of this, hydrate, then we can—"

"Fuck." I finish for him through a smile.

# Chapter Twenty-Five

*Say it again and again. And while I'm inside you, you'll say it again.*

*Brock*

-

Jesus Christ, listening to Brooke curse is hot.

Her crass words are a mix of insult, foreplay, and comedy all rolled into one. Hearing her say 'fuck' and labeling it as I did for exactly what I'm doing to her in my bed brings that simple word new meaning.

"Repeat that," I hiss, driving into her with powering thrusts I couldn't stop if I wanted to. Once again, she's got me too worked up. "Say it again," I insist.

I bite down on the soft skin of her neck. My finger runs over her clit three times in quick succession as my cock swells inside her. This gets the little minx's attention.

"Right now we fuck," she breathes out on a gasp. "Got it."

Fuck, she *is* getting it. She's getting everything.

My cock.

My mouth.

My entire body.

But, also my complete attention.

Since the moment I met her, Brooke's taken everything, all without a second thought. The nervous girl I first laid eyes on as she walked off the elevator into the swarming crowd of chatty women has acquired everything I have to give.

The same woman who played disinterest in a bar full of men who couldn't look away from her is clawing her way beneath my skin. As if this isn't already enough, the woman I've been inside of for the past three nights has let me *take* everything I want from her in return.

*Almost everything.*

"There," she grinds out through her clenched jaw. "Don't stop. I'm there."

She gives me only a second's warning. With her ankles locked at my back, her body growing stiff, and my hands binding her hips to the mattress, I last only three more powerful thrusts before letting go.

As my racing heart settles in my chest, beads of sweat fall from my temples. I lift my head to find Brooke looking as drained as I am.

She's biting her bottom lip, assuredly thinking of some smartass thing to say, but thankfully she holds it in. Once I've pulled out of her, I rest my cheek against her chest. She's no longer wearing her shirt as she did the first time. Further proof Brooke's slowly getting inside my head, as I prefer the women in my bed to be naked.

"You're staying the night again," I suggest, albeit strongly.

I'm not ready for her to leave. After my session of insanity, which was labeled as a first date, I appreciate Brooke's company all the more. I've come to realize how alone I'm starting to feel, being in this city. Or maybe more so alone without her close.

"Okay," she softly replies. "I'll stay the night."

Her fingers run through my dampened hair. Every time she does this I'm reminded of how good her hands feel anywhere they touch me.

I close my eyes in weariness.

"You're still on top of me," she says, squirming to get free.

"Can you breathe?"

"Yes."

"Then settle, woman. I'm tired."

Laughing, she pulls the hair she was just messing, so I crane my neck to look up at her. Her eyes are glossy, and her eyebrows are furrowed. The late nights of a lot of sex and small conversation are beginning to take a toll, and it's day three.

When I reluctantly release her to stand, she drags the bed sheet up her body and gets comfortable. Her long hair looks good splashed against my sheets. Her half-smile as she looks at my chest is telling.

"It's already fading," she quietly observes, at the same time pointing in my direction.

Looking down, I find the hickey she put there has started to change in color. When I first caught a glimpse of it in the bathroom mirror, I laughed. I haven't had a hickey since high school—junior prom to be exact. Normally, at my age, I'd find the notion of a blood blotch repulsive. Carrying Brooke's mark, though, hasn't been so bad.

"Bloodsucking temptress," I call her as I turn around to remove the condom. "I'll be back in a second."

Once inside the bathroom, I get a good look at myself in the mirror. My lips are red and swollen. My chest has her fingernail marks everywhere. As tired as I am, my just-fucked appearance shouldn't be a green light, but the recollections of Brooke in my bed have recently been the cause for my cock standing at attention all the time.

Discarding the condom and closing up the bathroom, I return to the bed to find she's adjusted herself on her side, looking absolutely sexy and completely sated.

Once our heads are to the pillows, neither of us are able to sleep. Everything between us is different and new. The idea of sleeping through any of it doesn't appeal to me.

"So, if you *had* to choose one, who would it be?" She starts in with conversation, as if we're in the middle of it. "Adam Levine or Keith Urban?"

"What?"

Brooke pushes, "If you had to pick a guy crush, which one would it be?"

"I don't have crushes on guys. Sorry to disappoint."

Smirking, she lifts her hand to her face to move the hair that's fallen. I lift mine, swatting hers away to finish what she started.

"I love Sam Hunt," she tells me. "His voice, his eyes, his—"

"No," I clip. My voice isn't nearly as irritated as I am in joining this insane conversation, but my words are direct. "Don't talk about another man in this bed."

Turning to her back, she rests her arm over her eyes and sighs. "Come on. Play the game."

If she wants to play the game, I'll be sure we're on the same playing field.

"Taylor Swift," I answer at random.

I don't give two shits about Taylor Swift, other than I like her voice. However, Brooke's knee-jerk reaction is amusing. Sitting straight up in bed, she tosses out an overly dramatic sigh, coupled with a look of disgust.

"She's still a kid!" she dramatically accuses. "What's the matter with you?"

Trying not to laugh at her ridiculous and very *ignorant* observation, I barely hold myself together.

"What do you mean what's the matter with me? She's hot."

Lifting a spare pillow, she throws it at me. She's not strong by any means, but fueled by anger, I'd bet had that been her fist, I'd be bruised by morning.

"Brock. She's like what, seventeen?"

"Twenty-six," I correct, then note, "She's your age."

"No way."

"*Yes* way. Where the fuck have you been?"

"Taylor Swift is twenty-six?"

"Yep, and she's a hot as fuck twenty-six-year old, too," I poke. "So, there's my pick. You have it now. What else you got?"

The narrowing of her eyes tells me I've not made her happy with my chosen celebrity. However, the words she used earlier to describe Sam Hunt, a country artist I've only listened to a few times, were equally as outrageous, but also annoyed the fuck out of me. I have nice eyes and a good voice. She can admire those.

Slamming her head back down on the pillow, she looks to the ceiling and crosses her hands over her stomach.

"You disappoint me, Brock LaDuece."

"How so?"

"Taylor is rich, blonde, and has a great voice."

Now she's jealous. This, I revel in because I like it.

Turning to face her, my finger traces slowly down her temple, then down to rest at the bottom of her cheek.

She doesn't give me the attention I'm silently asking for, so I prod, "Brooke?"

When her head turns to look at me, her expression is blank.

"You're jealous," I accuse.

"I'm not."

"You are. I like it."

Sighing, she concedes, but not completely. "While you're off in your imagination with Taylor, you should know I'll be off with Sam in mine."

This I do *not* like. Not the image, thought, reason, or the remotest possibility.

"Tell me about your sister." She's maneuvering toward a subject change.

I'd talk about anything else if it got her to stop imagining Sam Hunt so soon after we've had sex.

Lying on my back, I rest my arm under my head and my hand on my chest. I'm not touching Brooke, which is good, considering she may be pretty sore.

"Tate's a tyrant."

She laughs. "She's not."

At the same time, I turn to her and lift my eyebrows. "In *every* way. She's spoiled rotten, has a sailor's mouth that'll put most truckers to shame, and lives every day to drive me nuts. I'm convinced."

"She sounds wonderful," Brooke jests at my expense. "She's sixteen?"

"Yeah, newly sixteen at that. She was my parents' late-in-life mistake."

"Harsh," she remarks, regarding the label.

"I'm their disappointment." I shrug. "Guess that makes us even."

"I have a brother. His name is Ashton. He's not a tyrant, and he's not spoiled. He's a good guy."

"You two are close?"

"Very," she expands. "Our whole family is. I'm probably closest with my dad."

This is the second time, in the short amount of time we've spent together, where she's mentioned her family and how tight they are. I'm glad she has this. I didn't know my own father, and Martin and I aren't as close as we used to be. I'm still hopeful to change that.

"Why'd you come here? To L.A.," I probe. She's already told me she's not looking to get married, so I'm guessing there's another reason.

Her short answer doesn't lend much information. "Bored, I guess. Addie pushed, so did my dad."

"Do you have anyone waiting for you to get back?"

Shaking her head, she understands what I'm asking. "No. I did, but not anymore. You?"

"Nope," I confirm.

"How long was your last relationship?"

Now that's a pointed question with no real answer. The longest relationship I've ever been in was in part what got me into this mess.

"A few months. I work a lot."

"A few months?" she questions, but lightheartedly so. Her small smirk does a shit job in hiding her sarcasm. "You're like what? Thirty-five?"

"Thirty," I defend. "I haven't found the right girl."

Laughing out loud, she adds, "So you came here to find her? I would think there would've been less dramatic ways."

Shrugging, I admit, "I was coerced. My dad helped make this decision for me."

"I understand," she assures, "completely."

"What will you do after this is over?"

"Not sure."

"What do you *want* to do?"

Shaking her head, she says, "No clue, really."

"Kids?"

"Yeah. Later, though. I'm staying at my parents' until I can get another place. My roommate and I had a disagreement. I left without much notice."

I don't fault her for living with her parents. There have been times in my adult life I've actually missed living at home, Tate the Tyrant or not.

"I'm tired," she puts in while rubbing her eyes.

"Sleep," I suggest, pulling her into me before draping my arm around her waist and sliding my thigh between her legs.

To say I've never actually 'slept' with a woman would be true. I'm not so much the sleepover type of guy, as much as I am the sleep-with-and-go type of guy. The last two nights with her in my bed has all been new, and so far it's not as bad as I imagined it to be.

Not even close.

# Chapter Twenty-Six

*Kylee Simmons is the head bitch of the reality show cheerleading squad.*

*Brooke*

-

"I haven't heard if he nixed her yet or not." Leslie Miles, one of Brock's soon-to-be dates, sneers her gossip to Kylee Simmons. "But I bet he does."

I'm standing in the dining room of the hotel lounge holding a plate full of eggs, bacon, and toast. At the same time, I'm wishing I were anywhere else but here.

"She's too..." Kylee pauses, and I assume it's to lower her voice, but she doesn't. Instead, she raises it and continues with, "*Plain*. He'll choose someone more suited for him."

In high school, my friends and I had a few run-ins with girls who were a lot like Leslie and Kylee. We called them bitches.

We all know those women who challenge others behind their backs in order to lift themselves higher or bring themselves further into the spotlight. Those same girls often got pregnant as teenagers and became cashiers at Dollar General because they'd given away the goods too early and had pissed off every vendor on the block with their holier than thou teenage attitudes. I'm not sure if this is exactly how Leslie or Kylee are, but no matter—bitches are bitches.

"Whatever," Kylee snaps, turning around to find me at her side. As she continues with her rant, she looks me up and down, and her lip curls up in disgust. "In the end, he'll see each little girl for who she really is."

"Right," Leslie adds, now looking at me and mirroring Kylee's snobbish pose.

*Sniveling bitches.*

"You agree, don't you, Brooke?" Kylee fakes a smile, clearing away all traces of nasty from her face. "Most of these women are still young girls."

"I think it's up to Brock to decide what most of these women are," I reply, feigning a smile for her, too.

Surprised by my response, Kylee's façade of friendship quickly fades. I'm not a member of her Barbie club, nor do I have any desire to be.

Tilting her head to the side, she states, "You seem to know Brock. I'm curious how that's possible."

Nodding, I agree, but not entirely. "I met him here, just like everyone else."

Leslie, chiming in with her absurdity, advises, "You'd be good to remember we have weeks to go. We're all in this together."

*Right.*

"If you two will excuse me," I nod in the direction of the exit. "I'll see you both later."

"You will," Kylee surmises, her eyes narrowing as she does. "Good luck with that." She points to my plate and smirks before turning in place to give me her back.

*Such a bitch.*

"Hi, Brooke," Ryleigh cheerfully greets, walking in front of me and making it so I can no longer see the Barbie Doll duo. "I'm not an early riser," she explains.

Unsure as to how she can say this, considering she looks absolutely adorable in her small green and white sundress. The ties at her golden shoulders accentuate every curve of her oh-so-perfect body.

"I am," I admit.

"Your girl, Addie, is definitely not. She slept through my shower and panic of what to wear."

She's right about that. Addie hates mornings more than most. She's not a nice person if she's woken up a single second before she needs to be.

"Are you eating down here?" I ask. The white to-go box in her hands dashes my hope of finding anyone to sit with. This is so much like high school.

"No, I'm eating with Mary Ann. I'm taking this to her room. She's upset."

*I'll bet she is.*

Ryleigh looks to her left, then right, to ensure the coast is clear. Leaning down to my height, she whispers, "Mary Ann said the date last night didn't go so good."

"No?" I passively inquire.

Shaking her head, she continues in a rush, "No. She said Brock's a really nice guy. Raved about him, too."

Green jealous hate for Mary Ann bubbles inside of me, but I tap it down enough to keep listening.

"She said he was distracted."

"Distracted?" I question with too much enthusiasm. Saving face, I tone it down. "Distracted by what?"

"No idea. But Mary Ann heard an earful this morning from some of the others that Kylee had a lot to say about her inability to catch a man like Brock."

*Witch!*

"So between her date not going as she'd hoped, then all she heard today, Mary Ann's not having a good start to this."

"It's sweet of you to be there for her," I advise, truly appreciating what a great friend Ryleigh appears to be.

"Yeah, I'll do what I can. Catch you later." Ryleigh turns and walks away.

As I scan the room, looking for Leslie Dee and Kylee Doo, I catch Emilee near the coffee machine. She's standing alone and staring at it as if she's confused to how it works. Her long, dark hair hangs straight at her back. She too is wearing an adorable dress. Hers is white, accenting her naturally bronzed complexion.

"Good morning, Brooke," she greets me as I get close, then reaches to grab her own plate of food.

The bright colors of the fruit she's carefully chosen stare back at me. I second guess the helping of hash browns I was looking forward to when I woke up in Brock's bed an hour ago.

After our small talk last night, followed by this morning's semi-platonic shower, where I found he's not much of a morning person either, I told him I *really* needed to go. My suggestion of a quick departure led to a speedy, but frenzied make-out session before he walked me to the door and kissed me goodbye.

Looking at Emilee, I note she looks flustered. "Hey, Em. How are you?"

"Nervous," she replies, looking down and moving her hair from her eyes.

I've found the woman to be painfully shy, and I've wondered why she ever came to a place like this. L.A. is a big city.

"Nervous about what?"

"Brock had his first date last night," she tells me, though I already knew.

Everyone knew because it was announced at the end of the day yesterday. Also, I already knew because he was texting me during said date, following up with having sex with me after, *twice.*

*I'm a terrible person.*

"I heard it ended well, too. *Very* well."

My eyes narrow. "How so?"

"Some of the girls...um...they kind of heard things."

*Christ.* Please tell me they weren't loitering around his room. If so, they heard *my* things. My one-time, ever-epic, mind blowing, double penetration orgasm was the shout heard round the world. Suddenly, I look to my food and am no longer hungry.

"I heard from Joelle that Brock looks worn out and tired this morning."

A sad and pathetic satisfaction is taken from this. If the other girls think Brock's already swooning over someone, I suppose it doesn't have to be me who takes the fall.

Damn it. I'm a *terrible* person.

"Joelle said Willow knocked on his door this morning and he didn't answer. She said Willow wasn't happy and went screaming in a rant to find Matt."

Joelle, I'm quickly finding, is also a gossip. Unfortunately for Emilee, she got stuck with her as a roommate.

"Jo is ticked because her date with him is next week. She doesn't want him thinking about Mary Ann while his attention is supposed to be on her."

God, all my assumptions are correct. I've just travelled back ten years. I'm not only back in high school, but Brock is the captain of the football team and we're all the makeshift cheerleaders who are cattily scheming for his attention.

I'll say now, I hated high school for this very reason.

"Don't believe everything you hear, Em. Truly. There's still weeks to go."

Surprisingly, Emilee confesses, "I don't want Brock to pick me."

Turning my eyes to hers, I find her no longer leveling me with her undivided attention. She's lost in her own head.

"Why do you say that?"

Emilee's eyes change from sweet to semi-glossy before she says, "I came out here from Arizona because my boyfriend dumped me a couple months ago. He called me a boring cow. He said a wet blanket had more elasticity."

*Damn.*

"So, you're here to prove to him you're not?"

"Yes," she quietly confirms. "I'm not a cow," she bravely snips. "Or a wet blanket."

"Come on, Em. Eat breakfast with me. I'll take some food up to Addie, and we'll hang out in my room until it's time for the bus to take us to the studio. How's that?"

She smiles, and it's genuine. "Thank you."

# Chapter Twenty-Seven

*Step away from the makeup brushes, Taylor Van Buren.*

*Brock*

-

"How are things going for you so far, Brock?" Matt inquires as he walks into the men's dressing room, where we both now wait for the makeup crew to arrive.

I've never, not once in my life, held any sort of appreciation for women having to wear all this shit.

Shine-free powder, lip balm, and Vaseline over my teeth to 'ease my smile' has shed enough light on what women go through that I've mentally noted to forbid Tate from wasting her life applying it.

When Taylor, the guy in charge of wardrobe and makeup, came *at me* with a sharp pencil of black eyeliner, too happy to advise the coal in the stick would bring out my eyes in front of the camera, I uncompromisingly called foul.

Powder to avoid a glare, fine.

Lip balm to smooth my lips, okay.

Even the Vaseline held its purpose.

But eyeliner? That was an immediate *fuck no*.

Matt laughed at my reaction. Taylor hasn't spoken to me since. I must've hurt his feelings.

"Things are going good, I think," I answer. "Maybe a little exhausting."

Matt shrugs and smiles at me in the reflection of the mirror we're both now sitting in front of. His chair is black, mine's gold. Both are cushioned and comfortable.

"Has Jerry gotten with you yet this morning?"

"For?"

"He needs to get  your vote on which girl you'll no longer consider."

"Yeah, he did."

I chose, and it was rough. I didn't realize my pick to remove a girl from the dashboard of my life was needed *first* thing this morning.

Apparently, from what Jerry advised earlier, Willow came to my room to collect the girl's name and I didn't answer. I heard the knock, but was in the shower after saying goodbye to Brooke. I didn't want company, and I sure as hell didn't want *that* woman squawking at me for *any* reason. She told me herself she was here to support the girls. So be it. She can see to them. I prefer Matt, as he's much more laid back.

When I instructed Jerry on my choice to remove Mary Ann, he didn't offer a word in counsel. He just said, "I'll see the board gets your pick," and let me off the phone.

"Don't feel bad about any of the decisions you make here, Brock. If you overthink, you'll undoubtedly make the wrong choice. Go with your gut."

My gut says Brooke. I'm not so sure she's there with me, though. Other than in passing, she hasn't mentioned the weight of importance to why she's here, which to be fair, she hasn't exactly gotten an opportunity. When we're together, we're either fucking, rattling on about our impersonal likes and dislikes, or sleeping. However, as odd as it may be, I'm content with what we have, and I haven't been this content with any woman, ever.

And I've been with a lot.

 "And don't forget one thing as you cast each woman aside," Matt injects.

"What's that?"

"In the end, the woman you choose has every right to refuse your proposal. If she does, the matter is out of your hands."

"It goes to the audience," I recall.

"They'll cast their vote each week. We'll tape what we can until then. After that, you'll take a few days to breathe and come back to ask your girl to marry you."

"And hope to hell she says yes," I surmise.

Matt laughs. Looking into the mirror, running his hand through his hair, he returns, "Exactly."

"What if the woman the audience picks isn't who I want?"

"The woman the audience chooses will most definitely not be the one you want since you'll have already casted them out."

"Right."

"You have an obligation to marry *someone*, your pick or not. The contract stands until the catch-up episode airs. If you decide before then it's not a fit, you deal with the ramifications of the contract. However, you can file for divorce after."

"The other contestants," I start query next. "How'd this all turn out for them?"

Matt takes a breath before answering. "The lawyer, Marcus Wellman is now single. The plumber, who had a *very* disappointing year, ended up being happily married to the woman the audience chose. You're the third, and we're hoping for good things."

I'd heard rumors, from Nick and Drew of course, that last year's ratings had suffered, and this is why they chose a groom with money. They were hoping to turn the viewers' heads with motivation of the rich, yet not so famous.

"Not to be a dick, but I've heard about the show's complications."

Matt smiles tightly in the mirror's reflection, his gaze piercing mine with venom. I've struck a nerve.

"This show is Willow's baby. She doesn't take kindly to the tabloids calling her idea a sham. I love the woman, but she can be vexing."

I hardly know her, but agree.

"I want it to succeed. I hope your presence here can help us make it what she hopes it to be."

Getting off the topic of audience chosen brides, I ask, "Where am I taking Joelle on our date?"

"Ice skating," he answers, dusting off a piece of invisible lint from his shoulder. Taylor steps in between us now, analyzing his next touch up opportunity. "Jerry has the rest of the details," Matt informs me.

One problem. "Uh, Matt? I don't ice skate."

"You don't have to skate," he claims. "Jo's application stated she was a semi-professional ice dancer at one time. Just relax, have fun, and enjoy her company."

At best, this is weak advice, considering I really do *not* ice skate, but all right.

# Chapter Twenty-Eight

*Reservations are for three, and I'm not invited.*

*Brooke*

-

After finishing breakfast in my room with Addie and Emilee, we barely made it to the bus before it took off toward the studio. There, we endured a mass screening of skin products, which supposedly will 'agree with the camera.' Then we were instructed to form a line to file out into another room, where we were told by Willow to wait.

Wait for what, I'm not sure.

When I passed Mary Ann on the way into the dressing room an hour ago, her expression appeared wounded. Ryleigh must not have been able to cheer her up much because no doubt a jealous and ill-hearted Kylee had already managed to suck the life out of her just as she did me. Except I only had to hear her voice for her to accomplish that.

"He's out there," Kate whispers at my side.

Kate Sanders is the daintiest woman I've ever met. However small in stature, she's also the most enthusiastic. Like Ryleigh, Kate's also one of the most genuine women I've met since being here.

While we were getting our makeup done, Kate sat next to me. She expressed how truly interested she is in marrying Brock, calling him her life's catch. She went on to explain that she wants kids and thinks with her dark hair and dark blue eyes, coupled with his dark hair and honey colored eyes, the kids would be born beautiful. I didn't love hearing her hopes and wishes, but I agreed. Children born between Brock and Kate would be stunning.

"Have you talked to Brock since that first night?" she questions.

Talk, *check.*

Touch, *check.*

Had sex with, *check check check.*

"Yeah, a little."

Grabbing my arm, she talks to me as though we've bonded. By being here for the reasons we are, in some crazy way, I suppose we have.

"He's so nice, isn't he? He has the sexiest voice. What if he picks me?"

*Oh God.*

Again with the god damn flutters of jealousy, but now add some shallow hate for one of the only women here I don't want to stab with my lunch fork.

I play off my irritation toward the beautifully dark-haired, exotic woman with, "Then you'll win."

"I will win!" she shrieks with added enthusiasm. "I mean, I have a chance, anyway."

Kate's too much to take in at ten thirty in the morning.

I haven't talked to Brock since I left him in his suite hours ago. I wanted to text, and I started to, but refused to come off as needy. I wanted to simply say 'good morning,' but ended up typing 'good luck today,' then backspaced to delete that message as well.

Sending the man who gave me one great orgasm with his dick, and another just as great with his hand before our shower, off with a 'Hey, good luck on your date' would've sufficed.

I've been stewing. *Obviously.*

The chaos that ensued all morning has played like a gale of annoyance on my every last nerve. My thoughts are being muddled with uncertainty and challenging my resolve to continue this relationship—if that's what this is—with Brock any further.

This is business.

The cameras rolling aren't stage props. The viewers at home, watching from their living room couches, are real. The choice Brock makes for himself may or may not withstand to his liking. It's *these* women around me who hold the cards, not him.

The consequences of Brock and my actions now, as this plays out, could render as disastrous for only him later.

Admittedly, I don't want to see him hurt. But I'm jumping in where I know I don't belong. And, if this relationship continues as it is, only being based on sex, eventually has the potential to end badly for us both.

"It's time, ladies," Willow hollers to the group, while snapping her fingers above her head, then clapping them together.

*Jerry should teach her his whistle.*

"This morning, Brock was given a choice," she starts, and the girls immediately quiet. "He's chosen two girls from the group who he'd like to take to lunch."

All eyes move around the room, looking to one another as we stand quietly in place and wait.

Willow continues. "If you're not chosen, it doesn't mean he didn't deem you worthy. He doesn't know any of you well enough to determine this, so don't get riled up."

*Other than Mary Ann, who was chosen as a date, seemingly only to tell her pocketful of carnal animal stories, she means.* I don't voice this, but if Brock were standing beside me, I may be inclined to laugh.

"Leslie Miles and Kate Sanders, please come see me at the front counter. The rest of you can all go enjoy a free day in this great city. Shuttle buses will be providing tours. They pull away in fifteen minutes. Have fun!"

Other than Kylee's look of absolute disgust, sad and hopeless faces surround me. Unfortunately, I'm in a mood right along with Kylee. I'm ticked, and even knowing it's without reason, I'm still ticked.

"Hey." I hear Brock's deep voice coming from behind to whisper in my ear.

When I turn in place, hiding my internal and irrational jealousy, I smile back. "Hey."

"I'm killing two birds with one stone," he admits.

I don't understand.

Behind his shoulder, I notice Kylee walking in a small circle, carefully studying every move Brock makes. Her eyes are squinted. She's straining them in order to see more than she can from the distance.

"I'm not a fan of Leslie," he admits. "And if I take her to lunch, I don't have to take her to dinner alone."

I get it, and I don't blame him. But what about Kate?

"You look nice," he compliments, standing close and looking down. His eyes aim for my chest, and his hand grazes my lower back.

Jerry's whistle sounds off, forcing Brock to take two steps back. The loss of his touch sucks, but I get it.

"Ladies." Jerry addresses the women of the hour. "Brock," he addresses next, "let's roll out!"

"I'll call you later," he whispers before adding, "Wish me luck."

Without giving him my eyes, I look past him to Leslie and Kate. Kate waves at me with a huge smile on her face, while Leslie sneers.

"Good luck," I decide to tell him, but he's already gone.

# Chapter Twenty-Nine

*Check, please.*

*Brock*

-

Me 01:46 p.m.: *Meet me in my suite at 4.*

Taking in a deep breath, I walk back inside the restaurant to the table I left Leslie and Kate to talk among themselves.

Correction... I left Leslie to talk and poor Kate to endure.

Leslie, a snide-mouthed department store retail clerk from Denver, has been anything but cordial to Kate, who is her, for lack of a better term, competition. She's interrupted Kate multiple times, only to be curtly dismissed by me when she did. Leslie's mentioned Kylee's name during several discussions, and I already know how I feel about women who use themselves as mouthpieces for others, no matter the situation or circumstance.

Leslie's sour disposition, however, has not deterred sweet Kate's excitement in getting to be a part of this semi-third wheel lunch date. In my opinion—if I were to care to form one—Kate's the type of girl you grew up next door to as a kid. She's the one platonic female friend every guy in the neighborhood had, who they'd play basketball with in the afternoon before hanging out in her parents' living room that evening to watch movies. She'd let you choose whichever action movie you wanted to watch, too, because to her, it wasn't about the movie. She'd be there if only to share your company. I'm guessing, by her continuing excitement, she's chosen to ignore Leslie's rudeness and not let it interfere with her day of fun.

"Was it an important call you just took?" Leslie questions when I take my seat. "You ran out of here pretty fast."

My head turns in her direction, where I tighten my jaw and say none of what I'd love to. She doesn't deserve a response to her unwelcome inquiry.

"So, Brock!" Kate starts. When I turn my gaze to her, I don't hold back my smile; it helps to enhance Leslie's already well-sulking state. "I was thinking after we leave here, we could maybe head down to the Santa Monica beach for a late afternoon stroll, just the three of us. We could get to know each other better. What do you think?"

I *think* if Kate were Brooke, it would sound like an absolutely amazing way to spend an afternoon. However, she's not, so I pocket the idea and press forward with, "Not sure how much time we have today, but I'm sure there will be other days to do some sight seeing."

"Sight seeing?" Leslie scoffs. "In this city?"

Jesus Christ, the man who ends up with her will pray for death, and unfortunately for him, it'll be slow in coming.

"Will there be anything else today, sir?" the waiter, casually known to us as Frank, shows just in the nick of time. His welcome interruption adds to the generous tip I'd already planned to give him since Leslie sent her 'saggy' sandwich back to the kitchen in exchange for an entirely different choice of entrée.

Yep, Mr. Leslie, whoever the poor sap may be, better be happy giving his balls away.

*Just don't let it be me.*

Grabbing the heavy, black receipt folder from the waiter's hand, I shake my head. "No, we're about finished. Thank you."

Frank stands quietly between Kate and I. He looks both ways; first at me, then her. He ignores Leslie all together.

"If you don't mind me being nosey..." he stops, looks to Clive holding the camera from across the room, then back to me before he continues, "We usually don't get many celebrities in here, so can I ask...who are you?"

Kate giggles, while Leslie sits up further in her chair. Her mildly generous chest pushes forward, calling for Frank's attention, which again he immediately denies.

"Long story, Frank. And I'm doubting you'd believe me if I told you."

Clive takes this opportunity to step in and zoom close. Leslie sits up for the second time, but this time puckers her lips in a pout as Kate reaches over to touch my arm.

"I need to use the ladies' room," Kate whispers in my ear. "I'll be back."

As Kate moves to stand, she takes a quick look at Leslie, and for the first time since we sat down, she defies all I believe her sweet demeanor to be. The evil glare Kate disperses throws Leslie for a loop. She narrows her eyes, then relaxes them once she catches me watching.

These women are ridiculous. High school girls had more class.

After handing Frank back the folder and advising him to keep the change, I check my phone again. No return text from Brooke. Although I'm half-pissed, I'm also genuinely concerned. When she told me goodbye just before leaving, there was a feigned look of passiveness, as though my going to lunch with any of the girls didn't bother her. I didn't not only like the look, but how it made me feel.

*Alone.*

I owe her an explanation, the explanation in its entirety; who I am, what I'm doing here, and why I'd choose a television show in order to find a woman to make mine. My fear, as it always is, is that she'll realize my being here is in part an act of desperation, which is true. But since meeting her, that same desperation has turned to hope. The hope that someone like her, if not absolutely her, exists if only to make my life a normal, uncomplicated, and satisfying place to be.

Thinking more of it, I decide to send another text. If she needs pushed to meet me, then I'll shove her in to doing so.

Smiling to myself, I put the phone back in my jacket and wait for Kate to return, all while avoiding eye contact with the snapping viper who is Leslie Miles.

She's the next woman to be cast aside and hopefully for fucking good.

# Chapter Thirty

*Bossy isn't always hot, sometimes it's just annoyingly hot.*

*Brooke*

-

Brock 01:57 p.m.: *If you don't meet me in my room by 4, I'm coming to yours and won't do it quietly. Don't you room with Ryleigh?*

Seriously? *Seriously*!

*So bossy and such an asshole.*

"Oh, you look good and pissed," Addie observes as she sits next to me at the hotel bar.

About an hour ago, we got bored and decided to settle in for a drink. The bartender, Tad, is super nice. He's also very easy on the eyes.

"I am pissed," I bite out. "I've known the man a matter of days, and already he's impossible."

Impossible isn't the only word I'd use to describe Brock LaDuece. But, unfortunately, everything else I have for him is complimentary.

"You don't act like this," Addie discerns, taking another drink of her wine.

It's only three thirty in the afternoon and when I ordered a beer to go with my late lunch, she looked at me like I was nuts. So be it. I suppose I am.

"What do you mean I don't act like this?"

"You don't sit in a bar, stare at your phone, and wait for someone to either text or call."

"I'm not doing that." I quickly spit the lie so I don't lose my angry momentum.

Addie smiles, points to my second empty bottle of beer, and says, "You're worked up. All over a man you just met."

I admit to myself that I am as I take the last drink of the warm beer, which puts me in a worse mood. Slamming it down on the bar, I notice I've got Tad's attention, so I bring it up to order another.

"He wants me to go to his room."

"To talk," she assumes with a smile. "Because that went so well the morning after."

It so didn't, but it so *did*. There's no point in rehashing or debating with Addie. She'll win, so I stay quiet.

"Ya know," she says, turning around in her bar stool to fully face me. "I don't mean to sound like a critic."

"Sure you do," I counter, now turning to face her. "But go ahead."

"Go to him. Really talk about whatever it is you two are doing and decide together if it's such a good idea."

I turn again, this time to avoid her. All day I thought about doing exactly what she's saying, but came to quick terms that no matter what I decide, or we decide, him going on other dates while still seeing me is nothing but an invitation to heartache. Eventually, he'll get his fill of me, replace me with another girl, then go on to marry her. Because even if he chooses me to marry, it's not exactly what I want.

"What have I done by coming here, Add?"

Addie stays quiet at my side. A true friend, allowing another to stew in her own despair.

"Seriously. I'm an idiot."

"You are," she confirms. "But only if you don't march your ass upstairs and sort this shit once and for all. Either way you look at it, you'll come out ahead because things will be clearer to you both."

I suppose she's right.

When the fresh beer comes, Tad places it in front of me and smiles, but insists, "This one's on the house. When you're done, go see to your man. He's a lucky guy."

I don't bother to look over at Addie. I already know she's basking in the validation of her own advice.

# Chapter Thirty-One

*Now that that's finally out of the way.*

*Brock*

-

Fuck, but I want to touch her.

Sitting across my hotel room from Brooke has proven to be an impossible feat. She's wearing another silk blouse and short skirt. Her tanned, athletic legs are staring back at me in a way that makes me want to part them and prove to her the one way I know how, just how badly I want her here.

Every day.

Every night.

Until the clock strikes twelve and I have to make the choice of who to marry.

This is the effect she has on me and it's one I haven't taken the time to figure out. But, slowly but surely, I am. I like her. I like her company. Her humor. Her willingness to trust me with her body. Only she hasn't trusted me with anything else, which is understandable considering we've not only just met, but met under these precarious circumstances.

For the last hour, since I got back from having lunch with the girls, we've been sitting across from each other in my suite. So far, our discussion has gotten us nowhere, other than admitting we find pleasure in each other's company.

More evasive action is needed. I've got to be honest.

"Brooke, look. I've told you how I feel. I enjoy you. I enjoy my time with you. You've made this whole situation so much better that I ever thought it would be."

"I get that," she replies quietly, studying her hands, and not giving me her eyes. "You've done the same for me."

"I like you as a person," I add next, in case she hasn't gotten that. I've been in my head so much, I'm not sure what exactly I've conveyed to her directly.

"I hate this," she tells me. "I'm going to keep hating it. It's wrong. I feel like I'm standing in the way of something I don't have a stake in."

"My choice of a woman to marry," I deduce.

This subject hasn't been hanging over my head too much since I talked to Matt and figured one year of marriage to a woman of my choosing can't be all bad. Not to mention, what if I like her? I could take the time to get to know my new wife without all this static of outside influence and could end up happy.

On the other hand, if I asked Brooke, she could say no.

"What if it's you left at the end? What if you're my choice?"

Her head snaps up, and her eyes drill into mine before she says, "I don't know that I'd say yes, Brock. This is what I'm talking about. We don't even know each other."

"I don't know any of those girls."

"But you will because you'll *date them*."

"I'll date them each once, maybe twice."

I watch her flinch. My dating those other women is obviously bothering her. I hadn't realized in her mind those dates were really dates. So far, they haven't been that to me. They were nothing more than suffering to get to know another person I'd never met before.

"Will you come over here please?" I ask nicely.

"No," she clips. "You'll touch me."

Smirking, I compromise, "I will, but only if you want me to."

Her eyes narrow. I've hit the exact reason she pressed this shitty seating arrangement as she walked in, smelling like Brooke and beer. She told me she and Addie had indulged in a few downstairs. I didn't love the idea of Brooke sitting in the same bar I picked her up in, but was able to beat back my annoyance long enough to ensure she got her wish.

She also said it was Addie who sent her ass up here to talk to me in the first place. I'm going to high five Addison Tindal the next time I see her. I may even hug her and invite her to my wedding. Which may suck if she came to a wedding Brooke refused to be a part of.

"Brooke, really. Get your ass over here."

Again with the dirty look.

Standing up, I walk to her. She watches every step. Once I'm close, I kneel on the floor, but make it a point not to touch her. Not per her request, but for my sanity.

"If you're walking away, okay. Tell me now. I'll understand. I won't try to convince you of anything you don't already believe." I stop, hoping she says something, anything to deny she wants to leave. She doesn't, so I push. "We're in this shitty situation, and there's nothing I can do about it."

"What are you saying?"

"I'm saying, if you're willing to explore what we have, I'm in."

Closing her eyes, she thinks. Leaving her to do this may not be such a good idea, considering it hasn't worked out well up to now.

"Brooke?"

"Okay," she states. "I was jealous. I admit it. Seeing you traipse around with these women isn't easy. Hearing about *you* from *them* is even harder, but that's not your fault."

"Define what you think we're doing," I request. If I can get in her head, it evens the playing field.

"We're having sex," she simply states.

Part of me is good with her version of what we are. The part where I get to enjoy her when I can. The part that makes me feel less lost and alone in this entire course.

The other part of me doesn't appreciate her candidness regarding this so-called relationship. I like her. I really like her. It's possible she'll never believe this.

"There's nothing wrong with two people having sex." I aim to convince her.

Her eyes pin mine with a determined look.

"No?" she questions. "You're dating all these other women, but you're texting *me* to meet you in *your* room during those dates. That's not wrong?"

"I'm not sleeping with them," I state with conviction. "I'm sleeping with you."

The weariness on her face is evident. I can't say with certainty that if we were to exchange places, I would be so good with her going on these 'dates' either. Fuck that, I know I wouldn't be. But, as it stands right now, I don't have Brooke in any real way.

I don't relish in what her response may be, but I demand it anyway. "Tell me what you want. No matter what it is, I'll do it."

Cocking an eyebrow, she suggests, "Sex." Before I can agree or not, she adds, "That's all. I like being with you, too. But you're here for reasons I'm not. If I can't commit to being your pick, I can admit to enjoying our time together until it's done."

This is fair, but it's not. I risk losing the one woman here I've come to like more than any of the others—more than any I've been with in the past.

I'll take what I can get. "Done. Whatever you want."

"Okay," she returns, and if I'm right, I just saw a faint shred of disappointment cross her face.

"But, Brooke?"

"Yeah?"

"You're going to marry me."

# Chapter Thirty-Two

*Gumby has some fierce competition.*

*Brooke*

-

"Oh hell," Addie states to my surprise. "At least the woman's...um...limber?"

"Limber?" I protest. "Addie, did you watch the whole video? She's so limber she could be Gumby's stunt double."

Standing next to me, Addie is holding my phone as she views the latest video Brock sent of Joelle ice-skating. It was his night to take her out. On the clip, the woman is wearing a leotard, shaking her ass. It also appears she's trying to tempt Brock with every twist and turn. Clive is standing beside him; I can't hear him talking, but his camera is in the video, and he's aiming it at Joelle.

Once Addie and I finished lunch this afternoon, Willow and Jerry came to track down all the girls one by one. Today is our appointments with outside interviewers. We're supposed to tell the audience how we're handling things thus far into the 'game.' We're not supposed to leave out any feelings, good or bad, we've developed for Brock, either.

Willow had called the girls for a meeting first thing this morning and explained that they were going to change a few appointments on the itinerary. The reasons for this was being held from us. I'll admit I found it peculiar, but my concentration hasn't always been in the game.

As it turns out, he'll be taking women on 'dates' at a quicker pace than had originally been planned. This meant his time alone, more importantly his time with me, would be substantially less.

"Brooke, I don't think he's at all interested in Gumby's stunt double," Addie claims. "I mean, sure, he's sending you pictures of her or whatever. But, if he were interested, my guess is he'd have her off the ice already instead of texting you the entire day."

She probably has a small point. He has been texting me all day. Before the clips started rolling in, he was going on about our new 'arrangement' and that I had to live up to my side of it; meaning, after his date with Joelle, I'd meet him in his room.

Since our talk, I do feel better about us being together in the capacity we are. Keeping emotional ties clean in order to survive the break at the end will do us both good. I like him, genuinely, but I don't want to marry him. We just met.

All this said, the unwelcome fluster of fury in my belly ignites. Images of Brock tearing Joelle's prissy sequined pink leotard from her body, then ravishing her the way he ravishes me sits in my gut like dead weight.

Grabbing my phone from Addie's hand, I don't turn it off before throwing it in my bag. The background music continues to play as Addie and I take a seat at the table closest to the door.

"So glad you and Brock talked," she snorts, rolling her eyes, and crossing her arms over her chest. "Lot of good it did."

"Shush," I hiss. "We're not talking about this here. I'm next." I look down at the blinking box in my hand, which the set director told me would light up before my time came.

I haven't been front and center of the cameras since being here, other than when we're all together in a group. I don't relish in having to talk to interviewers who are out to make a story stick for public consumption.

All I really want to do is go up to Brock's room and wait for him to finish his date.

*How insane does this sound?*

"Maybe all this with Brock is a mistake," I tell Addie. I hate the notion itself, but it does have merit. "I mean, what if I'm getting in the way of something he could have with someone else."

"You are getting in the way of that," she assures. "But, then again, Brock has to make the decision, too. It'll work out the way it's supposed to."

I hate that phrase.

The night with Jason, Addie had said the same. He was cheating on me, and she said exactly that. I didn't want to hear it then, and I don't love hearing it now. Especially, since the way it will undoubtedly work out is Brock marrying someone else. I'm torn.

"There's Kylee." She points as the doors to the interview room open.

Kylee's smiling big for the camera, which is recording her exit from the interview room. She's wearing an all white, one-piece romper. Her shoulders are bare, and her skin is flawless. I imagine the audience will eat that up. I'm wearing what I always do, nothing special. A small frilly yellow blouse and khakis.

Addie nudges my elbow. "If Kylee does the queen's wave as she walks by that camera, I'll give you forty dollars."

"Stop it," I hiss.

"What?" she smarts. "I wanna see it."

I don't.

We both turn our heads to see Kylee walking toward us. Just as I assume she's about to pass us without speaking, she stops. When she places her hands to her hips, her long, red painted fingernails stand out against the white romper she's wearing.

"The audience *loves* me," she happily chirps. There's got to be a camera rolling if this she-devil is being so cordial. "When we were done, the lady who interviewed me told me I was a shoo-in for audience pick."

*Oh God. Poor Brock.*

"Girl, don't you want the man to want to marry you?" Addie throws down. "Or don't you care about being sloppy seconds to someone with class?"

"Why are you here? You're not in this," Kylee snaps, clearly having a distaste for my best friend.

"Nope. I'm not. I'm just one of the audience," Addie confirms. "And my vote is for Brooke."

"Addie," I snap. Picking a fight with Kylee in front of all those who surround us isn't a good idea.

Kylee rolls her eyes. "All right. I gotta go. Good luck in there, Brooke. If you get flustered, just look sweet and smile for the camera," she coaches.

"Thanks," I mutter, still unsure which camera is rolling. Kylee is never nice.

After Kylee walks away, Addie turns to me and states, "I'd marry Brock before having to watch him marry her. She's a nut job."

"I'm sure she's a nice person if you get to know her."

Addie shakes her head. "Fuck that." When her focus moves to the direction of the interviewing room door, she nods. "There's your cue. Knock 'em dead, Brooke."

# Chapter Thirty-Three

*Mom is rooting for the animal rescuer.*

*Brock*

-

> Brooke 06:32 p.m.: *Interviews are done. Did you know you've been coined this year's reality show heartthrob?*

Yes, unfortunately, I did. Joelle mentioned it on our way back from the skating rink. We were supposed to have dinner afterward, but ended up skipping the rest of the date because she coerced me into trying my luck on ice.

Turns out, I don't *have* luck on ice. What I do have now is a sprained ankle, which has been continuously throbbing like a bitch ever since I fell on it. Can't say I was embarrassed about the fall, either. I didn't have a chance to be. After going down as hard as I did, I was swarmed by girls—*teenage girls*. No women my age, or mothers, or any nurses rushed to my aid. Nope. Teenage girls came to my rescue as Clive stood in front of me, safely planted on the pavement, holding the camera steady as to not miss a moment of my glory.

> Me 06:41 p.m.: *Yes, Brooke. I'm aware. Come to my room.*

> Brooke 06:42 p.m.: *I'm having sex with a reality show heartthrob. I could be famous.*

She's such a smartass.

Me 06:43 p.m.: *You could be a lot of things if you'd get your ass up to my room.*

Prior to my fall, I stood next to Clive most of the day, watching as Joelle did spin after spin. She created an audience of onlookers who cheered her on for more. Jo was lost in the music, and it appeared she either didn't notice I was still there or didn't care to acknowledge me.

Those in the crowd didn't forget about me, though. Between the tweens vying for my ridiculous autograph, the women congratulating me on the choice of women I have to choose from, and the men telling me how crazy I'd be not to pick Kylee Simmons, I'm worn down.

I want to see Brooke. Whatever's happened thus far into this crazy mess, she's been the one who has centered me.

Brooke 06:45 p.m.: *Be there in a bit. I'm having a drink first.*

*What?*

Me 06:46 p.m.: *A bit? How long is a bit?*

Brooke 06:47 p.m.: *Keep your pants on, Tiny Dancer. I'm finishing up here and will be up in A BIT.*

"Okay, I think I have you all set up in here," Jerry informs me, handing me a glass of water after he all but carried me to my room. "Water by the bed, remote on the table, path cleared of all your clothes to the pisser."

"Thank you," I reply.

"I think you should see a doctor, Brock. Your ankle is quite swollen."

If the shame in not being able to walk two feet without stumbling on my ankle wasn't bad enough, I had to listen to Willow lecture me on the way up here as well. The woman was relentless as she emphatically advised me on how important my well being is, as in order to make the finale.

*Fuck the finale.*

"I'm good. Thank you."

Jerry grins. "Safe to assume you've removed Joelle from the list?"

*Fuck yeah, it's safe to assume.*

"Yes."

"Very well, then. If you're sure," Jerry returns. "I'll get word out and let the panel know."

"I'm sure."

Again, making these decisions suck. I hate hurting women's feelings, whether I know them personally or not. I hate being the reason they cry. Lucky for me, they won't know they haven't been chosen until the final taping.

I've all but decided Brooke is my choice, but now I need to convince her that getting married isn't only a good idea, but a fucking *great* one.

We've spent every night together for weeks. Whether she admits it or not, she's falling for me. During the night, if let her go, she moves in to get closer. During the day, if we're in the same room along with everyone else, I catch her watching me. The jealous and possessive gene she'd never admit to having is there.

"Matt mentioned Kate again this morning. He asked that I encourage you to take her out, just the two of you. He doesn't feel she got a fair shot since she went to lunch with you and *that* Leslie."

Yes, *that* Leslie.

Kate's a sweetheart. I talked to her again last night after we wrapped up the 'Are you ready to face your family?' segment of the taping. She told me she wanted another opportunity for us to get to know each other better. Even though life around here has been chaotic, by all rights, if it wasn't Brooke, it'd be Kate I'd choose to spend more time with.

"I'll think about it. For now, though—"

"Scratch Joelle."

"Yes. Thank you."

"So, all that's left is Kate, Ryleigh, Kylee, Emilee, and Brooke. All good women with solid ratings with the audience," he summarizes. "With four gone for certain, I'd say you're narrowing your choices down quite nicely."

Sure *he'd* say this. He's not the one stewing under the collar about every decision he's made so far. Matt told me to go with my gut and not to overthink. I'm doing just as he's instructed. Mary Ann, Joelle, Leslie, and Nancy aren't in the running.

Nancy was the only girl I didn't have to so much as speak to before I casted her out. She's a badass. I'm not a wimp, but I don't find women who have the same size chest and back as mine attractive.

Looking around the room, most likely noting I have nowhere to go, he asks, "Want me to bring up dinner? You didn't get a chance to eat."

Shrugging away his offer, hoping Brooke will handle it, I advise, "No. I'm good. I'll watch the game and order room service later."

Moving forward, he advises, "You'll be going home this weekend. Will you be happy to see your friends and family?"

*Will I?*

I'm not sure. I'm not happy about having to be away from Brooke for a week. She'll go home, get comfortable, and possibly rethink being here. She's told me she wanted an adventure. My fear is she'll realize this adventure turned into more than what she thought it would and bail.

I don't admit any of this. If Jerry or anyone here knew what Brooke and I have been up to, I imagine our covert actions would be frowned upon.

On the other hand, I am looking forward to seeing my friends again, as well as my sister and my parents.

"It'll be nice not to have Clive hanging around so much," I joke. "He probably feels the same."

"It's his job," Jerry reassures. "It's everyone's job. But yes, we'll enjoy the break, too." As he heads for the door, he turns quickly and tells me, "Three weeks and you'll be a married man."

I wish he wouldn't have said that. A simple goodbye would've sufficed.

As soon as he closes the door behind him, my cell phone rings. Hoping it's Brooke, I grab it quickly to answer.

It's not her, though. It's my mother.

*Christ.*

Letting it go to voicemail won't do any good. When my mother desires my attention, she tends to get creative. If I don't take the call, she's likely to call the network. If they don't answer, she'd likely try the president of the network. Martin has contacts, ones she'd have no shame in using.

"Hey," I answer cautiously, masking the pain exuding from my ankle. Mom's always seem to know what's up. If I told mine that I was hurt, she'd come here to help, or worse. She could send Tate in her place.

"Brock, honey, you sound different," she observes first. "Is everything okay?"

"Yes, Mom. I'm fine."

"Tate said you texted her your flight information and you'll be back here Sunday evening."

Tele-Tate relay system is still a go, I see. "That's right."

"I'm looking forward to hearing how things are going for you so far. We've been watching. Last night's airing, you were sitting at lunch with two of those women."

"Leslie and Kate."

"Yes. Any interest in either?"

Nope. Not really.

Rather than have to explain why, I go with, "We'll see. Still early."

"That host, what's his name?"

"Matt Sutton."

"Right. He mentioned you've narrowed your choices. Does your mother get to hear the inside scoop?"

Already exhausted from my day on ice, I placate her by saying, "I'll explain more when I get home. How's that?"

"Evasive answer," she accuses. "I didn't love you going there in the first place. The least you could do is tell me you foresee good things to come."

I do foresee good things; however, she's not in front of me at the moment. I clench my jaw, hoping to hell she doesn't plan to be gone the entire evening. We haven't spent a night apart in weeks, and I have no interest in being alone on this one.

"Yes. Good things," I lie. "How's Dad?"

"Tickled pink," she says, smiling through her words. "He couldn't be happier to see you have so many good ones to choose from."

*Good ones? Obviously, he has no idea what I'm dealing with.*

"His favorite is that small Mexican-American girl. What's her name?"

"Emilee," I inform. "Emilee Cruz."

"Ah, yes. She's cute. I like the tall, red-haired woman myself. She's seems smart."

"Mary Ann?"

"Yes."

Mary Ann is smart, but she's a *not*. My family shamelessly devours small animals at every meal. Mary Ann would be done with us all before dessert ever hit the table.

*How is she a farmer's daughter, anyway?*

"You're coming here for Sunday dinner, right?"

"I'll be there. Flight gets in at five."

"Good," she returns. "I look forward to hearing more about Mary Ann."

*Jesus.*

"See you then."

# Chapter Thirty-Four

*Okay. I'm doing this. I am. I don't have to be the woman the man I'm sleeping with is dating.*

*Brooke*

-

"Again, tell me how you managed to do this to yourself," I groan, pulling off Brock's shoe and tossing it into the corner with his other one. "If you *knew* you couldn't ice skate, why try to impress her?"

"I wasn't skating to impress her, Brooke," he bites back through a clenched jaw. "What else was I supposed to do?"

*Why do men lie?*

Obviously, Brock was, at the very least, inspired after seeing the way Joelle carried herself, which was understandable. After, for whatever reason, he felt compelled to show her what he could do to impress her. Which, as it turns out, was nothing.

The last week has flown by, so I haven't had much time with him. Between mid-season contestant interviews and spending time with Addie, I haven't had a lot of time alone to think. So while he was out on another date, I found myself hating how much I missed him.

By the time I filed out of the interviews, Brock was waiting at the front entrance of the hotel, where he was bidding his goodbye to Jo, and doing so with a severe limp. He didn't offer me a second glance. I hated how much his passive behavior hurt. Since discussing this relationship, going about it as we said we would, the only time we spend together is in his room are those very early hours of the morning.

Oddly, Ryleigh has continued to either ignore or not pry into my mysterious whereabouts. Addie said she has it covered, so I'm trusting she does.

"What do you think the others would say if they knew we were sleeping together?" I question, not so carefully lifting his sprained ankle to sit on my lap before grabbing the bandage to wrap it.

"I don't know. I imagine they'd be pissed," he replies with a wince. His focus is obviously on the pain shooting through his leg, not the conversation I'm trying to have.

He didn't suffer a bad sprain, but still one I'd say he deserves. He was showing off. At the very least, he was trying to prove to himself he could ice skate.

*Men are so stupid.*

"But we're not ending this, if that's what you're thinking," he warns once I have his ankle secured on my lap. "I like fucking you," he then confesses with a smile.

"If the other girls find out about me, there wouldn't be much left to fuck. Those women are here for you, and they're a catty bunch, Brock."

Resting the back of his head on his arm beneath it, he looks to the ceiling. He keeps his leg still to let me work. I'm not a nurse, and I've never wrapped a wounded ankle, but I think he's overreacting to the pain, if only to get sympathy.

"They want to see Brooke swim with the fishes," he jokes.

Flicking his big toe with my finger, I visualize this to be true. The Godfather, Michael Corleone himself, would gut me for my traitorous acts.

"Not funny. I'm serious."

"They are here for me, yes," he agrees, "but I don't know any of them."

"If you had to make a choice today, though," I query, unsure if I'm ready to hear his answer. If he has one, it'll give me a face to despise, a woman I wish to sleep with the fishes. Not nice, I know. "Who would you choose?"

His chin dips to his chest, and he looks down to aim his eyes at me. "You."

"I'm still not in love with you, Romeo," I tell him.

"Why not? I'm a catch."

Over the last week, we've found humor in each girl's enthusiasm, or lack thereof, in being here. Kate still swears she's his perfect match. Consequently, she's been letting everyone know what a catch she thinks him to be.

"Besides, Brooke, who am I coming back to every night?"

"You mean when you're not dating other women?" I smirk. His argument holds very little weight as far as our situation goes. "You're cheating on me every day."

With the increased schedule, Brock's been out most afternoons with a different girl. Whether they go to lunch or sit on set, cameras rolling, he's not been with me.

Shaking my head and focusing on the bandage, I explain, "I came here because I wanted to get out of Peace Hope for a while. My life at home was too quiet."

"So you chose a reality show to spice things up?" he laughs. "I still don't get that."

He's taken the news of my not being in love him well. Too well.

"Do you have a second choice? In case if you asked me today and I refused?"

"Yeah, I guess."

My spine steels, and my heart feels heavy. This second place decision is obviously something he's given thought to. I can't blame him, being that it's his future at stake.

"I like Kate."

*Kate.* The name incites me without warning. Of all the girls, it would be her. Perfect little faces, perfect little images of what he and Kate's kids would look like sully my train of thought.

"Why her?"

"I've talked to her a few times," he swiftly replies. "Kate's sweet, and she's already told me she hopes she's my 'one.'"

I laugh, but it's fake as he lifts his hands and uses his finger to gesture air quotes around 'the one.'

"She's pretty, too," I add.

"You're pretty," he returns to my surprise. "Matt wants me to consider taking her out again."

"You did already."

"Lunch," he reminds me. "It wasn't a formal date."

"She really likes you," I tell him, though it hurts to be the one to tell him what he probably already knows.

With a knowing smirk, he counters, "But I like you. And I'm already fucking you, so—"

*Ass.*

Pinching his wounded ankle, I let out a feminine growl as I set it down and start to stand.

Looking down at him so helpless on the bed, I chastise myself for asking the question. I'm not Kate. I'm not exotic, cute, or sweet. I'm me. I'm light, fun, and a lot of times a wreck. Suddenly, the idea of sleeping in his bed, in his arms tonight feels small.

Gathering my posture, along with my courage, I advise, "You're all set to heal. I'm going to leave you to it."

His elbows adjust beneath him, giving him support from the bed. The tight abs I've come to love viewing, touching, and licking, mock me from where I stand. They're baiting me to come back for more.

"You're leaving me?"

"Yes, twinkle toes. For now."

His concern is evident, but I don't let it stop me from walking toward the door.

Glancing back, concern turns to hurt. The same hurt I feel. "I'll be back in a couple of hours with more ice and dinner. Even wannabe ice skaters gotta eat."

"Even beautiful girls who deny their feelings have to admit them sooner or later," he snaps back.

My mouth slams shut; I have nothing to return. His laugh breaks the tension, so I quickly shut the door to avoid hearing it. I wish I found humor in this, but I don't.

Whatever we have between us is getting more complicated with each 'date' that passes.

# Chapter Thirty-Five

*I'm his pick.*

*Brooke*

-

"No more for me," I insist, pushing my plate away and leaning my back against Brock's headboard.

I don't have an appetite for anything. The two beers I had downstairs with Addie didn't taste good, either.

After we packed our bags to go home for the week, Brock texted, asking me to come back to his room. For whatever reason, being with him, knowing all this will remain casual, taints everything I once loved about it. I didn't expect to feel this jealous or annoyed. At the time, I thought discussing what we had was a good thing.

"Do you have plans for your visit home?" he asks, moving the tray of dishes from the bed and making himself comfortable at my side. His foot is propped up on a pillow. The wrapping I'd done earlier has held.

"Not really. I told Dad I'd help get him caught up at the Inn, but other than that, I don't have anything going on."

"You'll text me next week?"

"I might," I reply.

I'm certain, of course, that I will.

"You're upset about something," he accuses. "What is it?"

"I'm not upset," I lie. "I'm just ready for a break."

A tense expression blankets his face. "From what?"

Sighing, I admit, "All of this. I miss home. I miss my friends and family."

Grabbing my hand, Brock brings it to his lap, where he caresses the top of it. "Before you leave in the morning, I need you to know I'm choosing you." When I pull back my hand and attempt to interrupt, he squeezes and keeps it close. "Whether you tell me no or not, I've already made up my mind."

"This was sex," I recall. "We agreed."

Nodding, but not looking at me as he does, he informs me, "We also agreed we liked each other. I know you like me. Or parts of me," he adds suggestively.

This time I pull my hand and he frees it. "You don't know me."

"I know enough. I know you can be stubborn, and that you're jealous of those other women when you shouldn't be. You're a smartass."

"If those are compliments, they're not complimentary."

Clearing his throat, he adjusts his position and turns to look at me while being careful not to move his ankle.

"I also know you love your family, and you feel bad about what we're doing."

"I do," I agree. "Both."

"I'm going to choose you, Brooke. I'm not going to ask if you'll say yes, either. That's how positive I am. I'll risk you throwing me to the wolves."

Turning my eyes from his, I study the blank television across the room. He's so sure he'd be happiest with me, and he's willing to risk it if I refuse.

"I should go. Addie's waiting. Our flight leaves at six in the morning."

"Okay," he concedes. "I won't beg you to stay."

This is a first, so much different than all the nights before. How odd it is I've never spent a night without him since I've been here. Ryleigh won't know what to do if she wakes in the morning to find me there.

"What are you smiling at? You're leaving me here with a bad ankle, and you're smiling."

Shaking my head, I stand. "Nothing's funny. I'm gonna go." Bending down and closing the distance between us, I kiss his cheek, then start to straighten.

His hand wraps around my neck, pulling me to him closely before his mouth crashes against mine. The kiss isn't seductive or sweet, but rather punishing. My leaving irritates him. I'd be full of crap if I didn't admit I like this, even after hearing I'm his pick.

I need time to think.

# Chapter Thirty-Six

*I think he missed me.*

*Brooke*

-

"Fucking hell, I've missed you." My response gets lost as Brock's mouth takes mine.

I've missed him, too. His smell, taste, the sound of his voice, and his hands as they aggressively explore my body.

The six-day visit home wasn't all I'd hoped it to be. My concentration wasn't on my family and friends. There was no way it could've been. Between Brock texting all hours of the day, then calling at random hours during the night, he held my focus.

And, just to say, phone sex is hot. At least it was with him.

By the time I started repacking to come back, my body was hanging in a precarious balance of emotional torment and heated desire. Thoughts of being with him again, not only to sate ourselves, but to hang out as we had before, caused me to pack faster and with a lot less care than I had the first time Addie and I flew to L.A.

"Tell me you finally get it, Brooke," Brock encourages, taking off my shirt and discarding it to the floor next to his. "We're supposed to be together."

On the plane ride back, I rehearsed the speech I was certain would withstand Brock's temptations. However, when he opened the door to his suite, I was at a complete loss. None of the words came out. Rather, they buried themselves so deep, I lost what I was determined to say.

"After," I insist. "Take these off."

My hands work the zipper of his pants, but he grabs them, bringing his gaze to mine.

"Brooke, damn it, I said I missed you," he whispers.

His expressive determination shifts into something more...something I'm not sure has ever been between us. And there's been a lot of firsts with Brock.

"Say something already."

"I missed you, too," I admit as his hand cups my cheek.

Doubt blankets his face. If only he didn't look so lost, because my statement is true. I did miss him, more than I want to admit.

"We'll talk after," he offers, placing my hands back at his zipper. "Right now..."

"We fuck," I quip. The dark, possessive gleam in his eyes stops the breath I was about to take.

"Yeah," he concurs, pulling my waist and slamming my body against his chest. "We fuck."

"Well?" Brock prompts, running his fingers through my hair.

My head is on his chest, listening attentively to his rapidly beating heart as we lay in bed, both sated and tired. We've been laying here for about an hour, not paying attention to the time or minding where we're supposed to be. We don't even know *what* we're supposed to be doing. Tonight is the first time he's ever grabbed me from my side of the bed and held me like he's doing now. All the other times before, we either fell asleep or talked without touching. This position feels much more intimate.

Taping doesn't start again until tomorrow at lunch, where we're all scheduled to be together again. After, he's taking Emilee on her date. She's told me she's nervous, and that her break home was an eye opener. She doesn't want to be here at all anymore, let alone with Brock.

When I saw Ryleigh earlier, she insisted some of the girls get back together to go check out a club downtown. She said it's young and hip—all the things I dread. Addie's excited, but more so excited that I agreed to go without complaining...much.

"Will you agree to let everything outside of us go?" he questions.

Lifting my head, I rest my chin on his chest. His hair is mussed up, sticking out in all directions. I didn't think it was possible for Brock to get any cuter, but since we last saw each other a week ago, it's hard to deny he did. At the same time, I love and hate this realization.

"You agree you won't sleep with any of them?"

"Yes," he quickly complies.

Making myself clear, I state further, "No kissing either. Even if they try."

Brock scrunches his face, remembering the date he had with Joelle, who tried to kiss him before making her way off the elevator. He wasn't interested in her, but must not have made it clear enough for her.

"I'll agree to that, too."

"And no matter what, when this is over..."

I feel his hand squeeze the back of my neck, so I'm unable to finish.

"I'll agree to whatever else you want me to, but nothing will change, Brooke."

In the overall scheme of things, even if he were to go back on his promise, I could hardly hold it against him. He's here to find what some of those other women are—a life with someone they feel they're compatible with. He's said it's me, but there's still time, and more dates to be had.

"Okay, then," I concede. "I'm yours for as long as this lasts."

His lips form a lopsided grin. "You *are* mine, to do with as I please."

"Within reason," I reply, rolling over on my back to avoid his determined and smug excitement. "Don't get greedy."

Lifting himself to sit, he turns quickly. My back dips into the mattress before he comes down on top of me in a quick, eager movement. His hand trails my side before positioning it between my thighs where he stops, refusing the intimate contact I crave.

"I have so many things I want to do to you, Brooke Malloy. And now, when I do them, I'll know I get to do them *repeatedly*," he whispers before sliding his tongue along my bottom lip.

His finger caresses my clit, and my thighs open to grant him further access. When his lips trail small kisses down my jaw and to my neck, his finger probes my ready entrance. I haven't had time to come down from the first time he took me.

"Fuck, you feel so fucking good," he mumbles against my skin. "I've missed not being inside you."

Another stomach flutter, added now with the sensation of his fingers driving deep into me. He's near the spot I know will promise release before he bites down on my ear. My hips shift, helping him deepen the connection.

"Say my name when you come. Say it again and again."

My body jolts with his demand, causing my nails to dig into the skin of his back. Using my legs as leverage, I wrap them around his waist so the only thing between us is his hand. Brock uses his thumb, adding pressure to my clit as another finger breeches my rear entrance. The heady mix of being taken everywhere transforms my simmering body from a faint sizzle to full heat.

"Fuck, I want this, too," he hisses, thrusting his hips and running his cock along my inner thigh. "Your ass is fuckin' perfect."

Braving my composure, I return, "Soon."

Another hiss escapes his clenched jaw as he drives that finger further in. The exact measures of his thrusts at each angle sends a piercing shock up my spine and my mouth opens. No words come out, only a whimper of surrender.

"Give it up, Brooke. You want this. Take it," he urges, pumping his fingers in and out, running his thumb against my clit with every grind.

"Brock...it's too much."

*And it is too much.*

My eyes stay closed, and my breathing stops. Every touch, every movement has become overwhelming.

"I'm coming, damn it," he seethes. "All over you. Say when."

At his demand, I lift my hips for the last time, feeling him driving his fingers deep, then stifle a moan loudly into his ear, "*When, Brock. Now.*"

His warm liquid coats my thigh as his thrusts continue against me in rapid fury. A string of quiet curses moves along the skin of my chest as Brock keeps his head down while releasing all he has.

"Only one woman could make me lose my shit without being inside her. Jesus Christ, who the fuck are you, and why couldn't I have found you sooner?"

# Chapter Thirty-Seven

*These women are driving me nuts.*

*Brock*

-

"Your date with Emilee is tonight," Brooke reminds me as we're seated around a big table in the conference room, which Jerry has turned into a lunchroom. I sure as fuck don't need to be reminded since Brooke's mentioned this four fucking times since we left my room this morning.

Immediately after I'd gotten back to the hotel yesterday, Matt and Willow asked Jerry to escort me directly into Matt's office. The audience members who were polled all agreed they'd like to see more camera time with everyone at once. Being in a room with all those women I've casted off without them even knowing, then stringing them along with the hope I'll still choose them, bothers me.

Jerry gave me the itinerary for the rest of the show. I caught Kylee's name, along with her plans for the date, and cringed. She didn't want dinner, skating, or any of the like. She plans to take me to a sports bar.

I already have a well-developed opinion of Kylee Simmons, and she can kiss my ass. The first time I saw her in the elevator, I knew she was trouble. Since, she's added a list of obnoxious offenses and reasons not to choose her.

Kylee's outwardly abusive, but passively so. I've heard the others talk when they think I'm not listening. I've seen the sad, defeated faces of those left behind from the crowd Kylee has reined in around her.

Some women find men delusional or ignorant to their behavior, but I'm not most men. I have a little sister, a tormenter in her own right, and she's taught me a lot about how women think.

When Jerry expected me to nix Kate and I didn't, he faltered with his opinion by saying, "Cute girl, that one. She'd make a man very happy, I think."

She would, and she will. Just not me.

"Emilee isn't interested in me," I return. Brooke is looking into the crowd around us.

She smiles, turns her face to mine, and replies with a meaningful, "I know."

"How do you know?"

"Because I told her you had bad breath."

I laugh. This is probably why Emilee's kept herself from getting too close since the first time I spoke with her at the meet and greet.

"That's not fair," I reply with a shake of my head. "What if she was my final pick?"

Brooke's face falls, and I realize the joke was a bad one. Not because she's yet to show any direct interest in marrying me, but because I've surprised her with my own passiveness.

Resting my arm around the back of her chair, I try to relax. A few eyes are on us, but not many. Most of the women are too busy chatting with each other.

Brooke gets tense, then sits straight up to avoid physical contact.

"Sit back," I clip. "No one knows anything."

Turning in her seat, she notes the position of my arm. For all outsiders, the gesture is comfortable and simple. To her, it's deliberate and telling.

"Don't do this here," she instructs. "They'll assume something's up."

Leaning toward her, I use my finger to move the hair from her neck before bending mine to catch her scent.

"Fuck, you smell good. You smell like me."

When she inches away, I reach my end and start to get annoyed.

All these weeks, Brooke and I have slinked around like criminals. I've snuck her in and out of my suite too many times to count, and I'm growing tired of this game. When we were on break, I missed having her close. Now that we're back and in the cameras' lens, I don't have all of her attention.

There are three dates left before I get to take her on ours, where I *will* touch her. I'll do whatever the fuck I please.

"If you don't relax, I'm going to put my hand up your skirt and slide my fingers inside of you," I seethe with crass words, all while placing my hand on her shoulder. "Then I'll suck them clean so the others can watch."

"And what does that make you, Brock?"

"Hard," I immediately return.

"Oh my. Aren't you two adorable?" Kylee sarcastically drawls, coming to stand on the other side of Brooke.

My arm is still draped over her chair, and Brooke's still leaning into my side in order to finish our conversation. She doesn't take her eyes off me, but I look up to Kylee and smile. The cameras are rolling, and I'm not willing to cause a scene which would put Brooke into a negative light.

"Kylee," I nod to greet, then lie. "Good to see you again."

Kylee moves her gaze to Brooke, then to the position of my arm where her top lip curls. She soon recovers and paints on another plastic smile.

"I'm looking forward to our time together. I've heard you're *very* entertaining."

At her accusation, Brooke's back tenses again. She leans toward the table to grab her water, taking a long sip. She hasn't touched her plate of food, nor have I. The tension from her has caused my loss of appetite; no doubt Kylee has caused Brooke's.

"Well, I'll leave you two to it. Just wanted to come say hello. Brooke's been taking up all your time this afternoon, and I wanted my share."

*Not a fucking chance.*

"Sorry," Brooke mumbles, looking up at Kylee, then back to me. "But if you wait, I need to get going. He's all yours." She sets her napkin on the table and moves to stand.

Kylee immediately takes her seat and gets comfortable. I move my arm back to my place and take a drink of the wine that I ordered with lunch.

Clive, my favorite crewman, nods once as he lowers his camera. Good man that he is, he must see the same thing in this amazon woman that I do—pure, unadulterated trouble.

"Ya know, Brock," Kylee starts while I fight not to roll my eyes. Just the sound of her voice annoys the fuck out of me.

Turning in place to look over her shoulder, we both watch as Brooke makes her way out of the room, but not without stopping to say goodbye to Ryleigh, Emilee, and Kate.

"I think you and me could make beautiful babies together. I'm not so much into kids as I am into making them."

*Yeah, she just said that.*

"I love kids," I tell her. "I want a dozen, and the woman I marry will have them, or she'll get nothing from me at all."

Kylee's eyes widen. If I'm not mistaken, there's a vast amount of fear in their empty depths.

"Good luck with that," she tells me. "We'll talk about the future next week."

*No, we won't.*

"Until then," she bids while standing. "I need to get back. I have a lot to do before the episode airs tonight. All my friends and family call to get the lowdown on what really happened."

"Yeah, you should go tell them."

Kylee, being the bitch she is, leans down and kisses my cheek before I can back away. She also allows her lips to linger much longer than she should. I realize this when Brooke's stark expression of betrayal stares at us both with a hurt like I've never seen.

# Chapter Thirty-Eight

*Brooke*

-

"Brooke, honey. You're done. You've had enough to drink," Addie preaches, sounding more like my mother than my best friend.

She's not trying to mother me, though. She's attempting to reason with the jealous fury that has violently invaded my once calm and happy soul. This whole situation is ludicrous, ridiculous in every way.

"She fucking *kissed* him, Addie," I curse with venom. "That scaly, dragon-breathing hooker *kissed* my Brock," I slur loudly and with drunken conviction. "And he let her do it right in front of me."

Addie hasn't said much since we found a table near the back of the club and sat down. Other than demanding I keep my mouth shut as to not slip in front of Ryleigh, she hasn't talked to me at all. On the drive over, she insisted everything was going to work out as it should and I'd be okay, no matter what else happened.

Well, fuck that. I'm not okay. Nothing is *okay*.

"You knew he'd be dating those women before you two officially agreed to get involved," she insists. "And being that he's the one man all these women are here for, not to mention he's been sleeping with you all this time, you don't have the right to be ass hurt."

Disregarding Addie's self-proclaimed words of wisdom, I slam down another shot glass, then unsteadily lift my eyes to hers. She's scowling.

"Get me another drink," I strongly request.

Ryleigh is sitting between us in the half-moon booth, which is our table. Her oh-so-perfect blonde hair is swept up in an oh-so-perfect bun, and her oh-so-perfect chest is staring at me oh-so-perkily.

It's possible I've skated past a little drunk and veered into being an overly emotional mess. This, I'm guessing, happened about thirty minutes ago. However, I'm not keeping track.

"I fucking like him, Addie!" I shriek so loud it pierces my own ears.

Both Addie and Ryleigh wince. The music in this club is loud, so it goes unsaid I've made my point.

Just in case I haven't, I push, "I mean, I *committed* myself to him."

"Brooke," Addie charges, grabbing my forearm from across the table. "Enough, honey. You need to stop talking."

"Don't have her stop on my account, Adds." The cute nickname oh-so-perfect Ryleigh coined Addie with weeks ago doesn't sound so cute tonight, more so annoying.

*Everything is annoying.*

"God, you even have perfect teeth," I compliment, and she smiles wide. "Does it hurt to be so pretty? It must be painful. Has to be," I continue.

"Brooke," Addie calls. "Let's find the ladies' room.""For what?" I snip. Her face is fuzzy. She looks like Donald Duck. "I don't want to go to the bathroom. I want another drink. I'm celebrating."

"What are you celebrating?" Ryleigh smiles her question, doing all she can not to bust out into fits of laughter at my expense, I'm sure.

"I'm celebrating how single I am," I smart.

Ryleigh nods once, sits back in the booth, and traces her oh-so-perfect, lush bottom lip.

"You're not single," she denies. "Not even. No way."

Addie clears her throat, tosses me a disgusted eye roll, and sits back in her own seat.

"I *am* single," I insist.

"No," Ryleigh disagrees. "Girl, you haven't been single since I met you."

*Come again?*

"What?"

"It's okay," she pleads, lifting her hands up in surrender. "All is fair in love and war. I get it. I'm happy for you and for him."

*Shit.*

Little miss oh-so-perfect knows more than she's let on.

*Shit. Shit. Shit.*

Drunkenly feigning ignorance, I question, "Happy for who? Who are you happy for?"

"Brooke," she sighs out as an answer. "And Brock."

I gasp from shock. Addie looks to the ceiling and starts counting to ten. Ryleigh laughs.

"Shit," I whisper to myself. My eyes are wide; the dry sensation begs me to blink, but I can't. I can only hyperventilate. "Shit."

"Brooke, you don't volunteer at the zoo."

My eyebrows furrow, but because of my drunken state of misery, my eyes close as they do.

Ryleigh clears her throat before advising, "You're gone every night. Adds told me you volunteered at the zoo overnight. No one volunteers that many hours."

"I don't," I concur, looking down with shame.

Placing her hand on my arm, Ryleigh soothes, "Don't worry. I've known for a while. I'm telling you, I've known about you guys since before you knew he was..."

She trails off before saying more, clearly understanding the precarious predicament I've put myself in.

"You don't hate me?"

Her neck rears back, and she scrunches her nose. "Hate you? *No!* Why would I hate you?"

"Because I'm sleeping with the man who's supposed to be unattached."

"I would hate you if you were *only* sleeping with him. But you're not."

I'm confused. I look to Addie to find her just as confused. She's biting her thumbnail while trading glances between Ryleigh and me.

"You're in a relationship with Brock. If you were just messing with him so the other girls wouldn't have a chance, I'd hate you. But you like him. He likes you."

"How do you know that?" I whisper the question because I've lost my voice, along with my buzz.

Tilting her head to the side, Ryleigh doesn't smile this time, but rather asks with sincerity, "Are you new at this?"

"New at what?"

"Dating, woman," she exasperates. "My goodness, you're adorable."

Ryleigh labeling me as adorable due to my inexperience frustrates me, but I'm too thirsty to care.

"I need another drink, Ry. Addie won't help. Will you?"

Addie's eyes narrow. Ryleigh grins wide, and reaches for her purse.

"If you're getting drunk because you're pissed at a man, I'm getting drunk because I don't have one," she decrees.

"Well, okay," I return.

Addie scoots to where Ryleigh was sitting. Her parental shaming expression comes too quick for me to get away.

"Okay, friend. I have a few things to say about your hour of confession."

*Shit.*

I'm not sure I can sit up long enough to endure this. But, it's Addie, so I try.

"By now, you know I love you," she starts. "But stop it."

She levels me with a knowing glare. I can't help but cower slightly.

"You've been my best friend since the first grade, and I want good things for you. But getting drunk and pining over a man who you already know is here for the reasons he is, isn't going to work for me. Slow your roll."

"I'm trying," I aimlessly advise, then quickly process Ryleigh's knowledge about me and Brock. "You told her I worked at the *zoo*?"

Addie flinches. Not her best lie. "I ran out of things to say! She'd ask every night, and it wasn't as if I could tell her you were upstairs bumping uglies with the hot man she's supposed to date."

"Oh God, Addie. Think she'll rat me out to the others?"

Shaking her head, Addie moves back to her seat in the booth. She takes a drink of her margarita and replies, "No. She's a good friend, and she told me she has no interest in Brock. She prefers a man covered in tattoos and rides a Harley."

This surprises me, so I laugh. "She's really not mad, is she?"

"Nope, but there are other women here who will be, so control yourself, please."

Heeding her warning, I agree. "I'll do better."

"Good. Now, if you think you're sober enough, I'd like to dance. That's what we came here to do."

I hate dancing. I'm not a good dancer. I don't have the sexy or fluent moves other women seem to possess. However, to decide to appease my best friend. "One more shot, then I'm yours."

"Has he texted?" she asks, changing the subject back to Brock. "Or have you shut him out with your jealousy?"

"Shut him out," I admit.

I haven't returned any of the text messages Brock sent this afternoon. He's with Emilee tonight, and even though I know she isn't interested in him, knowing she's with him and I'm not burns.

"Throw the guy a bone, Brooke. He can't do any more than you can."

I see Ryleigh heading back to our table, so I grab my phone from my purse where Brock's latest text was left unanswered.

Brock 04:47 p.m.: *You're changing the rules because you're pissed. If the game's been called off, tell me now.*

*Game. Right. Because all of this is a game.*

Still too infuriated to answer, I stand from the booth and take the shot out of Ryleigh's hand and down it quickly.

"We're dancing!" I announce. I grab both Ryleigh and Addie's hand, and lead them to my certain display of public embarrassment.

# Chapter Thirty-Nine

*This should be interesting.*

*Brock*

-

"Holy fuck, you look pissed," Drew observes as soon as he gets close.

Although I'm elated my friend is here, I'm still livid at Brooke for her bullshit play to ignore me.

"When did you get in?" I ask once we're standing just outside the elevator. "I didn't think you'd be here until tomorrow morning."

"I caught an earlier flight," he advises. "I met Clive. He's everything you said. Cool cat."

"He's good people."

Drew and I step into the elevator where he drops his bag and turns to me once the doors close. "What's up with you?"

"Long day, longer night."

"Date?" he questions. "'Cause it doesn't look like it ended well."

"Date was fine," I answer, then admit, "It's Brooke."

During my break at home, I filled in both Nick and Drew about Brooke and what's happened since before even knowing she was part of this production. Nick slapped my shoulder and congratulated me on getting laid, which is typical. Drew's reaction was different. I saw his look of concern, laced with hesitation. He found it hard to believe I'd met someone, as in *truly* met someone. This is when he insisted he not only come for a visit, but stay the remainder of my time here to ensure I made good decisions.

"Ah, Brooke," he replies. "Well, I'm here now, and I want a drink. Where to?"

The last thing I want to do is go back into the swarming crowd of people I just left.

The date with Emilee went as I predicted. She has no interest in me, and after about an hour of trying to make light conversation, I ended up asking her to be truthful. The woman is painfully shy, but she was honest.

As it turned out, Emilee Cruz wants to be here as much as I do. Once all the cards were on the table, we ended up having a decent conversation. It was a breath of fresh air, considering my day started with Kylee's bullshit, which led itself to Brooke's.

"We can grab a drink in my room," I suggest.

Once the elevator opens, Drew grabs his bags, and we make our way into my suite.

He takes in the area and points to the couch. "This mine?"

"It is," I return. "You're not sleeping with me."

"Doesn't sound like Brooke will be either. What's going on?"

My chest tightens. I'm not used to feeling out of place inside any relationship. I'm not used to *being* in a relationship, and if this is what one feels like, I don't necessarily like how crazy it's made me.

"Brooke's a pain in the ass."

"That's so not how you described her before you left Dallas. You couldn't get on the plane fast enough."

"She wasn't ignoring me then."

Drew laughs. "Shit, that must hurt."

I've changed my mind on staying in, so I point to my room. "I need to change. Be ready in ten."

"To go where? You have a stocked bar here. We can stay in."

"Be ready in ten," I advise again, this time walking to my room.

Thirty minutes later, we're standing in the foyer of the hotel, waiting for Jerry to bring the car around. He's recommended a new club downtown, which I thought was odd, considering Jerry's well over the age I'd consider him to being in the know. However, seeing as he babysits single contestants for a living, it's probably me not giving him enough credit.

"So, who do you take out next?" Drew asks at my side. "And how many of these things do you have left?"

"I have three dates left. Ryleigh's next."

"Ryleigh," he repeats. "She the hot blonde, right?"

Turning in place to look at him, I narrow my eyes. Drew's been watching the aired episodes. Ryleigh's the girl who's caught his eye. Obviously, during the trip home, I didn't make myself clear about Brooke. Though, the woman is driving me nuts right now.

"Yeah, I guess. After her, it's Kylee. Don't ask if she's hot, either."

Drew laughs. "Already pegged her for a bitch. She's good in front of the camera, though. All smiles and giggles."

So true. Cameras roll and Kylee sheds her talons and shows herself as the sweet, girl next door your parents would love. It's the scariest transformation from bitch to troll I've ever seen in my life.

"Then Brooke," I explain. "I'm taking her out last."

"'Cause she's the one," he knowingly states.

I thought so. I'm too irritated right now to admit it.

"Fellas," Clive greets with his camera bag hanging from his hand. "I'm going with you tonight, cool?"

"What?" I clip. "Why? Who—"

Clive lifts his free hand and shakes his head. "Jerry insists. You're out on the town with a friend from home. He said it's camera worthy."

Fucking hell. Not a moment of peace.

"So, I'll follow in the van. If I happen to get detoured and lag behind an hour or so, you won't get upset, will you?"

Reading him clearly, I turn and slap Drew on the chest as the limo pulls up the drive.

"Thanks for the head start, Clive. Appreciate you."

"No problem, brother. Remember something tonight, okay?"

His tone is cautious. I don't like it.

"What's up?" Drew asks, eyebrows lifted.

My buddy is new to this, so he doesn't understand what 'cameras rolling' actually means. Anything can happen, and thus far, I've kept the sordid *true* stories to a minimum. The press can do whatever they want. They will anyway.

"Jerry's a good guy, but he's also Matt's guy. Remember that. See you in a bit," Clive bids as he turns in the direction of his van just behind the limo.

# Chapter Forty

*He wants to date other people – fine.*

*He wants to let other women kiss him – fine.*

*He wants to marry another girl – fine.*

*All is fine.*

*Brooke*

-

The crowd of young and single patrons is nearly out of hand. Everything is blurry since I'm a bit drunk, so my observations could be skewed.

It's well past midnight and I've learned, after so many shots of tequila, that I'm not *awkward* on the dance floor, I'm a *master* on the dance floor. My body is moving in ways I've only known it to move when Brock touches me.

The warm touch of his fingertips burned my skin as I gyrated to the music.

The soft texture of his lips on my neck provoked me to stay lost inside the music.

His coarse voice at my back whispered against my ear, igniting my skin there to flames.

"Brooke!" Addie screams. "What the hell are you doing?"

"Talking!" I yell back. Just as I sit back in my chair, I find a hand on my thigh.

Addie's lips purse, and she shoots an evil glare to the man beside me. In reaction, my body tenses and I turn to see her target. This is where I find a very tall, very broad chested, extremely handsome blond man with perfect teeth staring back at me. His eyes are a mix of gold and green. The depths of them appear heated.

*Shit.*

"Brooke, I think we've had enough. Are you about ready?"

"Where's Ryleigh?" I question, straightening my posture to get a look at the crowd.

"She's getting us a cab. Come on, it's time to go."

Pushing the man's hand from my thigh, I turn in place to get a better look at him. He'd been on the dance floor earlier, and had been following me through the crowd. If I stopped, he stopped. We'd dance a bit before I moved away, where he would then follow.

"Evan," he tells me after he has his hands to himself. "Evan Carson."

"I don't know you." I scowl. "And you're touching me."

Evan laughs. It's a sweet and carefree sound that relaxes me in a way it should *not*. Nothing about him screams ax-murderer, but I don't know him.

"You don't know me," he offers. Did I say that out loud? "I was watching, though."

The memory of Charles, the creepy skin man, comes to mind. He *was* creepy, though. Evan isn't.

"Watching me?"

Nodding, he looks up to Addie standing by my side and winks. "Until your friends showed up. You shouldn't drink so much and wander off alone."

"I didn't wander off alone," I lie. I did, but only because Addie got lost in the crowd, and I wasn't so drunk to know I needed to get myself out of it.

Tilting his gorgeous head, Evan smiles wide. "A girl like you shouldn't drink so much."

"Thanks, *Daddy*," I smart.

Setting his beer down on the table next to my empty vodka-cranberry, he sits back and eyes me before bringing his gaze back to Addie. "She's cute."

"Not cute. My name is Brooke," I say haughtily. "I'm also leaving."

His eyebrows lift, probably surprised I'm not thanking him generously for babysitting me until my friends came to find me.

"I hope to see you again," he suspiciously adds.

Leaning into me, he kisses my cheek. His lips are chilled from his beer, and he smells good. This scent is doctored in a manly way, but still, he smells fresh and clean.

"Brooke..." Addie pauses.

I turn to find out what she intended to say, only to note her eyes are wider than I've ever seen them. She swallows hard, and I catch that, too.

Evan has to move out from the table as I'm sitting next to him, blocking his way. My shoulder hits his as I turn in place.

"Shit," Addie curses. "This is bad, Brooke. Bad."

Narrowing my eyes, I stand next to her and scan to see what she does. I don't see anything out of the ordinary, so I ask, "What're you talking about?"

Evan, *as I now know him*, stands next, coming to my back from behind. I feel his chest, the entire iron wall of it, and don't move to step forward. The look on Addie's face frightens me.

Evan clutches my waist and positions me to stand behind him. I go willingly, still completely lost as to what in the hell is happening. Visions of a gunman, driving at us mid-aim crosses my mind. A sword-wielding ex-girlfriend of one of the men here comes next. It's not until I've regrouped that I peer over Evan's shoulder and see Ryleigh making a beeline for our position in the crowd. Her face is tense as she walks in quick steps with another man I don't know following closely behind her.

Then, I finally discover who else is coming. My breath hitches, and my knees get weak.

*Brock.*

As I take in his full view, my stomach pangs with longing. Brock's wearing a maroon Henley that covers what I already know is a perfect, smooth, and richly defined chest. His hands are clutched at his sides as each heavily booted footstep brings him closer.

He looks livid.

"Do you know him, sweetheart?" Evan queries, turning his head to the side and asking in a low and very deep voice. The same voice I heard talking in my ear earlier. The same ear which now burns with betrayal.

I wasn't doing anything wrong, per se. I was having a conversation with a nice guy who thought enough to see I was safe. Other than his hand on my thigh, he hadn't touched me at all, other than to push a bottled water at me so I wouldn't be sick.

"Yeah," I whisper. "I know him."

"Do you want him here?" he asks, turning his gaze back to Brock just as he approaches.

Brock stands in front of us but says nothing. The man coming up to stand at Ryleigh's side takes me in, and he judgingly observes. I don't love that. He doesn't know anything about what's going on, and it's not nice to come to assumptions about people you've never met, drunk or not.

"Brooke," Brock snarls. "A word?"

"Um-uh," I stutter as I attempt to push Evan out of my way. My new friend is having none of it, so I look over his shoulder to Addie for help.

"Brooke, come here," Addie instructs. "Brock, you need to step back."

"What the fuck are you doing?" Brock seethes. "And who the fuck is this?"

"Brock, there's Clive." The man, I assume is Brock's friend, warns. This leads to Brock no longer focusing so much disdain at me, but rather the camera now holding a microphone over our heads.

The recently rowdy crowd slowly goes quiet, and the loudly beating song overhead comes to a halt. No longer are the walls bouncing with music; the chaos has stalled out completely.

This is the first time since being in L.A. where I've been put under the spotlight. And here I am, certainly not sober, and most likely not looking my best. Not that those facts matter because under Brock's infuriated gaze, I'm melting into a puddle of uncertainty.

"Let's go," Addie insists, grabbing my hand, and pulling me to her.

Brock doesn't spare me a glance. Instead, he turns to his friend and a string of quiet curses flies from his mouth. I've never heard him talk like that in anger. Once he's settled, he runs his hands through his hair, but scores Evan with a gaze meant to insult, then finally takes two steps in my direction.

At first, I assume he'll stop. Maybe even apologize for being ridiculously angry and ask me nicely to explain. He doesn't, though.

Before he passes, I feel his breath on my face as he hisses, "So, I take it we're over. Fine."

*What? No. This is not over. No!*

"Brock..." I try to gather a thought, but my voice trails off. In the eye of the camera, centered between us, I gather up only enough courage to say, "It's not what it looks like."

He doesn't answer. He wastes no time in walking away before my plea of innocence can be heard.

*Shit.*

# Chapter Forty-One

*She was never mine.*

*Brock*

-

"Jesus Christ. Would you slow down?" Drew yells out as he trails not too far behind on my way to the limo. "You're pissed. I get it, but I'm thinkin' maybe you should listen to her."

"Her?" I bite back. Turning around, I watch him stumble in place as to not bump straight into me. If he did, I may punch him for no real reason, other than to let off steam.

"Really?" he questions. "You're gonna tell me that girl back there isn't *the* girl?"

"No, I'm not going to tell you that," I confess, my voice bitter. "But she's hardly the *girl* if she's dancing with another *guy*."

As I turn to continue making my way out of the parking lot, Drew's footsteps falter. "Brock, just stop for a second. Just one."

I turn in place, but continue walking backward to the car. "Stop for what?"

I want out of here. Watching Brooke from across the room as I've done so many times before, but this time sitting at a small table with another guy, has done me in. I'm finished with everything.

"They were talking. So what? Who the fuck cares?" he exclaims, trying to excuse Brooke's actions.

"Right." I agree, if only to assuage him so we can go. "Are you getting in the fucking car or not?"

"I wasn't doing anything else with him!" Brooke's voice calls from the side of where Drew and I stand. When we turn in her direction, she's standing alone. However, Ryleigh and Addie aren't far behind. "I mean, I was talking to him," she tries to explain. "But he was taking care of me so no one would—"

*Oh, even better.*

"Honey, maybe you shouldn't say anything else," Addie smartly advises as she grabs Brooke's hand and pulls her two steps away from me.

Brooke's having none of it. She jerks herself from Addie's grasp and takes the steps she lost, back toward me. Her eyes are dazed, reminding me of the girl I met at the hotel bar so many weeks ago. She was oblivious as to how men looked at her without her notice. She's in the same oblivious state now, except it's me looking at her, and apparently, she's clueless as to my reason for being angry.

"He really wasn't hitting on her," Ryleigh pipes up next in Brooke's defense. "I'm sure it looked that way, but Brooke wasn't doing anything wrong."

Turning my gaze to Ryleigh, it hits me that the cameras inside were rolling. I don't know how much of the scene was recorded.

"She knows," Brooke stage whispers loudly, too loudly, as she points to Ryleigh.

Ryleigh smiles. "It's okay, really. You're not my type. Well, unless you happen to be a closet dirty talking hair puller."

Brooke turns only her head and nods with a smug smile before confirming, "He's every bit of that."

*Jesus Christ.*

"Oh my," Addie breathes. "Not sure we can recover from that."

Drew steps between Brooke and I, and as he does, Brooke positions to her tiptoes. Her chin lifts as far as it'll go while still remaining connected to her neck. If I weren't so fucking pissed, I'd laugh.

"I'll catch a ride back to the hotel with her girls," Drew tells me. "You take Brooke with you in the limo."

"This will work," Addie agrees. "We can get a drink in the bar while you two talk."

Drew turns around, nods his thanks to Addie then asks me, "Sound good?"

Turning in place, I find Clive standing near his van parked behind the limo with his black camera bag sitting at his feet. When I furrow my eyebrows and tilt my head with question, he shrugs. Surely, he should be taping every bit of this mess for Matt and his precious ratings.

"Not sure what happened, but I think my camera broke," he casually explains.

For the tenth time, I take a moment to appreciate what a great guy Clive Masters is. Also, how my first order of official business with my father is putting in for a donation to the "Clive Masters is a cool guy foundation."

Looking down and trying to hold back a smile, Clive light-heartedly suggests, "Take your girl back with you. I'll explain to Willow and Matt what happened to the lens. Too late to do anything about it now."

And now I'll add that the donation is going to be a fucking *big* one.

Turning my eyes back to Brooke, I note hers are smiling. I'm still pissed, so I don't return so much as a smirk. Her drunken smile falls quickly, and she looks down before leaning into Addie.

"Brock?" Drew prods. "We good?"

Without giving me another second to contemplate, Brooke walks around Drew, places her hands on my chest, and looks up. With eyes as glazed as goddamn doughnuts, she grins happily and sweetly says, "I've never been inside of a limousine."

"Really," I return, not about to give away that she's still as adorable as I remember her being the last time she was this drunk. "Never?"

"Nope. And I'd be willing to—"

"Stop talking," I hiss as soon as I hear Drew stifling his laugh and Addie doing a shit job covering hers.

"Would you two just go already!" Ryleigh shrieks. "Good God. I said I didn't mind you two together, but I don't wanna watch you guys go at it."

Brooke giggles, then plants her forehead against my chest. I finally give in to my frustration long enough to bend my neck to kiss her head. Annoyingly so, the woman's made me unrecognizable to myself.

"We'll see you guys back at the hotel."

Drew slaps my back and leans in for man hug. "In the morning."

He looks down to Brooke, who's looking up at me, close enough I could easily kiss her, and grins.

"Yeah," he says. "She's a pain in the ass."

"Bye, guys." Ryleigh waves as she turns to walk away with Addie in tow.

I wait a few seconds until Drew catches up with them before turning Brooke around and walking her to the car.

After the two-minute tour of the limo Brooke demanded I give her is over, we're sitting side by side in silence. She's looking out the window as the city passes by, and I'm contemplating my first true adult spanking. If it weren't for the driver, who luckily for him has kept his eyes on the road since we got in, I may have decided to give her that spanking.

Instead, she breaks the quiet by turning her head toward mine and offering a confession. "I really didn't think I was doing anything wrong, Brock. When I was talking to him, I was just talking. It wasn't a big deal."

"It was to me," I counter. At the reminder, I'm furious all over again.

The image of her sitting at his side, sipping on a bottle of water, frays my already worn-out nerves. We were in this together, this fucked up version of a dating triangle with *eight* other women. I thought, at the very least, she was interested in staying inside that triangle until it was time to let her go.

"I'm sorry," she whispers.

Her hand reaches across the seat to grab mine, where she laces her fingers and squeezes gently to get my attention. I don't remember ever holding Brooke's hand. It fits in mine. Perfectly. I should've held it long before now. I'm an idiot.

"I'm sorry," she pleads again, this time taking off her seatbelt and inching her way closer.

Once she reaches my lap, she straddles herself on top of me. Her hand cups my cheek as she says, "Don't be mad."

Her lips touch mine briefly before they trace my jaw, then she moves down to kiss my neck. This is where her tongue starts at the base of my throat before making its way to the back of my ear.

When her hands cover my chest and she draws them up to wrap them around my shoulders, I ask, "How drunk are you?"

Personally, I'm a man who enjoys drunk sex, but only with a willing and semi-alert partner. Brooke's willing, but I'm not so certain of her degree of drunkenness.

"Drunk enough to admit I was pissed when Kylee kissed you. Not drunk enough to know I should've talked to you about it."

"Yes, you should've."

"I know."

"Do you trust me?"

She nods in answer, but then stays quiet.

"Prove it."

Up to now, I've done all I can not to touch her. A simple apology would be too easy. If I'm giving her a way out of this, she'll be giving something back in return. She's got to trust me, because there's no one but her who holds my interest.

"Prove you trust me, Brooke."

"Prove to you?"

"Take off your shirt."

Sitting straight, she purses her lips. She hesitates, but moves her hands to her chest. My eyes stay trained on her fingers as they unbutton each button of her silk, black blouse. Slowly and seductively, even in her drunken haze, Brooke seduces me with her slow, coaxing gestures until her lacy black bra comes into full view. With a quick unsnap of her bra, her chest is on display. With the weight of her tits so heavy and the tips so pink, my mouth waters, so I lean my head back to avoid devouring them the way I'd love to.

Shifting her body back and forth, Brooke inches her skirt up until it tightens against her upper thighs. The warmth of her center rests heatedly against the material of my pants. My knee jerks in reaction, and our eyes move to each other.

"Keep going," I encourage, before she starts to overthink it. "Touch yourself."

When her hands attempt to make contact with her chest, I grab them both and shake my head. "Not there. Let me watch."

She smirks, but it's spiked with nervous tension. She steals a look behind her, I'm sure to verify the window for privacy is in place.

"Use your fingers. Spread yourself for me."

Her quick intake of breath signals she's more than ready. If I didn't already know, her tight chest and flushed neck serve as confirmation.

My eyes don't leave her fingers as she moves them down the tight expanse of her abs until meeting the material of her skirt. Resting one hand on my chest for balance, she uses the other to push through the top of it before going down in search for purchase.

No longer able to resist touching her, I use both hands to push her skirt up further so I can watch as she begins to work herself. In and out, her finger disappears before coming back to run against her swollen clit. Her head falls back, and her mouth parts as she takes shallow, but laboring breaths.

"Fuck, you're beautiful," I hiss on a thrust as my cock strains against my zipper. My hand wraps around her long, delicate throat, feeling her pulse racing beneath my fingertips. "Ride your hand harder, baby. Don't come, but keep going until you're close."

Doing exactly as she's told, her eyes close and her head dips down to her chest. She's watching herself. Her hair falls to her sides, obstructing my view of her self-giving pleasure. I reach to grab a handful, then fist the soft, thick strands before pulling her head back.

Her heaving breaths brush my face as I demand, "*My* name when you come, Brooke."

Nodding, she continues picking up speed. Using her tanned and toned thighs, she rocks herself back and forth, up and down. Her flawless skin starts to sweat as she continues straddling my lap.

*I can't fucking watch this.*

Although she's close to release, I can't sit back and let this play out without me. I don't have the self-control it takes to watch her reach her own end.

Grabbing her hand and bringing it to my mouth, I suck her fingers while using the fingers of my other hand to delve deep inside her.

The gasp she emits and the smell of her pending arousal is my undoing.

"I'm fucking you in here. Any objections?" I advise, while unbuttoning my pants and not hesitating to hear her response. She's ready. Once I've freed myself, I tap her thigh lightly. She lifts ever so slightly until my heavy cock is positioned beneath her. "Now, ride *me.*"

She slowly sinks down, taking me all in. I grab her, bringing her body flush with mine. My fingers dig into the skin at her waist, and using all my frustration, I lift her enough to slam her back down.

"Fuck yes," I hiss into her ear.

For the first time since being with Brooke, I'm not wearing a condom. There's nothing between us. In every way, I've exposed us to each other.

"Brock," she breathes unsteadily. My name coming from her lips in the close confines of the limo spurs me on. I thrust my hips from beneath her, meeting her halfway, but I'm still not able to get enough at once.

After she's coaxed us into a steady rhythm, I sit back and regard her carefully. Her face is flush, and her eyes are glossy.

"I was pissed," she tells me. Focusing on my chest, her fingers wrap around my tie. Her words come out as confession as she pulls on it, bringing my mouth toward hers. There she admits, "I was pissed you *let* her kiss you." Her hips continue moving back and forth, up and down, again and again before she quietly relents, "I hate seeing you with any of them."

This isn't the first time Brooke's outright admitted to being crazy jealous, but it's the first time we've ever argued and she's readily seduced me after. If I can get her to admit the true reason for her jealousy, maybe I can get her to admit we're more than what she believes.

"Why?" I prod. "Tell me why you hate it. Say it."

Her body rocks once, twice, then for the third and final time. She stills above me, clutching my shoulders and digging her nails in over my shirt. My cock pulses inside her as her body contracts at every angle. Willfully knowing Brooke's going to take everything I have to give, I empty into her, holding her tightly against my chest.

There is where she finally answers. "Because I know at the end of this, it'll be one of them who gets to keep you."

# Chapter Forty-Two

*I didn't see that coming.*

*Brooke*

-

"This sucks," I mumble, low enough that I doubt Brock can hear anything I'm saying. "I feel sick."

Lying in his bed and staring at the ceiling, I listen as he paces around the room while preparing for this morning's meeting. All the contestants got a group text message from Matt instructing us to be downstairs in an hour.

"You should be sick. Exactly how much did you drink last night?"

"Too much and not enough?" I answer cautiously.

Something happened last night.

Even before the limo pulled up to the hotel, I felt a discernible disconnect. After we had sex, Brock helped me dress, but it was in complete silence. He didn't hold my hand as we made our way from the lobby to the elevator. This was understandable as we were still in public and he never does. But then once we stepped on and the doors closed behind us, I reached to grab his hand and he kept his still. He put no effort into holding mine back. I wasn't so drunk I didn't notice he remained quiet and detached the rest of the night, right up until I fell asleep beside him.

*Beside him*, not next to him or on top of him as I've come to do. All night, I was left alone and untouched.

Not minding my absence of clothes, I sit up and rest my weight on my elbows. The bright light from the sun delivers a sharp pain to the back of my eyes.

"You're leaving?"

Straightening his tie, he looks at me in the dresser mirror and replies, "Yeah. I got a text from Matt after the one he sent everyone together. Either Clive showed him footage from last night and he wants to discuss it, or something else is up. I don't know what it is."

"Clive was taping?"

Turning to me, Brock frowns. "Do you not remember what the hell happened?"

*Oh, I remember. But evidently, I only remember my version.*

I remember the ride home where, fueled by copious amounts of alcohol, I went from being restless and angry to downright sex-starved and feral. Then I remember having sex, without a condom, which led to one of the most memorable orgasms I've ever had. Last, I remember how quiet Brock was the rest of the night and how I spent my first night feeling ultimately alone in his company.

"Shower," he commands, pointing to his silver watch to signal the time before grabbing his shoes and taking a seat next to me on the bed.

"You're awfully bossy, Brock LaDuece," I return. The alcohol no longer serves as carnal courage, and after waking to his still somber mood, I'm in many ways exposed, so I grab the blankets and lay back again.

"Bossy, maybe. But at least I'm sober," he smarts, then adds to further insult, "No guarantee you are."

As he heads to the door without so much as a kiss goodbye, I narrow my eyes and wonder what the hell I missed.

After I showered off the drunken remains of last night and managed to make myself passably presentable, I head downstairs where I find Ryleigh, Emilee, and Joelle sitting together at a small table near the back of the room. The other women are scattered among the camera crews as last minute makeup touches are done.

Brock's nowhere to be found.

"How are you standing in front of me right now?" Ryleigh asks, handing me a much-appreciated bottle of lukewarm water.

"I'm sick," I confirm. "But I don't feel as bad as I look."

"Thank God for that," she returns. "How was last night?"

Feeling my face flush, but not from embarrassment, rather from worry, I go vague. "Good. I slept well."

"Oh, right. I'm sure you did." Ryleigh pats my shoulder. She leans in right after to explain some of what I didn't know. "Drew slept in our room last night. He's upstairs, testing Addie's morning disposition as we speak."

Shit, Drew. I forgot about Brock's friend.

"He slept in our room?"

Nodding, she takes a drink of her water, and as she snaps the lid back into place, she keeps going. "He came here from Dallas. Apparently, he's here for the week. I like him, he's really sweet. But I think he might be gay. I didn't get a good read."

"How was Addie with him staying there?" I question, not because I care about Drew, but Addie doesn't like unexpected company. Or company at all.

Ryleigh shrugs, turns in her seat, and scans the area. "She was okay. She woke up long enough to tell me to tell you that you owe her dinner tonight."

I accept that. Last night was the first time I've ever gotten drunk like that in public. As a general rule, I stick to drinking at home with the girls. Or, as it were, with Jason. Public drunkenness in no way has ever been on my social bucket list, if I ever was to have one.

Emilee's face pales as I step in closer and take my chair between her and Ryleigh.

"I heard something this morning," she tells us quietly.

"Oh God. What now?" Ryleigh quips. "After last night, I don't think I'm ready for more crazy."

I bump her elbow with mine to get her to stop talking, then turn my attention toward Emilee. "What did you hear?"

Sweet and shy, but seemingly honest as the day is long, Emilee leans forward in her chair as if she's about to offer a state secret. "I heard we have another contestant on the show."

"Another what?" I'm confused.

"Yep. She's right," Ryleigh answers, then continues. "I'm not one hundred percent sure, so don't quote me until we know more, but I heard from Leslie, who was talking to Kylee, that she heard from one of her minions in wardrobe that Matt and Willow have pulled a fast one."

Nothing she said just registered other than, "A fast one?"

"There's a new member starting soon. A new contestant on the show," Emilee whispers. "And we're being introduced to whoever it is this morning."

This is unexpected, and it has to be said I hate surprises. An unexpected guest this late in the game is bad news.

"I've heard Brock's choices are down to four, and rumor has it that someone else is coming in today. And if these rumors are true, that someone is also being sent in to help with ratings," Ryleigh continues to impart.

As if more drama is needed.

"Brock's down to four girls?" I ask.

I haven't talked to Brock directly in regards to who he's already casted off. Before we left on break, he told me his second choice was Kate. I stewed on this and hated myself for it. I decided to let it go since we agreed to live between us until the time we no longer can comes. However, I wasn't completely unaware he'd been making decisions all along.

"We don't know who's left," Emilee conveys. "None of us do until the end. I hope I'm not one of them, though."

"Me either," Ryleigh adds. "Bet I know who *is* left." She cheers in my direction.

I widen my eyes and look at Emilee, who remains oblivious with her attention bouncing between her lap and glass of water on the table.

"Can I get your attention up here for a minute please?"

All heads turn to the front of the room as Matt stands in front of a small wooden podium. He's wearing his signature black suit, and his hair as is perfectly in place, per usual. Willow is standing at his side, wearing a simple but elegant black suit as well. She's smiling into the crowd and making eye contact with each of this year's chosen contestants.

Kylee is seated front and center, legs crossed and posture perfect. Leslie is sitting at her side, ever the lowly mirroring sidekick. Kate is sitting behind both of them, beaming up with a bright smile at Matt as the makeup crew adds a few final touches to his already perfect appearance.

Scanning the crowd further, I find Mary Ann is sitting far off to our left on her own. Since she was the first to be chosen to date Brock, and being she was labeled the first true competition, she's understandably shied away from the others. I'd bet my last dollar she wants the same as Ryleigh and Emilee. She wants no part of Brock LaDuece.

If only I felt the same.

"Brock will be joining us in just a few minutes." Matt clues in the group. "However, I have a few quick announcements to settle before we can begin."

Matt nods to Clive, who's standing ten feet in front of the impromptu stage. A microphone is slowly being put in position above where Matt stands. The man holding it looks to Clive, where he nods, then lifts three fingers in the air and silently counts them down.

"What in the world are they up to?" Ryleigh whispers in my ear. "The cameras are all rolling, and Matt's text said this was going to be an *informal* briefing."

Had I not been reveling in my post epic sexual adventure with Brock last night, followed by my hungover wave of added uncertainty this morning, I would've known more about what's going on.

"This week's rating results have come in," Matt advises directly, without preamble. "This season, so far, has done better than last. Yet, we've found there to be many marked areas for improvement."

Matt stresses the word improvement at the same time Brock steps into the room.

He doesn't look into the crowd in front of him, but instead walks with weighted steps before taking a seat directly behind Willow. I don't get more than a few quick glimpses of his face here and there; however, his hand is on his knee as it bounces a mile a minute. He's either still put off by whatever it is I don't remember from last night, or Matt's news is about to shake the very ground we all cattily stand on.

"Oh shit," Emilee whispers beside Ryleigh. "Brock looks pissed."

"Because of this," Matt pushes forward, "we're adding to the members of this year's..." he pauses, lifts his hand, and motions in air quotes, "cast of characters."

All the women turn to look at each other while Emilee, Ryleigh, and I keep our eyes trained to the front. More female contestants will inevitably bring more drama. More would also mean additional dates for Brock, and less time for us together.

I swallow hard and wait to find out how many I'll undoubtedly have to share him with.

"Evan?" Matt calls, focusing to his right just as *that* Evan walks out onto the makeshift stage.

"Holy shit, Brooke!" Ryleigh shrieks.

All eyes in our small proximity come to her as she holds my wrist tightly in her grasp. Once collecting herself, she sinks slightly in her chair and fakes removing a piece of invisible lint from her dress.

Once most of the eyes are off us, I whisper, "What the hell?"

"Evan is here to duel," Matt jokingly describes his position. "All in fun, of course."

Willow steps in where Matt steps back. She grabs the mic from the stand and takes a step beside the podium. This leaves a clear, unobstructed view of Brock. His cheeks are red, and his eyes are narrow. They're also aimed at me.

"Ladies, I have great news!" she bellows in her usual jovial, shrieking tone. "We have another bachelor. I know you'll have questions, and answers will come. In the meantime, please know we're so proud of Brock for his work here, and in no way does this addition take away from his choice of women. However..." She trails off, turns back to Brock, then looks to Matt and winks. "Evan, too, will have the opportunity to get to know a few of you. I can assure you he's caught up on all the names and faces, and we're happy to say he's assured Matt and I he's up for the challenge."

"Oh my," Ryleigh sighs. "This just took an interesting turn."

Taking my eyes from Brock, I move my gaze to Ryleigh, where I find her looking worried on my behalf.

"That's the guy, right?" she asks as Evan steps up in front of the crowd and adjusts his suit jacket. "From last night. Same Evan?"

I don't answer as Evan greets us, using the deep voice I definitely remember from last night. "Good morning, ladies." He turns in place, nods to Brock and adds, "And gentleman."

Hushed whispers and excited smiles paint the crowd. Even Emilee appears to be tucking in a shy grin.

"I'll keep my introduction short. My name is Evan Carson, and I'm looking..."

Through the hazy static in my head, I hold no interest in Evan's introduction. I don't hear his voice. I don't see his face. I don't care about his story. All I can focus on is Brock. The hurt centering in my chest pales in comparison to the betrayal blanketing his expression.

# Chapter Forty-Three

*I almost told the first woman in my life that I loved*
*her and she cried.*

*Brock*

-

"This will be a great opportunity." Evan extends his appreciation as he stands across from me and next to Matt.

*Great opportunity.*

Last night was a set up. Either Brooke didn't know she was being tailed to the club, or she did and in her drunken state forgot to mention it. Somewhere between her intimate conversation with Evan and her fucking me as hard as she did in the limo, she left out the part about his new role in this ridiculous charade.

"I assume you still have the list of women who are left." Jerry pops in at my right, speaking directly to Evan. "Any of those girls are available. The others, unfortunately, are not."

Evan pats his suit pocket twice while confirming, "I do. Thank you, Jerry."

"How's this work?" I question, my voice as coarse as my annoyance to this sick new twist I hadn't seen coming. "Is Evan supposed to pick from the girls I've already dated?"

Walking up to my side, I hear Willow clear her throat. She doesn't add anything to the conversation, but looks to Matt. It's then we all do, waiting for his answer. When he doesn't offer one, I surmise this is about to go in a worse direction than I originally thought.

"So he'll be choosing from those I still have to choose from?"

Matt nods. His jaw is tight, so it's obvious he doesn't want to be challenged. However, neither do I, so we're on fair ground.

"Evan will be dating those same girls," he finally voices. "Your role won't change. However, the game already has."

"I see that," I seethe. My jaw aches from clenching it as I have been over the last hour.

"Evan will take out the same girls you are, on different nights of course, where he'll get to know them. In the end, if you two should choose the same woman, it'll be up to her to decide which proposal she'll accept, if either."

*All of this is fucked.*

Taking in a desperately needed breath of air, I nod in the other direction and take a few steps back. Close at my heels comes Matt.

Before I have a chance to say my piece, he rushes in. "This isn't how you imagined the rest of the show to go, Brock. I understand and can appreciate that."

"No," I bite out. "You can't."

"The point of this is simple," he starts, while dismissing my curt tone. "And I'll tell you now, this most likely will not interfere with Brooke at all."

My neck snaps back, and a sharp pain curses my temples. "What did just you say?"

Smiling, Matt clarifies. "I assume since you've not said anything about dating her, talking to her, or so much as mentioning her at all, that she's already your pick."

"You assume this how exactly?"

"Experience, my friend. You forget this is my job. As such, it's my job to know who comes from whose hotel room and when."

*Fucking hell.*

"No matter," he eases. "Nothing truly matters at this point. Not until the last card has been played and the bachelors cast their final vote."

Funny he mentions cards so casually, considering it was a game of cards that got me into this shit storm in the first place.

"I'll have Jerry send the finalized itinerary to you. Now that there are two bachelors, we need to use our time wisely. Your date with Ryleigh Summers is tonight, which leaves only Kylee and Brooke."

"Right," I confirm, now with a voice fully vexed.

"And Kate is still in the running, right?" he queries. The hair on the back of my neck stands at end. Knowing he's conspired all this time causes my hand to twitch. I'd love nothing more than to level him, but as always, the cameras are in motion.

"Yes, she is."

Looking down, Matt puts his hands in his suit pockets. His dimple belies his sincerity when he mumbles, "Kate or Brooke."

"What?"

"Oh, nothing. Willow and I had both agreed. For you, the decision would come down to either Kate or Brooke."

"And Evan's pick?" I question, feeling my blood race with anger. My temples are throbbing. Surely, he can see I'm pissed.

With a blank expression, Matt straightens to look me in the eye. "The same."

*Fuck this shit.*

"You set this up from the beginning."

Sighing, Matt crosses his arms over his chest. "I never lied to you, Brock. This is business."

A callous mock of laughter bursts from my chest. Willow turns in place and Evan follows after. Their eyes are on us, as is the camera, though probably not close enough to hear.

"This isn't how a business runs, Matt. You set me up."

"I was very honest when I told you I hoped your presence on the show would give it the push it needs to prevail through another season. Reality television isn't new. Viewers have grown tired of the same old, same old."

"You're an asshole," I clip, not that it matters. He must already know.

Matt, so suave and discerning, once again refuses to acknowledge what a prick he truly is. Rather, he offers, "Well, then. May the best man win."

As he walks back to where he came, I stand alone and watch as Evan extends his hand to Matt, then Jerry. Willow straightens her pose as Evan kisses her cheek.

May the best man win, my ass. Everything in my life can't always be a fucking set up.

"Matt knows we're sleeping together, Brooke. Ryleigh knows. Clive knows. Christ, is there anyone who doesn't?"

I'm standing in Brooke's room waiting for Ryleigh, Addie, and Drew to get back from dinner. Drew doesn't know it yet, but he's about to be my wingman for tonight's date with his new pal Ryleigh. That's if the asshat ever finds his way back to the hotel.

Apparently, after spending one night in each other's company, our mutual friends have somehow undoubtedly formed a bond. Visions of the next Thursday night reality show now include those three idiots being the cast of characters in the remake edition of Three's Company.

Brooke sent me a text message as I was dealing with Matt. She said she'd be in her room waiting after I finished downstairs. Nothing felt right about storming in here as I did. Nothing's felt right since finding out she's all but given me away to another woman before our time to end this is over.

*Because I know at the end of this, it'll be one of them who gets to keep you.*

I don't know what pisses me off more. The fact Brooke, the *only* person I've been sleeping with, can't see her hand in front of her face because she's so stubborn, or the fact that Evan gets a shot at taking her from me. The notion she may find him to be everything I'm not hasn't escaped me, but rather, it continues to fuel my already well-lit fury.

"Maybe he doesn't know anything, but he thinks he does," Brooke reaches. She's been grasping at straws since I got here and explained what the man said, word for word.

Adding to all this cluster, I have a date with Ryleigh in three hours. No doubt, Janet is discussing me and Brooke with Jack and Chrissy at the Regal Beagle right now.

"Maybe we should take a break," I strongly suggest.

I can't take back the words once I've said them, and for the first time since meeting Brooke, a stark look of undeniable doubt, coupled with sudden grief, passes over her face. She quickly tries to hide it, but it's too late. Like my words, she can't take back what she feels. She's not as unaffected by me as she portrays. Though, all of this remains, and I need a mental break before I have a break*down*.

"You don't mean that," she tells me, walking away from me to take a seat on the bed.

Last night I didn't touch her as she slept. Not once did I let myself reach over to assure myself she was there. I've only slept alone in my room once since I got here, and that fact alone is enough to convince me I need to catch my breath. I've got to find out if it's truly Brooke I care about, or if I've been using her the same way she's been using me. I want to know if we're anything more than a crutch to each other.

"I think I do mean it, Brooke. I'm not saying it's over."

"Not yet," she adds in a vindictive tone, looking up and leveling me with her eyes. "There's only three weeks left of taping..." She pauses, looks down, then finishes, "Then you're getting married."

"I am," I confirm. Everything I've worked my entire life to procure hangs on the balance of what transpires in the next three weeks. Brooke's not committed anything to my future, and I know because I've pushed.

I'm tired of pushing.

"He'll choose you," I brazenly assure her. "Evan will. I know it."

Though I haven't had a lot of time to process what happened today with our new guest, I have no doubt, if given the choice, he'll choose Brooke. Not because Matt may clue him in on what's happened between her and me, either. But because Evan will see the same in her that I do—a fun, beautiful, carefree woman who completes a man before he's ever realized the other half of him was missing.

The thought of them together sickens me.

With my hands shaking in fury and my heart already exposed, I summarize what she believes we've been doing. "It was sex. We were having fun and having sex. You've said it yourself. Once your 'adventure' is over, you'll move back to your family and you'll forget about me."

"About us," she corrects. The sad look in her eyes gives me another glimpse of her wavering uncertainty.

*God damn it, admit it. Something. Anything.*

"Yes," I confirm without wanting it to be true. "It'll be the end of us."

"If this is what you want?" she starts. Her mouth shuts, and she looks down. I can't see her face to know if she's close to breaking.

"Brooke," I call. "Look at me."

"No," she whispers. "You're right. I will go home. My life will go on and so will yours."

"Separately," I include.

Nodding, she folds her hands in her lap. "Separately."

"All this would be a fuck of a lot easier if you'd just admit you care about me."

Looking up, Brooke's eyes narrow. "Of course I care about you." Her head rears back as though I've physically struck her. "What did you think? For you to..."

"What?" I spit when she trails off.

"Yes," she confirms simply. "I care about you."

"But not enough," I add. "You're willing to let me marry someone else."

"What else do you want, Brock?" she questions in exasperation. "You want a break from us, take it. It's yours. I don't know what to say."

"I do," I insist. I hate the fact it was Evan who drove me to this, fueling me to the point of desperation. Somehow, though, no matter the cause of my self-discovery, in many ways, I already knew. "What if I told you I love you?"

When her hotel door bursts open, both our heads turn. Addie's smile falls flat the second she takes in Brooke sitting on her bed alone. Ryleigh's does the same. Drew immediately moves his gaze to mine, disappointment seeping from every angle.

Turning my focus back to Brooke, I stand stock-still above her. Looking down, as if in slow motion, two tears fall heavily against her cheeks. She swipes them away and stands.

I told her I loved her and she cried.

"We didn't mean to interrupt," Addie bids. "We came back because Ryleigh has to get ready…"

"Addie, no," Drew interrupts before closing his eyes.

*Yeah, all of this is fucked.*

"She has to get ready for her date with Brock," Brooke bites out. "It's okay," she tells them as she stands. Once she passes me on her way to the still open door, she turns quickly to tell the others, "We were done anyway."

Ryleigh was downstairs waiting for me at the hotel bar as agreed. I had Drew tell her I'd meet her there rather than going back to Brooke's room. It was easier this way. Not to mention, Matt eluding that he knows who leaves whose room at all hours of the day and night. In his eyes, we're no better than high school kids sneaking out of the closet after a quick game of seven minutes in heaven. In a way, Brooke and I haven't been far from that, partaking in our own secret version of Reality High.

"Have you talked to her since you left?" Ryleigh, sitting beside me in the same Italian Bistro I took Mary Ann, gently questions.

"I haven't," I reply. "I'm sorry you walked in on that."

Ryleigh waves her hand around her face. "Don't be. I'll say, if anything, you and Brooke have made things here more interesting."

"More interesting than Evan?"

Ryleigh exhales dramatically. "Oh, thank God, you brought him up! I was afraid to say anything."

Smiling for the first time, I'm thankful that of all nights, tonight is Ryleigh's.

"Did you know he had the audacity to ask me about her?"

My smile abruptly falls.

"He did," she continues. "Right before Drew and Addie came to get me for lunch. He asked if I had a second. I said sure, cause why not, right?"

*Right.*

"I thought maybe he wanted to ask me out for a drink or tell me I was his choice for tonight. But he didn't."

This isn't going to be good. My life would be too easy, too predictable, had he asked about Ryleigh. She's one of a few who I know have no interest in being there at the end.

"Then he asks *me*, her competition, if I knew anything about her past relationships."

"He asked you what?"

Annoyed, she exclaims, "Seriously! He asked me if I knew anything about where she came from, who she dated, what *experience* she's had."

*Seriously.*

Ryleigh catches on quick. Sensing this is the last thing I want to hear of Evan, she says, "Let's order. Dinner is on Matt and Willow, and Clive looks bored."

When I look over to Clive, he's holding the camera directly at us, but his posture is faltering. He looks like he's about to fall asleep.

"If you want, I can make a huge scene and act like you're breaking my heart," she offers. "But after dinner. I'm starving."

"I'm good," I reply. "Thanks, though."

"No?" Her eyebrows lift in mischief. "You could act like you're about to kiss me if you want. I've got no problems steering the attention my way if it takes it off Brooke and Evan."

My head tilts, and my eyes narrow. Her passive comment holds a truth she can't take back.

I need confirmation, so I ask, "Why would you need to take attention off Brooke and Evan?"

Ryleigh's face pales. Her mouth opens, but she doesn't say anything.

"Tell me," I encourage. "Tell me they're together right now on a date."

"Brock, wait."

"Unbelievable," I hiss. Running my hands through my hair, I pull it in frustration. "He chose her first, didn't he?"

With an expression of absolute defeat, Ryleigh lends the truth. "Yes. She didn't want to go. I know she didn't, Brock."

"How's that?" I question before downing the entire glass of wine I hadn't yet touched.

"She likes you. She said it last night. If Kylee had been there, she may have punched her."

Fuck it. I told the woman I loved her and she shed tears.

Turning around in my chair, I find our waiter. I don't care if I'm sitting in a crowded restaurant, yet to be served my dinner. I'm livid. It's time to go.

"Check!" I call out, just as Ryleigh whispers, "Oh shit."

Once I stand and grab my suit jacket from the back of my chair, I take out my wallet and toss the money for the food we haven't eaten, as well as a healthy tip to the table.

"Brock, maybe you should take a minute. Calm down a little."

"Up," I demand. "Let's go."

When she doesn't move, I walk around the table and pull out her chair. This gives her no choice other than to stand or start screaming out loud, making good on the scene she promised.

"I didn't mean anything. I just meant…"

"They're out tonight, aren't they?" I push. "That's exactly what you meant."

"Not yet. He wasn't taking her to dinner. He was taking her for a drink and not picking her up until nine. Addie said—"

As her hand reaches to grab my arm, I pull it back and step out of reach. My phone messages show zero, other than the one from Brooke earlier, requesting I meet her in her room.

In record time, I shoot her a message back.

Me 07:48 p.m.: *Where are you?*

Without waiting for a response, I shove the phone back in my suit pocket and grab Ryleigh's hand to walk her to the door.

I'm not going back to the hotel, and neither is she. I need a drink, and since she's who I'm supposed to be with, she's going along.

On the way out of the restaurant, I snap my fingers to Clive who immediately comes out of his daze and stands at attention.

"We're leaving. Do you know the sports bar on Roosevelt?"

"Capes?"

"Yes, Capes."

"Yeah," he answers, smiling wide.

"If that camera should happen to break again, tonight's drinks are on me."

Nodding with enthusiasm, Clive grabs his bag to follow us out.

I'm not positive, but if I don't have answers to all my fucking headaches, Jack Daniels might.

# Chapter Forty-Four

*I want an old man to kiss my hand, too.*

*Brooke*

-

After leaving without a word to the others in my room, I walked to a park across the street from the hotel and found a quiet bench away from all the people. There, I watched an elderly couple strolling up and down the same sidewalk again and again. They were in no hurry. No one was calling them on their cell phones, or texting them where to be and when. There were no busy or conflicting schedules herding them apart, shuffling them along from building to building.

They were happy just to be together.

And, for what it's worth, I was happy for them.

My relationship with Brock isn't what they have at all. Our time together lately has been filled with anger, jealously, resentment, and threats to our sanity. But not until the old man in a black pea coat took his wife's hand in his, brought it to his lips and kissed her, did the weight of what's happened since we got back from our break settle.

*I love him.*

Brock isn't perfect; he never claimed to be. His reasons for being here, in part, are like mine. Our lives separately weren't being fulfilled according to those who love us. Together, he's made this experience something I'll never regret. It was a foolish chance I took that's made me crazy happy that I did. Yet, because of my stubbornness, I never stopped to see Brock for who he really is. Aside from the cameras and the circumstances that surround us being here, I shut him out before he ever had a chance to get in.

I gave him only pieces of myself I was willing to leave behind when I should've been giving him all I have.

Earlier, as I was strolling through the grass alone, Willow called. I didn't answer the first time; however, the woman is hell on persistence and kept calling until I finally did. When she explained I was Evan's first pick, I laughed. I waited for her to ask about last night and if I had in fact already met him, but she didn't, and I didn't give up any more information. Part of me thinks she knew anyway. The whole scenario was too coincidental.

*Maybe we should take a break.*

*He'll choose you. Evan will. I know it.*

*It'll be the end of us.*

*What if I told you I love you?*

"You are entirely too distracted to be having any fun," Evan observes before taking a sip of his wine and peering at me over its rim. "Want to talk about it?"

Do I want to talk about it? No. Not with him.

"You set me up, Evan. You set this all up," I jauntily accuse. "So, not only am I distracted, but I don't like you."

With a grin I vaguely remember from the other night, he tells me, "You're already his, Brooke Malloy. I have no intention of taking someone else's place."

"Then why all this?" I gesture around the restaurant, pointing to the bald cameraman standing in the corner.

*I miss Clive.*

"Because it's television. Ratings."

"That's not an answer."

Placing his glass back down on the table, he scoffs. "That's exactly what this is, and mind you, you came here for the same reasons I did."

He's right, and I hate that he is. However, a keen and dawning realization strikes me with escalating force. I did come here, whether it was under subtle protest or not. But I found my strength here, as well as finding Brock.

"I'd like you to take me back to the hotel if you don't mind."

Shaking his head, he grabs the black folder holding our tab sitting beside him. He opens it and scans the bill. "I'll take you back." Looking up, he pins me with a determined expression. "On one condition."

Folding my arms across my chest and sitting back in my chair, I narrow my eyes. "And that is?"

"Have a drink with me at the hotel bar, for no other reason than I picked you first and the cameras are still rolling. The result of my first date can't be the woman I chose, demanding to go back to the man she really wants to be with."

"No," I deny without a second thought. "I want to go back to the hotel and to my room."

One dimple appears, then another, as his boyish smile widens. Evan is an outsider, a foreigner to my world here as it is. I hate that smile.

"I'm not holding you hostage, Brooke. I like you. You're cute and sweet."

I scoff.

"Or you were, anyway. I'm not so sure anymore."

The tension fades from my body as I remember my dad's advice. I'm supposed to be nice. I'm nice to everyone, even those who cross me. It's not necessarily Evan who caused mine and Brock's fallout. It was bound to happen, given where we are and the situation surrounding us.

"One drink," I relent.

"One drink." He lifts his chin and holds up the bill. "Well, Brooke, if I've just bought more time with you, we should go."

# Chapter Forty-Five

*How much longer can I endure?*

*Brooke*

-

It's been over a week since I left Brock standing in my room, alone with our friends. The last text he sent still sits alone and unanswered on my screen.

Brock 07:48 p.m.: *Where are you?*

Both anger and pride kept me from answering. He knew where I was. Ryleigh had told him. Through no fault of her own, of course, she charismatically relayed his heated reaction to my 'date' with the newest groom.

"I don't see Evan," Kate frets, standing at my side near the corner of the room as we wait for final makeup and hair approval. We're the last to enter the informal living room. "And Brock's not here, either."

Glancing around the open area, I'm careful not to let my gaze linger in any one place for too long. The Barbie twins will surely be around here somewhere. Since all the drama between Brock and I played out, I've done a good job so far of avoiding them. All I've heard is that Brock had his date with Kylee, and per those rumors, their time together was interesting. I didn't probe to find out how 'interesting' it had gotten. I knew I wasn't ready, but also knew I'd never be.

*Ignorance is bliss.*

Yesterday, during the group lunch, I avoided eye contact with both Brock and Evan. The cameras were rolling and they were standing close, probably zooming closer. The nearer we get to the end of this, the more the viewers are waiting with bated breath for drama to add to their viewing pleasure. I have none to give them.

When I called my dad this morning to hear his voice, the urge to pack my bags and book a plane ticket home was overwhelming. The consequences of doing that would suck, though. The contract is solid. I'd be ridiculed not only in the public eye, but most likely be sued for breach of contract, as well.

I'll say in my defense, though, that even Addie has had enough. She's as over this shit as I am. Thankfully, she's been the one true crutch I've leaned on, and I appreciate all she's done this week to help me keep my shit together. Between her and Brock's friend Drew, I shudder to think how Brock's cold shoulder could've affected me had they not been here.

Caring about someone, but knowing you've disappointed them is painful. Adding to that, knowing you'll never be together like that again—well, the notion is crippling in its own right.

Memories are all I'll take with me. And, after all that's happened, those feel empty.

"Girls," Willow beckons, standing at the front of the room as she usually does. "Give me your attention, please."

All quiet chatter fades, and the women turn in their positions to listen. Other than a few heavy sighs, Willow begins her command of the room.

"The audience has voted." Of course they did, but I'm tired of hearing about what the audience wants. "Brock and Evan will have dates tonight, but not of their choosing. They'll be taking who's been selected for them."

Small gasps and more sighs, along with a few eye rolls come from those around me.

"And here we go," Ryleigh whispers, coming to stand at my side. She looks flustered, which I've never seen before. She's also smiling wide, which I have seen, but not to this grade. "More surprises," she grins, then lifts her eyebrows in mischief. "Can't wait."

*I can.*

"Evan, can you step up here with me, please?" Willow requests. Looking to the side door, we all watch Evan enter the room.

As he takes the makeshift stage, a few women clap, while a few speak quietly to the girls beside them. Others, like me, say nothing.

"Evan has been here a couple of weeks, as you know. He's taken a few of you out. So, before the guys go on their final dates, we've let the audience decide who they will take out next."

*Shit.*

The idea of having to witness who the audience wants Brock to spend more time with sickens me. Not to mention, what if I've been chosen to go with Evan?

*Oh God.*

Turning to the proud new bachelor, mic in hand, Willow smiles. Her white teeth glisten under the lights as the camera aims its lens to capture what's about to play out.

"Evan," she addresses, holding a white card in her hand. "Tonight, Leslie will be with you."

Evan smiles, but so do I. Not because he is, but because he's uncomfortable in doing so. Leslie is nasty, just as nasty as Kylee, if not more so.

When he looks into the crowd, he finds Leslie at Kylee's side and nods to her with acknowledgement. After, he leaves the stage, and he does it quickly.

*Yeah, he's excited.*

"Brock, our leading man, come on out."

Brock, being around the longest, knowing all of us more than Evan, is met with cheers and claps all around. Except I don't clap or cheer. I can't move. My heart hurts too much for motion.

Brock's wearing another suit. His hair is styled to perfection. His posture stands both rigid and strong. His confidence as always is unwavering. As he stands next to Willow facing the room, he clutches his hands in front of him and looks down.

"Brock, the audience chose..." Willow waits, holding the card in front of her as if she's surprised at the result. "Kate!"

*Fuck. No, please. No. Not Kate.*

Turning in place, I give no thought as to how my running may look to the others or Brock because I don't care.

I want to go home.

# Chapter Forty-Six

*Women are so fucking infuriating.*

*Brock*

-

"Are you *sure* you don't need me to fly out there, Brock? 'Cause I'll do it. I'll get on a plane tomorrow. Just tell Mom and Dad you need backup."

"*Tatum Lee*," I hiss, using her full name to garner her attention. "No, damn it. I don't need you here."

"Bullshit," she spouts. "Drew told Nick you were miserable. I say misery calls for company. Let me come out there, Brock. Please!"

*My sister is unyielding.*

"You have school. Not to mention, Dad would never let you get on a plane alone."

"Let me handle Dad. He's so sick of hearing me complain about the reporters around here, I bet he'd put me on a plane himself."

The last thing I need is Tate.

The first thing I need is a drink.

"Don't ask Dad for anything," I order, hitting the elevator button to my suite.

As I step in, Tate suggests, "What if I got Mom to come with me? Then would you let me come to L.A.?"

*My mother in L.A.? Fuck no.*

"I'm about to hang up on you, Tate."

"No, you're not. You're homesick. Admit it."

I am homesick. Homesick for the days when my life was spent solely on me; what I wanted, what I planned. Hell, if it got me away from all this, I'd agree to lunch with George McLain every day for a week. I'd turn myself inside out to ensure I was more worthy in every way that made my dad proud.

Stepping off the elevator, continuing to listen to my sister's pleas for me to call Dad, I run into the absolute unexpected.

"Tate, I need to go."

"You said this already, but I think you need..."

Dropping the phone in my pocket once I've disconnected the call, I take a few cautious steps toward Brooke. She's sitting outside my hotel door, elbows to her knees with her head looking to the floor.

"Brooke?"

When her eyes come to mine, they're swollen from tears. The puffiness on the outside adds to the redness within. She looks as miserable as I feel.

In broken words, sounding a lot like broken English, Brooke rushes out, "I fucked up, Brock. I did this. I'm so sorry. I don't know what to—"

"Stop talking," I demand. Brooke Malloy in tears is gut wrenching. The sadness is comparable to a broken bird trying to take flight.

Wiping her cheeks, she asks, "Can I come in? I promise what I have to say won't take but a minute."

I want to tell her to come in, to stay the night. Fuck, I still want her to stay forever, and I'd say or do whatever it took to convince to her never leave. The issue, though, is that this *has* to be her decision. She needs to make any and all choices for herself without my influence.

"Come on. Get up. You look terrible," I instruct, but joking, of course. Crying or not, Brooke's beautiful to me.

Wiping her face as she stands, she smiles. "Now you're being bossy *and* rude."

Once I've opened the door to my suite, I push it further and step out of the way for her to pass. The familiar scent of her hair travels the small distance, and I have to plead with myself to stay in control.

With her arms crossed over her waist, Brooke looks around my suite, as if for the first time. I've hardly spoken to her once after admitting I was falling in love with her, at least not about anything that mattered. Her reticent reaction broke my heart, crushed my hope, and admittedly damaged my ego.

"Our official date is Friday," she starts, finally turning around to face me. My back is against the door, supporting my weight in case this doesn't go the way I want it to. "Two days from now," she adds.

"Yeah?"

"I'm here to give you the chance to call it off. I can tell Matt and Willow—"

"I'm not doing that," I assure. "I planned this date to my exact specifications."

"You did?"

"Yes. Jerry had no input."

"He didn't?" Her voice is hopeful, as is my resilience to keep going.

Walking toward her with careful steps, I'm hesitant in case she bolts. At the very least, I wait for her to back away. When she doesn't, I keep moving in her direction.

"Tell me why you're here," I insist. "Tell me you're not here, expecting me to cancel our date."

Shaking her head as I hold her cheek, Brooke gazes at my chest. "No," she mumbles. "I didn't want you to cancel it."

"Tell me why you're here then."

Lifting her head, I note not only are her eyes swollen, but they're tired. Brooke's exhausted.

"I miss talking to you," she says first. "I don't have anyone but Ryleigh and Addie. They're sick of me."

"I bet they are," I concur. "I bet they're sick to death of you."

"What?" she gasps, hardly able to get her reply out.

Smiling down at her, I pull her into me. Once I know she's not going to battle to get away, I whisper into the top of her head, "Tell me why you came here."

"I just did," she speaks into my chest, her words muffled and unclear.

"You came to hear me tell you I was sorry," I press, knowing that's not the reason, but offering us both an out anyway. I owe her an apology. One delivered face-to-face, if not heart to heart.

"Yes," she tells me. "That's exactly why I'm here. So, go ahead."

"If I say it, are you staying?"

Pulling her head back from my chest, her neck cranes as she looks up. "If I say it, will you let me?"

"For as long as you want."

# Chapter Forty-Seven

*If only I had realized all this sooner.*

*Brooke*

-

Everything is dark, and the room is quiet.

Brock's arm holds me tightly to his chest. His breathing isn't steady, so I know he's awake. The lazy graze of his fingertips circling my outer thigh is light, but there. Giving into my body's shiver, I close my eyes and savor our time alone. Our time hasn't been like this, just he and I, for weeks.

After Brock apologized, I did the same. We talked, but not for long. The sex that came after wasn't about releasing our pent-up frustrations, or encouraging the playful banter that often times precedes it.

Brock *made love* to me.

For the first time in my life, I found such a notion existed. Even before, when things began to change between us, I never felt this between us.

His kisses weren't pressing. His touch wasn't deliberate. Brock was taking his time, slow and easy. Since the first night we met, I didn't try to freeze the moment and save it to memory. Not because it wasn't beautiful, because it was. After I tell him what I have yet to tell him, my hope is that it's always like this. The threat of forgetting what we once had together won't be there anymore. Because if I'm blessed, I'll always have him.

"You're awake," I whisper, covering his hand on my thigh with my own.

He kisses the back of my head, and the warmth from his breath lingers through his question. "Have you slept at all?"

No, I haven't slept.

I tried closing my eyes, but the urgency for me to say what I came here to say has kept me awake. The fear he wouldn't return it, or worse, wouldn't accept it, clouded my thoughts.

"Not yet."

Moving his arm around my waist, tucking his fingers beneath my side, he continues to hold me as close as he can.

"Why not?"

"There's more to say," I explain. "And I want to say it before we leave this room."

His voice is raspy. From worry or sleep, I can't tell. "Brooke? What is it?"

Staring outside the hotel window to the glowing city in all its beauty, I admit, "I love you. I should've told you before you left—"

"Don't say it," he clips. "I was an ass. I fucked up."

Smiling at the memory, now that it hurts less to remember, I agree. "You were an ass. But I knew how you felt, and I should've told you then."

"You love me," he states plainly. The vibration of Brock's chest against my back sends a shiver down my spine. "This is good," he says with relief.

Continuing my gaze to the outside world, I wait for him to return the sentiment. When he doesn't, I prod, "Are you okay?"

Sighing heavily, he answers. "I'm debating."

"Debating on what?"

His hand drops from my waist, and in that millisecond, I start to panic. The knee-jerk reaction would be for me to get up, dress, and run as fast as I can. I beat it back though and wait.

When I feel his hand drop below my stomach, inching between my thighs, I close my eyes and inhale.

"I could say it now, because I really want to. Or I can wait until I'm inside you, showing you how I feel when you hear me say it."

His fingers dip into the skin of my inner thigh, so I spread them to grant him access.

"You're with me?" he questions, his fingers prodding my entrance, but then hesitating. "You're with me at the end of this?"

All things considered, I hadn't given thought to marrying him. With everything that's happened, all the good and all the bad, I do know I'd take everything Brock was willing to give me.

"Yes."

He releases a heavy sigh and sits up. Without delay, he positions me beneath him and blankets his body over mine. The city lights cast a glow on the side of his face. The sincerity in his eyes is evident, the sincerity in his voice is blatant, as he slides into me while saying, "I love you."

Tears I hadn't realized I was holding streak my temples as they cascade effortlessly on each side of my face. The ache of relief floods my stomach as I wrap my legs around his waist. Our hips move in sync as he pushes inside before pulling out, rocking our bodies in unison.

This is what I've waited all my adult life to feel.

Desire.

Passion.

Peace and understanding.

"I love you," he whispers again, this time peppering small kisses to each tear that's fallen. "And I'm sorry."

When Brock positions his hands beneath me, tilting my hips to his, he drives deep. Fast and furious, the spiraling moments of all our times together come back piece by piece.

My body shakes, readying for release, while at the same time, Brock slides inside one last time. "Don't walk away from this again," he whispers.

# Chapter Forty-Eight

*Blood-sucking temptress does one better.*

*Brock*

-

"So, do you live on a farm?" Drew ignorantly questions, grabbing a beer from my mini-fridge and not offering anyone else one of their own. "I mean, like, do you have cows and shit?"

Addie, being the spitfire she is, takes immediate offense. "Cows and shit?" she hisses. Janet's frustration with Jack is funny. Brooke and I have enjoyed their never-ending banter. "Not everyone in the Midwest owns a farm. And there's nothing wrong with farming, anyway."

"Unless you're Mary Ann," Brooke mumbles to herself at my side, but I clearly caught it.

"That's funny?" I snap, grabbing her chair and pulling her in close.

Rather than go out and see the city as Matt suggested to us all to do, the four of us grabbed a set of playing cards from the break room, sent Clive to get a couple of cases of beer, and came back to my room to play strip poker.

"Is it funny you dated a vegetarian farmer's daughter? Yes."

"I came out of it okay."

"Because you thought of me the whole time."

"I did," I freely admit. "Your body and your mouth, actually."

Shaking her head and feigning insult, she *tsks*. "I came out on top that night."

"Could you guys lay off the public displays? Brock, you lost. Lose something."

Looking down, I contemplate. Addie's in a bra, as is Brooke, but to save Drew the trouble of getting a fist to the face for gawking at her, I made her hold a pillow between her and the table. He doesn't get to see what I now know is mine.

Grabbing the back of my shirt, I pull it off in one quick motion. Brooke gasps, and Addie laughs. When I turn to look at Brooke, her eyes are wide as she stares at my chest. Her face turns red.

"Jesus Christ," Drew gasps. "What the fuck?"

Looking down, taking in what I already know is there, I turn my head to the side and smirk. Not one, but two hickeys decorate my chest.

"She's a sucker," I say.

"Oh my," Addie breathes. "Brooke...oh, my."

Grabbing the pillow from her chest, Brooke throws it at me. Drew turns to Brooke, where as any natural born man would look, he zones in on her chest.

"Drew," I clip, shaking my head. "No way."

Turning in his place, Drew looks to Addie at his side. "I'm not looking. Just tell me when it's my turn."

"I can't look away," Addie informs, studying my chest. "I'm not sure if I'm jealous or turned on."

Suddenly, Drew stands, throws the cards on the table, then grabs Addie's arm.

"You're leaving?" Brooke admonishes. "I was about to win the pot."

Pointing to my chest, Addie hisses, "Like you haven't already won the biggest jackpot. I'm going back to my room. I'm going to shower, put on my pjs, and watch a movie."

Brooke sits back in her chair, thankfully taking the pillow with her as she does, and mumbles inaudibly under her breath.

"We'll catch you guys after your date tomorrow," Drew bids, following Addie to the door. "Brooke," he nods. "My buddy bruises like a peach. Go easy."

"Oh my God," she whispers in return.

After Drew and Addie file out, I turn to my flushed soon-to-be fiancée and grin.

I mean, she's already undressed. What else are we going to do?

# Chapter Forty-Nine

*She'll say yes. She has to say yes.*

*Brock*

-

I'm ready.

In my pocket, I have the ring I picked out myself, the proposal speech I've rehearsed in my head hundreds of times, and the confidence I've somehow seemed to muster. I'm ready.

I'm lying. I'm a fucking mess.

Sitting alone at a table for two in the seemingly popular Mexican restaurant as the cameras roll in every corner, I'm doing a shit job in beating back the nerves that twist in my gut.

Brooke's the *one*.

It doesn't matter where, how, or why we met, all of this was meant to happen. She's the girl I've waited for. Brooke fits my life. All the craziness, cattiness, and emotional torture we've endured will soon be worth it.

Technically, I'm supposed to wait until that final episode. Theoretically, I should give her the chance to turn Evan down in front of viewers should he ask for her hand himself. However, nothing about our relationship thus far has been conventional. Brooke deserves a proper proposal, and that's what she'll get from me. The only thing I couldn't cover was calling her dad and asking permission. I've never met him, but from hearing Brooke talk about their relationship, he trusts her.

"Can I get you another drink while you wait, Mr. LaDuece?" the tall, young waiter questions as he holds a bottle of wine at my side.

I look down to my second empty glass and then to my watch. Brooke's late. Thirty-minutes late.

"No, thank you. I'm okay."

The sweat on my brow has to be shining for the cameras. The patrons sitting at the bar next to me continue to stare as they wait for Brooke to arrive. Those who were dining when we got here were all clued in on what was about to take place. The women swooned in their chairs. The men smiled with mockery and agreed to watch and stay quiet until it was over.

But, Brooke's late for her own proposal.

Clearing my throat first, I pull out my cell phone to check for messages. When I find there's nothing, I send her a quick text.

Me 07:43 p.m.: *Where are you? And why am spending our first official date alone?*

Setting the phone on the table, I wait for a response.

"Brock," Clive calls for my attention.

Once at my side, he stands close. As I crane my neck to look up, I immediately note his expression is grave. Clive's one of the easiest going men I've ever met. So, to see him appear stricken with whatever news he's about to impart is unsettling.

"What is it?"

Quietly, he leans down and informs me, "Matt needs you to go back to the hotel."

*What the fuck?*

"I'm a little busy," I bite back. I don't give a shit what Matt thinks he needs me to do. Now's not a good time. "Tell him I'll call him when Brooke and I are finished."

Clive's hand comes to rest on my shoulder. Being as I've never seen him look so uneasy, his added gesture of comfort is alarming.

"What is it?" I ask again. "Just tell me."

His head lifts, and his eyes scan the restaurant as he takes in a deep breath.

"He didn't say, man. He called and said you have a meeting with both him and Willow in an hour."

"Willow?"

"Yeah. And, if I had to guess, all this is about Brooke. I'm thinkin' something's happened."

Standing, I toss my napkin on the table and shake my head quickly to clear it. A thousand possibilities plague my mind, filtering through slowly, one a time. *Brooke refused the date. Brooke's been in an accident. Brooke's chosen Evan.* All my contemplations soon turn to irrational reasoning and my blood burns in response.

"What the fuck is going on? Where is she?"

"I'm telling you, Brock, he didn't say. Come on. You can ride with me so cameras don't follow."

On the way back to the hotel, Clive stays quiet. There's no conversation or music to interrupt my thoughts. The ring is still in my pocket. The speech I was ready to give alongside my proposal has been left unsaid.

*Where the fuck is Brooke?*

# Chapter Fifty

*My heart is sick, too.*

*Brooke*

-

"Deep breaths, Brooke. Come on, honey. You're not thinking clearly."

Hell no, I'm not.

In a matter of seconds, my life has flipped upside down, completely turning itself inside out. I have no balance. My body has become no heavier than a feather in the wind, mindlessly attempting to adhere itself to something safe and true, but in the empty void of time and circumstance, there's nothing within my grasp.

When I initially heard my little brother's ringtone, I lunged at my phone to answer right away. I was excited when his name popped up on my caller ID. Ashton knew tonight was mine and Brock's first formal and official date. He was nervous about it going as it should, and the cameras rolling if things didn't. Initially, I thought he was calling to offer a piece of his immature nineteen-year-old advice. But when his voice came out broken, I knew he was close to tears.

*Dad's sick, Brooke. He's in the hospital. Mom's a mess. You need to come home.*

Those words hit my chest, settling in as dead weight, and doing their best to suffocate me. My eyes closed, angry at Ashton because he wouldn't take them back. I wanted him to tell me he was kidding. I nearly demanded he admit it was one of his jokes said in bad taste.

He didn't.

Rather he went on to explain that Mom has refused to budge from my father's bedside, and that the medical staff are finding her impossible to deal with. Ashton said he needs me to come home to take care of her because he doesn't have the wherewithal to do it himself.

"Willow and Matt are on their way up now," Addie advises me as she grabs my second suitcase. She filters through the mess I've already started to make and hands me an old T-shirt and pair of jeans. "Here. I need you to put these on."

I'm still wearing the same dress I chose to wear tonight for Brock. I'd been looking forward to spending tonight in the public eye with the man I've started to fall in love with. He promised Mexican and margaritas. After, he promised a night together I'd remember forever. Looking down at my matching high heel stiletto shoes, I frown in shame.

Anything and everything that's happened since being in L.A. is trivial.

*Dad's sick, Brooke.*

"Addie," I call out, grabbing her arm before I fall.

My knees are weak, and my head is light. Childhood memories of my dad and I invade my mine. In my own, I feel his large hands, which I've always found safety in holding. His broad shoulders that I've cried on countless times beckon me to burrow myself against them again, and his gentle voice as he always called me 'Button,' chastises my ears in memory.

With tears streaming down my face, I chance a look at Addie, only to find her tears doing the same.

"My dad, Addie" I croak.

Within minutes of hanging up with Ashton, I'd emptied every drawer, grabbed all the clothes from my closet, all the toiletries from the bathroom, and had both suitcases out of the closet and open to pack. My irrational thoughts were reeling, brainstorming ways to get home as fast as I could.

"Honey, let's get you changed first before we finish packing. Focus for me, okay?"

Nodding, more tears fall, and I wipe them away as I follow her to the dresser where she starts to unzip the back of the black dress I'd put on only hours before.

"I'll call the airlines after Willow and Matt get here. They'll sit with you while I make all the arrangements to get us home. Don't worry about anything else, okay?"

"Why did I come here?" I question, looking into the dresser mirror. It's a question I ask out loud, but only to myself.

If something happens to my dad before I'm able to make it home, I'll always regret the time this absurd trip caused me to lose with him.

"You came here because the man you're rushing home to see told you to come, Brooke. He's proud of you."

*Do you remember when you were six years old and I took you to the fair?*

*You never let go of my hand.*

*And don't think about us back here missing you, either. We'll see you soon enough.*

What if I don't see him again?

Once my dress is off, Addie tosses it on the bed and moves in to finish putting my clothes on. My eyes are red and swollen, leaving my makeup an unfortunate mess. My hair, which was loosely swept up from my neck earlier, now hangs in dangled strands at my shoulders. In my panic, I run my fingers through it again and again.

"Arms, honey," Addie gently prods.

When I pull the hem of my shirt down, it's then I notice it's grossly oversized. The Van Halen logo stares back at me in the mirror. Addie recognizes who it belongs to.

*Brock.*

"Shit," she curses. "Do you want me to call him? Let him know?"

"No."

It's irrational why I feel any anger toward him, I know this. None of this is his fault. He didn't ask me come to L.A., to leave my family behind and set out on some selfish exploit. He had no way of knowing the time I spent with him was ultimately taking me away from what could possibly be the last with my dad.

"No?" Addie questions. Her eyebrows are furrowed. She doesn't understand, and I don't have time to explain.

"I just want to get home, Add. I need to find out what exactly happened. I'll call Brock then."

"Okay," she hesitantly agrees. "Whatever you want."

The knock at the door comes. In a way, it serves as a rescue, so I inhale a quick but nervous breath. Sharing my burden with my best friend is one thing. In her company, I'm allowed to cry, scream, panic, and shake. Sharing my heartache and worry in front of people I still deem as mere strangers is another.

"I'll get it," Addie advises, pointing to the small round table in our room. "You sit. Drink this." She pushes a lukewarm bottle of water in my hand, and I turn to do as she's asked.

Once the door opens and Willow's sad eyes, along with Matt's concerned gaze turn to me, I look down and bite my lip.

*Yes, facing strangers in a time like this sucks.*

"We've already made all the arrangements." I hear Willow explain to Addie.

Addie turns back to me and offers a careful smile.

"I'm sorry this happened," Matt quietly expresses, coming to stand at my side. "I spoke with the hospital administration, verifying all the information they were willing to give. In light of what's happened, you've been released from any and all contractual obligations to the show."

It's of small relief, but at least there's that.

"Is there anything else we can do?" Willow gently asks. The care in her eyes is heart-wrenching. Her pity feeds my already weary state.

"The press." I have the forethought to consider. "I don't want them to know—"

"Won't happen," Matt tersely advises. "This is a private matter, and we'll explain it as such. No room for negotiation."

"Thank you," I utter, genuinely thankful for another small piece they've offered.

"And as far as Brock is concerned—" Willow starts.

I stop her immediately. "I don't want him to know anything either."

Willow's head tilts to the side. "But I thought you two—"

"No, not now. I don't want him to know," I assert, this time with added confidence. "I'll contact him when I can."

"Anything you say," she replies with sincerity.

Matt comes to my side again and gently rests his hand on my shoulder. "It was really nice to meet you, Brooke. I can say, even without knowing him, I'm sure your father would be proud of how you've handled yourself during your stay here. Dignity and grace are characteristics not too many of the contestants we've had on this show have had an abundance of."

I turn my gaze to Addie, wishing she'd get them both out of here. I'm appreciative of his sentiment, but my only focus is getting home to see my dad.

Willow comes to me next, her arms extended for a hug, so I stand.

"Addie has all the travel information, and there's a driver waiting downstairs to take you to the airport. If you need anything from us here, anything at all, you have my number."

"Thank you," I tell them both as they turn to file out.

# Chapter Fifty-One

*And so it goes.*

*Brock*

-

"My guess was spot on," Matt comments as he hangs up the phone. He looks up at me, sitting in the chair in front of his desk. "As of now, all indications tell us the audience will no doubt choose Kylee."

*Fuck me.*

Neither Willow nor Matt has told me anything in regards to why Brooke left me sitting in that fucking restaurant alone. He's kept tight-lipped about her reasons for fleeing the show as she did. His version suggested nothing more than she had a change of heart and found a loophole in her contract big enough to get her out of it.

*All of that is fucking bullshit.*

"Why the hell did the audience choose Kylee?" I snap.

Thus far into the airings and audience polls, they don't have Brooke as a match for me. And it's understandable they wouldn't, considering they haven't seen much of her on camera. I've done my best to keep Brooke out of the spotlight, and now my overprotective worry for her privacy has bitten me in the ass.

"Kylee has no reservations in putting herself front and center, Brock. Surely you can understand why the audience has gravitated toward her."

I can in a way, and that further pisses me off. Home viewers love drama. I know this firsthand, as my sister is one of those very same people.

"She's beautiful. She's friendly," he attests in Kylee's defense.

"When the cameras are rolling, sure," I counter back. Matt's been around. He'll get it.

"When the cameras are on, yes," he replies. "Unfortunately, she's who it appears they'll choose. You've cast aside each girl so far, meaning you can't backtrack and choose from them. The panel already has your votes."

"Brooke was it for me, Matt. I didn't have a choice but to cast them aside."

Looking around and taking in the large expanse of his office, my thoughts tread to more anger in wondering why Brooke left. I could text her, but at the same time, I highly doubt she'd answer. If she did, I doubt I'd listen to what she had to say anyway.

I know she cares about me. If I'm right, she may have truly loved me. Just not enough to commit to that love in a way that encompassed marriage.

"What do I do now?"

"We won't need you again until the final taping. I've talked to Willow, and she agrees in light of what's happened, you could use some time off to take this in. Last year, we did the same for the groom."

"Time off to do what?"

"Go home. Be with your family, prepare them if you have to. Get your thoughts clear and ready yourself for what's to come."

"How long do I have?"

"Two weeks. That's solid. When you return, we'll help settle you back in before the final episode is aired live."

*The final episode.*

"The wedding," I correct. I want to hear him confirm it.

"Yes. You're welcome to bring your family back with you, as well. They'll have a section in the audience reserved just for them."

To sit front and center as witnesses to my life's biggest fuck up? No thanks.

"When will the announcement of who I'm to marry be made?"

"Very soon," he answers. "We'll run the last taping a few days prior to the wedding."

Throwing back the third shot Matt poured me before breaking the news as gently as he could, I finish and immediately thirst for another.

And another.

And another.

But drinking myself into oblivion would be pointless. It won't change the fact that Brooke left, and it's highly unlikely I'll ever see her again.

"Is there nothing I can do to stop this?"

"Aside from moving to another country?" he half-heartedly quips. "No."

"No way to buy myself out of this, either?"

Shaking his head, his jaw gets tight. "No. You signed a contract."

"And if I break the contract?"

"Public ridicule for one. The sad eyes of Kylee Simmons will haunt you as I'm sure she'd be more than happy to ruin your name in any way she can. They'll believe her side of the story because they love her."

"Right," I clip.

"Not to mention, the network has a legal panel with enough backing to take down anyone who may cross them."

Fuck, I know he's right again. My father has a similar team of men at Merritt.

Looking at me with careful caution, Matt suggests, "This may not be what you want right now, Brock. However, there's still opportunity here. You may find after Kylee settles away from the spotlight, she's not such a bad person. Women are fickle when they feel they're being threatened by other women."

"I won't be happy with Kylee," I assure, but avoid going into detail of how much I already hate the woman. The label bitch comes to mind, but I don't voice it.

"Then you'll have to endure her temporarily until you're legally allowed to let her go. It's not my business; however, I suggest you have her sign a prenup."

Of course it's not a bad idea, I just hadn't gotten that far into thinking this through. I had my hopes on marrying Brooke. Now that that has fallen through, I have all the more to think about.

And, to add to my frustration, the realization of how much my mom will hate Kylee clouds my thoughts. I'm going to lose Merritt Media, no matter what happens from here.

"Is there anything else you need from me right now?" he questions.

"No," I reply as I stand. "That's it."

"Then we'll see you in two weeks, Brock."

# Chapter Fifty-Two

*I still don't want to ride the pony.*

*Brooke*

-

"Whatever business we have left at the inn can wait," my mother assures, resting her hand on the small of my back.

I'm standing at my father's side, willing him to wake up so I can tell him I've come home. Since fleeing L.A. as fast as I did, and feeling the stress of what I was coming back to, I haven't seen the light in his eyes that I wish so badly for now.

"I can go in and cover a shift, Mom. Really."

Mom's eyes are glassy. Her tears have been endless, yet she's still trying to be strong for Ashton and me.

When I stepped out of the airport terminal, Ashton rushed me. His embrace was strong. On the way home, he told me Mom wasn't good, and Dad's heart attack was bad. He'd slipped into a coma soon after they revived him. I hated myself for not being close when my family needed my support the most.

"You could work, yes, but you're not going to. Ashton hasn't come to see your father, Brooke. I need you to stay with Dad while I talk to him."

"Ashton hasn't been here at all?"

I'm incensed. It's an emotion I've rarely felt. Being that most of my life has been both carefully planned and executed, surrounded by the love and continuity of my family, it's rare I've ever felt bitterness toward any of them.

Mom's head shakes, and her lips quiver. "Ashton can't..." she pauses. "He's so young, and doesn't realize this time could be all he has left."

Turning back to Dad, I study him closely and pause for his eyes to open, his brows to furrow, anything at all that tells me he's listening. He'd know what to do about Ashton. He'd know what to do about Mom. I don't know what to do about anything because the one person who'd give me guidance doesn't even know I'm in the room.

"I'll talk to Ash," I whisper, taking the seat next to Dad's bed. "Because you're right, he'll regret this."

Mom places her hand to the top of my head where she strokes gently before running it down my back, just as she did when I was a kid. My eyes close, allowing me a moment to appreciate all I had growing up, but also regretting everything I always took for granted.

"I know he will, Button. But you won't, so you're not going to work. If needed, I'll close the inn until we're ready to reopen."

"Okay," I reply.

Mom walks to the door where she stops to turn and say, "Addie needs to talk to you. She said it's urgent. You know whatever it is she has to say must be urgent if she's called me three times and you not once."

Addie has called me, but since coming home to find my father so sick and frail, I've not answered. She'll have to forgive me, and she will. I need this time to myself.

"I'll call her later."

My mom's expression turns to thought. "I haven't given her any updates about Dad. I thought you would do it once your grandmother gets in. This is our time now."

"Thank you," I return, truly appreciative for her forethought. I have none.

Before Willow left my room three days ago, the look on her face as I pleaded for silence was concerning. As we sat at the airport, she called again to ensure Addie and I had made it to our flight. She advised me the plan was to play off my absence with, "Well, this is why we have an extra girl this season," then promised she'd cover things from there.

I still have no idea who the audience will choose for Brock to marry, or if he's chosen anyone for himself. I'd be lying if I didn't admit I hated the fact that it could be Kate. He liked her. I think they'd be good together.

But who am I to decide? I don't know anything.

I don't know how to get time back with my dad.

I don't know how to make him hear me.

I don't know the first thing about how to push forward with my life without him.

The slow steady pulls of the machines helping him breathe hum around us, so I break the silence with sarcasm I know he'd appreciate. "You know, Dad, if you'd wake up, I'd have a lot to tell you. My drama would keep your mind spinning for hours. You could help keep track of everything I've messed up."

A small voice in my head, which in my exhausted state I believe is his, urges me to keep going.

"I knew Brock was going to choose me. I don't know, maybe I'm wrong. I've been wrong before."

*Would you have said yes?* In my head, his strong and steady voice lovingly questions.

Tears come that I can't control. They spill down my cheeks one at a time, each taking their turn in submitting to my grief.

"I would've said yes," I confirm. "You would've liked him for me, I think. He's fun. He makes me laugh."

*Humor is the most important element in any relationship, Button. You know that.*

"And he's protective...and kind of bossy."

*As long as he takes care of my little girl, he can be whatever he needs to be.*

"And I think he loves me."

*My sweet Brooke, you make that easy. Your mother and I love you, too.*

God, this is heartbreaking. The heaviness in my chest is only second to the infinite relay of memories that play on endless reels in my mind.

Thankfully, I'm granted a distraction when the nurse opens his hospital room door. She's wearing Mickey Mouse scrubs and a white surgical cap. Her sympathetic look of understanding offers only a small comfort.

"Your mother said I'd find you with Mr. Malloy," she whispers, moving around files and logging into a small computer across the room. "Seems we have a celebrity up in our midst today."

I don't know about that. What I do know is we have a broken hearted daughter who wants nothing more than to see the reassurance in her father's eyes.

"I need to have him bathed, sweetheart," she insists, still typing notes on the screen. "After, the doctor will make his rounds."

"Can I come back?"

"You most certainly can," she replies, standing up and walking toward me. She eyes my father first, then turns her gaze to mine. "But you look like you could use some rest."

"I don't need rest," I petulantly return. My father would be disappointed in me, throwing attitude at an innocent person who's only trying to help. I can't help it, I'm not leaving.

"He's as stable as he can be right now," she eases. "He's big and strong, too. You're very lucky he's taken care of himself."

Playing with the edge of the sheet that covers him, I ask, "Then how'd this happen?"

"Genetics," she shrugs. "Maybe he's tired. The body has a way of telling us we're taking on too much. We can't control how it decides to clue us in."

"Do you think he'll be okay?"

Shaking her head and coming to my side, she looks down at my dad. "Time is the only true test right now. In time, his body will heal, or it won't."

This isn't what I want to hear. She's being honest, and I should appreciate her gesture. Still, her words are hard to accept.

"He's always been so careful," I explain.

"Like I said, he's been taking good care of himself," she returns.

Shaking my head now, I try to clear it. I'm talking to a total stranger, and in ways I don't understand, the fact I don't know this woman makes my attempt to explain my dad easier.

"No. I mean, he's always been so careful with *us*. My mom, Ashton, me..."

"I see," she puts in when I can't keep going. "He's a family man."

"Yes," I whisper. "But now that he's not here, I don't know what to do."

As she wraps her arm around my shoulders, more tears come.

"You're doing exactly what he would expect you to do because he raised you to do it. Believe in that."

"Thank you," I return, but offer no more insight to what I'm thinking.

As the room becomes basked in silence, the nurse moves a few things around, here and there. At this point, I don't think she's here to do her job, but more so to ensure I don't fall completely apart.

"You look just like him," she utters, grabbing her files and heading toward the door. "The resemblance is striking."

As a kid, I hated the notion that I was my father's small female twin. People used to comment about it everywhere we went. I don't look anything like my mom. Not like Ashton does, anyway.

For the first time in all my life, the thought of looking like my father couldn't make me a prouder daughter.

"Thank you."

"Go on now. Tell your mother we'll have him cleaned and ready for more visitors within an hour."

On her way out, she turns one more time to find Dad still hasn't moved. And, it's in that moment, as a complete stranger regards me sitting at my father's side, that I realize something significant I never understood before.

Even if I wasn't scared that day at the fair, I'd still refuse the chance to ride Magnificent because I'd rather stand at my dad's side if it meant I got to hold his hand.

# Chapter Fifty-Three

*Teenagers watch entirely too much reality television.*

*Brock*

-

"Brock, I think you're gonna wanna see this," Tate states calmly as she walks into the living room I'm currently sulking in.

I've been staying at my parents' place the last couple of days. When I called to let them know I was coming home for an unexpected visit, I found out our mother was visiting my aunt in Chicago, and Dad's been away on business. They didn't want to leave Tate alone. Had I not showed, she would've stayed with friends. She wasn't as excited to see me as much as she was excited for me to be home.

When Tate flips on the overhead light, my eyes squeeze shut at its bright intrusion. The silver iPad mini my sister carries dangles from her right hand. As she walks in my direction, I also notice her typical disapproving scowl.

*What the fuck did I do now?*

"What is it?"

Plopping herself down next to me on the couch, Tate lifts her feet to rest them on the table in front of us before settling the iPad on her thighs. The screen is frozen, framed with a picture of what I imagine to be one of those late night entertainment shows she's always so enamored with.

"It's fucked up is what it is," she responds.

I don't have time to scold her for her mouth because a picture of Willow Ellis comes into view before I can.

"Have you seen these?"

Narrowing my eyes, I grab the iPad from her grasp to get a closer look.

"Hit the big play button," she instructs, pointing to the middle of the screen.

Doing as she says, I hit it and the screen immediately starts to move.

Willow Ellis and another woman, one I assume is interviewing her, are sitting on a red couch with the camera pointed at them both. They're smiling as a large television screen next to where they're sitting boasts the logo of this year's reality theme…

*Marry a Millionaire.* Or as I now refer to it as, *Ruin a Millionaire.*

"What is this?"

Tate clears her throat before pointing to the screen again. "Bloopers."

"Bloopers?"

"Yeah," she answers, as if I'm some lost or random idiot for not understanding. "Every year, the show puts together and airs a reel of bloopers on how and where they found that year's contestants. According to them, it's a way for the public to pick apart the groom's choice."

"Right," I agree, as if I knew. Which, of course, I did not.

"Last year…" she *tsks.* I see a bit of compassion in my sister's expression, which is rare, so I hold my breath. "Luke Marks was the contestant."

"The plumber," I confirm.

Tate's lips get tight. The same sympathetic expression now increases on his behalf. "Yeah, that poor guy. They found him working at a high school. He was pulling tampons from…"

"Tate," I clip. "Move it along."

"Fine," she snaps. "Anyway, they gave his story, too. Just like on here."

"On here?" I question, looking back to the screen.

"Yeah. Your girl is there."

"My girl?"

Unfortunately, I don't know which 'girl' my sister is referring. Kylee, the bitch I'm set to marry soon, or Brooke, the one who fled from my soon-to-be proposal without so much as a single word.

"Your future bride, Brock. Look!"

As the clip starts to play, I sit back further on the couch and put my feet up next to Tate's. In twisted shock, I cover my mouth with my hand.

*You've gotta be fuckin' kiddin' me.*

Kylee, my audience-chosen fiancée, and soon to be wife, is front and center of the camera wearing a flimsy, black G-string bikini. She's pouring a large bottle of what appears to be vodka down her neck, chest, and stomach. She's laughing herself into hysterics while a large blond-haired man at her right licks the liquid from her neck, and a dark-haired man on her left does the same, but with his tongue in her navel.

"Your future wife is a slut," my sister sneers. Thankfully, Tate sees traits in people as I do. "Hit fast forward. Your other girl is on there, too."

Again, doing as she's instructed, I roll through to the bottom until I find Brooke's face on the screen. My chest constricts as I take in the sight of her.

Her amber eyes look pained, and her posture stands defeated. She's standing just outside what I guess is to be a women's public bathroom with a crowd of people surrounding her. Addie's standing at her side, talking to Willow before turning to the mass of people and telling them to 'fuck off.' The curse has been bleeped for television viewers.

A blond man I don't know stands alone at the end of the hallway. His shirt is wet, and his hair is standing at all ends, as though he's run his hands through it several times in frustration. Brooke's watching him with anger and disgust.

"That was her boyfriend," Tate informs me. "Took some googling, but I found out his name is Jason Evers. From what the news said—"

"Tabloids, Tate," I correct. "The news doesn't report shit like this."

"Not shit. Bloopers, Brock," she corrects me, just as I did her. "The news doesn't report bloopers, but tabloids do. Keep watching."

Leaving her with an eye roll, I turn back to the screen.

"Anyway, I guess that's how Willow found your Brooke."

*Your Brooke.*

Fuck, if only that were true. She was once, at least I thought so.

"She threw a drink at him. As in *on* him. Apparently, he broke her heart. That night he showed up at some bar with the woman who he cheated on her with."

"Jesus Christ," I utter to myself.

"Shocking, eh?" Tate queries. "I'm not sure, but I think if you look at this and compare the two women, we both know who you should've chosen."

I attempt to hand her back the iPad, but she refuses it. Pushing it back in my direction, she adds more of what I didn't know.

"Um, keep going. There's something else."

*Great.*

Settling the screen in front of me, I hit play as it fades from Brooke's instance to what I clearly recognize as mine.

Drew and Nick are somewhere we've all been together, and they're clearly drunk. Drew is going on and on about a buddy of his who'd be perfect for the part of the groom, if only they would hold the auditions in our area.

Nick is standing at his side, nodding his head repeatedly, then adds, "He's great with the ladies, too. He's rich *and* good looking."

*I'm going to kill my friends.*

Looking back, I thought it peculiar that I was accepted on the spot the day of the audition. Seems Matt Sutton already had an informer within his midst who gave him the scoop to my life as I would never want it to be told.

After having enough, I toss the iPad back to my sister and grab my drink from the table. The burn of whiskey blazes down my throat, but does nothing to assuage my nerves.

"I think I've told you your friends are idiots." Tate slams my *ex*-friends in one breath, but comes back in the next, saying, "I'm sure they meant well, but still—*idiots*."

"Yeah," I agree, sitting quietly and focusing on the table, also the colorful images of me wringing both their necks the next chance I get.

"You're not going to do anything about this?" she asks curtly.

"About what?"

"There's still time, Brock. You still have time to get to Brooke before it's too late."

"Believe me, Tate, there's not. I signed that contract with the show. I'm fucked."

"In more ways than one," she states smugly.

I can't argue. She speaks the truth. I've lost Brooke and Merritt Media, along with the respect of my parents. I'm fucked in all ways, none of them good.

"What if Dad can help?" she suggests. "Maybe if you talk to him? He's due back today, as in any time."

"What if Dad can help with what?" Both Tate and I turn our heads to the side to find my father leaning against the door's entry.

Tate stands, taking her iPad with her. With kind eyes, she looks to me and softly whispers, "Ask him, Brock. Maybe he can do something. And if you go get her, I'm going with you."

"Tate," I state firmly.

She's not going anywhere because *I'm* not going anywhere. She's being a teenage girl, wishing and dreaming for something that can't possibly happen. I hate to let her down when she's looking up to me for the first time in her life, but no.

"If you're going, I'm going. If you're doing something crazy, I'm doing it with you. This whole mess should tell you that you still need supervision."

Hearing enough of my little sister's torment, Dad instructs, "Tate, go upstairs and call your mother. Give me a few minutes to talk to Brock alone."

Tate does as she's told and walks around me, but not without reaching down to run her fingers playfully in my hair. This is her way of releasing the stress we're both feeling, and also her way of reminding me she loves me.

Even as the fucked up big brother that I am.

Once she's gone, I turn my focus back to the muted television and wait as my dad comes to take a seat next to me on the couch where Tate had been.

"So, what's going on?" he asks.

Part of me wants to beg for his help. He has a vast variety of lawyers at his beck and call, each with extensive contractual experience. It would take only a phone call and an order to have the documents I signed tediously examined.

"I don't want to marry Kylee."

"You'd rather marry Brooke? The girl who refused your proposal?"

"She didn't refuse it," I respond quickly. "She left without hearing it."

Dad laughs, but it's the truth. Brooke left before she knew my final choice was her. Or she did know and took off for the same reason. Although, after spending all these weeks together as we did, it wouldn't or shouldn't have come as a surprise.

"Have you spoken to her at all?"

"No," I admit.

I haven't. I've tried several times; texts, calls, voicemails. The only thing I haven't done is send a telegram, and as the days have passed, I've started to consider that as a viable option. I've never been as letdown as I was when I found out she fled. And, fuck me, but I still want to know why she did.

"Do you think you should go to her? Maybe find out the reason she left?"

"One problem at a time," I advise.

"Yes, there are a few," he lightheartedly counters.

"I hate to ask you for help, because you seem to know more about me than I do—"

"Not true, son," he denies, but follows with, "I only know how you get when you don't enjoy what you have. And from what your mother and Tate have both told me, it seems you enjoyed your time with Brooke very much."

"Yes," I confirm in a broken whisper.

I enjoyed my time with her more than anything I've ever done. She made everything about my life easy to accept, except *this*. Marrying someone I hate will slowly kill me.

Dad sits at my side, staring at the same commercial I am.

"Think there's anything I can do to get myself out of this?"

"I'm not sure what you're truly asking, but I'm here, and I'm willing to listen."

To be honest, I don't know what I'm asking. I want Brooke to come back, let me in on what spooked her. Then maybe we could work things out from there. I already know marrying Kylee Simmons will go down as a galactic mistake, and I sure as hell don't want that on my already tarnished record with my family.

"You've gotten yourself into quite a mess this time," Dad states plainly, but I can hear the hint of humor at my expense in his words.

*This shit is not funny.*

"Yeah, another disappointment."

"Brock," he sighs. "It's not the end of the world."

"Isn't it?" I snap, turning my furious gaze to his lenient one.

"I've been thinking."

"Yeah?" I ask. "'Cause I'm trying not to do just that."

He smiles, turns his eyes from mine, and looks ahead. After clearing his throat, he informs me, "For the first time in your life, I'm going to give you an opportunity to redeem yourself."

I keep my gaze casually aimed at the television as he is, fearing what he's about to offer.

"There's a potential client that lives in Des Moines, Iowa. I believe that's not too far from where your Brooke lives."

"Yeah?"

"I had originally considered George to be the one who scouts the area, but maybe now I've changed my mind."

"We don't have business in Iowa, Dad."

"*We* don't," he agrees. "But *you* do. And nothing in that contract says you're expected to sit home during your time off before the wedding. You have some time before you commit to Kylee. Is what Tate told me correct?"

"Yes," I answer.

"Then, you have a job requirement to see to. You'll do this for me."

"Okay."

"You'll do this for *you*," he pressures. "In the meantime, I'm going to have Darrin and his group take a closer look at what you signed. If there's a loophole anywhere to be found, you know he'll find it."

"There isn't," I reply. "I'm not a lawyer, but all that contract said to me is that I was fucked."

"Fucked," he laughs. It's not often my dad curses, even in jest. "Maybe so, but let me worry about this, and you worry about that." He points to the television where a commercial preview for the finale *of my life* is playing.

The same life that has now become a complete self-sabotaging fuck up in every way.

# Chapter Fifty-Four

*Brooke*

-

The unanswered texts have stopped.

The calls are no longer coming through.

My voicemail is empty.

Brock must have finally come to terms with my leaving.

In a way, I'm relieved. I want Brock to be happy. He deserves this more than most. While we were together, he told me why he came to the show in the first place. I'm hoping his mother will love whoever he chooses.

On the other hand, I'm not sure I can face ever finding out who his decision will end up being. Knowing she'll have what I left hurts. It won't be me sharing late night conversations after sex. Nor will it be me he'll find standing across the room before tilting his head in a way that communicates the things we could never let others see.

"Are you okay?" Mom asks as she stands at the kitchen counter making our lunch.

My father's condition hasn't changed. His stats are steady, but he hasn't improved. It's wearing on us all, but now that my grandmother is here, Mom's been able to take more time away to see to things at home and the inn. It's helped her to step away, even an hour or so at a time.

"I'm good."

"Good." She turns around with two plates full of sandwiches and chips. "You haven't been 'good' since you've come home."

"Do you blame me?" I question, pointing to my father's empty chair.

Mom shakes her head, takes a seat, and slides a small plate on my place setting. I'm not hungry. Since coming home, I've all but lost my appetite.

"Your sorrowful mood has to do with more than just your father, Brooklyn Paige."

"I don't know."

"It's that man, isn't it?"

Hearing her call Brock 'that man' forces a smile to my lips. My Dad refused to give Brock a name, too. I don't think any of us thought my visit to L.A. would turn out the way it did.

I fell in love. And maybe I did it even before I knew who Brock really was.

"It doesn't matter," I explain. "I left to come here and now he's there. He'll choose someone he believes is good for him."

"You would've been good for him," she states to my surprise.

My mom doesn't know Brock. Her random assumption seems out of place.

After taking a small drink of her iced tea, Mom sets it down, sits back in her chair, and surveys me in a way she's done all my life. My mom and I may not be as close as I've always wished we were, but that said, she still knows me better than most.

"Do you think he'd have chosen you if you'd have stayed?"

"I don't know. I think, maybe...yes."

"And what would you have said?"

Her calm tone indicates she's come to terms with the possibilities of Brock and I. She was so angry when I first brought up the notion of taking part in any of this, so her inquiry is another surprise.

Mom's subtle smile presses for my answer. "Well?"

"I don't know."

"Have you talked to him?"

"No," I reply, shaking my head. "He's tried, but with everything happening here and Grandma coming to visit, I haven't had time."

Narrowing her eyes, Mom questions, "Did I ever tell you that your father asked me to marry him a year before I said yes?"

"No?"

She nods and grabs a chip from her plate. "He did. I was young and inexperienced. He scared me. Your father is a big man, but not just physically. He had big plans of owning his own business. He said he only wanted to make enough money to care for his family. I used to think his dreams were too big for my life."

I understand how she feels. After being front and center to all those other girls, begging for Brock's promise of marriage, I felt the very same. Brock's larger than life, whether he believes that or not.

"It took a year for your father to convince me. He said he fell in love with me because I was everything those other women he dated before weren't."

"What's that?"

Mom's face reddens. "His."

A sad frown crowds my face. I know it's there, but I can't muster the strength to change it. I was Brock's. He was mine. Maybe it was only for a short time, but during those weeks we spent together, our lives settled into each other's with ease. Even while being challenged by the chaos and drama of the show.

To my next surprise, Mom wonders aloud, "What's Addie have to say about all this?"

"Not a lot," I return.

"That's hardly true. Addie *always* has something to say. What is it?"

"She wants me to talk to him, but I don't see the point. I left. When I did, my obligations were void, and I'm no longer accredited to the show."

"You can't go back?" she asks.

I'm not sure I could, and if I did, it would be risky. Brock's surely chosen by now, or worse, the audience has surely chosen for him. Aside from that, my being there would be a hazard to my emotional health. Maybe his, as well.

"You're in love with him, sweetheart," Mom expresses quietly.

Pushing my plate of food away, I give her honesty. "I don't know what love looks like. Jason-"

"Jason is a fool," she spouts angrily. "He's an idiot."

*Whoa.*

I've never heard my mother talk about my first and only long-term relationship in such a way. Sure, she never was overly excited at the sight of Jason, but she's never outwardly called him names.

"Jason called your brother yesterday."

"He did *what*?"

She nods, wiping her hands on her napkin. "He called to ask how you were doing and when you were coming home."

"That *asshole*," I hiss, tightening my jaw.

Mom smirks, no doubt loving I agree with her on what a jackass my ex-boyfriend is.

"From what Ashton told me, Jason has been watching the show. I think he's starstruck."

"Lightning would strike him better than I could."

"So very true," she chuckles. Once she notes I'm festering in more ways than one, she instructs, "Eat your lunch. We'll go see your dad later. Ashton's coming home after class so he can come with us."

Well, at least there's that.

# Chapter Fifty-Five

*If women take classes in secret keeping, Addison Tindal gets an A.*

*Brock*

-

"I already told you this on the phone," Addie reminds me, yet again. "She won't talk to me. She's not taking any of my calls. When I spoke with her mom, she said Brooke wasn't ready to talk to *anyone*."

"Try her again. Call her now," I insist.

Addie purses her lips and places her hand to her hip as she angrily stands at my side. After I was able to catch a late-night flight and arrived first thing this morning, I didn't go to my hotel. I came straight to the address Addie had given me to a truck stop on the outskirts of town where she works.

"I can keep calling her, but Brock, I'm telling you it won't matter."

"What's her home address? Give it to me."

"She's not there," she replies, shaking her head. Nevertheless, she pulls out a pen from her apron and jots the address down on a white napkin. "They haven't been home. I've driven by a thousand times."

Sitting back in the booth and grabbing the beer I'd been drinking before Addie finally was able to take a break, I clutch it in both hands.

"You talked to her mom?" I query next.

Addie nods, then comes to take a seat across from me in the booth I'm sitting in.

"I did. Her mom's kind of..." she pauses, thinks, then finishes, "uptight. Brock, it's a private matter. I know me explaining everything as that doesn't help, but you need to trust me."

"A private matter," I repeat, resting my posture to slouch. Private matters are never good. Especially those that would force Brooke to leave as she did.

"I called Ashton and he answered, but when I started asking where Brooke was, he told me he had to go. Again, you've got to trust me."

Reaching in my pocket, I slide a twenty across the table in her direction. She raises her hand to stop me.

"Keep your money. Beer's on me," she advises. As I start to stand, she asks, "Where are you off to now?"

"Hotel, I guess. I don't have anywhere else to go."

"Where are you staying?"

Honestly, I have no idea. "In Triade somewhere. Not sure."

"Triade is about thirty miles from here. Can't miss it. Just drive north, the way you came."

"Thanks again, Add."

The restaurant is crowded; the noise is loud. As I walk away, I hear Addie call for my attention.

When I turn to face her, she observes, "Brooke was the one you were going to ask to marry you, wasn't she?"

Nodding, I answer with what she most likely already knows. "Yes, it was Brooke. I knew it was her the night you led me to her in the hotel bar."

Addie's face falls, and tears flood her eyes. She's flushed as she sighs and offers a small wave of her hand, which I don't return.

*How hard is it to find the woman I love in this godforsaken state?*

Thirty minutes later, I'm parked directly across the street from the address Addie wrote down. It's exactly the kind of house I imagined Brooke's family to own. During our time together, she vaguely mentioned she'd been staying with her parents temporarily as she was looking for a new place. I didn't pry into her circumstance, only because when she addressed her situation, she did it unenthusiastically.

Two empty trashcans sit next to the curb, as well as the overstuffed mailbox against the house. Several newspapers line the end of the driveway, indicating no one's been home for a few days, and if they have, they haven't done the everyday things a person normally would.

*What the fuck is going on?*

The phone in my jacket rings so I remove my seatbelt to answer. Caller ID tells me it's Tate.

"Yeah, what's up?" I answer, skipping the formal greeting.

Her heavy sigh leads, followed by, "I can't believe you went without me, Brock. I wanted to go."

"I know you did, but this is something I have to do alone."

"I'm glad you went," she tells me. "I heard Dad talking to Darrin."

I haven't heard from my father since I told him I'd booked my flight and he wished me luck. I could tell his words were sincere as he said them. I felt a connection between us for the first time in a long time—too long, in fact.

"What's he saying?"

Tate clears her throat before she talks low. I imagine her to be home, holed up in some closet as she speaks covertly into the line. "He told Darrin to keep looking. He kind of threatened him. I've never heard Dad talk like that."

Smiling to myself, I *know* she hasn't. She doesn't work for Dad. I've heard the same tone I imagine he used with Darrin time and time again.

"Do you think she'll forgive you?" Tate queries.

"Forgive me?"

My sister's voice rises, but only a little. "Yeah, forgive you. For whatever it is you did to make her run. I mean, she *bolted*. I can't wait to find out why."

*God, she's such a fucking brat.*

"Let me worry about forgiveness, Tate. I'll handle it."

In the background, I hear static across the line, then the voices in the background get louder and louder before a door slams.

"Jesus," she hisses once she's back. "I gotta go. Dad's in a mood, and Mom's out with friends."

"He doesn't know you're calling me, does he?"

She laughs, but it's hushed. "Nope. Well, now he does. He told me to tell you to get off the phone and get to doing what you're supposed to be doing."

"Tell him I said he needs to do the same."

"Fine," she huffs. "You and Dad have all the fun. This sucks."

"Talk to you soon, Tate."

"Go get her, Tiger," she asserts before I hear her voice trail off and the call ends.

My sister isn't always a brat, I guess. She has a good heart, but uses it only when it suits her.

"Hello?" a voice calls at my window.

When I turn my head, I find a middle-aged woman with brown hair, graying at the sides. It's swept back into a low hanging ponytail. She's wearing a running suit, but doesn't appear to have been running anywhere.

"Can I help you?" she questions as I lower my window. Her eyes squint as she scans my face, the phone in my hand, then the inside of my car.

"I was looking for Brooke Malloy. I got this address from Addie Tindal."

"Addie," the woman *tsks*. "We aren't doing interviews. So, if that's why you've come, you're wasting your time."

"No," I immediately correct. "I'm here to talk to Brooke. My name is Brock LaDuece. She knows me."

The narrowing of the woman's eyes is a little frightening. I consider starting the car and backing away until she repeats my name as if to herself. It's familiar.

"You've come all this way to see Brooke?"

"Yes, and if you could tell me..." I stop talking when Brooke steps out of a black SUV I hadn't seen pull into the driveway. She doesn't offer a glance in our direction.

"I don't know that she wants to see anyone," the woman tells me. "But I'm Nora. I'm Brooke's mother."

The faint resemblance is there, but it's not obvious. I wouldn't have guessed.

"Can I get a minute with her?" I press.

As I reach for the car door handle, Nora steps aside and crosses her arms against her chest. When I look up, Brooke's gone.

"She assumed you were another reporter," Nora tells me in a hiss. "We've been hounded by those scoundrels since she's come home. Things here have nearly been impossible to deal with."

"Things?" I question. "What things?"

"Come in," she insists. "I'll get her for you. It's not my place to fill you in."

As we make our way up to the house, my heart can't find its rhythm. I haven't slept at all since arriving yesterday.

What if Brooke doesn't want to see me? What if she throws me out without a word of explanation? If I'm doomed to marry Kylee, I'd appreciate knowing why I'm being forced to.

Clearing my thoughts, I walk the long expanse of the drive in step with Nora Malloy.

As we walk inside Brooke's house, everything I remember about her comes back at once. Her taste, her touch, her voice... all of it. With only the hope of seeing her again, my stomach twists in both longing and regret. It's calming and confusing, all at the same time.

"Brooke, honey," Nora calls. "Someone's here to see you."

As Brooke rounds the corner to the foyer we're standing in, she drops the envelopes she'd been holding. They fall at her feet, but she doesn't look down. Her eyes widen, and shock takes over every feature of her face.

"Why?" she whispers so low I almost miss it. "What are you doing here?"

Turning to Nora, I wordlessly ask to be left alone. This works as Nora says, "I'll give you two a minute."

"Why?" Brooke pushes. "I left you," she says next, before her mother is out of the room.

Her summarization strikes a nerve. Hearing her admit she left me sitting in that restaurant alone doesn't come as a surprise, it comes as a stark reminder she wants nothing to do with me. However, I came all this way for an explanation, and I'll be damned if I don't get to hear it.

"Where the fuck did you go?"

"Where did I go?" she asks, her brows furrowed with confusion.

"Yes," I sneer. "*Why* did you go?"

"I came home, *Brock*," she smarts, gesturing her hands about the room.

"I get that, *Brooke*," I snap as she did. "But why? Why did you take off?"

Her lips get tight, narrowing themselves together and she doesn't answer.

"What the fuck?" I question again, this time taking a step toward her. The shine in her eyes hold her unshed tears. She's not unaffected with either being in my presence or having to answer for vanishing from it.

"Brock..." she grouses, but stops as her hand reaches her mouth to cover it.

"Why?" I push again, this time in a low, subtle plea. "I waited for you at the restaurant. The cameras were rolling the entire time. I wanted to ask—"

"No!" she shrieks. Her hands come up and out in front of her when I take another step in her direction. "Don't say it."

"I was going to ask you to marry me, Brooke. It was you."

"And now it's not," she says quietly. "You can't be here."

"Is there someone else? You didn't want to get married..."

"Not that," she assures after I can't quite get the words out. "I don't have anyone else. It just can't be you."

I don't get it. My chest is heavy. The confusion bears down like a heavy weight.

"Brooke," Nora addresses.

I turn around to find her mother standing alone in the mouth of the hall. Her eyes are pinned on Brooke, but her request is on my behalf. "I think you should tell Brock why you're home. I think he not only deserves to know, but he should hear it from you. Don't you agree?"

"Mom?" Brooke's tone reveals the hurt and betrayal. "Stop."

"Tell him about your father, honey. It's okay."

Brooke's head lowers. Her gaze hits the floor as her hands ball into fists at her sides.

"Brooke?" I whisper.

Just as I'm about to take another step toward her, her head lifts and countless tears fall against her cheeks. Other than the night I found her outside my room, I've never seen her cry. In comparison, this is so much worse. Her spirit is broken.

"I have to go," she announces. "I *need* to go," she says, this time stronger.

As she moves to pass me, I grab her arm, but she doesn't stop pressing to get away.

"Brock, no," Nora jumps in, so I release Brooke to watch her walk out the front door alone.

*What the fuck have I missed?*

"You see? She wasn't running away from someone. She was running toward someone."

"I get it."

Brooke's mother just finished filling me on everything I'd never have guessed. Over the last month and a half, while spending time with Brooke, I thought I understood the degree of admiration and love she held for her father. It wasn't until today that I learned not only are Brooke and her father close, but as far as she's concerned, he not only hangs the moon, he named all the stars after her.

"She talks about you guys a lot," I aimlessly advise. "She did, I mean. When we were together."

"They're very close. Brooke's always been the apple of her father's eye." Nora winks. "Her brother and myself have always tried to keep up with the two of them."

There's no anger in her reference for how close her daughter is to her husband—no trace of underlying jealousy at all. I imagine Nora has had years of watching them together and has come to appreciate them as they are.

"If you give Brooke time, as well as her father, they'll come around."

"He's going to be okay then?"

The way Nora had described his heart attack and the coma he fell into after, I hadn't taken his condition as good.

"He will. He has to wake up for this," she says.

"For this?"

"Yes, *this*," she charges, sitting up and leaning forward. "Decklan has never seen his daughter in love," she continues with a smile. "And if he hasn't already heard it in her voice, he will soon."

Guilt of our situation strikes. Her mom must not have any idea of what's happened, nor how it's all about to play out. Which is to say on live television, in front of hundreds of thousands of viewers.

"I need to see her," I advise. Running my hands through my hair, I feel my body readying to race to wherever Brooke could be. "Do you have any idea where she may have gone?"

"No, I don't. But I meant what I said. She'll come around. Be patient."

Giving her my card first, I stand and she follows, doing the same.

"I'm staying at a hotel in Triade. The name and number of my hotel and cell phone are on the back. I'll be in town as long as I think Brooke needs me. Tell her that for me, will you?"

"Of course. Anything else?"

Anything else?

*Tell her I love her.*

*Tell her I forgive her for leaving.*

*Tell her I need her to forgive me when I do the same.*

"No, that's all. Thanks again."

"Any time, Brock. Good luck."

# Chapter Fifty-Six

*Your heart will guide you where you need to be.*

*Brooke*

-

"Finally!" Addie exclaims her relief into the phone. "I haven't heard from you in a week!" she shrieks next. "Thank God everything is okay so I can forgive you now."

As I sit on the couch outside Dad's room, filling her in on his progress, explaining first that thirty minutes ago, he woke up. I wasn't here when, from out of nowhere, he opened his eyes, but thankfully Mom was. She called me as I was seeing to business at the inn. Mom was beside herself and could hardly speak through her thankful tears.

"So, he's going to be okay?" Addie probes, her hopes as high as mine.

"The doctor is with him now. So far, all he's said is that everything looks stable, but Dad still has some ways to go as far as recovery. I'm going in as soon as they're finished."

"How's your mom?"

"Ecstatic. She hasn't stopped crying, but she's relieved."

Addie exhales. "So am I."

Three days ago, after leaving Brock standing in the living room with my mother, I made my way to the inn. There, I was met with the angry eyes of my brother who tried to get me to call Brock and tell him me leaving was a mistake. I convinced him to let it alone. It took some time, and a few tears on my part, but he finally saw things as I did.

There's no easy way out of what's happened. Brock's destiny has been signed in ink. There are no loopholes to slide his way through. If Matt and Willow hadn't been as generous and understanding as they were, there wouldn't have been any for me, either.

"He came to see me at work," Addie advises quietly. "I was trying to give you space. I didn't tell or give him anything but your address. He looked so lost and confused."

"He knows we're over, Add. I saw him, too."

An exasperated sigh comes through the line before she says, "You told him you were done?"

"What am I supposed to tell him? I can't tell him it's okay for him to be here when he should be home, thinking about who he'll choose to pick a wife. That's crazy."

"Oh, Brooke."

She sounds as though I've let her down. But seriously, what other choice is there? Maybe my forethought into our future is born from self-preservation, or maybe denial, but Addie was there in L.A. with Brock and I. She was witness to what we were doing. There's no way she didn't see that what we were doing was wrong.

"I don't want to talk about it, okay? Sleeping with a man who wasn't engaged is one thing. Sleeping with one who is—"

"Do you at least know who he chose?" she questions, not caring that I haven't finished my thought.

When the nurse I've come to love steps out of my father's room and smiles wide, I cut Addie off with, "I have to go. I'll call or text when I'm finished here."

"Okay, honey. Tell your dad I'll come by this week and to get plenty of rest, because I'm bringing the UNO cards. Love you."

"Thanks, Add. He'll love that," I return. "Talk soon."

The sterile hospital room has more life in it now than I've been privy to since this started. As if my father can already tell something's not right, his head turns and he studies my way from the door.

"Button," he quietly breathes.

My name spoken in one word—one sentimental word of adoration—relaxes me. I feel the release of my pent-up emotions bursting out everywhere.

Walking toward him at a faster pace, I call out, "Well, thank God you're finally awake."

"You have so much to tell me." He smiles.

No matter the circumstance, this feels no different than any other time I've come home with a lot on my mind. In the past, it's always been Dad who I immediately go in search of to share whatever was happening. He's my moral compass; my sounding board when all else I tried on my own had failed.

The IV in his hand doesn't allow me to squeeze it as I'd like to. I hold it steady in mine regardless, and smile down at his tired and broken body with appreciation.

"I'll leave you two for a few minutes. I need to make some calls and find out where Ashton's gone," Mom offers before leaning down over Dad and kissing his cheek like I've seen her do a million times.

"You stay in bed. Do what the doctor says, and I'll be back soon," she tells him.

"I don't have anywhere else to go, Nora. I'll be here."

"Brooke," she sternly addresses. "We'll talk later."

In a turn, I've gone from thankful daughter to scorned child standing in between her parents. Obviously, I've got a severe talking to coming. Being as I'm an adult, I'm not afraid of the consequences of my actions.

*I'm twenty-six, not twelve.*

"We'll be here." I smile brightly, hiding my inner thoughts.

Once she's gone, I turn around and get a better look at Dad. He's smiling, but it's for my benefit. His lips are chapped and his skin is pale, but it doesn't stop his determination to discuss what's on his mind. I feel parental lecture part one about to play out, and he's only just woken up.

"You look different, Button," he tells me first. "I don't know if you're happy or sad. Have I been gone so long I can no longer read you like I used to?"

"You haven't been gone," I laugh. "You never left. You were resting." Squeezing his hand tighter than I should, I freely admit, "I've missed you so much."

"You came back," he observes. "Your mother says you left everything behind in a rush."

Furrowing my eyebrows, my confusion comes with my response. "Of course I did. You were sick."

"I was fine."

Rolling my eyes at his absurdity, I confirm, "Yes, I left. The show was almost finished anyway."

"And you had fun?"

Now that Dad's better and the burden of worry has lifted from my shoulders, I pull up a chair and sit next to him. I don't know where to begin, but now that he's awake, there will be plenty of time to catch up.

"I had a lot of fun. I met a lot of people and saw a lot of places I wouldn't have seen if I hadn't gone."

Dad moves his hand from mine, but only to aid in sitting up further. The wince of pain strikes his face, and I feel bad for talking so much about myself.

"I'll come back later. We can catch up then."

Dad looks to the door, then back to me. "We'll talk now. Your mother filled me in on all things Brock LaDuece."

He says his name, which is not only surprising, but the way he said it was sincere.

"She did?"

"Of course she did. She's concerned."

Shaking my head, I insist, "She shouldn't be concerned. No one should. I'm fine."

Reaching up, Dad pecks my nose with the tip of his finger. My face scrunches. The gesture isn't meant to make me feel small, but it does.

"I want to know something, Brooke," he insists. "And I want you to be honest with me, if not yourself."

"Okay," I reply meekly.

Dad grabs my hand and looks at me with a serious expression before clearing his throat. "You may not think any of this is my concern, but I can assure you it is."

"Yeah?"

"Yeah," he answers. "Mom told me Brock came here to see you. Is this right?"

He knows it is. Mom wouldn't lie about something like that. This is how Dad gets me to talk about things I don't want to discuss. He makes me own up to every facet of whatever situation I've found myself in.

"He's still here. He's in Triade."

"Did you talk to him?"

"Yes." I briefly told him goodbye, but don't admit this.

"How did he take the news of you ending things with him?"

"Um..." I trail off, unable to think fast enough. Brock and Mom talked after my mad dash from the house.

"Brooklyn Paige Malloy," he states sternly. I much prefer Button.

"He told Mom he wasn't leaving," I admit. "Then he wanted to know if there was anything he could do."

"Interesting," Dad comments. His smile doesn't reach his eyes, but those same eyes are certainly dancing with humor.

Releasing his hand and sitting back in my chair, I cross my arms over my chest and wait.

"Your mother didn't tell me everything there was to know, did she?"

*That I've fallen in love with Brock?* No, she must not have mentioned this.

*That he's set to marry someone else because I up and left with good reason?* She must've left that out, too.

*Or, maybe from the moment my dad opened his eyes and I knew he'd be okay, I've regretted leaving Brock with my cheap, generic version of goodbye.* No, she couldn't have told him this because I just realized it myself.

"No," I answer. "I don't think she filled you in."

"You know, kiddo, I don't think there's ever been a time in your life that I've seen you glow," he notes, to my initial panic.

My first thought at hearing him say 'glow' lends itself to pregnancy. However, I'm on birth control, and Brock and I have always used a condom—well, except a few times. The first being the limo, and when he took what I let him have, which he did gloriously. In front of my *father,* my face heats with remembrance.

*Jesus.*

"Scared you, didn't I?" He smirks.

"Noooo," I draw out for exaggeration. "I'm not pregnant, Dad."

"Well, thank God for that."

"Aren't you tired?" I smart my rhetorical question while pretending to be serious.

Dad laughs. It's quiet, and his body doesn't shake with it because of his weakened state.

"When I say you glow, I mean to say I've never seen you in love."

*In love.*

Am I so transparent?

"Dad, you hardly—"

"Don't tell a father he doesn't see what he sees in his children. You'd be wasting your breath. You've fallen in love."

"Things aren't so simple."

"They are if you live in the now, sweetheart. And even though I'm so happy to see your bright face again, I'd be happier if you'd go share your time with a man who cared enough to travel the country to ensure my daughter was okay."

Tears well in my eyes. I know where Brock is. I also know if I went to him, told him how I felt, we'd be no better off than we are now. Eventually, he'll leave me, go back to L.A., get married, and live his life. I'll be left here alone, trying to pick up the pieces of whatever we've lost.

"I'm not sure that's a good idea."

"It's not," Dad convincingly admits. "But me, all but putting you on that plane myself didn't feel like such a good idea either. I've been worried sick."

"I'm sorry."

"No, Button." He smiles. "There's nothing for you to apologize for. I wanted you to live and you have. You still would be if I wasn't stuck in here. Go to him, Brooke. Talk to the man. I'd like to meet him, if that's possible."

"You'd like to meet him?"

Dad's eyebrows furrow this time. "Well, of course I would. Your mother and I both."

*Oh God.*

"I'll see what I can do," I tell him. "Addie's coming by this week. She told me to tell you to rest because she's busting out the UNO cards."

My dad, clearly not accepting the subject change, instructs, "I'll rest once you're on your way to where you already know you should be. Give your father a hug, and go do exactly as he's told you."

With a faint smile, I do as he's asked, all while thinking how annoying it is that Brock and my dad are just as bossy as the other.

# Chapter Fifty-Seven

*Brock*

-

"No, I think I'll stick around here for a few more days." I'm explaining this to Drew as I sit in my hotel room, drinking another beer, and wondering who the hell I'm sticking around for.

With no word from Brooke in three days, my patience is waning. Even with her reaction as I showed up at her house, I still left with hope. Nora Malloy is in part how Addie described her— quietly reserved and partially uptight. However, not exactly the way I initially thought. The woman is a mother who loves her children, wants what's best for them, even if they can't see what's best for themselves. The way she insisted Brooke would come around eventually said a lot about their relationship. She was certain it would happen. So, rather than catch a plane the next morning, I've decided to give her a few more days.

Unfortunately, that's all I can afford her because I'm running out of time.

"Fuck, Brock. But really? Why the hell does it have to be Kylee?" he snaps.

When I broke the news to my friends that the audience poll was now official, and the announcement of my future bride would be aired in a few days, I thought Drew was going to get sick. We were all sitting around Drew's living room table, trying to think of what I could say to Brooke to change her mind once I got here.

Until now, both my friends have been supportive, but eventually their support won't be enough to shield me from my impending future.

"Yeah. Still don't have your head around it either, do you?"

"No," he sighs. "That she-dog is easy on the eyes, sure, but damn, I bet she breathes fire."

This, I agree with. She's a fire-breathing, man-eating bitch. And this is my future wife I'm describing. I don't foresee good things to come, as I don't expect her to change.

"Your dad hasn't found anything that could help?"

"Nope. Not yet."

When my dad called earlier and advised me that Darrin had hit a wall in finding anything pertinent which could get me out of this, I wanted to throw my phone to the floor and stomp on it like a child. The defeat in his voice in telling me he had nothing mirrored mine as I thanked him again for trying.

Before letting me off the phone, he wanted to know if I thought Matt or Willow knew of any name Kylee may have used in the past. When I told him I had no clue, he then admitted that pushing me to marry wasn't the best parental decision he's ever made. I didn't agree and still don't. If it hadn't been for his interference, I wouldn't have met Brooke.

"Should I fly back out to L.A. for the finale?" Drew inquires. "Nick said he wants to take the week off so we can be there to wish you well."

"I appreciate the offer, but I'll be back in Dallas as soon as it's over. I'll see you guys then."

I haven't spoken to Kylee about where we'll live. As far as I'm concerned, there's no reason for her to come to Dallas. Our marriage is only temporary. Even if I have to live in misery with the press until the divorce is final, it'll be worth it not to have her near my family, in my house, or in my bed.

"If there's anything I can do, Brock. Me or Nick, you say the word."

"No more fuckin' poker parties, asshat."

Drew laughs. "Right. Definitely not. No more dares, either," he agrees, just as room service knocks on my door.

"Gotta eat. I'll call you if something changes."

"Hope it does, 'cause seriously, Kylee?"

"Asshat," I mumble, disconnecting and tossing my phone to the table.

As I open the door, fully expecting to find my dinner, I'm taken aback. It's not room service.

Brooke's standing just outside my door. She's clutching the handle to a small, black suitcase, which sits at her side. She looks happier, livelier, than the last time I saw her at home.

"He's awake," she breathes. "Dad woke up."

Her face is flushed, and her smile is wide; her relief undeniable.

"Brooke," I whisper.

I don't know what else to say. The woman I love, who I've come all this way to see again, is standing outside my hotel door, and I can't put together a cohesive thought.

"Can I come in?" she prompts, straightening the bag in her other hand. "Can we talk?"

Looking down, taking in all she's brought with her, I question, "Are you going somewhere?"

Shaking her head, she smirks. "No, Brock."

As I step to the side, Brooke aims to rush past me. I grab the suitcase and bag before she can get away, then settle them in the corner. As I turn around, I don't get a single word out before she's at my chest. Her arms are draped over my shoulders as she stands on her tiptoes, clutching me as if I'll disappear.

"Hey there," I greet, taking in the smell of her hair, the scent of her skin, and the feel of her body against mine.

My hands reach to her waist, where I try to push her away, but Brooke's having none of it. It's not until I hear her quiet sob and feel her body's subtle trembles that I know she's crying.

"I..." she hiccups. "I'm so sorry, Brock. This is all my fault."

Stepping back, her hands cup my cheeks as I stay quiet and take her in.

Her eyebrows are furrowed as she scans my face. "When are you leaving? When do you have to go..."

"Back to L.A.?" I fill in when her words trail off. "Three days."

"So soon," she utters. "Three days is so soon."

It is, but only now that she's with me. An hour ago, I was contemplating, counting the minutes until I left.

"Why are you here?"

Brooke takes one step back, then another. The distance between us serves as a reminder to all I've been missing. I hate how much I've missed her. Using both hands, I reach out and grab her waist. She stumbles into my chest, bracing her hands there for balance.

"I'm here because there's nowhere else I want to be," she quietly admits. "And Dad's okay right now, so I packed my bag and took a chance you'd want—"

"Yes," I cut her off. "I'm not here because I like Iowa, Brooke."

When a small smirk tips her lips, my mouth crashes down on hers. She doesn't hesitate. She opens, inviting me in as she always has, but this time, she's attempting to take control. Her soft lips and gentle moans ignite an already fueling flame. My hand fists her hair. When my other reaches her waist, the skin beneath her shirt welcomes it.

Grabbing the hem and lifting it over her head, my greed demands, "Everything off. All of it."

Momentarily she studies me, but says nothing more. Without waiting, I grab my shirt from behind my shoulders, then toss it to the floor. With appreciation, she bites her bottom lip, looking up at me as if for the first time. My cock strains against my jeans, rigid and aching to be inside her. When I step close, the hasty and painful score of her fingernails glide down my stomach until she reaches the button and zipper of my jeans.

"How long can you stay?" I curtly question, stepping into her before pushing her on the bed. When she doesn't answer, I find her eyes are soft and appreciative. "Baby, tell me how long?"

"I'm here until you leave," she explains, then robotically adds, "I thought there would be more time."

"Hey," I call. She's lying on the bed, her weight held beneath her elbows, and she looks lost. "What's wrong?"

"I couldn't remember what you looked like," she admits. Her gaze stays trained to mine in reflection.

"What?"

"I just realized I couldn't remember your face," she adds.

Crawling up on top of her, I brace my elbows on either side of her head and use my thumbs to wipe away the tears.

"I'm here now, right?"

She nods and swallows hard.

"Help me," I prod, using one hand to remove the rest of her clothes.

Once we've settled, I slide into her without warning. She gasps, but spreads her thighs to grant me further access. My mouth tastes the skin of her neck, while my hands explore her body. My mind burns every part of her to memory.

"Three days, Brooke," I tell her. Reaching beneath her, I cup her ass in both hands, then tilt her hips in line with mine, lending room to drive in harder, deeper. "For now, don't think past that."

When she locks her ankles, securing them tightly behind my back, she grabs my face and brings it to hers, where her kiss serves as her promise.

*Three fucking days.*

*Seventy-two hours.*

*Then time as we know it ends.*

And, eventually, all I'll have left are these moments of memory with a great girl who made me laugh, frustrated me to no end, but loved me the only way she knew how.

*Fuck you, Karma. Fuck you, Fate.*

Three days left.

# Chapter Fifty-Eight

*He's going to meet my family.*

*Brooke*

-

"She's awake," I hear Brock tell the lie into the room before I have a chance to open my eyes.

The bright sun is casting its harsh rays against the bed I'm still comfortable in. The subtle sounds of the television play in the background.

*Baseball.*

"After she gets her ass up and moving to eat, I'll bring her by," he says next.

Lifting my head, I watch Brock toss random pieces of clothing into a pile next to the dresser. He's up and showered, but hasn't shaved. When he smiles and winks, I almost miss the fact that he has my phone.

*My phone.*

"Who is it? Who are you talking to?"

*Who is he making plans with?*

"All right," he bids, then waits as the caller speaks. "It's no problem at all. I'm happy to help," he says next. "See you then."

Tossing the phone to the hotel chair, Brock turns to me with an expression I can't place.

"That was your brother."

"Ashton?"

Brock walks slowly to get closer. His playful smirk wreaks havoc on my already aching body.

"Yep. He called twice. When your phone went off the second time, you didn't budge, so I answered."

I didn't hear it. After all that's happened over the last two weeks, I was finally able to get a good night's sleep. Maybe it's because Dad waking up came as such relief, or maybe because I spent last night with Brock holding me tightly against him. Either way, I'm thankful for it.

"Is my dad okay?"

"He is," he assures. "But Ashton said he's awake, and he's waiting for you."

No, he's not.

Dad's awake and waiting to meet Brock, Ashton meant to say. I know my dad, and the way we left things yesterday, I also know he'll soon get impatient.

Sitting up, I run my fingers through my hair, then rest my arms over my knees. Brock takes a step forward, but not in my direction. He gets comfortable in the chair not far from the bed. I bite my lip to keep from laughing.

"What's funny?" he questions, sounding almost irritated.

Pointing to this chest, I note, "I gave you another hickey."

Brock smiles, but doesn't look down. "Bloodsucker," he jokes. "Saw it when I showered."

Noticing the space between us, I ask, "Is everything okay?"

His just jovial expression morphs to suddenly pained.

"Brock?" I push.

"We're down to two," he says quietly. "I leave Wednesday morning."

"I know," I confirm, with a sadness I don't bother masking.

Last night after sex, Brock and I talked, but it wasn't about plans for the future. We lay in bed, talking as we always did. He asked about my dad, so I explained his long road ahead to recovery. Brock talked about his family and friends, and how nice it was to see them again.

Neither of us mentioned the future, already knowing ours was undoubtedly about to end.

"There are things to say," he advises.

My voice trembles when I reply. "I'm not ready to say them."

"I'm not either," he agrees. "But before we leave this room, we should."

"Can I shower first?"

Brock smiles. "Am I invited?"

Shaking my head, knowing what's to come, I say, "Talk first, play later."

Looking down at his chest, he studies his new mark. He's wearing only a pair of old jeans—no shirt or socks. His hair has grown since I last saw him. It's not styled for the cameras, but rather it's been left wavy and natural.

Without looking at me, Brock says, "My dad is helping. He's looking into the contract and doing what he can to get me out of it."

This comes as a surprise, considering his dad is the one who pushed him so hard to get married. "Your dad is helping?"

"A lot has happened," he says.

He's right. Uninvited events have detoured everything I thought was going to play out. I would've told Brock yes. I didn't believe this before Dad got sick, but I believe it now.

"You're going to get married." I needlessly remind him.

Leaning up, bracing his elbows to his knees, Brock laces his fingers together.

"I'll get married," he assures. "But only if there's nothing I can do to stop it."

Swallowing hard, I brace for his answer before I've even asked. "Who will you choose now?"

Kate. I know it's Kate. Part of me will be happy for him. She's so nice and sweet— genuinely so.

"I'm not choosing anyone, Brooke. Because none of them matter. Whoever the audience picks, fine. But I don't want anyone else."

Standing, Brock takes two steps in my direction. My eyes cloud with tears, realizing that in two days all of this will be gone. There won't be his voice, his laugh, his touch, or us together. Not anymore.

Sitting at my side, Brock rests his hand on mine. "I told Ashton I'd bring you by the hospital."

"Then let me shower so we can go."

"Brooke, honey, shouldn't you and Brock be heading out soon?" my mother suggests quietly. She's standing next to my dad, who's sitting up in the hospital recliner, reading the paper. When he peers over its edges, he finds me standing next to Brock and winks.

"He has an early flight tomorrow morning," Dad remembers.

They all know what's about to happen and not by my voice either. Brock wasted no time in shaking both my parents' hands, then Ashton's, before he spoke the inevitable truth into a room filled with my family. Eventually, they'd have found out anyway, but hearing him break the news to them the way he did was rough.

*Rough.*

My dad's jaw ticked, my mom's eyes widened, and my brother walked out of the room without so much as a word, good or bad. An hour passed before Ashton found his way back with a deck of cards in his hands. I assume he used this time to calm down since he walked in a lot less angry than he walked out.

*Thank you, God.*

"Yeah, we're going," I return, not about to chance a look in Brock's direction.

Ashton and Brock are still sitting at the small round table playing cards. The two haven't said much to each other, but Dad's been at Brock with non-stop questions about his life in Dallas, the show, and his future plans. All this led me to shoving the morning paper in his lap and my request for him to tell us about next week's weather.

"We'll head back to the hotel when you're ready," Brock assures.

Ashton, obviously sensing I could use a distraction, grabs the television remote and flips it on. Muted sounds of commercials dance across the screen as everyone goes back to what they were doing.

"Jason came by here earlier," Mom announces, and my jaw drops. "He came to check on your Dad and find out if you'd be coming to visit him today."

The clearing of Brock's throat focuses me to drop my head and look to him. "Jason is my—"

"Ex," Brock clips. "Got it."

"He's an idiot," Mom announces, much to Brock's satisfaction. "Anyway, we sent him on his way. Can't say he'll be visiting again anytime soon," she states casually, running her fingers through Dad's hair as he ignores her for whatever he's reading.

"Do you think you're really going to have to marry one of those women?" my brother questions, throwing down another card. "And if you do, do you get to choose?"

"He doesn't," I assert.

"I was going to choose Brooke," Brock informs, doing the same as Ashton and tossing in another card. "That's not an option anymore," he says quietly. "So, yeah. I'm going to have to marry one of those girls."

"That's messed up," my brother comments. When his eyes come to mine, the support in his gaze is there as always. "So, what happens between you two?"

Brock lays down all his cards before standing. His heavy sigh is heard, and my dad steps in for reassurance.

"Things work out the way they're supposed to, Ashton. Leave Brooke and Brock alone."

As Brock explained to my parents the role his dad was playing in trying to get him out of the contract, my parents took this in and appeared seemingly relieved. At least if Brock is forced to marry someone, it wasn't because he hadn't tried to get out of it.

"Brock," My father drops the paper and extends his hand. "If there's anything you need from us before you go…"

My dad stops talking as Ashton rudely turns up the television. The sound of Matt's voice so close after being away this long causes a daunting shiver to crawl up my spine. He's standing in the same room Brock and I saw each other for the first time. No one is with him as he stands alone in front of the camera with that million-dollar plastic smile.

"Shut it off," I snap, but I'm ignored. "I don't want..."

As my words trail off, a photo of Kylee Simmons comes first, front and center, before it's positioned at the side. She's wearing a small red dress and clutching a diamond studded purse.

Next, a picture of Brock enters the screen before it's positioned at her side. He's wearing a suit. I remember it being one he wore right after the tapings had begun.

"They chose her," I whisper to no one. The ticker at the bottom of the screen reads, 'Kylee Simmons to marry Brock LaDuece in this season's Marry A Millionaire.'

Bile and anger make its way to the back of my throat, sitting there twirling like dead weight before I finally gasp for a shred of air. My heart beats heavily in my chest as I drop my focus from the television screen, only to find Brock carefully waiting for my reaction.

*He already knew.*

"Her?" my brother spits, turning from the television to Brock. "She's such a little bitch!"

"Ashton!" Mom admonishes. "Mouth!"

"She's awful," he sends back without delay. "You said it yourself."

"Brock, I'm sorry," my mom apologizes. For what, I don't know.

Leaving Brock's heavy gaze, I turn back to the screen. A picture of Evan, in all his stated glory comes as Kylee's did. The next picture is Leslie. Barbie girl number two. The screen settles their pictures together as well. 'Leslie Miles to marry bachelor number two, Evan.'

*Dear God, it's all really happening.*

Standing, I run my hands down my thighs to dry them. Brock stands as well and comes to me in quick steps. His hands grasp my shoulders, and his head positions back and forth in an attempt to get me to look at him, but I can't.

"I need a ride back home," I whisper to myself. In my panic, I finally meet his eyes. They're soft, gentle, but above all, *knowing*. He knew this was coming, and he said nothing. "Can you take me home?"

Nodding, he holds me steady and turns to my parents, where Dad speaks first. "Son, I'm not sure what your dad can do, but tell him to do something."

Brock doesn't answer, but nods, then turns to look at my mom. She's got her hand on my dad's shoulder, biting her bottom lip as her eyes flood with tears—for me.

"Good luck, Brock," she murmurs before we turn to go.

Brock's going to marry Kylee Simmons, head bitch of reality television and heartless cow to those who know her as I do. He's leaving in less than twelve hours, and I'll never see him again.

I want to go home.

# Chapter Fifty-Nine

*No, really. Fuck my life.*

*Brock*

-

The ride home is quiet. Brooke hasn't said a word since I grabbed the keys from her hand and loaded her in the car.

As soon as I looked up and saw Matt Sutton on the hospital television screen, readying to make the announcement, I knew there was nothing more I could do to shield Brooke from the truth.

*Kylee fucking Simmons.*

"Baby, I'll fix this," I express in false assurance.

If my dad can't find a hole in that contract in less than seventy-two hours, the wedding will go on. I'll have lost Brooke, along with my self-respect, and the respect of those who've stood by me.

"You can't fix this," she replies, sullen with truth and drowning in doubt. "You heard Matt. Everyone did."

Grabbing her hand, I squeeze it gently.

Brooke stares out the window as we finally make it to the hotel. With the same sad voice, she opens the door while whispering, "It's been a shitty week. I almost lost my dad, and the man I love is leaving in the morning to get married."

Fuck, that hurt.

Grabbing her hand on the way to my room, I stay a step in front of her. The same solemn spirit I recognize from the day I arrived is back. She's broken, and once again I'm the cause.

Brooke passes me as she enters, skipping over the lights. It's dark with only the moon coming through the curtains.

"I can take you home," I offer. "If you need to go, I'll understand."

"No," she returns, heading toward the bathroom and removing her shirt before she gets to the door. "I'm going to shower."

While Brooke's busy, I grab my phone. I'm hopeful for word from my dad, but the only text I have is from Tate.

Tate 06:47 p.m.: *Have you thought about running away?*

The answer is yes.

Fuck. Yes.

# Chapter Sixty

*How long does it take for your heart to forgive you?*

*Brooke*

-

"Man, Willow looks good. How old is she, anyway?" Sam questions, holding the tub of popcorn to her chest, not looking at any of us as she voices her curiosity. She's studying the screen as if the breaking of my heart isn't being broadcasted for the world to see.

"Forty, maybe?" Addie answers.

My mind is numb. My heart is crushed. My spirit is broken.

The weariness I've succumbed to continues as Kylee's face is plastered across the screen, showcasing her plastic smile. The other girls I came to know during my time there are all sitting behind her in high-rise chairs. Ryleigh is smiling, though it's not real. Emilee is scowling in Kylee's direction, not caring that the cameras can see her. The others are sitting straight, not offering so much as a glance to the audience.

"He looks mortified," Addie observes. "As in, he's about to throw up."

"Wouldn't you?" Sam counters. "Kylee is the devil in a dress. Why did the audience choose her, anyway? I mean, really. The woman is awful."

"She's going to hurt him," I whisper between us from my middle seat on the couch. "He doesn't want this."

"No, honey," Addie replies, wrapping her arm around my shoulders and pulling me to her. "He doesn't."

"Oh God. I'm such a witch," Sam breathes, sitting up and freeing her hands. She turns to me and says, "The wedding is next weekend. I'm getting married, and yet I'm sitting here watching the man you love marry someone else."

Smiling, though it's small, I reply, "This doesn't change anything about your big day, Sam. No way. Everything that's happened happened for a reason, right?"

Shaking her head, she returns, "No, Brooke. Everything that's happened is shit luck. I'm sorry."

"Well," I tell her, reaching for the remote and clicking the television off. "What's done is done, and if you don't mind, I think I'd like to be alone, if that's okay."

Patting my thigh, Addie eases my sadness, if only a little. "For what it's worth, he picked you. I know that probably doesn't make any of this okay, but it's the truth. He loves you, Brooke. Take at least some comfort in that."

Tears fill my eyes, but I don't allow them to fall. Taking heed in Addie's truth does help. Not much, but it does.

"I'll be fine. You two go on home. I'll call you tomorrow."

"We have the final fitting in the morning. If you can't make it—"

Cutting Sam off, I advise, "I'll be there, I promise. And by the time the sun comes up, I'm going to be back to the person you remember."

She doesn't believe me. Neither of my friends do.

"If you're not the old Brooke, that's okay," Addie jokes. "I like the new girl. She's crazy."

"You're crazy," I retort.

Sam isn't deterred by my façade. "I'm so sorry," she says, pulling me in for another hug.

"Go home. I'll see you both tomorrow."

An hour later, I'm still sitting in front of the television. It's not on, but I haven't found the motivation to move. Not because I don't have a thousand things I should be doing, but because why bother? My mind is heavy, and my heart is breaking.

Pulling out my phone, I check for messages to find only one. It was sent from Brock right before the show began.

Brock 06:51 p.m.: *I love you. Don't give up on me.*

Letting the tears finally fall, I run my fingertips over the screen, as if I can feel his doing the same.

Then I type my final response before blocking his number from my phone.

Me 07:48 p.m.: *Congratulations, Brock. Be happy.*

After I've blocked his number and removed him from my contacts, I shut the phone off completely, lay it down, close my eyes, and pray he doesn't find me in my dreams.

# Chapter Sixty-One

*Who the hell is Leah Wilson?*

*Brock*

-

"You'll stand here, and Kylee will meet you as soon as the music starts," Jerry explains, pointing to the door my soon-to-be wife and forever she-devil will enter.

Over the past two days, Jerry has transformed from an uptight assistant to a complete head case. He's been popping antacids like Skittles, and clutching the same bottle of thick, pink liquid as if it's the last bottle ever made to be sold.

"I'm ready, Jerry," I reassure him again. Looking around the decorated area where I'll pledge my oath as a husband for as long as I have to, I ask, "Where's Clive?"

I wouldn't let anyone from home come to witness my demise. The live broadcast will hurt them enough. I would find some comfort in Clive's company, though.

"He's on his way," Jerry promises. "There have been some..." Pausing, he looks to the sky while curling his top lip. "I've heard there are some ends to be clipped before we can officially start. Matt invited last year's couple back tonight to start things off. We have time."

"Ends to clip?"

Nodding, he brushes me off with, "No worries. Everything is set."

Scanning the area, I notice that not only is Clive missing, but also Matt and Willow. To be honest, the only people around is Taylor, the one man makeup brigade, and Kate.

Kate's standing by the door, leaning against its jamb, and watching me closely.

"I'll be back. Sit tight. There's a bar across the way." Jerry points to a gazebo. The bartender on duty looks as bored as I am stressed. "Have yourself a stiff drink, Brock. It'll most likely be your last as a single man."

Hearing him put it like that, my stomach twists.

"Thanks," I reply, walking around him and toward Kate.

Once I approach, her curious gaze finds mine. She's up to something. The sweet face I've come to appreciate in the midst of all this shit appears both full of mischief and excitement. I don't share in either.

"Kate," I call. "Where are the other girls?"

Still smirking, she answers, "Wardrobe."

"You okay?"

"I'm okay," she states simply. "Brock, Kylee is awful."

Smiling for the first time today, I reply, "She is."

"She's evil," she adds, looking down. "Do you know who Evan chose?"

Evan's happy nuptials follow directly after mine. I don't know who he chose, nor do I care in the least.

"I have no idea."

When Kate's eyes come back to mine, her expression softens. "I heard something."

Intrigued, I ask, "Oh yeah?"

"Yeah. I heard Matt in his office this morning. He was yelling at Willow."

I don't particularly care for Willow, but knowing she may be getting her ass reamed, I don't like Matt now either.

"I think the show is in for another twist."

Shit. I'm so tired of these 'twists.' "What?"

"I'm going to congratulate you now in case I don't see you later." Kate's small body shakes with her giggle. Women make me suspicious. Lifting her hand, she waves. "Good luck, Brock."

As she walks away, I turn in the other direction to go see about that drink.

"Brock, you got a minute?" Matt pulls my attention away from Taylor, also saving me from another round of last minute face powder. Taylor huffs and rolls his eyes, but steps back.

"What's up?"

His jaw tightens. Through clenched teeth, he hisses, "We have a problem."

*What now?*

"I didn't do it," I clip. "Whatever it is, I had nothing to do with it."

Nodding, relaxing only a little, he assures, "No, I know. But—"

Before he can finish, an extremely irate Kylee bursts through the door, wearing only a white silk robe and a pair of god awful fuzzy slippers. Her hair is in rollers, her makeup half done, and her expression is furious. Not for the first time, I wonder how someone can look as she does but be so insecure she thrives to bring others down.

"Matt!" she shrieks, coming at us in a rapid pace. "Matt!" she calls again as he keeps his gaze on mine before rolling his eyes and turning around.

"What the fuck?" I ask, now standing at his side. "What's happening?"

Leaning closer, he advises, "Let me handle this."

When he turns to Clive, who I finally see smiling ear to ear and coming up behind Kylee, Matt nods. Clive bends to grab his camera, props it up on his shoulder, and starts to tape.

"I thought tonight was supposed to be live?"

"Oh, it will be. But we'll want this for later."

Matt's sudden feigned relaxed state causes my pulse to quicken. *So, really. What the fuck?*

"You had no right to do that!" Kylee snaps, getting in Matt's face once she's close.

I step back, wanting in no way to be a target of her fury.

Pointing her finger to his chest, she claims, "What happened prior to any of this was none of your business."

"It absolutely was my business," Matt replies, as if bored. "You lied, Kylee. You signed that contract."

"Lied?" I pipe up with vested interest. "Lied about what?"

Kylee turns to me, smiling sweetly and aiming to look innocent. "Nothing," she answers. "This is all just a small misunderstanding."

I like misunderstandings, those that could potentially free me from this mess, anyway.

"Matt," she addresses calmly. "I need to talk to you." Looking to me, she speaks, but her words are still for him. "I need to talk to you in private."

"We have nothing to talk about, Kylee. It's done. Over."

"Over?" I question.

*Jesus Christ, what's over?*

Turning in place, Matt nods to me. I don't know what that means, so I probe, "Matt, what's happening?"

"Brock, to make up for this, we're inviting you back next year. If you'd be willing to come back, that is."

"Come back?"

"No!" Kylee screams. Her hair is starting to fall from its rollers. Her hands shake at her sides, and her usually flawless face turns a nasty shade of putrid gray.

"Brock, you're not getting married."

Blinking twice, I find his words impossible, but hopeful.

"I'm not getting married," I confirm for myself, tasting the promise and savoring its meaning.

Coming up from behind Kylee, Willow appears just as angry. Her face is pensive, her posture rigid.

"Kylee, let's go now," Willow demands. "You're done."

"I'm not done!" she shrieks. "I'm getting married!"

Her face has contorted to utter fear. The woman I once thought had too much confidence looks downright terrified not to be getting what she wants. If all this is right and I'm not marrying this lunatic, I dodged one hell of a fucking bullet.

Slowing her roll, Kylee's entire demeanor morphs from anger to defeat.

Turning in place, Matt and I watch Kylee being led out of the area, not only by Willow, but also two overly enthused security guards. When one reaches to grab her arm, she fists her hand and pulls herself from his grasp. Turning in place, she levels her eyes to Willow and hisses something I miss.

Matt and I stand and watch as she loses a slipper on her way, but doesn't look back to claim it. Thank fuck I'm not her Prince Charming anymore. I'm not touching the damn thing.

"What the hell was that?"

"That was..." Matt stops, smiles, then covers his mouth with his hand. "That was desperation. Her name isn't Kylee Simmons. Her given name is Leah Wilson."

"Leah Wilson? As in the *ex-cheerleader*?"

*What?*

I watch a lot of sports, baseball mainly, but I had heard the story of a rogue cheerleader out of Seattle who'd been jailed a few years ago for stalking a player *in* his home. She'd approached his wife and children on several occasions, going so far as to applying for a job as their nanny, even though the position was never posted.

"This will make headlines, I think," he justifies.

"You hope," I correct. "And headlines will—"

"Will help Willow with her ratings," he finishes.

"Son of a bitch," I mumble.

"So, you're free. I hope you consider coming back next season. The viewers at home loved you. They'll feel sorry for you after hearing about this."

"I'm not coming back, Matt." I don't have to think twice. He knows this, I'm sure.

Confirming, he replies. "Well, then. You're free to go get your girl. Give my best to Brooke, will you?"

*Hell yes, I'm going to get my girl.*

Shaking his hand, I smile the first true smile I have since I left her in the first place. "Good luck, Matt. Tell Willow the same."

I don't wait for his response, but rather turn in place to ask Clive for a much needed ride out of this crazy town and all the madness that dwells within it.

# Chapter Sixty-Two

*My dad is a traitor.*

*One week later...*

*Brooke*

-

"Are you sure you don't want another drink?" Sam asks, grabbing the chair next to mine before taking a seat. Elbows to the table, her hand holding her chin, she tells me, "I'll have the bartender make whatever you want."

Brushing her sweet offer away, I advise, "I'm okay. I'm not staying too much longer. When do you throw the bridal bouquet?"

"Soon."

Sam's wedding was beautiful, the reception fun, and finally the evening is almost over. I studiously completed all of the maid of honor duties. I spent all morning prepping with the others and doting on what a beautiful bride Sam made, along with gloating about how gorgeous her groom was. I stood at her side in the mirror, reassuring all her last minute doubts, while ignoring the pangs of jealousy and heartache in longing for what she had.

My family showed up in the nick of time. My brother was wearing a suit, my dad a nice shirt and khakis, and my mom wore her Sunday best. I nearly broke.

It's been a week since Brock left a *felon* at the altar before Willow made the announcement of 'complications which caused the season for Brock to come to an end.' The reporters have been relentless toward Kylee and her past life's indiscretions. Some went as far as to personally ridicule the audience's chosen bride for Brock.

I'll admit, the image of Kylee Simmons sporting orange prison gear, if only for the term of ninety days, made my broken heart smirk in rebellion.

When Addie came storming into the inn after seeing the episode, her intent was to give me the inside story. Adamantly, not wanting to hear a word about it, good or bad, I pushed her away. She was startled at my reaction, citing this was good news, great news, and that I should be excited. She went on to counsel me about calling Brock at once, then book a flight to wherever he was. But, in truth, after the last few months of drama and heartache, I had nothing else to give.

And I still don't.

"You look sad," Sam comments, running her hand through the back of my hair. "I wish you'd rethink--"

Shaking my head as tears fill my eyes, I cut her off. "Sam, no."

"Talk to her, Addie," Sam exhales, sitting back in her chair with defeat. "I need to find Sean. I don't want him worrying that I've fled the scene."

The touch of Addie's hand to my shoulder doesn't help. Addie takes the seat Sam leaves before grabbing a random glass of champagne from the table and downing it quickly. Once finished, she wipes her mouth with the back of her hand and slumps her shoulders.

"Nothing from Brock?" she questions for the eleventh time this evening.

"Addie," I whine. "No."

I blocked his number. She doesn't know this, and there's no reason to explain my reason in doing so. They're mine.

"You know..." She smiles.

Have I mentioned I hate her smiles?

"What?"

"Brad Woodbury came to tell the happy couple congratulations."

Rolling my eyes, I sit back and pin her with my best third grade evil eye.

Raising her hands in surrender, Addie promises, "I said nothing. But, he's alone."

"Again, Addie. Stop."

Shrugging, she gives in and says nothing else.

An hour later, I'm still sitting at the same table alone, scanning the crowd. Addie is dancing with my dad, a faster song than I'd prefer he jive to considering he was just released from the hospital after a heart attack that had him in a coma for the longest six days of my life. My brother is standing near the bar, probably wishing he was old enough to drink. And my mom is talking to Sam's parents, enjoying the banter between them.

A tall, thin, beautiful blonde woman wearing a short, red evening gown, accented with heavy, but elegant jewels, strides through the door. Her hair is swept up from her neck; wistful strands hanging from the clip holding it all together. Her bronze skin shimmers in the light. Ashton takes notice and turns his entire body in her direction. She smiles, he smiles, and I think what it would be like to turn a man's head the way that woman just did.

I did turn a head that way, but a lot of good it did me. I'm alone, sitting at a table, watching guests be merry.

*Sad.*

Just as the woman makes a move toward Ashton, Addie's back at my side in a flash. I hadn't even seen her coming.

"Brooke, stand!" she demands, grabbing my arm and pulling me rudely from my chair.

"What are you doing?" I snap. "Addie, stop."

"Brooke!" she hisses in my ear, placing her hands to my cheeks from behind. Once she positions my head where she's focused, I see him.

He's dressed in a suave suit, filling out every inch, as if it were made for only him. His hair is kept, as always combed and styled. His hands are in his pockets as he watches the woman in the red dress flirt with Ashton.

*Brock is here.*

"Why did he come?" I whisper to myself, but Addie's there.

"I think the question should be, 'who did he come here for?'"

Green. All I see is green. The anger, the sadness, the inevitable heartache I've been suffering pushes the envy to that one woman left in the room that I can see.

And she's talking to my brother!

"Addie, who is she?"

"No idea," she breathes. "But damn, Brock looks good."

"I'm leaving," I cop out. Grabbing my purse, I turn to run the other way.

Surprisingly, I make it four steps before my dad's big chest blocks my way.

"No, Button," he says. I don't look up. I can't.

The disappointment that I know is sketching his face will be too much. And I've already had a bad day. It can't get worse, can it?

"Dad, I want to leave."

"He called, you know," Dad baits.

"Who called?" I question, finally moving my eyes to meet his. "Who?"

"Brock."

*He called my dad?*

"He has a question for you."

*Shit.*

"I haven't talked to him."

Nodding, Dad's disappointment shines only a little. "I know. He told me that, too. He called Ashton, asking for me. Ashton gave him my number. He called two days ago."

"You told him to come here?"

"I told him he had my permission."

"He's with someone," I remind him with regret.

"Brooke," he says quietly. "No. That's his little sister."

"Tate," I remember.

Nodding, Dad bends to kiss my forehead. "I love you, Button."

"Baby." The familiar voice I've missed since last hearing it comes with a gale force wind of mixed emotions from behind me.

"You got this?" Dad questions, looking over my head and talking to Brock.

I hear Brock respond, and without seeing it, I know he's smiling. "I've got this. Thank you."

Wrapping his strong arms around me, Dad whispers into my ear, "I approve of him, Brooke. Now talk to him."

"I never figured you for a traitor," I smart. "Really, Dad. Mom, maybe. You? Never."

Laughing, Dad pulls me back and holds me by the arms. Squeezing, he says, "Go do what you should've done a week ago."

# Chapter Sixty-Three

*I told her she was going to marry me.*

*Brock*

-

My life would be much easier if the first woman I ever fell in love with were a lot less stubborn.

"You wouldn't return my texts," I accuse, hiding my impatience if only for the sake of Sam's guests who are dancing around us. "And you wouldn't answer my calls."

Guilt washes over Brooke's face before she half-smiles. I've missed that fucking smile more than I thought I had.

"I've been busy," she passes off.

"You blocked my number," I correct.

More guilt wades, but this time she gives me the truth in doubt. "I wasn't sure you'd still want--"

Pulling her into me as close as she'll allow, I lean down and take in a deep, relieving breath. "I love you, Brooke. I'm not leaving again. I'm staying here and I'll stalk you into being with me if I have to."

Brooke looks up and for the first time in as many miserable weeks we've been apart, I see exactly what I hoped I would.

Her answer is yes, and I didn't even have to ask.

But I will.

"You're not leaving?"

"Never."

"What about your company? Your job?"

"Brooke--"

"What about your family? Your friends? What about Drew!"

"Brooke--"

"What if you miss them and--"

Losing more of my already weary patience, I interrupt, "Woman, if I miss them then we'll go see them together. I have a job here with Ashton. I agreed to partner with your families' business. Now if you'd shut up and let me finish what I came here to do, I can get you out of here, out of that dress, and do what I want to do *to* you."

"Oh my," she breathes as I pull the black box from the inside pocket of my suit. When I start to take a knee, she releases another breath and her eyes fill with happy tears.

"I love you, Brooke Malloy. You're a pain in the ass, and fuck me but I love you. I told you you'd marry me. Now I'm asking."

"Brock--" she hesitates.

"Marry me, Brooke."

"I love you," she replies without an answer.

"Marry me."

"Yes!" she *finally* agrees with excitement.

As I stand, sliding on her finger the simple but elegant ring I bought what feels so long ago, the guests around us cheer and clap.

Brooke awkwardly drops to her knees where she hugs me so tight I can hardly breathe.

Everything I've done in my life has come to this. Every frustrating moment with her has been worth it.

Brooke is who I was always supposed to spend the rest of my life with.

And thank God our life together is about to start.

# Epilogue

*That's a wrap*

*Brooke*

-

"If you keep touching me, you'll make us late," I protest, but doing so just barely as Brock's hands are exactly where I like them to be.

"Fuck them," he hisses in my ear before biting down, sending a violent shiver of lust between my legs. "Fuck everyone here."

"Brock, stop. We came all this way for a reason. Why not make the most of it?"

When Matt and Willow tag teamed to coerce Brock and I into coming back to L.A. to do one final follow-up show, Brock refused. I had mixed feelings.

On one hand, I had no desire to ever step foot back in this city and all its crazy again. On the other, I wanted closure. Part of me also wanted the world, namely Kylee Simmons, to know Brock was really mine.

Sighing, Brock lifts his head. His beautiful eyes scan my face. "Doing this today will cause another shit storm. I know it. All the same people will be there."

He's lying. That's not the reason. Though our time in being hounded by the press has passed, Brock's more worried about who I'll see again.

"You're jealous," I smart, running my fingers down his cheek and tracing the line of his jaw. "Evan is happy. I wasn't the woman for him."

"No?" He smirks. "You were, but the asshat wasn't the man for you."

Sucking in my lips to hide my smile, I test his patience.

"Brooke," he growls. "Don't start."

"Who is the man for me?" I ask as his hands lift the hem of his shirt I'm wearing in our hotel room bed.

"Not Evan. Not Sam Hunt," he mumbles, dragging my panties past my knees and stopping long enough to kiss my inner thigh.

As he brings his body above mine, positioning himself at my entrance, I lift my head from the pillow to kiss him. Soft, slow, and with a familiarity that comes with truly knowing you're exactly where you're supposed to be.

*Brock*

-

"So, we understand there's going to be a wedding?" Matt asserts, sitting on the couch across from ours.

The small stage isn't set in front of an audience. The only people in the room are those running the cameras, Matt, Brooke, and me. I negotiated this to save my sanity. I didn't want to look at any of the women I'd met here before. There aren't any good memories of lasting friendships I'd consider keeping other than Ryleigh who has already become a staple in Brooke's life.

"Yes," Brooke answers when I don't. Her hand squeezes my knee, reading the annoyance I'm asserting as I endure all of this against my will. "In September."

"Congratulations," Matt extends. "Where will you two live?"

This was a discussion that did and didn't take place. The decision was made by me and explained to Brooke in a way she understood I had no intentions of debating or compromising.

After meeting her, shortly after falling in love with her, I knew my life wouldn't ever go back to being as it was.

In truth, I hate my job. I hate Dallas. I hate living in the shadow of my father.

So when I walked into his office three days after Brooke finally accepted my proposal, I had planned to quit. But, being that Martin Merritt is not only a genius of a man, but also my father, he knew what I was going to say and said it for me.

For the first time since graduating college, I left his office feeling as though he was proud.

"We're going to live near Brooke's family," I put in. Matt's eyes move to mine. "And you don't need to know where."

Brooke's face blushes but she smiles. I'm tired of living my life with others watching. She's the only person on earth who understands.

"Brock is going to help my little brother run our family business," she adds in an attempt to smooth my rudeness. "So, after this we're going house hunting."

"I hope you keep us all up to date on your future plans. You're always welcome here."

"Thank you," Brooke returns. I say nothing.

"We have our next year's contestant picked out. We're in negotiations as we speak. Would you like to meet her?"

"No," I clip over Brooke's, "Sure."

"Let's bring her out."

When Matt stands, directing his attention to the door opening behind us, I continue looking forward, but Brooke's gasp as she walks in the room has me curious.

"I don't think introductions aren't necessary," Matt says, smiling down at me.

When Brooke's best friend Addie comes to kiss Brooke on the cheek, I stand.

"You didn't..." Brooke starts, but stops, obviously unsure what to say next. "You're not doing this."

Shaking her head, breaking into a huge smile, she winks while coming to me and slapping me hard on the back. "Marry The Hostess."

*Oh, fuck no.*

I don't take from Addie's enthusiasm. I can't. Brooke looks so happy as they hug and whisper between them.

"I'm going to be on *television*," she chides at us both. "My name. In big lights. With men begging at my feet."

*This woman has no idea.*

"Reality TV!" she continues, lifting her hands above her head. "Here I come!"

Matt smirks. Brooke and Addie giggle. I say nothing. I just want to go home. To my new home, with Brooke.

Fuck reality television.